Carmen Reid is the bestselling author of, most recently, *The Personal Shopper*, *Late Night Shopping* and *How Not to Shop*, all starring Annie Valentine. She has worked as a newspaper journalist and columnist, but now writes fiction full time. Carmen also writes a series for teen readers, *Secrets at St Jude's*. She lives in Glasgow, Scotland with her husband and two children.

For more information on Carmen Reid and her books visit her website at www.carmenreid.com

www.**rbooks**.co.uk

Did the Earth Move?

Carmen Reid

CORGI BOOKS

TRANSWORLD PUBLISHERS
61-63 Uxbridge Road, London W5 5SA
a division of The Random House Group Ltd
www.rbooks.co.uk

DID THE EARTH MOVE?
A CORGI BOOK : 9780552155809

First publication in Great Britain
Corgi edition published 2003
Corgi edition reissued 2007

Addresses for Random House Group Ltd companies outside
the UK can be found at: www.randomhouse.co.uk
The Random House Group Ltd Reg. No. 954009.

The Random House Group Limited makes every effort to
ensure that the papers used in its books are made from trees
that have been legally sourced from well-managed and
credibly certified forests. Our paper procurement policy can
be found on www.randomhouse.co.uk

Typeset in 11/12pt Palatino by
Phoenix Typesetting, Burley-in-Wharfedale, West Yorkshire.
Printed in the UK by CPI Cox & Wyman, Reading, RG1 8EX.

8 10 9

Acknowledgements

Thank you so very much to:

Thomas. No way would I have managed this without you, your tireless support, (almost!) unfailing humour and our gorgeous, exhausting children.

My wonderful parents for helping out way beyond the call of duty.

The people who look after me and work so hard to make sure I do it better than I ever thought I could: my agents, Darley Anderson and Carrie Neilson, and Diana Beaumont at Transworld.

Debbie Turnham for helping me to find my own way.

Sophie Ransom at Midas.

The people who loved the first book, had faith and got all their friends to buy it, especially Tash, Son, Sarah, Lucy, Georgina, Ali and Jo.

My East End Mummy friends.

And so much love and thanks to Scott – for evenings in the garden, for always making time and for being such a modern Cool Dad to the boys. We're all heart-broken and miss you terribly.

Chapter One

'Nils.'

'Yes?'

'Nothing. I'm just trying it out. Nils . . . Nils,' she repeated slowly, resting her head back against his arm and feeling dangerously close to falling asleep, right there in the middle of the afternoon. This was so good. How come she had forgotten how good this was?

Eve turned and smiled at the broad, freckled face beside hers on the pillow. 'It might be quite fun to do this all again some time,' she said, already with a little stomach flip replaying the best bits in her mind.

'Yes please,' he answered, in the Dutch, butter-melting-on-toast accent which had landed her here in the first place.

He rolled onto his side and propped his head up with a hand to take a better look at her. So pretty in the way he thought of as totally English: skinny as a whippet, perfect nose, thin lips, hair

7

too blond, too long and scruffy, *nails* . . . endearingly, the worst he'd ever seen. Had she been digging with her bare hands?

Without another word, just smiling, he ran a fingertip slowly, slowly from her chin to her belly button.

'You're very nice naked,' he said.

'Likewise,' was her answer and she moved in close so they were pressed up against each other. 'And now I know you're a natural blond,' she teased, moving her fingers down his chest to the damp curl of hair at the very base of his stomach.

He put both arms round her, squeezed her tightly and she felt herself sighing with relief. This was OK. It was good. It was fun. She was going to be all right. She was going to be able to move on.

She heard a vigorous scratching and turned out of the hug to see one of her grey cats sprawled over the bottom of the bed, pawing at its ear.

'So they should make a full recovery?' she asked Nils.

'A week of the drops and there shouldn't be any more problems. But I hope you'll call me anyway.'

Because Nils was her vet, well, the cats' vet. She'd known him for almost a year now. They had laughed and flirted in his surgery, and she had been to his above-the-practice flat twice before for an elegant blue and white cup of scalding coffee. But this was the first time she and the cats had charmed their way into the plain, tidy bedroom which she was looking at properly now: white walls, white sheets, dark wooden furniture neatly stacked with books and clothes and shoes, a bed which had creaked, groaned and wobbled quite alarmingly all afternoon.

There was one big window, framed with masculine green-striped curtains, and filled up with the bare branches of a cherry tree. It was a clear, early February day, but the sunlight slanting in through the window was lukewarm.

'South facing,' she said, prompted by her own thoughts, 'You could grow all sorts of exotic stuff in windowboxes . . . chilli peppers, tomatoes, basil . . . I could plant some up for you, if you like.'

'Windowboxes?' he replied. 'This is what you mad Englishwomen do instead of sex, isn't it?'

'No! I have sex . . . sometimes. Occasionally.' But you couldn't really call one afternoon of sex in three years 'occasionally', could you? Three years!! How had this happened?

'I'm a busy girl,' she said.

'I know.'

'I have four children, two exes, a full-time job, two cats, one garden, a very messy flat and an old car . . .' She counted this all off on her fingers then gave a shrug . . . As if that little summary did her weird and intricate past any justice at all. But just how much would a new lover want to know about her children and their histories?

9

Denny, aged 22, Tom just turned 20 (not to mention their long-lost dad), then Anna, nine, Robbie, two, and their father Joseph. The complicated one. The man she'd most loved, most hated, most wanted, most pushed away. She twiddled at Joseph's ring, still encircling her fourth finger. No, a new lover would particularly not want to hear about him.

'You are busy,' Nils agreed. 'But I'm very glad you took an afternoon off.'

'Do you think your receptionist suspects us?' She twined a leg round his and registered all the interested stirrings going on between them.

'How could she? I didn't even suspect us,' he said.

'Oh, but I did.' There was a throatiness to her delicious giggle which he hoped meant they were going to start all over again.

He put his warm coffee-tasting mouth over hers, rolled her on top of him and she felt another big surge of interest. Whoa. Light touchpaper and retire.

'Like riding a bike' were the words popping up somewhere at the back of her mind. It may have been three years, but you didn't forget how to do this. His tongue was now exploring places he was making it very difficult to feel shy about because she felt turned on, touched, brushed against from fingertip to toe.

She could even hear herself groaning in a strange out-of-body kind of way: '*Yeah. Yeah. Ohhhh . . . More . . .*' More? That was the problem.

More. She'd done it now. She'd reactivated the sex button and now she was going to want Nils morning, noon and night. And really, as she kept telling herself, she was TOO BUSY.

'What?' His head ducked up from under the duvet and her eyes snapped open.

'What?' she asked but suspected she'd said that last bit out loud.

'You're feeling dizzy?'

'No, no. Fine.' What was the etiquette here? Did you just say 'carry on, please'?

'Are you sure?'

'Of course I'm sure.'

He was holding himself up on his arms over her and she had to have a little squeeze of his hard, blond biceps, 'You're lovely,' she said and meant it. He was. In a totally different way to . . . oh no, don't go that route . . . never mind . . . concentrate please on the muscular vet who is licking and breathing against the side of your neck, whose fingertips are tracing, circling there, there . . . oh yeah . . .

She wrapped her legs round him and he was inside again. No sex for three years then three shots in one afternoon. Was this a record? It was certainly an overdose. And how was she going to explain away the growing stubble rash on the side of her face?

But she was very pleased that she had decided to give in to her growing conviction that Nils van der Hoeven should probably be the one who was going to help her make the transition from separated to single to back out there again. She had made the appointment for the cats – which did actually have sore ears, she hadn't deliberately infected them or anything – but she had booked in for the end of the vet's day, hoping that he didn't have much else planned and wondering if she could still remember the slightest thing about seducing men or at least letting them know it was OK to go about seducing you.

So that was how she'd ended up in Nils's little consulting room scooping her cats onto the table in a way that just happened to make a silver G-string pop up over the top of her tight combat trousers, and when she turned round she could see his gaze was straying, as intended, to the cleavage Wonderbra-ed up underneath her slinky pink cardigan.

'Ear infection, I think.' She had run an armful of jangling bangles through her hair and smiled glossy lipstick at him, thinking she was maybe overdoing this a little. He had examined them carefully and the two fat ladies – as she thought of the cats now – had purred and sat still for him.

'I've been away, so I don't know how long they've been like this,' she'd said.

'OK . . . so, where have you been?' he'd asked in the accent which had a strangely hypnotic, unzipping effect on her.

'Oh nowhere interesting, visiting family out of town.'

'Nowhere interesting . . . hmmm . . . my most

12

interesting client says "nowhere interesting",' he'd teased.

'And what makes you think I'm so interesting?' she'd smiled at him. Ah, standing there in the beam of his warm, amber eyes was like basking in the sun. She'd felt so happy and relaxed, she'd had to fight the overwhelming desire to start taking her clothes off right there and then.

For a moment, all she'd been able to think about was sex on the disinfected linoleum floor with the cats watching and a waiting room full of pensioners with constipated dogs and moulting budgies tut-tutting about the delay and wondering what the rhythmic banging noise was.

God, Eve get a grip. She'd tried to click that daydream off.

But he was so nice and *solid*. The rolled-up sleeves of his white coat revealed chunky forearms dusted with freckles and golden hair and she couldn't help picturing the strong, golden-downed body underneath the coat. She'd looked up at his face, big jaw, blond and brown tousled hair in a messy pudding bowl kind of thing. He was gorgeous. And at least 35-ish . . . not too young. Still inexplicably single?

'Well,' he was answering the question she'd now completely forgotten about, 'I still don't know why someone like you is wearing an engagement ring, dressing like a teenager and living alone with children and cats in this part of town. I think it is probably a very interesting story . . . huh?'

'Well . . . maybe. I like it here,' she'd smiled back, answering the easy part of the question.

'I do too.'

'And anyway, why is anyone single?' Big smile, little flick through hair. 'Are you still single?'

'Yes.' This said decisively as he crossed his arms over his broad chest and squared up to her: 'I'm nearly finished for the day. Would you like to come up for some coffee?'

'Of course. I'd have invited myself, if you hadn't asked,' she'd confessed.

'Really?'

She'd gone back to the waiting room with the cats, feeling almost breathless with the suspense. Surreptitiously fluffing her hair, hoiking up the cleavage and tugging down the combat trousers, she'd wondered if she still had any idea how to do this: let someone know you wanted just a little bit more than their friendship. Not too much more – just a little bit.

'I have wine too,' he'd said as she followed him up the stairs to his flat. 'Maybe you'd prefer a glass of wine.'

'Yeah, if you like or ketamine? You know, the horse tranquillizer: apparently that works much faster.' *Oh my God, I've clearly gone insane.*

They were in the hallway now and he'd turned to look at her with amusement.

14

'Sorry, why am I making jokes about horse tranquillizer? Jut shoot me now. I mean – I don't mean you shoot horses . . . well probably you do . . . but only when you have to.' *This wasn't exactly easy was it?*

But Nils had smiled at her a little too broadly, as if he'd been trying not to laugh, then added: 'There isn't much call for shooting horses in Hackney. Do you want to let your cats out? They can wander about.'

She'd bent down in the dim little hall to unclip the latch on the basket and when she'd stood up again, they'd kissed.

That was it. So easy she couldn't really work out how it had happened. Bend down, cat latch, stand up and kiss.

And they must have both decided at the same time because she met him halfway, mouth on mouth. At first they were kissing lip to lip, then so tentatively, tongue on tongue.

Only when it had started to happen had she realized just how much she'd wanted this. A kiss . . . kissing . . . God, she had been *starved* of kissing. She'd wrapped her arms around him, not wanting to let him stop, her very turned-on Dutchman . . . in a white coat . . . which smelled of Dettol . . . Several fantasies rolled into one.

She'd felt her bra ping open at the back and his hands on her bare skin, shyly moving to her breasts. The excitement of doing this with some-one new was so intense, it was close to terror. A different face, a wider, softer mouth, a whole new island of person to work her way around. She'd groped for the buttons on the starchy white coat and began to undo them, needing to have him warm and naked against her.

'Yeeeeeouwl!' He'd stood on a cat, but who cared?

Oh, he did, obviously.

'I'm so sorry.' He'd let go of her and followed the cat into the bedroom.

'She'll be fine.' Eve, thick-voiced, went into the room too, her arms folded over her undone cardigan and bra, to watch him give the cat a quick check over.

'You must stand on cats all the time, in your line of work,' she'd joked.

'My line of *work*,' – which came out '*vuuuerkk*' and almost made her knees buckle – 'is trying *not* to stand on cats.'

Then he'd gone to stand very close beside her, hoping he hadn't killed the moment, as well as very nearly the cat.

'Where were we?' she'd said, wrapping hands around his waist, hooking her fingers into the belt loops of his cords and pulling him up against her.

'Remind me,' he'd said, leaning in, moving his mouth onto hers, running his hands through her hair, circling against her neck and shoulders until the possibility of taking off every shred of clothing and getting into bed with this strange, new man was becoming very real.

She let him undo the top button of her

trousers, then he sat down on the bed and pulled her down beside him. Pushing back the insistent thoughts that this wasn't Joseph . . . this was a new . . . a first . . . she'd let him peel back her clothes and move his mouth down, skimming over cold nipples, soft stomach and arched hip bones until he was *there*; tasting, touching, insistent and persuasive. And despite her whispered reservations – '*No . . . no . . . not . . . quite . . . just . . .*' because this felt so intimate and strange – it had become irresistible and she had slowly lowered her guard, closed her eyes and wound the unfamiliar curls round her fingers, opening to the flickering touch, the breathing, the steady rippling of underwater waves and – *no!* – she was going to come before she'd even undone his zip, she realized as it happened, with a quiet juddering.

Nils had stood up then and undressed, unselfconsciously, not breaking her gaze as she'd watched. He'd taken off his shirt and T-shirt, then he'd unbuttoned his trousers and pulled them off along with his trunks and socks. He had a square, strong body, as golden-haired as she'd expected, surprisingly freckly, but quite spectacularly attractive.

Unable to take her eyes off him, she'd waited naked on the bed – heart jumping in her chest – for him to fit on a condom and come back.

When he moved inside her, she'd had to bend her knees up and put her heels onto his buttocks to make room. But it was perfect to feel small, to

17

feel as if she was clinging to this great bear of a man for dear life. She'd held on, felt his size and warmth and managed to keep at bay all the tearful thoughts welling up.

He was going to come quickly too. She'd felt him make the momentary effort to slow and hold back, but then with a gasp he'd given in and collapsed down against her.

Later, they'd had much slower sex with talking. What Joseph had always called mantra sex. (Except, she wasn't supposed to be thinking about him.)

'So how come you're still single?' she'd asked Nils.

'British girls aren't into vets,' he'd told her. 'Too much exposure to *All Creatures Great and Small* at an impressionable age. They're always thinking about where my hands have been and am I *sure* I've washed them.'

'Yeurgh,' she'd giggled.

'I don't know,' he'd added, a little more seriously. 'Probably just haven't met the right person, yet.'

'I've always wanted to have sex with a Dutchman,' she'd told him then.

'Why?'

'Because you're all so liberal, nothing's supposed to shock you and I was hoping you'd have lots of good ideas.'

'I see,' he said switching positions and explaining that he was from one of the tiny Protestant, Puritan Dutch islands where he went

18

to church six days a week until he turned 19 and left for vet school.

'Ah.'

'But that doesn't mean I haven't got some good ideas and, please tell me you're going to come soon . . .'

'Oh yeah . . .'

'It's almost five o'clock, isn't it?' she asked him now, trying to move her head up from the pillow. 'I really have to go.'

She got out of bed, retrieved her tiny pants and then lay flat on her back on the floor. Raising her hips with her hands, she swung her legs up into the air, then down past her head to touch the floor on the other side.

'What are you doing?!' he asked, sitting up to watch.

'Just stretching out my back,' she said, smiling, looking surprisingly comfortable.

'Isn't that dangerous?'

'The plough? No, not when you've been doing yoga for as long as I have. Since *before* the Nineties,' she added, but then wished she hadn't, she didn't really want to remind him that she was, well . . . call it a few years older than him.

She held the position for several minutes, then unfolded herself and began to pull on her clothes. He asked if she would like to make another 'appointment'.

This was the part she wasn't so sure about.

'I've got a lot on . . . and little people to look after. I really don't know . . .' she trailed off.

'Do you want to see me again, Eve?' he asked, from the seriously rumpled bed.

'Yes. I just . . .'

'Shh!' he held a finger against his lips. 'It's OK. No rush. We'll see how it goes.'

'Thanks.' She sat down beside him and put her hands up against his face to draw him in for a kiss. And to his surprise it was a kiss on the forehead, a slightly mumsy goodbye.

'What does this have to do with things?' He held her left hand in his and put a thumb over the dainty emerald ring on her fourth finger.

'Oh, nothing . . . really. Just habit. We split up ages ago . . . you know that . . .' She felt a flush of pink heat up her cheeks, and it annoyed her, making her blush even more: 'But there hasn't been anyone since. So this is . . . all new.'

'No rush,' he said again, reassuringly.

'I'm sure I'll tell you all about it.' She shot him a smile, did up her trousers, slid her feet into her shoes and picked up her cardigan. 'But not today.'

Chapter Two

At 4p.m., most days of the year, Eve's stint at the office ended, although *work* didn't. She sometimes didn't think work ended until she sank into her bath at 10.30p.m. with a hefty glass of red wine in her hand.

But 4p.m. was the changeover, when Probation Officer Eve powered down the computer, closed the files on the big kids for the day and turned back into Mummy Eve, who did food and homework and bath time, laundry and hoovering and all that other stuff for the next few hours.

And today, Friday, was no different. Lap one, rush to the bus stop and catch the red double decker, which dropped her just a short walk from Robbie's childminder. She always rang Arlene's doorbell in short bursts of three so Robbie knew it was her and came hurtling down the corridor screaming with glee, ready to fly into her arms as soon as the door was opened.

'Hello, bunny,' she said into his hair, as he clasped her fiercely round the neck. Eve and Arlene had their doorstep chat – what they'd done today, how he'd eaten, how long he'd slept – then Robbie climbed into his buggy and they whizzed down the road to collect Anna from her after-school club.

Reunions with Anna were not nearly as gushy. Her tall, fair-haired daughter didn't see them coming in because she was at the table pushed against the wall in the club room, doing her homework, completely oblivious to the chaos going on around her with other kids playing ping-pong and pool, jostling for goes on the Play Station.

'Anna!' the club supervisor had to call several times, before Anna heard. Then she turned, flashed her mother a quick smile, turned back, finished her sentence, her sum, whatever it was she was doing and only then packed her books and jotters away, all neat and orderly, just like a mini executive sorting out her briefcase at the end of the day.

Anna allowed herself to be kissed on the cheek by Eve, but nothing more than that. Then she bent down to kiss Robbie hello, all sweetly condescending and so self-possessed for a nine-year-old.

'So tell me all about it,' Eve said when they were back outside, and the last fifteen-minute stretch home was full of school news and a little girl's gossip.

There was that house, she couldn't help noticing as they walked past, the big one on the corner, shabby and unloved, with the wild garden. Someone had finally put it up for sale.

It was close to 5p.m. when they were at last back at the little two-bedroomed basement flat which had been Eve's family base for over ten years now.

Opening the front door was always such a relief: all three of them loved to be home. Anna rushed to her room and Eve carried Robbie into her bedroom so he could sit on the bed and watch her slip out of the work suit into jeans, a bright top, woolly socks and a decrepit old pair of Birkenstocks. That was when she finally felt like her proper homebody, Mummy-self again.

She took out her earrings, brushed through her hair and tried to feel a tiny bit recharged for the final laps of the day ahead of her: suppertime, homework, Joseph handover, baths and bed.

'What are we eating tonight?' Anna called from next door.

'Soup, salad, bread and cheese,' Eve answered, knowing this was not exactly a break with routine.

'What kind of soup?'

'Carrot and lentil,' she answered, not expecting to hear a groan in reply. This was one of her more popular numbers.

Anna came into the room, dressed in sensible chinos and a white long-sleeved T-shirt. She found her mother's taste for sequined hipsters, splashy tops and bead jewellery hard to relate to.

'How's it going?' Eve asked but before Anna could reply, Robbie somersaulted straight off the bed and landed in a wailing heap on the wooden floor.

Once they'd both cuddled him up and patted him better, Anna replied with an: 'OK, surviving, trying to keep within my own boundaries and not get too involved with all the children stuck in the toddler stage in my class.'

'Hmmm,' Eve nodded, knowing from experience it was best not to get too caught up in a pop psychology conversation with Anna; it would only end with cries of: 'You just don't want to understand!'

Occasionally, Eve would worry if it was normal to have a nine-year-old who was desperate to be a psychiatrist and who spent most of her spare time reading psychology manuals. But, hell, what was normal? Best not to spend too much time wondering about that.

While her youngest children had supper – Robbie breaking all his bread into pieces to float it 'like ducks' on the soup and Anna having to cry because she blobbed the bright orange onto her T-shirt, 'and it will *never* come out' (theatrical wail) – Eve tried to take a call on the kitchen phone from her eldest son, Denny.

'Have you met Tom's new girlfriend yet?' Denny was asking above the increasing kitchen cacophony.

'Yes. Isn't she lovely? I'm cheering from the sidelines,' Eve said because this was beginning to look like Tom's first big romance. He'd always had girlfriends but no-one really serious until now. When she'd met Deepa, just a week ago, she'd seen the thrilled friendship between them and felt so happy for him. And Deepa was lovely: an attractive, intelligent medical student, full of fun – like Tom – but ambitious too, which was interesting because Tom was laid back, never took anything too seriously, was determined to be a carefree, software-designing surfer boy for as long as he could.

'I know,' Denny was agreeing. 'No idea what she's doing with Tom.'

'Denny! He's getting it together,' Eve said. 'His job is working out OK. His finances are improving.' Eve had limitless understanding for her kind, but chaotic, second son.

'But not his taste in clothes,' Denny added.

'Well . . . maybe Deepa will help him out. It's early days. How about you?' she asked, trying to ignore Robbie's discovery that he could ping soup across the table with his spoon. 'How's work going?'

'Fine. Big job next week hopefully, fingers crossed. And Patricia's well too.'

'Good.' Then Anna took a direct soup hit.

'I have to go,' she said to deafening shouts of 'Mum! Look what he's done!'

'You do,' Denny laughed. 'Give them a cuddle for me.'

'See you soon. Are you OK?' she added quickly.

'I'm fine.'

'OK you two . . .' She headed to the plastic-table-clothed war zone with paper towels. 'He's still stuck in the toddler stage,' she reminded a tearful Anna.

'Can we have the yoghurt now, Mummy?' Robbie looked up at her with the most heart-winning, charming smile he could muster.

'Yes, yes, just a minute.' She wiped everything and everyone down a bit, then plonked a fruit yoghurt in front of Anna and prepared for the evening debate with Robbie.

'Who have we got today?' Robbie asked gleefully.

She looked in the fridge: 'James, Thomas, Annie or the Fat Controller.' After months of resistance she had finally cracked and bought the Thomas the Tank Engine themed yoghurts and now she was enslaved. He only ever wanted to eat the Henry one. Really she should just wash out the Henry pot, refill it with normal yoghurt and slap the foil back on. Why did she never remember to do that?

'But I want Henry,' came the little wail now.

'Oh no, Thomas is going to cry.' Eve made sobbing noises into the fridge. 'Eat me Robbie, eat me,' she said in a silly voice.

Anna was rolling her eyes.

Finally Robbie relented and let her spoon the pale pink goo into his mouth.

After supper, she jammed the plates, cups and bowls into the pocket-sized dishwasher Denny and Tom had bought her for Christmas, and went into the sitting room with the children.

She flicked on the lights the room needed even in the middle of the day because it was below pavement level with a green curtain of ivy and clematis over the two small windows.

Eve liked the underwater green effect. She'd decorated with pale apricot paint, a saggy secondhand sofa, bookcases, stained-glass shaded lamps and ropes of white fairy lights. The wooden floor, like all the others in the flat, she had painstakingly sanded, smoothed, nailed down, fillered and varnished herself. There were no curtains on the windows because the trellis of leaves was enough.

Like every other room in the flat, the sitting room walls were covered in all sorts of interesting things: posters, paintings, Denny's family photos blown up, and lots of home-made art – framed bright blue handprints, salt dough trees, painted and glazed, glitter dinosaurs, dip dyed handkerchiefs, even a pink tulle baby's dress in a frame. It was a quirky collection begun way back when Denny and Tom were small.

Robbie hopped onto the biggest sofa and began rearranging the cushions. Eve slotted the Thomas the Tank video into the machine, hit play and lay beside him, curling herself so he had space to sit in the bend of her knees.

Anna unpacked her books and settled down at the table behind the sofa. This way, Eve could help with homework without having to prise herself up again.

The clonky theme tune started up and Eve felt her eyelids hover. She wondered how long she could just 'rest' them shut before Anna had a question or Robbie poked her in the face.

Barely fifteen seconds later, she got her answer: 'What's six times eight again?' Anna asked.

'Well, what's five times eight?' she asked back.

'Forty, so plus eight, forty-eight.'

'Well done. Are you all packed, by the way?' Eve asked just as the doorbell rang.

'Is it Daddy?' Anna's face lit up.

'Better go see.' Eve uncurled from the sofa and caught herself arranging her hair. Oh good grief. And there were the strange tummy flutterings along with the surge of tension Joseph always managed to provoke in her. She wondered if it was going to feel different to meet him today now that she had taken such a big step, had started to see someone else . . . properly.

She had never expected maintaining civil friendliness with Joseph to be easy. They had been together for seven years and she had loved him all the way. They'd had Anna together and several years of the kind of happiness you could never, ever regret, but things had begun to fall apart well before Robbie arrived.

In fact, Eve had called it off and moved Joseph out for what surely had to be the final time just a few months into the pregnancy. What had gone wrong? She would only ever explain it as 'He changed', which didn't really begin to describe the whole complicated set of circumstances but made it easier for her to cope with. Now, she considered herself still heartbroken and more than a little suspicious of new men, but determined not to be bitter, and some day to be able to get over it – as Joseph appeared to have done without too much problem.

So here they were: apart, trying to be civil and parenty, trying to ignore all the unresolved, difficult feelings still breaking out between them.

In some ways it had been easier when the father of Eve's two older boys, her husband Dennis, had left. He'd done the melodramatic, clean break, disappearing act. It might have been shocking and hell to adjust to, but at least there hadn't been all this confusion and toing and froing and on-ing and off-ing and having to try and be friends for the sake of the children.

'Hello, Joseph.' She stood up and smiled as he came into the room.

'Hi, Eve.' He did a quick stoop and brush of the cheek kiss. No, despite the afternoon of wild abandon with Nils, there was still a something, a little tiny rush . . . a jolt . . . when he did that. It annoyed her so much. And no, it was still hard to keep her eyes off him. But maybe she wasn't alone here. He was tall and muscular slim with dark eyes and thick, black hair. Plenty of women found him a pleasure to look at.

'Hello Jofus,' Robbie was saying from the sofa.

'Hello, buddy, how are you?' He settled down on the sofa to speak to the son he saw so little of. He and Eve had agreed that Robbie would come with Anna on the weekend visits to Joseph's flat in Manchester 'when he was older' but time had passed and so far neither of them had discussed when that would be. Each felt the other should make the offer first. It was just another little fly in the relationship ointment.

Joseph stayed long enough to have a cup of tea and the handover chat: How were Anna and Robbie doing? How much homework should Anna take? What was she reading? And all the time Eve was watching him, noticing all sorts of little, personal things and he was doing the same.

He'd been at meetings in town all day and his dark suit had that soft, perfect cut look to it of criminal expense, but he wore it casually with a black T-shirt and the world's tiniest mobile phone clipped to the top pocket, the ear wire tucked round his collar. He had a new laptop computer. She saw the small, light bag at his feet. No doubt something very sleek and top of the range. He was doing well, turning into a wealthy, successful businessman. Just as she'd suspected . . . and hated. She never accepted any child maintenance from him, but made sure he put the money into an account for the children when they were older. She tried not to interfere with his lavish treat buying.

Anna came back into the room with her small overnight bag.

'Are you sure you'll get it into the boot?' Eve asked because she couldn't resist. She couldn't remember what kind of car it was Joseph drove but it was the silliest, shiniest boy-toy ever and she loathed it.

'Miiiiiaaaaaooooow,' Joseph said but smiled at her anyway.

'Any plans for the weekend?' Eve tried out her 'being civil' voice again.

'Loads of plans. We'll have a great time, won't we, Anna?'

'Yeah. Is Michelle around?'

Joseph and Eve felt their involuntary intakes of breath. You could always rely on nine-year-olds to bring on those awkward questions.

'She's offered to make us dinner tomorrow, if you want.'

'Better eat before you go, darling.' Eve knew it was mean and evil and wicked, but she couldn't help herself.

Michelle, Joseph's girlfriend was – and Eve was only going on photographic evidence and what Anna had reported here – one of those perky gym bunnies always engrossed in the current diet fad. At the moment, Michelle didn't 'do' carbohydrates and apparently never even had so much as a mouthful of cake or chocolate or ice-cream or anything sugar-filled or fun

31

because of the terror that she would just let go, let rip, gorge herself until her thighs ballooned, or her bottom burst or the seams of her latest designer outfit exploded.

Some fun she must be, Eve consoled herself.

'Eve,' Joseph warned, 'Behave.'

'Sorry.'

But then he couldn't help adding: 'At least Michelle can cook something other than lentils.'

Owww, oww, ouch: 'Oh, please,' she managed, hoping it sounded offhand and unwounded.

'Have you got plans?' he asked then, maybe trying to make up for the dig.

'Yeah. I've got a date tomorrow night. Our new vet actually – a very nice guy.'

If Joseph was a surprised by this, he didn't show it. She was studying him to read his reaction, but all that came was a smile and a polite-sounding: 'That's good, I hope you have fun.'

Yes I bloody well will she told herself, surprisingly hurt at his lack of interest in this, the first ever date she was telling him about. *I will eat, drink and be merry and bring him home for a sexathon and not think of you for one moment.* Even though Nils hadn't invited her for dinner or any sort of date and she had made this up on the spur of the moment just to annoy him.

'You're going on a *date*? With the *vet*?' Anna was asking. Oh no, now she had shocked the one person in the world she least wanted to: 'Why

32

didn't you tell me?' She knelt down and said to Anna: 'Honey, it's just for fun. Robbie's coming and we're going to talk about the cats.' See. This is why she hardly ever lied. It always got far too complicated.

'OK.' Joseph picked up Anna's bag and started on the goodbyes.

'Give Mummy and Robbie a kiss, Anna. It's time to go.'

Robbie was in bed at 8p.m., cuddled into the bottom bunk with his bunnies, struggling to keep his eyes open as Eve read him a story.

She ate a solitary supper with the radio on and afterwards forced herself to go round the house doing the bare minimum of chores – washing in machine, cursory sweep of kitchen floor, wipe of surfaces, armfuls of child junk into toyboxes. In the kitchen she filled up the bread machine and clicked it on, then chopped up vegetables and threw them into boiling stock to simmer.

At least Michelle can cook something other than lentils, she couldn't help remembering as she stirred her soup. God, Joseph.

As if he'd been worried about her cooking skills on evenings when the big boys were away and Anna asleep in her cot, and they had come into the kitchen for supper, watching each other eat by candlelight, absolutely certain of what was going to come next.

She remembered him dripping salad dressing onto her warm, bare summer arm and licking it off all the way from her wrist to her shoulder, until she was sitting in his lap, tasting him, wanting him, but he was tilting back to look into the fridge and see what other props he could find.

'What about ice cubes . . . or butter? Oh . . . the classic: we have cream *and* strawberries.'

'Yes, please.'

He'd once invented some ridiculous smorgasbord of snacks to complement oral sex: taramasalata, cream cheese, slivers of smoked salmon.

And sometimes he would tell her all the way through a meal what they were going to do afterwards, until they were so breathless they could hardly finish the food. 'See this strawberry—' he'd dip it into chocolate or hot caramel or cream and start to lick it with the very tip of his tongue, as she was imagining he would do to her nipple, her clitoris, the tip of her nose.

'Lucky strawberry,' she'd say, not able to take her eyes from his face, wondering once again how she'd managed to land such an irresistible man.

Why was Joseph so hard to get over?

This was the question which could still wake her up at 3a.m. and make it difficult to get back to sleep.

He *looked* exactly like the man she'd been so in love with. But she just couldn't believe what he had turned into. It was as if she was still, after all this time, expecting him to one day give up the executive position, return the car, the phones, the laptop and the gadgets, and appear on the doorstep all rumpled, delicious and studenty again saying 'I'm back the way you want me, please let me in.' Where had that person gone? The one she'd been so in love with? Was he inside there somewhere? Was there even the slightest chance she could lure him out again? Or had he disappeared completely?

The two cats, winding and purring round her legs as she stood at the cooker, were fed and then it was time to go out into the garden.

Eve slipped on her fleece jacket and heavy boots at the back door and went out, flicking on the outdoor spotlights, which lit up the green haven she had been working on since the day she'd moved into the flat.

Over the years, her garden had evolved and taken shape. She'd started off tending the lawn and border arrangement she'd inherited, but soon she'd built up the confidence to change it into something much more interesting and private. She'd heightened the three walls around the space with trellises, so they were now eight-foot-high walls of ivy, then the lawn had been ripped up and replaced with winding paths of stone slab planted all around with tall shrubs and greenery in pots, dense bushes and fruit trees, so that slowly the garden had grown higher and more tangled, more secluded from the other houses all around.

Now, it was like entering a secluded green world with something interesting to see in every corner. Pots in all colours, sizes, patterns and glazes, spilling over with every kind of plant: flowering bushes, roses, tall sculptural spiky palms, earthbound knotted alpines. Every space was filled: she had planted indiscriminately, coaxing whatever she could get her hands on into vigorous life.

There wasn't any plan. Rosemary, mint, parsley, lettuce – in winter, Brussels sprouts and cabbage – grew haphazardly on the edges of the big terracotta tubs, or in the spaces between the perennials, wherever she could find room.

In the summer, tomato plants were trained up the sunniest wall alongside the sweet-smelling crumpled-up-handkerchief roses, the sun-flowers planted especially for Robbie and the wild and untameable courgette plants.

Her autumn bulbs were pushed into every available square centimetre of earth so that crocus, tulips, lilies, peonies, all sorts of multi-coloured blossoms popped up unexpectedly from February onwards.

At the end of the garden was a pocket-sized patio, surrounded by green and covered with a canopy of climbing roses and clematis. There was a comfortable wooden garden bench there, out all year, and at the very start of summer Eve would bring out the wrought-iron chairs and the large round table she had decorated herself with a detailed mosaic. Big containers full of scented stocks and pink geraniums would take up the rest of the patio space and when the weather was good, supper was eaten outside every night in the twinkly light of candles on the mosaic and strings of fairy lights wound through the flower canopy above.

She loved not just to garden – to move among her plants watering, pinching off deadheads, trimming back shoots, pulling out the few stray weeds – she loved the garden. It was a *place*, a 'living' room which she had created. It was a private park for Robbie, a reading bower for Anna, an oasis for her, a clandestine place to sit, talk and eat with her friends; it was a magical extension to her life and she had made it almost all by herself with her own two hands.

Tonight, she was picking off snails by torch-light and drowning them with some distaste in a bucket half filled with water. Still, this was a better way to go than the ones unlucky enough to be crunched under her boots as she walked about in the dark. She loved to be in her garden at night, feeling alone, but not lonely, feeling busy, but at peace.

Chapter Three

Patricia opened her eyes and for a moment couldn't remember where the hell she was. Oh yes, in the tiny flat her boyfriend, Denny, shared with his brother Tom. There was Denny, still fast asleep beside her. Nice guy, she thought, watching his sleeping face, he took very good pictures, especially when the photo sessions ended in bed.

He'd probably do very well in the future and it was a shame she wasn't in love with him. She'd decided that about a month ago now. She wasn't in love with him and she didn't think she ever could be. Not his fault, just one of those things.

She looked at the bedside alarm clock: 7.18a.m. Shit. She was due over on the other side of town by ten and she had a lot to do – shower, shave, quick eyebrow pluck, nails, hair, make-up. This would be a great job, if she could get it. Every model she knew was after a shampoo contract. The money was amazing!

She was preening herself in the tiny bathroom mirror when there was a banging on the door.

'I have to come in,' came the choked voice on the other side.

'Hang on,' Patricia said, peering closely at the eyebrows. Were they matching? Or was the left one just a little bit too high?

'Please, it's urgent.'

'Oh for God's sake.' She recognized the voice now. Tom's girlfriend Deepa, Miss Completely Bloody Worthy medical student, who could barely hide the fact that she thought Patricia was a total waste of space.

She unbolted the door and Deepa ran in, lifted the toilet lid, bent over and threw up loudly.

'Oh yuk,' Patricia gathered up her make-up tools and backed out of the room, shutting the door behind her. It reminded her of the early days, all that miserable puking to stay thin. She'd graduated long ago to the ballerina method of two days a week, soup and fruit juice only.

Deepa was heaving up again. She felt appalling. Beads of sweat were leaping out of her forehead, upper lip, back of her neck.

She grabbed at a handful of toilet paper and wiped her face, then lurched over to the sink to splash herself with water.

Finally, she felt able to let herself out of the bathroom and head back to Tom's room. She was going to have to tell him, oh no . . . just the thought of that and – she raced back to the toilet again.

'Are you OK?' Tom's messy head was surfacing from the tangle of mismatched pillows, sheets and blankets.

'No.' She sat down on the edge of the bed beside him and put her hands up to support her head.

'What's the matter?' He sat up now, stretched and put an arm round her, stroking her soft velvet brown shoulders and silky black bob.

'Tom . . .' She wasn't looking at him, she was focused on the battered old Oasis poster Blu-Tacked to the wall, 'I'm ten days late, I'm sick as a dog. I think I'm pregnant.'

'Nah,' he said and carried on stroking the shoulders.

'I wouldn't joke about this kind of shit.' She turned to face him now. 'I'm going to do a test today.'

'I'm sure it'll be fine. We've been very careful.'

'Hmmm.'

He slipped out of bed, naked, and she watched the slim white buttock and thigh move past her face. Even from the depths of this horrible nausea, bubbles of desire still managed to burst up and she touched him as he passed.

He went to the tumble of clothes heaped at the end of the bed and fished out black moleskin jeans, which he pulled on without anything underneath. Then came a long-sleeved T-shirt emblazoned 100% HEADSHRUNK TO FIT IN.

'Chop chop, today is a work day, Deepybeebs,' he said, as if pregnancies were announced at his bedside every day of the week. 'Do you want tea? Toast? Cereal? Other proof that I know how to keep house?' He was hopping about pulling on a sock, which she suspected was unwashed and maybe just a little bit crusty.

'I love you,' she blurted out, which was very spooky because she'd never said it before, to anyone. She really must be pregnant: this was exactly the kind of thing pregnant women did, wasn't it?

'I love you too,' Tom replied and carried on with the other sock. Totally unconcerned, because *he* said 'I love you' all the time – to every girlfriend, to his mum, to his brothers, to his sister, to his step-dad, to his boss, to the sandwich lady, the Australian barmaid at his local. He loved everyone. Thought there was quite enough crap flying about the world without people worrying so much about who they really loved and how much and should they tell them. Love everyone. That was his motto. And, in his way, he meant it.

Deepa yanked her nightie off and stood up to try and locate her clothes. Tom quickly moved in behind her, cupping her breasts up in his hands and kissing the back of her neck.

'This looks like a Benetton ad,' she said, looking at his white hands holding her brown breasts. We'd make a beautiful baby, she thought, just as he said it aloud.

'What!?' she asked, turning round to face him.

'We'd make a beautiful baby, you and me,' he repeated.

'Tom, I'm halfway through a degree I've wanted to do for my entire life. I don't want a baby right now,' she snapped, 'I can't have a baby.' And then, for the first time since she'd begun to suspect that this was what was wrong with her, she began to cry. Great, embarrassingly helpless sobs.

'Shhh,' Tom cuddled her against him and tried to soothe her. 'It'll be fine. You won't be pregnant, I know it . . . And you know, if . . . we'll do whatever you want Deeps. It'll be fine. People go through this stuff all the time.'

She was crying really hard now.

'Anyway, I love babies,' he added, hoping this would help.

She punched his back for that.

Now what? He couldn't exactly say: 'And I love abortions too.'

'We have choices,' he said and suddenly felt a wave of panic. Was she really pregnant? Was this really going to happen to them? Jesus. What the hell would his mother say?

'We need tea,' he said and gently set her down on the edge of the bed.

He opened the door on the flat's tiny kitchen and set about trying to find the kettle.

Chapter Four

Anna had woken as soon as the light filtered through the filmy curtains of her second bedroom, the one she had to herself and didn't have to share with her little brother.

She checked the clunky diving watch, which she wore even in bed, and saw that it was a quarter to seven. Good. Her father and Michelle wouldn't be up for about two hours, so she would have the flat to herself. She would be able to do the secret guilty thing that she could only do here, when everyone was asleep.

Wrapped in her blue dressing gown, she slipped out of the bedroom and into the sitting room where she quietly turned on the TV, then searched through the cabinet for the video which she knew was tucked down the back of the bottom shelf where she had left it last.

She slotted in into the recorder and before she pressed play, she went into the kitchen to pour herself a bowl of cereal – one of the sticky sweet kinds her dad allowed her, Coco Pops, Crunchy Nut Cornflakes – and a glass of milk. Then she came back into the room and switched the tape on.

She was planning to watch the full ninety minutes of action. Here was her mother breast-feeding while her dad videoed her, telling her how beautiful she was and how their baby, Anna, was perfect. Here, he reached out a hand and stroked them both as if he couldn't quite believe that the scene in front of him was real.

But the bit that always made Anna cry was later on in the tape. Her mother was sitting in a deckchair in the garden. A crawling Anna was now at her feet, rummaging through a selection of baby blocks on the grass and the footage bumped along, Joseph obviously walking quickly as he filmed:

'Hello there.' Eve was caught unawares, putting up her hand to shield her eyes from the sun.

'Hello.' The camera swooped as Joseph bent to kiss her face.

'What is it?' Eve asked with a laugh. 'You look incredibly secretive.'

'OK, performance time.'

'Oh . . . great.' Eve was trying to sound sincere. Then the camera was set down on the garden table and adjusted so that it focused on Eve in her deckchair.

'I want to film your reaction,' Joseph explained.

'I see. What, the full audience horror?'

'Maybe.'

Then he slung his guitar down from his shoulder, put his foot up on her chair and strummed a chord.

'This is a home-made number.'

'Oh, how . . . nice,' she settled on, but then couldn't resist, 'Should I cover the baby's ears?'

'Ha, ha . . . a one, two, three, four . . .' Then the most Godawful tuneless strum broke out and Joseph began to sing, equally tunelessly.

> *'Eeeeve . . . I can't belieeeeve,*
> *How fab you are.*
> *So much better than my playing*
> *Of this guitah . . . ah . . . ar.'*

At this, Eve almost doubled over with hysteria in her deckchair, but still the singing continued.

'I may not be able to sing . . .' Here, Joseph reached into his pocket for a small box and held it out to her.

'But I want you to wear my ring.'

This was always the point where Anna felt the throb well up in her throat, because her dad suddenly sounded so serious and sincere. And her mum looked astonished, taking the box and opening it up without a word. Looking up at him, quite bewildered, for further explanation.

'Eeeeve, I can't belieeeeve . . .'

'Oh God, don't sing this. What do you want to say?' Eve asked him.

'But this is the best bit . . .'

He took his hands off the guitar and added, in a low, half-sing now: *'Eve, do you want to wed? Or shall I just make you happy in . . .'*

She burst into laughter again and put her hands over Anna's ears: *'Joe!'*

'Instead . . . I was going to say "instead". But I'll do the other stuff too.'

He leaned over to kiss her and that was when Anna would see the smile – the secret, conspiratorial, sexy smile, which she'd never seen on her mother's face at any other time.

'This is just perfect,' she told him, looking at the ring now, taking it out of the box to admire. 'Can we afford it?'

'I might have to do some busking.'

They collapsed into giggles at the idea.

He took it from her and put it onto her fourth finger. 'When are you going to agree to marry me?' he asked.

'I love you,' she said and they began to kiss, him adding melodramatic groaning sounds.

'Then marry me,' he added.

'I don't know, Joseph . . . I don't know if I want all that again.'

'Me, Eve . . . Not "all that", just me. Don't you want me?'

'Are you going to turn that thing off?' she asked, looking directly at the video now, as if she'd just remembered it.

Clunk, darkness. That was where the clip ended.

That was when Anna would sob hard into the toilet paper she'd stuffed into her dressing-gown pockets, knowing that this moment would come. How could two people love each other so much, be so happy together and yet let it turn out like this? How could her dad be in Manchester with stupid, awful Michelle, while her mother was left alone?

Why had her parents let this happen?

She'd asked them both hundreds of times and she thought their answers were just rubbish.

'Well Anna, your daddy loves you very much, but we don't love each other any more.'

'Why not? Why do you stop loving someone?' Did that mean one day they would stop loving her?

'We don't get on any more . . . it's complicated, Anna.'

'Well you made Robbie together, didn't you?' Anna would storm. 'How did that happen, then?' How indeed, Eve would wonder.

'Anna, I'm sorry. I'm very, very sorry that your daddy and I aren't together any more. I'm so sorry for you, baby.' Her mother would hold her.

'But what about Robbie?' Anna would sob. 'He hasn't really got a daddy. How's he going to turn out?'

'Probably like Denny and Tom – really nice,' Eve would soothe, stroking her hair. 'And anyway, when Robbie's older he can go up on visits with you. He's just a bit small to spend the weekends away from home, right now. He does have a daddy, just like you do.'

But sometimes Anna still felt inconsolable about it. It wasn't something that got better. She missed her dad. She wanted him back living with them all the time. She didn't want to get used to living without him, seeing him every second weekend. Deep down, although she loved her parents very much, she thought they were both selfish to have done this to her and Robbie. Selfish, selfish, selfish. That's why she was determined to be a head doctor. She wanted to make everyone feel better. She wanted to stop these things happening. And she'd decided she was going to have one really good try at getting her parents back together again.

She heard a door opening and quickly hit the stop button on the video remote.

Michelle was standing in the doorway, all freshly showered, in a long white robe with her hair up in a towel. She smelled way too flowery for Anna's liking.

'Hi,' Michelle said.

'Hello.' Anna wasn't exactly filled with enthusiasm at the prospect of a conversation with Michelle.

'Are you watching TV?'

'I was. But I'm fed up with it now.'

'So, what would you like to do today, Anna?' Bright smile.

'Don't know. What are you doing?' Scowl.

'I was going to go into town. Maybe you and Joseph would like to come along?' Michelle was trying really hard here. 'Maybe you'd like something new? A dress or new shoes or something?'

'Ummm . . . No thanks. Why don't you go off shopping so Daddy and I can do something a bit more interesting instead.' With that Anna picked up the remote control, flicked the television on again and pretended to be incredibly interested in the Japanese action fighters cartoon bursting over the screen in front of her.

Michelle left the room without another word for one of her fierce whispers with Joseph.

'It doesn't matter what I do, she just doesn't like me,' Michelle complained. 'She doesn't want to like me.'

'Calm down,' he tried to reassure her. 'It's a big thing, your dad being with someone else. Just give her a chance.'

'But she's so snooty with me. You really should tell her not to be so rude.'

'Michelle, calm down.' Joseph put his hands on her shoulders and kissed her lightly on the lips, 'She's nine, you're . . .' Unfortunately, he couldn't remember.

'Twenty-seven,' she hissed at him.

'Sorry.' He gave what he hoped was a reassuring pat on the shoulder again and went to see his daughter.

'Morning honeybun,' he said as he came into the room.

49

'Morning.' He was treated to a rare full-beam Anna smile.

He sat down on the sofa beside her, cuddling her up against him. Then, noticing the video recorder lights on, he took the remote from her hand and pressed play. Footage of Eve laughing, holding a squirming almost-toddler Anna filled the screen.

'I'm just reminiscing.' Anna tried to sound casual.

Joseph laughed at his funny little nine-year-old, watching her toddler shots and coming out with a word like that.

'You were a lovely baby,' he said. 'You're a lovely girl.'

'Daddy?'

'Yes.'

'Why can't you and Mummy be nicer to each other?'

'Why can't you be nicer to Michelle?' he countered, but it was true, he and Eve were going through an embarrassingly snide phase at the moment.

Anna decided to ignore the Michelle remark and carry on: 'It's just so . . . childish,' she told him off. 'You're so nice to me and Mummy's so nice to me. Why do you have to be so stupid when you're together? It makes me feel really sad.'

'Sorry,' Joseph said and cuddled her in a little closer. 'I'll be much nicer to your mummy.'

'Promise?'

'Promise.'

Oh good, there was the very first step in her reconciliation programme already achieved and how easy had that been! Now, for step two.

'Anyway, I don't really like Michelle,' she confided, 'I think she's boring.'

There was just a trace of irritation in his voice as he replied: 'Well, just try a bit harder for me, honey, because I really like her.'

'Hmmm.' She was going to have to work fast, before her dad decided he *loved* Michelle or something awful like that.

'How did you and Mum meet?' Anna asked, because apparently focusing on happier times was a very important part of relationship counselling. She now had a book on it: *Make Your Marriage a Happier Place*, which she'd bought at a secondhand bookstall at the market for 50p.

'Bit young for that, ain't you?' the dealer had asked.

'It's for a friend,' she'd said coolly, handing over her 50p and hiding the book in her bag so her mother, over at the vegetable stall with Robbie, wouldn't see it. Plus, she'd discussed the subject at length, although not to her great satisfaction, with her mother's friend, confidante and hairdresser, Harry.

'How do you think I can get my parents back together again?' she'd asked him as he'd combed through her long wet locks.

'Pah!' he'd laughed, shrugged his shoulders and said '*Amore*!? You ask-a me about *amore*?'

Because although he'd been born and brought up about two centimetres from the Mile End Road, he liked to ramp up 'the Italian in him', believed to be a long since deceased grandparent.

'I think she still loves him,' Anna had observed, watching the neat comb and snip, comb and snip going on at the very bottom of her hair.

'For her, the door is still open. She hasn't found anyone else, maybe she doesn't want to find anyone else.' Big shrug. 'But for heeeeem? I don't-a know.'

'He has a girlfriend,' Anna told Harry, 'but she's awful. Young and dumb,' she added, sounding so like one of his Wednesday afternoon OAPs that it was hard not to laugh.

'But what can I do? You know, to get them back together?' Anna had asked again.

'Nothing,' was Harry's warning. 'If it was really love, the once in a lifetime stuff that everyone gets so excited about, they will wake up some day and realize.'

'But what if only one of them realizes?' she'd asked.

'Well, then it isn't meant to be.' Snip, snip. 'Two people have to be in love together, or else the whole thing falls apart, no?'

'But can't I just remind them that they still love each other?'

'How can you be sure?'

'I'm their daughter. I know this stuff.' She'd

crossed her arms and kicked her legs out with a clang against the wall.

So that was why she was now trying to remind her father of the night he first came across Eve.

'How did we meet?!' he was repeating her question. 'Oh, you know that story, don't you? Anyway, it was a long time ago.' For a moment, Anna thought he was about to get up and her chance would be gone.

So she quickly added: 'I know the first thing you ever said to her,' as a prompt.

'Do you?'

'Yeah, she told me ages ago. It was: "Do you believe in love at first sight or do I have to walk past you again?"'

Anna laughed and Joseph felt himself blush.

Partly because it was such an embarrassing line and partly because with those words he was, of course, there, in the sweaty little jazz club . . . ten years ago now . . . clapping eyes on Eve for the very first time and reliving the moment when he had gone to talk to her with a suddenly dry throat and knees in danger of actually knocking together.

She had been leaning on the bar, sticking out a small pert bottom, twiddling with long blond hair, and he'd only been able to see one side of her face, but the expression was a beguiling mixture of dreamy calm and mischief.

As he'd got closer, he'd realized that she was about ten years older than she had looked from afar and this had made him even more afraid and even more inflamed. He'd never felt anything like this. And even as he'd prepared to do the line – ironically, of course – he'd been convinced this was the *coup de foudre* (well, he was a French lit and philosophy student at the time). This was, on his part anyway, *love at first sight*.

Chapter Five

'Do you believe in love at first sight? Or do I have to walk past you again?'

She had laughed out loud and taken in the handsome face framed with overgrown dark hair. He was ridiculously young. But then so was everyone else in this dim, clammy little night-club she'd been taken to by her best friend Jen, Jen's husband Ryan and two other friends from work.

Jen and Eve had been looking forward to the rare night out for weeks, buying silly tight tops, new lipsticks and sparkly eye shadows at the shopping centre, scanning the listings pages for a club that sounded good.

Eve's boys had been taken to Jen's house to sleep over with her sons and a babysitter, and the five adults had piled into a shared cab to the funky little soul and salsa venue in Islington.

And how liberating it was to drink, dance and watch a different kind of world go by. Eve felt full of fun. Jen had been right, they needed to do this more often. Get out there. Remember the life beyond work and pre-school breakfasts, home-work, snot noses, nutritious suppers and all the other stuff they did day in, day out.

So when Jen was on the dance floor again and Eve was at the bar, ordering more drinks and taking in the scene, that was when Joseph had walked up to her and started talking.

About what, it was strangely hard to re-member. They had joked about their drinks and the dancing . . . oh, God knows.

Her looking at this handsome, handsome face as he distractedly pushed back locks of hair and smiled lots, a wide-open, disarming smile she couldn't help but smile back at.

As the conversation went on, she noticed Jen pointedly staying away, so as not to interrupt them, but it took a while for Eve to realize what this was about.

'So who are you here with tonight?' she'd asked.

'My mates,' Joseph had answered. 'If you look casually over your right shoulder, you will see a group of morons waving and cheering me on. That's who I'm here with tonight.'

So she'd looked and sure enough, a tableful of lads about 15 feet away started shouting and giving her the thumbs-up sign.

'So why are you over here talking to me?' She

wasn't being flirtatious, she was genuinely
curious.

'Because I really wanted to and they dared
me.'

'Oh.'

Oh . . . Oh! This was about flirting and chatting
up and maybe even snogging and dating and
things she had barely thought about – let alone
done for a long, long time. He was interested . . .
in her!! She'd looked at this young man properly
then. Broad shoulders, the low-hipped jeans
which bagged over bright blue trainers, the olive
tan hands, face and long fingers with smooth,
round nails. She had a vision of small wood-
brown nipples on a hairless chest and felt . . .
alive, alert – and suddenly nervous. He was
absolutely lovely. Their eyes kept meeting and
holding. His dark, liquid brown, hers an un-
fathomable steel grey, he thought.

'It's really corny,' he'd said as they'd grinned
at each other, both frantic to think of something incredibly interesting to say next, 'but
would you like to go outside to chat? It's quieter
and maybe there are stars . . . or at least street-
lights.'

She'd laughed at this, but just a little because
the thud, thud, thud in her heart was so loud she
could hardly hear him over it.

Once they'd stepped out of the club onto the
back street pavement it felt weird and very cold.
The air was frosty and their words made clouds.
He smiled a bit shyly at her now and they just

looked at each other for a breath-holdingly long time.

'Do I look a lot older than I did in there?' she'd blurted out.

'A bit – but that's making me feel shy, not putting me off . . . or anything . . . I mean . . . I don't . . . I didn't . . .' he'd petered out, embarrassed.

'How old are you?' she'd asked, hugging her bare arms tightly around her and trying to stop her teeth chattering.

'Twenty-two.'

'Ah! Well, that makes me ten years older than you, which is maybe a bit scary,' she'd told him, wondering if he was going to rush back inside.

'You know, it could be fun. We probably shouldn't even think about it,' he'd said encouragingly and leaned just slightly towards her, coming closer without actually moving.

It was a pivotal moment: should she just laugh this off and turn back into the club, which is what she thought she was about to do, or should she allow herself just a little bit of . . . what? Fun? Daring? Experiment? She thought of Jen's words to her earlier in the evening: 'You're turning into such a boring old drudge, Eve. Lighten up!'

So she hesitated for just a little moment between turning or staying, turning or staying, and then she moved, stepping towards the soft mouth that bumped down onto hers. Thud, thud, thud – she'd never felt so wired in her life. She couldn't breathe, could barely stand up, knew she was going to have to surface for air from this long, gasping underwater kiss.

'You're lovely,' he said when they broke apart and she felt the kind of embarrassed flush you'd hope to have grown out of by 32.

And so was he, so soft – soft mouth, soft stubble. Babyfaced. Oh God, that thought was embarrassing her even more.

'You too,' she'd managed back in a voice barely above a mumble. 'My friends will be wondering where I am. Why don't you come in and say hello?'

'In a minute.' He pulled her in to kiss her neck now, causing every hair the length of her spine to stand on end.

When they made it back inside, Jen, Ryan and Eve's other very intrigued looking friends had insisted Joseph sit down beside them and answer questions far nosier than any Eve would have dared to ask him.

It turned out he was a student – French and Philosophy. How romantic, she'd thought, forcing herself to look away now and again because she was staring at him, hungry for every little detail: the way he waved his hands about when he spoke, the cheekbones when he smiled, that little scoop of skin between the top of his lip and his nose.

He'd worked in France for three years, saving up money to do his degree, so he still had a couple of years of study ahead of him, he was telling them.

He looked a little French, she'd thought, and whenever he'd glanced up and met her gaze she'd felt the jolt of excitement that made it very hard to concentrate on anything other than him.

He'd insisted on buying everyone drinks and when he'd come back from the bar he'd squeezed himself onto the sofa next to her and begun tracing circles on the skin of her back with his fingers. She'd sipped the marguerita, which was making her head spin anyway, and thought only about where else she would like those fingers to go.

When she'd torn herself away to go in search of the toilets, she'd been tailed by all three of her friends, Jen, Liza and Jessie.

'You bad, bad girl,' Liza was telling her.

'What?! We've had one kiss.'

'You've already snogged!' Liza pretended to be shocked.

'One kiss. Well . . . maybe it was three. It's just for fun.' Eve had clicked open her handbag and was trying to be casual about the lipgloss, spritz of perfume, hair fuss she was going to do in front of the mirror now.

'Hmmm . . .' Jen rolled her eyes. 'He is gorgeous! Just what the doctor ordered, Eve. Please do yourself this favour . . . for my sake!'

'Don't be silly.'

'Toyboy!' Liza had teased.

'Has he offered you a lift home yet?' Jessie's voice from the other side of the cubicle. 'I bet he's mentioned how he lives "just around the corner" and it won't be any bother to share a cab?'

'For goodness sake!' Eve had protested but it was no use, the three of them were cackling now. And it was true, he didn't live too far away and they had made the arrangements, in excited whispers into each other's delicious little earlobes.

'Can I give you a lift?' he'd asked.

'Oh, it's out of your way,' she'd protested, all the time thinking: yes please, yes please.

'*Please*, can I give you a lift home? Please, please,' he'd whispered, 'I'll be very good.'

Oh. She'd thought of the back circles. Of course he would be. Very good.

'OK then,' she'd agreed. 'Just let me check with Jen.'

He'd gone off as well, to make sure all the friends he'd brought to the club were able to get home without him.

'Your boys will be fine,' Jen had told her. 'Go off, have fun. And there's no rush tomorrow, pick them up whenever you like.'

'What are you suggesting?!' Eve had tried to sound outraged but couldn't keep the grin off her face.

'What's going to happen, I bloody well hope. He's lovely!'

They both laughed at this.

'OK, night-night. I'll speak to you tomorrow. Don't let the boys eat everything in your cupboards for breakfast,' Eve warned.

Jen waved her away. 'Good night. Don't go to bed too early . . . *please*! For my sake!'

Eve turned from her friend and walked towards the smiling stranger waiting for her on the other side of the room.

What did she want to do? she'd wondered. Did she want to take him home? Did she want to sleep with him? She felt a blood rush just at the thought of that. And slight panic.

Oh God, just get over there girl, see what happens. He was fun to be with. Couldn't she just concentrate on being with him? Enjoy the moment, rather than fast-forward to the future where she was filing for divorce because he'd been cheating on her with A-Level students because 'they really understand me'. EVE!!

He'd put an arm round her, which they'd both pretended to be so casual about, then they'd walked out to his car – even smaller, older and rattier than her own – *sweet*! So there they were, sitting in the front seats, looking at each other over the handbrake as he started up the ignition.

'So . . . where to now?' she'd asked, wondering if this was going to be awkward. But he wasn't going to let it get awkward. He'd leaned over and kissed her again, making her pulse jump in her throat like a live thing.

'You know I don't have to take you home,' he'd said, stroking her cheek. 'And I don't have to drag you home with me. This is nice . . . we could go for a drive. Watch the sun come up, stay up till breakfast.'

Stay up till breakfast?! The last time she did that, vomit-soaked sheets and two small boys with raging fevers were involved. But Joseph didn't need to know that. She wasn't hiding anything, he already knew she was a single mother of two. But she didn't want to bore him with too much domestic stuff. She didn't want to bore herself with it either. He was right: this was nice.

So, he'd fired up the car and they'd driven off together. First, to the all night bagel shop in Brick Lane and then out through east London, the Docklands and Greenwich to a quiet street over-looking the river. He'd left the car stereo on and they'd moved to the back seat where, huddled under a blanket, they'd talked, joked, kissed and snogged and watched a pale pink wintry sun break through the low mist – or was it smog? – over the water.

Just a little bit after dawn, when the insides of the car windows were steamed up with the cold outside and the warm breaths inside, Joseph's kissing was too hot and persistent to ignore.

His breath was moving over her face as he licked at her eyelids, lips, earlobes. She felt herself undoing the buttons of his shirt as his hands moved up under hers, tugging her small breasts out of the stretchy little cotton bra, pulling her top up so he could lick her nipples.

She'd wanted to keep this strictly above waist level: it was night one – the first time she'd met the guy. But it was too good. Her eyes were closed and she was yearning for more, for all of this, for him. She wanted to touch his legs, his buttocks, the dark hair curled up in his groin . . . him.

He was tugging at the zip of her trousers now and pushing aside wringingly wet pants in the awkward fumble of trying to get intimate in the back seat of a tiny car. She blinked open to see his brown eyes locked onto hers with black pupils wide open, soft lips all rosy and flushed.

'You are so lovely,' she'd whispered, before her mouth was under his again and his fingers were finding the melting, dissolving place between her legs.

In a giggly tangle, she'd managed to unzip him and get the warm olive cock between her lips, before she'd scrambled up into his lap, taken him inside and sat over him watching his lovely face change, sigh, tense and finally come as she moved with him, breathed into his ear, kissed his eyebrows and told him how good he was.

And then came the awkward bit. Her not able to quite believe what had just happened, him knotting up a wet, filled condom and wondering where to put it.

Where did they go from here? she'd worried, tugging her jeans back up, suddenly feeling the cold and damp in the car.

'We need breakfast now,' he'd said with a smile and then crawled to the driver's seat to turn on the ignition and the fan heater up to full blast.

'You know, I don't really know what I want,' she'd tried to tell him. 'I mean from . . .' Big blush, why was all this stuff so hard to spit out? 'A man . . .' Oh cringe cringe.

'Neither do I,' he'd joked back.

'I've got the kids and I don't want to complicate anything or confuse them . . . or even spend much time away from them.'

'It's OK,' he'd said, 'I just wanted a quick shag in the back of a car and what's your name again?'

She'd looked at him in dismay.

'JOKE!' he'd said quickly. 'Joke . . . stupid, tasteless . . . strange moment after sex joke. Sorry. I'm sorry. I think you're lovely, you obviously like me, so why don't we hang out a bit and see how it goes? No promises, no-one doing anything they don't want to do. If you want to call a halt at any time, you can.' He put his arms out to help her squeeze through to the front seat again.

'But you haven't seen any of my good moves yet,' he'd added, smiling. 'My style was totally cramped in there. I know stuff that women can't resist.' When he'd said this in his sort of jokey, *amn't I so ironic?* way, it was funny and cute. Killer combination. Lady-slayer. Could he really be as nice and interested as he seemed? Or was this all a big seduction act?

He'd leaned over the handbrake to kiss her.

'We could have a lot of fun and I bet I love your kids.'

When she'd drawn back from his lips at this,

he'd added quickly; 'When I'm allowed to meet them . . . when you want me to.'

'You know what's really worrying me,' she'd told him, 'is that you seem too nice. These are the things men say when they're trying. I just can't believe you're really this genuinely nice.'

'Too good to be true.' He'd folded his hands under his chin, leaned against the steering wheel and smiled. 'Well, that's a new complaint, I have to admit and I'm not sure my last girlfriend would agree. I'm a bit asthmatic, I wheeze at night – does that make me less perfect?'

She'd laughed at this.

'But don't you think we behave differently with different people? Some people bring out the worst in each other and some people bring out the best.'

He'd left it there. No need to spell out the implication that maybe they could bring out the best because it was there, obvious as the dimply little grin tucked up under his left cheek.

So they'd gone for breakfast in some kitsch little café where even the growling, pissed-off waiter hadn't been able to burst their bubble. Then he'd dropped her at her door – she wouldn't let him in – swapped telephone numbers and he'd already made arrangements to see her again.

In fact, he'd called constantly, had begged to be allowed to come round much more often than she let him and had already met the boys within days of their first date. Eve soon found Joseph was an irrepressible force. He would have camped outside her door if she hadn't let him in.

He was smitten and gradually, very gradually, she allowed herself to be too. It turned out to be the perfect time for Eve to fall in love again. Her first marriage was six years behind her and her boys, Denny, then 12, and Tom 10, didn't need her as much. They had football practice, friends to visit, places to go . . . so there was Joseph all ready and waiting to take up her time and let her reclaim some of herself for fun, romance and life beyond the kids.

He made her laugh so much. There was a lightness to her which had rarely been there before.

Eve and Joseph's first whole weekend alone together had been unforgettable. For weeks they had sneaked sly sex in the bathroom with bathwater running or on her fold-down bed in the sitting room in the very small hours of the morning, with the boys' bedroom door barricaded shut – and even then it had to be in silence, total darkness and completely under the covers, all of which turned them on to the point of hysteria.

Finally, she'd agreed to Jen's nagging offers to have the boys for the weekend and Joseph had come to stay on Friday night and hadn't had to leave until Sunday late afternoon. Just like a proper couple.

He had arrived at the door weighed down with carrier bags full of stuff and she'd let him into the flat where their long, excited hello of a kiss had become the first breathless up against the wall session of the evening.

Then he'd been allowed to unpack his goodies and they'd made dinner together before going to bed very early, with the lights on and the covers off to drink in every little tiny physical detail. Afterwards, she'd touched every single one of his moles and he'd combed out her pubic hair in between taking little licks down there, telling her – to her mock screams of horror – that the area was in need of some serious attention. 'You've got a mummy muff and it really has to go. I don't know what I'm doing.'

'Joseph!!!! You're a rude, rude boy!'

'Oh yes, very rude.' And he moved his mouth down again and got to work for longer than she'd ever imagined she could want him to. Until she'd come all over again and felt picked clean of every last remaining shred of desire.

The next morning – or well, afternoon, by the time they'd had breakfast in bed, more sex, a bath, more sex, lunch – they'd gone out for supplies. Food, wine . . . and Joseph loading up a basket at the chemist's but refusing to let her see what was in it until much later that evening when she was giggly drunk, had smoked her first joint and was sprawled over the messed-up bed beside him.

Then he'd brought out the hairdressing scissors and begun to trim the hair between her legs, making silly hairdressery comments all the time: 'Ooooh darling, I think we could transform this with just a little wisp of gel . . . now be honest with me . . . how often do you shampoo? It's too much darling, you'll strip off all the natural oils.' She was just about hysterical with laughter and lust. He kept snipping, then touching, then groping. With care and dedication he coated the edges with Immac and when he was finally finished, she had a small, shorn, heart-shaped muff which they both wanted to take to bed straight away.

On Sunday morning, he persuaded her to bleach a great chunk of her fringe white and dye the rest of her hair pale copper. Then, he gave her the mini PVC nurse's outfit and stetson, hoping she would see the funny side . . . *and* put them on.

'Really, if it's too much . . . I'm OK with that . . . this is a 1990s, ironic, post-feminist, we're-all-consenting-adults, PVC outfit, honest.'

'Oh really?' she'd said, coaxing down the cheap, jamming zip. 'I'm not sure if I really want to know just how fearless you are in bed.'

'Oh yes you do, nurse, you do.'

'Now you can truly say you've had a dirty weekend,' he'd told her when they were having sex *again* for what they knew must be the last time on Sunday afternoon as the sun was setting, just an hour before the boys were due back.

She was chafed from her chin to her ankles and so was he. On top of him on the sofa, she moved slowly, neither of them sure if they could possibly come again.

'I want to live with you,' he'd said, all of a sudden. 'Please say yes. I think you should buy a bigger flat with two bedrooms. One for the boys and one soundproofed room for us . . . aaah' – slight change of position – 'and I'll be your lodger so you'll easily afford the mortgage and we'll get somewhere with a garden, so me and the boys can play football. And I'll put my desk in the bedroom so I can study all the time I'm not making love to you . . . or making you deliriously happy . . . please say yes, Eve. I think we could be really good for each other.'

He'd waited a long time for her reply. He'd slowed down until she just felt the pulse of him throbbing inside.

'I haven't met your parents,' she'd said finally with a little bit of a smile.

'That's very old fashioned of you!'

'I mean I'd like to meet your parents.'

'OK . . . but you're avoiding my question here. Can we move in together?'

'Well . . .'

'Please?'

'I need to think about it and sound out the boys. Buy a flat?' These were all huge steps, but Joseph made it sound easy, wanted it to be easy for them.

'Think about it, Eve. Oh fuck, I want to come but there isn't any sperm left inside me.'

Kids today, she thought, stroking the head moving between her breasts. They were so liberated, it was scary.

'You're going to love my mother,' he added.

'Stop . . . you're really scaring me now!'

Chapter Six

She'd finally found a dingy two-bedroomed basement flat with a charmless stretch of garden at the back, but she knew she could make this home, and when she and her sons moved in, Joseph came too.

They'd bought a bed together, but that was the only joint purchase she'd allowed. Eve had been on her own with her sons for too long to be able to let someone move easily into her life. He'd paid rent and she'd paid for all the other furniture, curtains, paints, plants, kitchen pots and pans – the stuff she gradually accumulated to make a real home. To make the home she'd always wanted for her sons.

But Joseph wouldn't let her keep him at arm's length. He loved her generously, unselfishly and wanted to be the love and the lover of her life. Until gradually, she'd let him in. No sooner had she started to return his 'I love yous', than he was

wanting to rush on into commitment, marriage
. . . babies!

'Slow down,' she seemed to be warning him
all the time.

'Why??!' was his response to this.

It maybe shouldn't have been such a surprise
to her that she became pregnant within months
of moving in with him. Had it been realistic to
expect a diaphragm to hold this amount of deter-
mination at bay?

The first few months of the pregnancy were
fraught for Eve: not only was she frightened
that they weren't ready for this – but she had
miscarried at the end of her first marriage and
it was terrifying to be pregnant again. She
was tearful, tired, sick and anxious. She would
lie awake in bed at night certain that the
slightest tummy twinge was the first sign of
another miscarriage. But finally, finally, their
fat, feisty little baby girl had arrived and
although Joseph and Anna had fallen in love at
first sight, Eve's first reaction to the baby had
been an emotional mess of love, relief and fresh
anxiety. For a long time after the birth, she'd
had to cry almost every day because this so
wanted baby was here at last and perfect. It
took months to rid herself of all the fears and
Eve found it hard to let the baby out of her sight
or even put her down until she was a robust
three-month-old.

*   *   *

Throughout Anna's baby and toddlerhood, Joseph was studying at home most of the time so he slipped quite naturally into the main carer role and loved it. He was absorbed by his tiny girl, would pace the flat with her when she fretted, coax her to sip at her bottles of breast milk and make up tuneless lullabies to soothe her to sleep. For Eve it was a revelation to have a man who was so interested in her and so interested in both Anna and her big boys. Her first husband, Dennis, wouldn't have had the slightest idea how to look after his sons and hadn't cared enough to learn.

'Look, look,' Joseph would point out, besotted: 'my eyes, your hair, your nose. I think she's got your top lip and my bottom one. Isn't that *amazing*?! She's the most perfect girl in the whole world.'

'Even better than *me*?' Eve would joke.

'Even better, because she's you *and me*.'

Now, three whole years had passed without him and she was still getting used to it. She felt contented most of the time, happy even, but it would be a lie to say she didn't miss him. She'd had to throw out their bed and buy a smaller one because the emptiness where he had once been would creep over and chill her. Small things could still lurch her back into how much she missed him, or rather, missed the way things once were.

She would catch a trace smell of him on Anna's

74

jumper when her daughter came back from a weekend away. She would see something he would have laughed at, or worst of all she would be reminded of the sex.

How effortlessly good it had become between them. They would roll up together in bed at night with kisses which were so wanted and well timed that sliding into one another was easy and unspoken. Sex was an easy rhythm, moving into different positions was mutual and coming together was almost always possible or just out by a few beats. They would fall apart and into sleep almost straight away, because there was never any need to say anything. It was totally good, totally satisfying. When she and Joseph had become live-in lovers she had finally understood what it was to 'know' someone, to 'move as one'.

She found it hard to sum up what had gone wrong between them over the years. Maybe she'd always felt too pressed by him for a commitment she didn't want to make; maybe she didn't like the person he was growing into. She'd fallen in love with a dreamy, home-based, idealistic student, but Joseph had graduated, landed a job, found out he loved it, wanted to be ambitious and make money. Eve, who had once been the wife of a wealthy workaholic, had panicked that her new, carefully reconstructed life was about to veer off in the direction she'd wanted to avoid.

*　*　*

'I've made the biggest ever mistake. I shacked up with a complete prat,' she'd told Jen when she'd finally flung Joseph out of the flat close to midnight after a stand up and scream row. Jen had arrived within the hour, bearing a large bottle of cheap Polish gin and a carton of apple juice, which was all she'd been able to rustle up in the rush.

They had drunk tall glasses of this odd apple gin concoction. 'The Dutch are really into this . . . or is it the Belgians?' Jen had told her, chucking in a few shrunken, frosty ice cubes hacked from the back of Eve's freezer.

After two glasses, they'd moved on to the biscuit tin of joints in the kitchen and had smoked and drunk their way into a numbed state that even Eve's trauma couldn't reach.

'He was so lovely,' she'd told Jen, as they curled up on the sofa together and shared the last joint. 'Such a great guy. Such a lovely dad to Anna.'

'Such a great fuck,' Jen had added, then quickly, 'I'm not speaking from experience, you idiot, I could just tell by how happy you were and you could never keep your hands off each other.'

'How did I manage to turn him into Richard Branson? Or a sort of good-looking version of Dennis?' This was the question Eve couldn't answer. What had she done? What had gone wrong?

When Joseph left university he had surprised

her by taking the first job he'd applied for, in tele-sales. Even more surprising, he was really good at it and was quickly earning a decent amount.

And no sooner earning it, than spending it. The flat had gained a silver Bang and Olufsen stereo, a flash video recorder, stacks and stacks of CDs and videos. Joseph's wardrobe had rapidly expanded to contain Hugo Boss this, Gieves and Hawkes that . . . Kenzo . . . Emporio Armani. She and the children were showered with gifts too, clothes from DKNY, Calvin Klein, expensive Nike trainers.

She knew all the labels of course – from her former life, the one she'd left behind and vowed never to return to. And she'd felt uneasy.

It wasn't hard to guess that Joseph was not putting anything away, he was spending flat out and maxing the credit cards too. But when she nudged him about it, there was always talk of promotion and next month's bonus and earning more commission.

'I want us to move to a bigger flat in a nicer part of town,' he'd tell her, forgetting that Denny and Tom would have to commute to school.

'I don't know if I want Anna to go to that school. Do you think we should look into sending her somewhere private?' This casual remark one supper had caused the most enor-mous row.

It wasn't just Joseph's wish for 'something better' for his daughter. Eve knew it had trig-gered her deep-seated fear. The fear that all would be lost again, that she would be alone and having to start from scratch. That everything would vanish overnight . . . all the nice clothes and treats and toys that you somehow invested emotionally in, the private school, the social lives constructed around it. This is what had happened to her before and now she only put her faith in things that were solid, that couldn't be taken away. State schools, healthy savings accounts, truly affordable mortgages, cheap clothes . . . human relationships based on solid, solid ground.

Joseph was changing the game plan all the time.

It was true, the flat was tiny for them now, her big teenage sons were crammed into the small back bedroom, Anna slept in a child bed at the foot of their own. But this was her home and besides, it had been very cheap and she had saved hard for it.

'I want what I have,' she would tell him in exasperation. 'I like this flat, Denny and Tom are going to be moving out soon, so Anna will have the second bedroom and we'll have far more space. I like it round here, this is where my friends live. The school is fine. I want Anna to go there.'

And they would stop rowing for a bit until Joseph's unstoppable tide of wants would break out again.

'Stop buying all this stuff!' she would scream at him. 'There isn't any room. No wonder the place is so small. It's got all your shit in every corner.' This had been a memorable outburst, complete with her hauling all the CDs off the racks and scattering them onto the floor.

Denny and Tom had moved out that year. She had given them the deposit to buy a little ex-council flat round the corner. She was sure they were a bit young, just 17 and 19, but her flat was too small for them and their friends and the problems between her and Joseph were too big for everything to fit in.

'Why can't I aim for something better than this? Why can't I want to do well and earn more and move us up just a little bit?' Joseph had ranted at her. 'Why is it so wrong to you? I'm not saying I don't love you, I don't love your life. I just want something . . . *more*. You had it all once, Eve, the cars, the house, the money. Why am I not allowed to even want a little bit of that? Just because it hurt to lose it doesn't mean it will all happen again.'

'This is better, Joseph. You have no fucking idea how much better this is,' she spat at him.

And then the big slap in the face: 'Christ, you're so set in your ways, Eve. Maybe you're just too old for me.'

There were tears and forgiveness and make-up sex but then, just days later, another round of fresh rows. Until their life together became unbearably stormy. So perhaps she should not have been so surprised when he came home one evening and announced that his firm was setting up a new office in Manchester and he was going to be in charge there.

'*Manchester!!!*' she'd shouted. 'We are *not* moving to Manchester.'

He'd taken off his shoes, gone to the fridge and poured himself a glass of orange juice before telling her calmly: 'No, I didn't think that for a moment. They're going to pay for me to have a flat up there so I can stay Monday to Friday and be back here at the weekends.'

It was all decided and he was not consulting her on this, he was telling her how it was going to be.

'I see.' She'd crumpled down into a chair at the kitchen table because she knew this was the beginning of the end and she felt distraught and yet oddly relieved. She was worn out by him. She couldn't take all this fighting and unrest any more. It had sent the boys away out of the house and she missed them Godawfully and knew they had grown up now and would probably never live with her on a day to day basis again.

'Oh Joseph,' she'd cried into her hands. 'You're moving out too.'

'I'm not, really I'm not,' he'd insisted, 'I love you and Anna and us all. I just think a bit of space would be good. We'll remember what we liked about each other so much. Not what we dislike.'

'Oh no. You won't be part of the family any more. Don't you see? You'll only have Anna at the weekends, you won't know about all the daily stuff. You won't be here to tuck her up in bed and read to her every night. She'll miss you so much. And what for? For more money?'

When she lifted her head to look at him, she'd seen the tears in his eyes too.

'Eve, of course I'll miss her all the time . . . and you. But if we carry on like this, we're not going to last another month together. I need to get out of this for a bit. Because I want us to stay together.'

'Space never solved anything. I promise you that.'

'Well what the hell am I supposed to do? They want me to do this job. I can't turn it down.'

'Of course you bloody can. You could get another job with another company here without even trying.'

'I haven't even been with this place for two years yet. How will it look on my CV if I up and leave now, when a promotion is being handed to me on a plate?'

She'd snorted at this. *How would it look on his CV*? Who was this person? What happened to the man who read French poetry aloud in bed?

How had she made such a big mistake? Had she completely misread his character? Had she changed him? Did he wake up one day and feel overwhelmed by his paternal responsibilities?

'I just knew,' she'd told Jen, feeling oddly calm. Probably the effect of Polish gin and the grass. 'There's no affair or anything, but we're not his focus, not even Anna. I could just tell. He was distracted, he was thinking about something else, he was somewhere else even when he was with us. He didn't seem to care enough about our problems any more. He didn't want to argue, he didn't want to get me to change my mind about stuff. It was like he'd already made the decision to move on, he was just waiting for the right time to tell me. And it was once so equal between us,' she added. 'Now it's not.'

'You mean you were once in charge,' Jen had pointed out.

'No I wasn't,' Eve had answered, a little irritated. 'He helped, he did his share, did the time. But now, it's work this . . . work that . . . I really resent it. I'm getting Dennis flashbacks.'

They'd sat in silence for a while, comfortably side by side on the sofa.

'Maybe he's pissed off you don't want to marry him,' Jen had suggested.

'Oh, I just can't do that again. It's too scary, I don't want to be a "wife" again. I did it all with bells on.'

'Don't you think you're confusing "marriage" with marriage to Dennis?' Jen had asked.

Eve had a suspicion that all marriages were fundamentally marriage to Dennis to varying degrees.

'I mean, I'm married, thank you very much,' Jen had reminded her. 'Do I seem a downtrodden doormat to you?'

'Why did you do it, though?'

'You were there. Is it so hard to work out?' Jen had asked. 'So we could have a bloody great, happy party and tell everyone we loved each other. And I think the paperwork helps. We're that bit more bound together.'

'And absolutely nothing changed between the two of you after marriage?'

'Hardly anything.'

'So something did?'

'My family started being nicer to him. They finally accepted Ryan as a permanent fixture. Is that so bad? And we argued more about housework. Otherwise, everything was exactly the same.'

'Hmmm.'

'I'm absolutely starving.'

They'd both begun to giggle.

'We've got the munchies. This is pathetic. If Anna gets out of bed and sees us like this, I'm going to be mortified.'

'It's organic, isn't it?' Jen had held up her stub. 'Well, that's fine. Let her try a puff. Might mellow her a bit. She's so uptight for a five-year-old.'

'Shut up!' Eve had given her a mock slap.

So Eve and Joseph split with bitter tears and a small removals van. She was distraught. He was distraught and so were all three children.

Denny shouted round the house and told his mother there had to be something wrong with her. Tom actually cried over it and Anna took weeks to comprehend that Daddy didn't live here any more and she wailed with distress when she was taken away to Manchester for the weekend, leaving Eve alone in her flat for what felt like the first time in her life. Unbearably alone. She'd gone out and got the two kittens that very first Saturday.

There had been brief, muddled reconciliations, including a final one when it had been agreed that Joseph would spend the three days of Christmas with them, for Anna's sake. Somehow wine, candlelight and the little girl's delight at having them both there together had led to tearful, nostalgic lovemaking in the bath with water splashing all over the floor and Anna's rubber ducks, boats and bath people falling on top of them. For a few hours they had felt happy and healed.

But he was seeing someone else by then, he'd moved out of London . . . and she felt far too defensive and protective of her hurt children to want to risk 'trying' any sort of relationship out again.

'This is all too complicated. I have no idea what I want and neither do you,' he'd told her, stroking her hair as he'd kissed her good night on the cheek and gone to sleep on the sofa.

For that one Christmas splashdown to have resulted in another pregnancy had felt like some appalling cosmic joke. She'd been 39, not the age when you expect your body to spring fertility surprises on you, and had left it till week 15 before breaking the news to Joseph. He'd offered to come back and they had spent a long, draining weekend talking terms. She'd somehow thought another baby might bring everything back to where it had once been – the perfection of life when Anna was tiny. But he'd not been prepared to give up the job or the Manchester commute.

'Not everything can stay the way it was, Eve. Just because we're changing doesn't mean it has to be for the worse,' he'd pleaded with her.

His final offer had been made on the phone, late at night, in tears and she'd turned him down, telling him no, it was over, despite the baby which she was determined to have.

'I'm never going to ask you again,' he'd shouted at her at the end of the call. 'Do you hear me, Eve? I'm not going to be the one who is ever, *ever* going to make the first move again. All you've ever done is shut me out. You never wanted to get married, maybe you never wanted me around. Maybe you prefer to be on your own with your children. Have you ever thought about that?'

She'd been too distraught to say anything.

'This is your last and final chance,' he'd warned, sobbing now. 'If you ever want me back again, you'll have to ask, I can't take this any more.'

Chapter Seven

Monday morning. Eve opened the door on her pokey office with a slightly heart-sinking feeling. No. The stack of files was still there where she'd left it on Friday. No paperwork pixies had been in at the weekend to go through it for her.

At least there was a square of sunlight on her desk and the smell of the hyacinths, which had opened up on her windowsill and were now drooping with thirst. It was the very start of April. She still had earth under her nails from a weekend of weeding and digging, planting and tending to seedlings. The daffodils were out, the tulips dotted all over were going to be colourful and the very first of her lettuces would almost be ready if she could just keep the slugs off them.

OK, but never mind all that. Here she was at work again, with a two-foot pile of case notes in front of her. But first she really had to water the plants, fill the kettle and consult with Liza and Jessie about a possible lunch venue.

Finally, unable to come up with any further distractions, she settled down to read the notes. Eve had been a supervisor of young offenders for the best part of fifteen years and there was very little wayward teens could come up with now that would take her by surprise.

So, these notes were all the usual stuff – poorly educated, badly parented kids getting into trouble. The same kind of trouble, the same kind of kids and it just seemed to happen over and over again. She saw the same names, the same faces and sometimes wondered if she was operating a dishearteningly revolving door service. But then, tucked in a bottom desk drawer were the reminder notes and sometimes even photos and letters from the ones who did get away. The ones who did learn something useful on community service or occupational therapy or who met someone new . . . or maybe, just maybe, took something she said or did for them to heart and got out, changed, stopped coming back for more.

Almost an hour of reading later and it was time for her first interviewee of the day, 19-year-old Darren Gilbert. Picked up by the police in a stolen car with a package of cocaine in the boot – nice.

He shuffled into her office, baseball hat jammed onto bald, shaven head. Hands shoved deep into pockets.

'Hello, Darren,' she said, but made it sound as headmistressy as possible. Even she thought he looked hard for a 19-year-old. He was wearing a tight red tracksuit top and baggy denim jeans that she recognized as some hip and culty label. Teenagers and their pathetic label fetishes! As if some label made you a better person or brought you closer to Posh and Becks. A metal ID bracelet and watch clanked together on his wrist.

He fell back into the chair, hoicked a heavily trainered foot up onto his knee and let it rest against the side of her desk, where she tried to ignore it.

So they did the interview, Eve making it clear she wasn't buying much of his 'just helping somebody out . . . didn't know the car was stolen' story.

'Has it ever occurred to you, Darren, that the owner of the "minicab" office is some hard nut drug dealer?'

'Nah,' he replied, but so unconvincingly she knew he'd already figured out exactly what was going on.

'You're just 19 and you're working for the kind of bloke who will probably send someone to put a bullet through your knees if you mess up. Nice one. And I don't think your mum is going to be too chuffed with you either, is she?' She'd read the case notes, she knew his mother was an A&E nurse.

Darren didn't say anything to this, but she had

his full attention now, absolutely no doubt about it.

Then came the bit where she spelled out her rules and explained to Darren what he was going to have to do if he didn't want to spend time in jail in the future. She liked to use as many 'tough cop' phrases as possible because teenagers raised on a diet of gangster films seemed to respond to that: 'Show some respect', 'Are you the man?' All that kind of thing.

'Maybe we can even train you up to do something a little bit more useful,' she told him at the end of her spiel.

Darren was looking out of the window, so she couldn't read the expression on his face. But the ankle had come off the knee, the trainer off the edge of the table. *Oh, I'm really quite good at this*, she couldn't help thinking.

'OK,' she started to write in his file now, 'we have another appointment next week. In the meantime, lie low. If you're contacted by the cab office, tell them you're not going to get anyone into trouble, but you can't help them out any more.'

Darren had hardly slouched his way out of the office when there was a rap on the door and Lester, her boss, put his head round.

'Hello, Eve, have you got a few minutes for a chat?' he asked.

'Yeah sure,' she replied.

'Big news,' he said, closing the door behind him and sitting down at her desk.

'Good news or bad news?' she wondered.

'Oh good, very good.' He smiled at her, folded his hands together with the index fingers pointing up under his chin and challenged her to guess.

'We're all getting a six-week sabbatical to go on a team building course in Tuscany?'

'No.'

'No? Didn't think so somehow.'

'I've got a new job and I'm leaving in six months' time.'

'Oh God!' was all she could manage for a moment, because it was such a surprise, but then she rallied and added, 'Lester, that's great, fantastic – but how the hell are we going to manage without you?'

'Well . . .'

'And where are you going?' she interrupted.

'Out of London. I've finally found a nice little position doing this job in a bigger department in Ipswich. Trish's family is from round there, as you know, so we're going to sell up, buy a place out in the countryside, get some dogs, hopefully the kids will come and visit once in a while, but you know teenagers . . .'

'Indeed I do. Personally and professionally.'

'They're not even teenagers any more,' he remembered. 'What's the term for moody young twenty-somethings?'

'Post-adolescents or "thresholders", that's very now.'

'Yeah, well . . .'

'That's great. I had no idea you were planning all this.'

'I don't tell you everything, Eve.' This said with a little smile, before he added, 'But I'm telling you ahead of everyone else because I'm going to recommend you for my job. What do you think of that?'

'What do I think of that?' she repeated. 'Now I really *am* surprised.'

Lester was a good man to work for: kind, fair, older, wiser. All the qualities you could have hoped for in a boss in this line of work. He was the reason she hadn't moved areas for an almost unheard-of amount of time. Well, that and the fact that she had never wanted much in the way of promotion. She'd been happy with her lot under Lester.

'You'd be really good,' he was telling her, leaning over the desk with enthusiasm. 'Everyone here trusts you and likes you. You'd be a very safe pair of hands and I know you'd like the pay rise. It doesn't have to be five long days a week, you could maybe do four longer days and a half-day on Friday, or something else like that. All sorts of things could work. You're the right person for the job. Make it work for you. I don't want them to have to go outside for someone else.'

They tossed it about a little longer and Eve promised to give it some thought. When he stood up to go, she stood up too.

'I'm going to really miss you, Lester,' she said.

'Likewise,' he answered and their eyes held for a moment over her desk.

'I don't want to make your life any more complicated than it already is,' he added, 'but maybe this would be good for you. You've seemed a bit . . . I don't know . . . unchallenged lately. Is that the right word? Maybe you need something to move forward in your life.'

'Maybe.' She held out a hand for him and he took it in a double-handed shake.

'Better let you get on,' he said, pointing at her desktop paper stack.

'Oh yes.' Bugger, now she wasn't going to enjoy lunch with the girls nearly so much. This was a secret she couldn't share with them yet.

And she'd been hoping to leave early because Jen was due for supper tonight, but the paper-work pile had to be diminished. She sat down and pulled open a fresh file.

By 10p.m. Eve was fading, but judging by the contents of the wine bottle between her and Jen on the garden table, the evening was still an hour or so away from being over.

'So,' Eve topped up their glasses, 'any improvement on . . .' her voice went down to a mock whisper: 'the sex problem?'

They both burst into cackles of laughter.

'No, no. Ryan still considers watching an episode of *Sex in the City* as foreplay,' Jen confided. 'No, I lie, he's got a new line: "Jen, I've taken out the rubbish"!'

Further giggles at this.

'At least he tries,' Eve told her. 'I don't think I could be bothered with sex.' Now why had she gone and said that? She often said it to Jen, but at the moment it wasn't true and anyway, it just invited trouble.

'So nothing to report on the vet front?' Jen was asking her. See? Now look what had happened.

'No, no . . .' Eve was trying to hide behind her wine glass.

'Nothing at all?! Are you sure there isn't a thing you want to tell Auntie JenJen?'

'I quite like the vet . . . the vet may or may not like me . . . that is absolutely all. And I haven't seen him for ages,' she lied. She'd last seen him two weeks ago, but she'd turned down two recent requests for 'an appointment'.

'Do you really want to spend the rest of your life alone?' Jen was leaning back in her chair, warming up for their favourite debate.

'I'm not alone!' Eve replied. 'I'm not alone for one minute of the sodding day! Alone would make quite a nice change.'

'But your bed is cold and unshared,' Jen reminded her. 'Your children will grow up and move away and you'll die a lonely old maid, all withered up inside.'

Eve snorted at this. 'I have electrical appliances,' she said.

It was Jen's turn to snort. 'Oh please. That's not the same.'

'Definitely not! Oh anyway . . . I couldn't fit a man in.' They both had to shriek at this.

'Into my schedule!' Eve explained. 'I've got kids, work, cooking, homework, cleaning, structured play, park time, paperwork, the older boys and all their stuff. There is no room in my life for a man needing sex and square dinners and patting and attention and weekends away and . . . all that stuff. And anyway,' Eve added, 'what would Anna and Robbie make of it all? No, no, no. I'm going to be celibate for years.'

'Well you're a sad old bag,' Jen said. 'But anyway, I don't believe you. Why do you still look so nice then, all highlighted and toned and dressed in girlie gear? If you really weren't interested you'd just frump out bigtime.'

'I'm a yummy mummy and anyway, I like to show you up.'

'Ha, ha.'

They both knew this was a joke because Jen was the most glamorous midwife this side of 40. She had made the decision many years ago that she might not be thin, but by God, was she sexy. This was a girl who could fill a pair of stretch bootlegs and a Wonderbra with plenty left to spare, and she was totally uninhibited about the overhang. 'Bloody body fascists,' she liked to shout out loud at adverts for Weight Watchers and the like.

Her hair was always a deep mahogany

brown, usually bundled up, and she liked scoop-necked tops, blouses unbuttoned one notch too low and to ooze from tight skirts and jeans. Eve didn't think she'd seen Jen without make-up for about ten years now and it was always deep, dark lipstick and smouldering eye shadow. The one thing Jen couldn't have was the long, painted nails she would have loved. Nails didn't really work in her profession. 'I can't go poking people in the pudenda,' she'd say. The two of them couldn't really have looked more different – Jen, short, dark haired, curvy and glammed up; Eve, tallish, willowy, fair and *au naturel*. She was your 'slap of moisturizer for every day', 'lipgloss and blusher for an event' kind of woman. Her long, highlighted hair was her one beauty extravagance and even that was done at mates' rates by Harry, her friend as well as hairdresser.

'I'm up for a promotion at work,' she told Jen now, watching the candles she'd lit for their outdoor chat flicker in the breeze. 'A *big* promotion. The boss is leaving and he wants me to apply for his job.'

'Fantastic.'

'Yeah but . . .'

'Yeah but . . . yeah but . . . I know what you're going to say you sad and over-anxious mother hen,' Jen teased. 'What about my kids? Who will meet them off the bus and cook them organic lentils?'

'God, I don't only eat lentils. Can we all get that straight?'

'OK.' Jen was a little taken aback by this outburst.

'Anyway, they're still really small, the little kids,' Eve protested. 'Robbie is two. And I worry about how I'll get all the mum stuff done on top of a big, scary job. I'm tired enough as it is. You know, being woken up too early, spending far too much of my life doing the domestic stuff instead of being down at the garden centre choosing new climbers.'

'You are so sad,' Jen told her.

There had been a burst of warm weather, so they'd decided to move their supper outside for the first time this year. And even though they were now in two jumpers each to keep out the chill, it was still wonderful to sit out and drink in the leafy dark, breathing in damp earth because Eve had been round with the hose.

'Maybe it would do you good, the new job,' Jen said.

'That's what Lester said,' Eve told her, feeling a little suspicious now. 'Why do I seem in need of being done good?'

'Well there's nothing much going on for you, is there?'

'Don't hold back, Jen, please.' She was a bit hurt now.

'Sorry. I just mean since you and Joseph broke up and Robbie was born, nothing has changed at all. And that's over two years ago now, isn't it?'

'What, you mean apart from having a new baby-toddler person to cope with?' Eve sounded a little snappy again and Jen thought she should probably leave it at that.

Eve felt rattled. Jen didn't know about the vet. No-one knew. Oh hell – what was there to know? A few afternoons of friendship sex wasn't exactly anything to report. Her friend was right: nothing had changed at all.

And maybe because it was dark, maybe because she was hurt, most likely because the best part of three bottles of wine had been emptied, Eve suddenly heard herself telling Jen something she had barely even let herself think.

'I think I want to give things another go with Joseph,' she said.

'*What!!!*' was Jen's response. 'What? With Richard frigging Branson the Second! Eve . . . Hello? I'm taking your wine glass away now.'

'Jen, don't.' Eve was hugely irritated by her confession.

'When did this happen?' Jen asked.

'It hasn't. Nothing's happened. I'm just going to tell him and see what he thinks.'

'Oh Eve!' Jen gave an exasperated sigh. 'He's got another girlfriend, in case you hadn't noticed. He lives in Manchester . . . he's moved on. All you're going to get is a great big, humiliating no.'

'Well, maybe that would help,' Eve said. 'No matter what I do, I can't stop wondering "what if?"'

'Oh pet.' Jen moved her chair closer, to put an arm round Eve. 'What's brought this on? I thought you were much better.'

'I'm not,' Eve said, recognizing the crack in her voice which meant she was going to have to try very hard not to cry. 'I've been sleeping with the vet and it's just not the same.'

'Of course it's not the same,' Jen soothed her, holding back the desperate urge to ask 'What? Where? When?' and other related questions.

'But it doesn't *mean* anything.' Eve was squeezing away tears now. 'It always meant something with Joseph, even from the very first night.'

Jen just patted and soothed.

'I can't go forward until I know for sure that I can't go back,' Eve told her.

'It's OK.' Jen rubbed her arm. 'But you can't just blurt this out to him, not without some sort of *sign* that he's interested.'

'Anna said she found a photo of me in the glove compartment of his car.' Now that Eve was saying this aloud, it sounded pathetic.

'Anna is an interested party,' Jen reminded her. 'Do you really think you should be listening to everything she says?'

'You're right . . . but the last few times I've seen him . . . I don't know, something seems to be changing. We've been really nice to each other and he wants to spend more time with Robbie – and he's planning to take Anna with him on a trip to Germany because he's investi-

98

gating *environmentally friendly* business ideas.'

She wanted to say: Doesn't that sound a bit more like the old Joseph . . . *my* Joseph? But the look on Jen's face was putting her off.

'Oh God, Jen,' she sighed, 'you're probably right. This is all ridiculous. You shouldn't let me drink this amount of wine.'

Eve found a scrap of tissue in the pocket of her jeans and dried her eyes. She blew her nose and smiled apologetically. 'I'd better take the plates in,' she said.

Jen managed to look sympathetic and stay quiet for about five seconds before she blurted out: 'I can't *believe* you didn't tell me about the vet!'

Chapter Eight

'Are you going out?' Anna was in Eve's bedroom watching her carefully apply a somewhat dried-out lipstick she'd found at the back of her underwear drawer.

'No.' She tried to sound offhand.

'But you're all dressed up, you look really nice.' This was true. She was in a dress, for starters, which was highly, highly unusual. It was a shimmery, satiny, grey-black, ladies-who-lunch kind of dress, which she'd bought for some special event, so long ago she couldn't remember what it was. She was even wearing little glittery earrings *and* stockings *and* high heels *and* perfume. How had she expected Anna not to notice or ask awkward questions? Oh, this was all too obvious.

She pulled off the shoes and stockings and put on beaded flip-flops instead. She tried on a little black cardy over the dress.

'Where are you going?' Anna was sitting on the bed, all packed up, dressed and ready to go off for the weekend with Joseph.

Because it was Joseph's visit that was causing Eve the flurry of beautifying activity. She had intended to look casually gorgeous, to be very, very nice to him and to see if this provoked any sort of sign . . . a sign that she should ask . . . suggest . . . offer that they take the first steps in getting back together again.

She wasn't going to say anything – or even really do anything – she just wanted to see if there was going to be any sort of, well . . . *sign*. She didn't know what it would be, but she felt sure she would recognize it.

'I'm not going anywhere, honey.' She was brushing her hair now, then shaking it into the 'I hope this doesn't look too brushed' thing.

'Is this for Daddy?' Little hopeful look on Anna's face.

'Don't be silly. But I am going to be nice to Daddy, like you want me to be. OK?'

'OK.' Big smile on Anna's face now. 'He's going to be nice to you too. I made him promise.'

'Good, well that's great. We'll all be friends.'

'Yes.' Anna had a lot more planned than 'friends', and look how well it was going. Her mother was in *a dress*, putting on *lipstick*, promising to be nice to him. In her estimation, they were just weeks away from being happily together again. Ha ha, Michelle.

*　　*　　*

It was almost exactly 7p.m. when the doorbell rang, but still Eve felt startled. Hell! Here he was. She bounced off the sofa, mussed hair, flung off cardigan and waited for Anna to open the door and show Joseph in.

Robbie was boinging up and down on the other sofa now, chanting 'Jofus! Jofus!'

'Hi, Daddy,' Eve heard her daughter say.

'Hello, Anna. How are you? Big kiss for Daddy.'

'Oh. Hello, Michelle.'

Michelle??

Michelle! What was she doing here? Smile, Eve, they are coming into the room now. 'Hello,' she said, stretching as wide a smile as possible over her cheeks.

'Hello, Eve.' Joseph hung back in the doorway, didn't come over to give her the usual kiss on the cheek.

'This is Michelle,' he said and put an arm round the shoulder of a small, pretty, blonde girl, who looked . . . well, exactly like Anna had said: groomed, made up, hair in a shiny ponytail, peachy, pouty lips, floor-length cream shearling coat. Very pretty.

'Hello, nice to meet you.' Michelle held out a hand, which when Eve took it, felt all soft and small and made hers feel like an ungainly, dried-out gardening mitt.

'I've heard lots about you,' Eve said with a smile. *Hardly any of it nice*, she didn't add.

102

'This is Robbie,' she introduced the toddler.

'Oh, hello, Robbie.' Michelle gave a little wave. Joseph went over to hug and tickle his son.

They all watched the playful, giggly fight.

'So, would you like a cup of tea, or glass of wine or something?' Eve suddenly remembered to ask.

'No, no. We're not going to stay,' Joseph told her. He was sitting on the sofa now with Robbie on his knee, rumpled from the toddler tussle, and he'd never looked more perfect in his life. She had to get him back – just had to.

'I wanted you to meet Michelle,' he was saying 'And erm . . . we wanted to tell you that . . . erm . . . we've decided to get engaged.'

'*Engaged*?!' This came from Anna, but echoed Eve's sentiments perfectly.

'Yes, Anna,' Joseph said calmly, although it was perfectly obvious to everyone that the little girl was furious.

'*Married*?' she demanded. Her face was quite white with a little pink spot on each cheek. She was looking from Michelle to Joseph and back again, challenging either of them to give her an explanation.

'Yes,' Joseph said. 'You get to be bridesmaid,' he added, in the vague hope that this would make things better. But Anna burst into tears and ran out of the room, pushing past Michelle on her way out.

Eve was left with a slightly frozen smile on her face. Bursting into tears and running out of the room was tempting, but she didn't think she should do that right now. Well, she'd wanted a sign, hadn't she? This was certainly a sign. A sign that she was completely *insane*.

'Congratulations,' she managed. Joseph looked shocked, so she added: 'I think Anna will need a little time to get to grips with this, but I'm sure she'll be OK. So, when did this . . . happen?'

'At the weekend,' came Michelle's reply. 'I wish I could say he got down on one knee with a big ring in a box.'

Like he did for me, Eve thought.

'But actually it was more . . . spontaneous than that,' Michelle added.

He proposed in bed, Eve concluded.

'Well, that's really nice. Congratulations,' Eve said again, then added: 'Joseph's always wanted to get married.' And now she wished the ground would swallow her up, because obviously that meant he'd always wanted to marry her.

Michelle was shooting him glances and had folded her arms in a fairly obviously angry kind of way.

'Let me go and see Anna,' Eve said. 'Are you sure you don't want some tea or something?'

Joseph decided he needed a glass of wine and Michelle wanted water.

'I'll get it,' he told Eve. 'You check Anna, or do you want me to do it?'

'Give us a few minutes,' she said.

She opened the door of the bedroom Anna and

Robbie shared and saw Anna lying face down on her top bunk, sobbing.

Eve patted her back and finally Anna sat up and let herself be hugged. She squashed her arms round Eve's neck and buried her streaming eyes and nose in Eve's satin dress, which served her right for putting it on in the first place.

'I want Daddy to marry you,' came the fierce, fierce sobs.

'I know, darling,' she whispered.

'Why did you and Daddy have to be so awful? If you'd just been nicer to each other, you could be married now. Now he's going to marry stupid Michelle.'

'Anna, Mummy and Daddy aren't together any more. We love you, we love Robbie, but you are going to have to get used to this.'

'Well why do you keep getting my hopes up then? Both of you? With your silly games. With your photos in drawers and pyjamas in the cupboard and putting on lipstick?' She was crying quite hysterically now. Eve wasn't sure what all this referred to. But she saw now that Anna had noticed far more of the unresolved emotions flying about between her and Joseph than she had ever suspected. Maybe there had been one reconciliation too many for Anna to truly believe that they were apart. Well, had Eve even really believed it, until tonight?

Now it was well and truly over.

'How's it going?' came Joseph's whisper from

the door and Eve blinked back the tears forming in her own eyes.

'I'm not coming with you,' Anna shouted from the bunk. 'I don't want to be in Manchester with you and Michelle,' and she burst into fresh sobs again.

'I'm really sorry, Anna.' Joseph took over on the back-patting while Eve carried on holding their daughter. 'I didn't know you'd feel like this.'

'I'm not coming with you,' Anna repeated. 'There isn't enough room in your car for three people' – which sounded horribly like 'There isn't enough room in your life for three people.'

Anna wouldn't be persuaded. She wouldn't even come out of her room. She didn't want to set eyes on Michelle again who, by now, had been roped into a complicated game of hide-and-seek with Robbie, which she didn't seem to be enjoying too much. 'You should probably just go,' Eve told Joseph. 'She'll be fine. Give her a phone tomorrow.'

'I hope we haven't spoiled your plans,' Joseph said at the door.

'Plans?' she asked. He gestured vaguely at her dress.

'Were you going out?'

'Oh no. No, no. A friend was dropping by later, but I'll cancel. No problem.'

A friend? he was thinking as he steered the car through the north London back roads he knew out onto the M1. Which friend? Who had she been waiting for in a dress he recognized from way back. A dress she'd bought for some special occasion they had all been at together. What was it again?

'So? I want to know what you think?' Michelle sounded exasperated. He hadn't been listening *again* and, quite rightly, she wasn't going to like that.

'I'm sorry. I missed the last bit of that.'

Big sigh.

'Joe. I'd like to talk about our wedding. I didn't really want any bridesmaids. I mean, if it's going to be really important to Anna . . .' She tailed off.

'I'm sorry. I should have thought about that. What else have you got in mind?'

'How about a grown-up, romantic wedding? How about taking off somewhere really glamorous and getting married there? The South of France, Italy . . . somewhere like that?'

'It would be great, but my children have to come to my wedding. Anna is having enough problems adjusting to the idea without me sneaking off to do it behind her back.'

'Anna has problems, full stop, let's just face it,' she snapped.

'Don't.'

He glanced over at her but she just stared straight ahead at the road, her mouth set in a scowl.

'Look, I'm tired.' He reached out to put a hand over hers. 'I don't really want to talk about all this right now, but we've got all weekend. And how about we go and look for a ring together tomorrow?'

She turned and smiled at him: 'Are you sure?'

'Yes, I'm very sure – about everything,' he answered and that was when he remembered . . . Eve's dress. She'd bought it for his parents' 30th wedding anniversary party. Scene of yet another of his rejected marriage proposals. Well if he'd wanted a sign from her that he was doing the right thing marrying Michelle, surely that was it?

He'd proposed to Eve seriously six times, light-heartedly at least a hundred times. And the closest he'd ever got to a yes was 'Ask me again really soon.'

This was better. Michelle had accepted before he'd even finished asking, which after his experiences with Eve had taken him somewhat by surprise. Michelle had wanted to talk about rings and dresses and venues and invitations almost constantly ever since. But he was finding it strangely hard to get enthusiastic about all that stuff and now he was worried about Anna.

Much later that evening, Eve tucked her daughter up in bed and stroked her forehead until her eyes finally closed. Together they had stayed up late on the sofa, wrapped in a blanket together eating the entire contents of the biscuit and cake tins and drinking hot chocolate, in Eve's case laced with a slug of brandy, while they watched comforting Friday night TV.

It was very late, so Eve was surprised when the phone rang, although not when she heard Jen's voice at the other end.

'Oh go away!' she said, exhausted at the thought of having to relay this saga to Jen.

'I'm just checking on you. I knew he was coming round tonight and I just wanted to make sure you didn't make a complete tit of yourself.'

There was a pause.

'Then again, if you did make a complete tit of yourself, I'll still be your friend, OK.'

'Jen,' Eve said with a deep sigh, 'he came round with Michelle . . .'

'Oh!'

'To tell us that they're engaged. They're getting married.'

'Oh.' It sounded as if even Jen hadn't seen that one coming. 'Well, you wanted a sign,' she added.

'I know!' Eve began to laugh, 'I got a bloody great big sign all right, didn't I?'

'Are you OK?' Jen asked.

'Yeah, I'm OK. Feeling slightly stupid, I have to say. And poor old Anna's very upset.'

'Oh, the little soul.'

'What about you? Are you at work?' Eve asked.

'Yeah, I'm fine. I should go. I was just checking on you.'

'You're the best.'

'I know. Eve?'

'Yeah?'

'Phone the vet.'

'Oh for goodness bloody sake . . . you're obsessed.'

'I'm not. It's just a useful quality men have, being able to help you get over other men. They're good at that. And at taking out the bins.'

'Good night, you mad woman.'

'Night-night.'

Chapter Nine

Eve was hacking hard at a particularly stubborn root with a garden trowel when Tom's head unexpectedly poked out of the back door.

'Hello,' he said with a smile and ambled into the garden, all rangy, blond-topped six-foot-two of him, gangling along in his oversized jeans and 'Porn Star' T-shirt.

'Hello there!' she answered and watched him walk over, taking in how handsome he looked – slim, big shoulders, a square face with long, surfer hair. She thought he was fabulous.

And she of course was her usual completely extraordinary self, he couldn't help thinking, grinning as he walked towards her: her blond mane tucked up into a hideous old khaki hat. The rest of her outfit was no better – a fuchsia and white, too tight, tie-dyed top, armfuls of bead bracelets, baggy combat trousers and a pair of filthy old walking boots. But he adored his mum.

'Come here,' she smiled and opened her arms.

111

He bent down to kiss her face and gave her a quick hug.

'Where are the kids?' he asked.

'They've gone to see Jen's new kittens,' she said. 'But you are just what I need.' She looked back down at the deep trough she'd dug all around the offending plant: 'Brute force. Will you pull this bloody bush out for me?'

'Oh bad karma, man! Why are you digging up the roses?'

'Only this one. It's all straggly and mangy despite everything I've done for it and look, don't debate it with me – just pull! Here, you'll need my gloves, it's really prickly.'

Tom forced his hands into her small gloves, stiff with earth, and grasped the base of the bush. He strained hard against it, and with a crack the root snapped and the bush tore away.

'There you go!' He tossed it onto the ground and they grinned at each other.

'What are you doing here anyway?' she asked, because it was a Friday afternoon, still not gone 5p.m. 'Shouldn't you be at work, dot.com.ing away?'

He laughed at this then his face switched to serious. Even a little bit nervous, she thought.

'Out early for good behaviour, but there's something I want to talk to you about. I wanted to see you on my own.'

'OK.' She took her hat off to get a better look at him. 'I'm all ears,' she smiled to reassure him.

'Right.' He ran his hands through his hair

and tried to smile back, 'here goes . . . Deepa is pregnant.'

Before this had even really registered with her, he added: 'And we're planning to have the baby – and get married.'

'Deepa's *pregnant*?' she asked, with the very slimmest of hopes that maybe she'd heard this all wrong and Tom was talking about someone other than his girlfriend of two minutes. Eve really liked Deepa but . . . *babies? Marriage?* She was still trying to come to terms with the last shock marriage announcement to hit her. This did not compute . . . did not compute. No!

'Yeah.' Tom stuffed his hands into his pockets and pulled his jeans up.

'How did this happen?' What kind of stupid question was that? she wondered, as soon as she'd asked it.

'Umm . . . the usual way, I suppose,' Hint of shy grin.

'You've known about contraception since you were *six*, Tom. There really isn't any excuse,' she snapped.

Tom gave a reply that was somewhere between a mumble and a giggle and hoicked his jeans up again, which was pointless because they were too wide and they sagged down as soon as he let them go.

She could feel the angry heat in her cheeks. Her son Tom, just turned 20, just landed his first proper job was seriously contemplating marriage – *parenthood* – with a student just a little

113

bit younger and a little less dizzy than him. He had no idea! They had no idea! And the worst thing – the part that was really bringing hot tears to the back of her eyes – was that this is what had happened to her. Pregnant at 20, married the bloke . . . and look how badly that had turned out.

She'd wanted things to be so different for her children.

Oh God.

Tom put an arm round her. 'Sorry,' he said, patting her head against his shoulder.

She put her hand on his back.

'Oh Tom. This is going to be so hard. A baby? Have you really thought this through?'

'Yeah, we have. We've given it a lot of thought. It's not what we planned, but what is?'

She was struck by the note of seriousness in his voice.

'Do you love her?' she asked.

'Yeah, I love her and she loves me and we'll work out the baby thing.'

He made it sound so simple. That's how it was when you were 20. Fairly straightforward, you didn't see all the other complicated stuff that proper, older, grown-ups suspected lay ahead for you.

But she felt a bit better.

'It'll be cool, Mum,' Tom said and did his jean-pull thing again.

'You need a belt,' she said and he just smiled.

'Robbie's going to be an uncle,' she added.

'And he's only two.' She wasn't sure whether to laugh or cry at this, didn't know which way it would go.

'It'll be cool.' Shrug, pull at jeans. She couldn't believe he was really 20. The same age she was when she'd had Denny. Tom still seemed such a *teenager* and she'd thought she was such a grown-up back then. It made her laugh to think of herself at 20, all tailored suits and blow-dried hair. She'd thought she was so adult, and look at me now . . . Not for the first time, did she wonder if she'd done everything a bit backwards. Back then she'd been a married, two-children, suburban housewife with a businessman husband, a proper swank house, antique furniture and clothes which almost all needed dry cleaning. Now, she was single, *dating*, muddling along with post-teens and young children, living in a basement flat, listening to pop music, dressing at Top Shop. Her own life had run in a strange and unpredictable way.

'When's the baby due?' she asked, pushing her hair back from her face and wiping her hands down on her trousers.

'The start of September. She's 18 weeks . . . I know we've taken a while to start telling people. It was a big decision.'

She noticed the 'eighteen weeks'; her son was already talking pregnancy terminology. 'Sick?' Eve asked.

'As a dog. It would be quite funny, if I didn't feel so sorry for her.'

115

'Poor thing. Has she tried ginger biscuits?'

'Mum, she's tried ginger everything – ginger biscuits, ginger tea, ginger wine. Raw grated ginger. Barfed it all up.'

'Poor, poor thing . . . Do her parents know yet?'

'Ermmm . . . I think she's going to tell them this weekend. I don't know if I'm going to go along or not. I don't want to get hit or anything.' Smile, shrug, tug at jeans.

'Oh God. Are they . . . ummm? Is Deepa . . .?' What was the currently PC way to ask about your son's Asian girlfriend's um . . . cultural heritage?

'D'you mean religion and stuff?' *Religion and stuff?!* Well that was one way of putting it.

'Yeah.'

'They're all C of E, lapsed. The missionaries must have got to their ancestors or something.'

'Can I make one suggestion?'

He nodded.

'Please don't wear that T-shirt when you go with her to meet the family.'

'Oh yeah . . . right.'

'Porn star!' He even had one top he'd worn round for Sunday lunch, quite blissfully unaware, emblazoned 'Masturbation is not a crime.'

'Do you really need to get married?' she asked. Marriage seemed far too complicated an arrangement for them both to rush into. 'Wouldn't it be better to try living together with the baby first?' she asked.

116

'We want to get married, Mum. Give it our best shot.'

She had to admire their enthusiasm . . . blind optimism: 'When?' she asked.

'Before the baby gets here. Deepa wants to go for June. The local church, hotel with a big garden. She wants the white dress, veil, wedding car – the lot. Bump and all!'

'And what do you think about that?' Eve wondered.

'Well, it's not really my style. But if that's what she wants . . . And she thinks it will bring her parents round . . . so . . . it's cool.'

'Hmmm. D'you want some tea?' she asked.

'Have you got cakes?' Even in a crisis, Tom could eat cakes.

'Yes. I have cakes. Joseph's getting married too,' she told him, trying to sound ultra casual.

'Oh yeah? Who to?'

'His girlfriend, Michelle.'

'Wedding frenzy then.' And that was all he seemed to want to say about it, which surprised her.

At the back door, as she stopped to kick off her muddy boots, he added: 'There's something else too . . .'

She turned to face him, foot dangling mid-air, and when he saw the hole in the toe of her sock Tom felt a stab of sympathy for his mother and wondered if he really had the right to put her through this.

'Yes?'

117

'I want to invite my dad . . . you know, Dennis, to the wedding. And maybe his family too, if they'll come.'

Eve carried on taking off her boots.

'I see,' she said finally. 'Well, you can't really expect me to be thrilled at the prospect of that.'

'No.'

She was beginning to wonder what she was going to be hit with next. Anna exposed as a playground drug dealer? Robbie offered chairmanship of Lego?

Dennis. Tom wanted to invite Dennis to the wedding . . . as simple as that. Dennis, the dad who had walked out on her and Denny and Tom about sixteen years ago now. They had, of course, seen him since then. He'd had to get back in touch for the divorce. Then followed erratic cheques and even more erratic visits, when he breezed into the country, phoned from his all-expenses-paid Trusthouse Forte suites and chaperoned his dazed sons through several days of money, treat and sugar rush highs. They got everything they wanted at Hamley's, ate sundaes for supper, went to the zoo, whizzed round Hyde Park on their brand new rollerblades, skateboards – whatever it was he'd bought them that time. Then, at the end of his visit, they would be handed over to her for a sobering detox and back-to-reality bump.

Dennis the Dog . . . Dennis the . . . whatever really ugly word began with D. Dope? No.

Dunce? No. Duplicitous dog shit. That was more like it.

'He's going to be a grandfather,' Tom was telling her. 'He might like to know.'

'Hmmm.' He'd never been too interested in playing at happy families in the past. Well . . . not with them, anyway.

'Careful you don't step on Robbie's cars,' Eve warned him as she put on the kettle and cleared a space for them both at the table in the chaotic kitchen. 'I'm going to break my neck one of these days.'

'Robbie's cars?!' Tom bent down to pick up a battered old tractor. 'I recognize this one.'

'Maybe Uncle Robbie will pass it on to his nephew – or niece,' she said and felt the 'laugh or cry? laugh or cry?' confusion coming over her again.

'I know, Mum,' Tom said. 'It's a bit weird . . . but we'll be cool. Think how much fun it will be for Robbie.'

'What would you like to drink?' she asked him as the kettle came to the boil. He knew the wide selection on offer: three types of tea – all decaffeinated, herbal teas, fruit flavours, Carob Cup, decaf coffee . . .

But his mother was pulling up a chair so she could reach to the top of the kitchen cupboards and she was bringing down the battered old biscuit tin, so now he knew just how rattled she was. This was the hard stuff, only to be used in emergencies – full strength Arabica roast. Still perched on the chair, she unwrapped the foil package and breathed in deeply with her eyes closed.

'Mmmm,' she said, 'I'm feeling better already.'

He was wondering if she still kept supplies of her other emergency drug when she jumped down from the chair and brought the tin over to him.

'Would you like one? Because I think I will. Counteracts the worst effects of the caffeine, you know.'

He looked into the tin and saw about six pencil-thin, three-centimeter-long joints, 'One hundred per cent organic grass,' his mother was saying now. 'Totally nicotine free and grown in a greenhouse in Brighton, so fairly clean conscience.' As he took one out, she added: 'Listen to me, I sound like a dealer. You know I only smoke in exceptional circumstances.'

'You old hippie,' he said.

'Oh thanks!'

They sat down, at the kitchen table in the disgracefully messy London flat he still thought of as home, to a steaming pot of coffee, lit up their spliffs releasing the unmistakable sweet smoke smell and talked it over a little.

'Is Deepa's family going to be OK about this?' Eve asked her son.

'We'll have to wait and see.'

'What's she studying again?' Eve felt embarrassed that she couldn't remember.

'Medicine. She's in her second year.'

'Ah, so I don't think "congratulations" is going to be the first word you hear from her parents.'

'No. But we're getting married. They'll like that.'

'They might not, Tom. Who knows? Twenty is young.'

'We'll be the same age you were,' Tom reminded her, unnecessarily.

'Yeah.' She breathed out a mouthful of smoke and swallowed down a cough. 'That's why I'm worried for you.' Her eyes were fixed to his. 'Twenty is young,' she repeated, 'especially nowadays. But we'll all try and help you out.'

Her hands settled down round the coffee mug again. Such nice hands, he thought, mummy hands. Small, warm and capable. The nails were short and often a little bit earthy and she always wore two clunky silver rings and, on her fourth finger, a chip of emerald on the daintiest of platinum bands. Despite the gardening, her touch was usually soft, due to some weekly ritual involving olive oil and salt and going to bed with socks as mitts. Completely fruity.

'Where is Dennis at the moment?' she asked. She let her sons handle any contact or correspondence they wanted to have with their father. She was determined to be uninterested.

'I'm sure he's still in Chicago. He'd have told us if there'd been any change there.'

Vigorously she stubbed out her remaining butt in the bronze ashtray she'd placed on the table, jangling all the bracelets wrapped around her arms.

'Deepa seems like a really good person, Tom,' she said. 'It might all work out very well. But promise me you'll do everything you can to be a great parent to your baby. Because every child deserves two good parents, even if they aren't together any more.'

'I promise,' he said and surprised her with a squeeze of the hand. 'Thanks, Mum.'

Once he'd gone, she opened all the windows and the back door, letting in a breeze, then sat down at the table again and reopened the emergency tin.

She was definitely going to smoke another joint. This was about four emergencies rolled into one: Joseph getting married, Tom getting married and becoming a father. The prospect of grandmotherhood, exactly two and a half years after the birth of her fourth child . . . and Dennis. Jesus Christ, a reunion with Dennis and maybe even his new family as well.

Chapter Ten

All of Eve's London 'family' had been invited to her house for lunch to meet Deepa, talk babies and celebrate, for God's sake. That had to be better than sitting on the sidelines with arms folded, disapproving, Eve had decided.

So all her children were going to come, along with the older boys' girlfriends, plus Jen and Ryan, of course. Their sons, Terry and John, were invited too, but as Jen put it: 'Oh, Sunday . . . I think that's their day for shoplifting cider, burning cars and doing smack.'

'Ha, ha.'

Two other guests had already accepted: Harry, family hairdresser and friend – camp, over-dyed, a tad too theatrical and always ramping up the *Italiano*, but nevertheless a man who had been very kind to Eve and her boys when she first moved to Hackney and who had grown from a friend into a surrogate uncle. And Nils.

To everyone, apart from Jen and an extremely suspicious Anna, Nils was the vet and a new 'friend'. But Eve could see they all had a bit of a sparkle in their eyes when she brought him into the noisy, packed kitchen and introduced him.

Everyone else knew Eve's kitchen and no longer paid any attention to it, but Nils, there for the first time, couldn't sit down straight away; he wanted to wander about because there was so much to look at.

The room was full. Chock-a-block. There were dressers and shelves and cupboards on all the walls and every one of them was brimming with an array of kitchen *stuff*. Pots, pans, plates, glasses – all the usual things, yes, and then all the unusual things too: antique butter-dishes, six of them, different coloured enamelled colanders, a range of graters, Japanese teapots, rows and rows of battered and ancient cookbooks, jugfuls of utensils. And plants jammed into every nook and cranny, in potted groupings on the windowsills, on the floor, high up on shelves, ready to kamikaze down if they got too dry.

This was obviously a woman at home in her kitchen.

'Pour wine, please,' she ordered, handing him a bottle and several glasses. 'Then sit.' She looked a little frazzled, hair in a messy bun, apron on, flitting between the rickety old gas cooker and the kitchen table where her guests were seated in a raucous huddle on mismatched chairs.

Her kitchen was scarily grubby for a hostess, she couldn't help noticing as she kicked toys and old toast crusts into a corner, hoping they weren't too visible.

It was her roasted roots lunch: chunks of sweet potato, squash, parsnip, carrot, shallots, garlic cloves, all baked and bronzed in oil and herbs from the garden, with mountains of home-grown salad. Then creamy meringues and strawberries for pudding.

Eve toed and froed from the table and the cooker, catching wisps of conversation and enjoying bumping into and brushing past Nils who was trying to help but seemed to be taking up all the available space round her work units.

Jen was talking pregnancy with Tom and Deepa, who now had a round, hard football of a bump tucked under her T-shirt.

Anna was wrapped up in the conversation Harry and Denny's model girlfriend, Patricia, were having about hair serums, which left Ryan, Denny and Robbie to debate engines.

'This is Duck, he's going back to the yard to see the Fat Controller.' Robbie was dredging along the tablecloth with a small green engine.

'Oh, I thought it was Percy,' Denny said.

'*No!*' Indignant little voice, chubby fist snatching up the toy and jamming it right under Denny's eye. 'Duck. He's a Great Western engine.' Sure enough, GWR was outlined on the side.

'How are you?' Nils asked her in semi-privacy at the kitchen sink.

125

'I'm OK,' Eve smiled at him. 'I'm sorry I've been so busy, I've had no time to see you till today.' This wasn't exactly true and they both knew it.

'It's fine,' he said, resisting the urge to touch her face, because whatever kind of an 'item' he and Eve were, it was still a secret one: 'It's nice to meet everyone.'

'OK, we're all done, come and sit down,' she told him, laden with the last platefuls of food for the table.

Finally, when everyone was served and all the glasses were topped up, she raised hers and said: 'Here's to Deepa and Tom. Congratulations you two, all the best days and worst nights of your lives are ahead of you!'

Everyone else chimed in and drank the toast.

Her eyes settled on her oldest son, Denny, who looked tired, she thought; blue-black circles under the eyes and his brown hair darker than usual because it was unwashed. She wondered if he was worrying about work or Tom or if he'd just been out late partying with Patricia.

She was trying to like Patricia, but it was against her natural instincts. Patricia was absolutely stunning, pale, pale, perfect skin, waist-long straight chestnut hair which she wore in a flawless ponytail with not the slightest strand out of place, and a figure that was 100 per cent pure model – the ideal woman pre-shrunk by 40 per cent in everything except height.

She held herself in a very self-conscious way, tipping her little chin up and down, laughing gently, somehow always aware she was being watched. Of course, she ate tiny mouthfuls of food and it bugged Eve that Anna watched and copied this skinny angel of perfection. Anna would be sending back her lunch plate barely touched, and tomorrow she would be going to school with a scraped-back ponytail in reverence of Patricia.

'So, Mum,' Tom leaned over the table to talk to her, 'How's it going?'

She smiled at him and said, 'Lovely, great . . . couldn't be better, hon. By the way, have you done anything about getting in touch with your father?'

'Yeah, I've spoken to him and . . . er . . . he says he'd like to come. If it's OK with everyone.'

'Our dad? What? Dennis?' Denny was asking, just loud enough to make everyone else turn their heads and tune in. 'Have you invited him to the wedding?'

'Yeah, sorry.' Tom looked embarrassed by the attention. 'I was going to tell you a bit later. I was coming round to it.'

'Oh for God's sake,' was Denny's reply.

Tom rumpled his hair and added, 'D'you realize it's been six years since we last saw him?'

'Well, exactly.'

Eve was sure Dennis had found the sulky teenagers who'd greeted him on his last visit – and been vastly unimpressed with his swank hotel suite and extravagant gifts – too much like hard work. Since then, it had been Christmas cards only. He never did anything about birthdays.

'Anyway,' Tom was saying, 'I got him on the phone and told him all about the wedding and the baby.' Here he nodded at Deepa who gave him a tight smile. 'And so . . . he said he'd like to come to the wedding and see us all. He's going to bring his wife and daughters too.'

'Well, aren't you the guy with all the shock announcements,' Denny said but Eve shut him up with a glance. Jen and Harry were open mouthed with surprise, and Eve caught the quizzical look on Anna's face and suspected the inevitable psychoanalytical remark was coming right up: 'There'll be no more denial now,' her daughter said and Eve couldn't help a laugh.

'So, what did he say?' Eve, feeling a surge of curiosity, wanted to hear this blow by blow. She picked up Robbie's fork to manoeuvre food into his mouth, but was still concentrating on Tom.

'From the beginning, everything you can remember.' She smiled.

'Well . . .' rumple, rumple, scratch at nose. 'Well . . . he wasn't too happy about the becoming a grandfather bit. I can tell you that for free.'

Eve cackled.

' "You're getting married and becoming a

father!"' Tom did a replica American boom for them. '"At 20! Are you *insane*?" That was his response.'

Tom carried on, quite animated now with lots of fake American accent: 'He's such a barker. He picks up the phone and says "Dennis Leigh" at top volume, like he's deaf or something. And I said "Hello, this is Tom Leigh from England". I thought he would know who I was, so I didn't add, "your son". But there was silence for ages, before he went "Tom Leigh? My son, Tom? Oh! Hello, how are you Tom?" He doesn't really think about us too much, does he?'

'Ermm . . . that would be a no,' Eve said. She'd stopped mid-forkful and Robbie, sitting with his mouth wide open, eyes fixed on the fork, baby bird like, was hoping the food would land on him eventually.

'So,' Tom continued, 'we chatted, I suppose. What was I doing? His reaction! He asked about Denny and you, Mum. He still calls you Evelyn. It sounds so bizarre. We talked about his work for ages. Well, he talked,' Eve rolled her eyes. 'I'm going to have to do overtime to pay the phone bill. Oh and that was the other thing, he told me: "You're with a dot.com company. Jeez Tom, just forget that. That is so over." I was trying to tell him "Well, we're developing pretty advanced software actually, Dad . . . Dennis,"' Tom corrected himself. It was too weird to be calling this stranger Dad. 'But he wasn't really listening.'

Eve could have regaled them with many other examples of how Dennis never listened, never took any interest in his kids, always thought his opinions were the most important, but she had always *tried* to be the kind of divorced mum who doesn't do down their ex the whole time; well at least not in front of the children.

'So, he'd like to come?' she asked.

'So he says.' They all knew nothing could be counted on with Dennis.

'Send them an invite, see what happens,' Eve said. 'Might be interesting.' That was an understatement.

'My God, does that mean we all get to meet him? And the new wife and kids?' Jen sounded almost hysterical with excitement. Dennis, the missing piece of Eve's past. She was actually going to meet him.

'She's not exactly a new wife. Been on the scene for years—' Eve, trying to sound breezy.

'But let's face it,' this from Tom, 'it's going to be interesting.'

Eve looked over at Denny who was eating, eyes fixed in the distance, not saying anything. 'What do you think?' she asked him.

'Oh . . . whatever,' was his answer. 'I couldn't give an arse about Dennis. I've no idea why you're so desperate for him to come,' he shot at Tom.

'He's family,' Tom said. 'In his way.'

Denny gave a snort and both Tom and Eve

decided to leave it at that. Denny angry was a scary sight.

Later, when almost everyone else had gone – Nils having sneaked several kisses on his obligatory tour of the, today, very damp garden and making her promise to call – Tom and Deepa hung about in the kitchen and offered to help Eve clear up. What *exactly* was it like getting married and having your first baby at 20? They wanted to know and started to quiz Eve over the pot scrubbing and dish scraping. 'Oh God,' she told them, pushing hair out of her face with rubber-gloved hands. 'I can tell you what it was like for me, but that doesn't mean it's going to be like that for you. In fact, I hope it will be *really* different for you both.

'I mean . . . I was with Dennis and he was such a grown-up, workaholic, thirty-something. He wanted all the grown-up stuff: house in the country, two point two children, housewife. And I thought I wanted that too. But it didn't work out.' Clatter, bang of bowls and pans, as she tried to distract even herself from the memories. 'Well, it did for a while . . . in a way.

'I dropped out of university,' she added. 'Drifted off to Surrey, lost all my student friends and the career that might have been at the end of that . . . But I got my boys.' She looked up from the sink here and flashed the couple a smile.

'So how come I hardly know about any of

this?' Deepa directed the question at Tom, but was hoping Eve might fill in some blanks. 'House in the country? Hot-shot dad?'

Eve's face was fixed firmly back on the sink now. 'Dennis is still quite hard to talk about. He let us all down really badly.'

Chapter Eleven

Mrs Evelyn Leigh she had been way back then. Such a different kind of person. The young and gleamingly well groomed wife of super-successful (or so she'd thought) financial fixer, Dennis Leigh. Mother of two, mega house in stockbroker Surrey, daily worries nothing more pressing than: what shade to choose for the dining room re-paint? How to fit in a manicure and leg wax before tennis? Was curried parsnip soup too boring to serve at Saturday night's dinner?

Dennis had swept her up at the age of just 19 with . . . with what, exactly? Love? Longing? Need? The promise of children and financial security?

She had been an anthropology student in London when she'd met him. Her father had wanted her to study law and that was what she had hoped for as well. She loved courtrooms, had sat in the back of these formal, reverent places to watch him at work since she was a girl. But her A Levels had been 'disappointing' – how she had lived down to her father's expectations – and she'd found herself scraping through the clearing system with degrees in art history and anthropology the only ones available to her in the capital. Because London was without a doubt where she wanted to be. Growing up in the cramped cosiness of a small town, she wanted the city. Wanted endless streets, crowds, adventure and anonymity.

'Evelyn' had drifted through the first year of her degree, mainly making new friends and hanging out in cafés and wine bars.

One night, she'd been introduced to Dennis, a casual acquaintance of someone in the group; the ex-boyfriend of someone's older sister, something like that. He'd come over to say hello and ended up sitting next to her.

From the moment they started talking, she'd been infatuated. He'd seemed so sophisticated, grown-up, in his immaculate City suit with watch chain, folded handkerchief in the top pocket, expensive cologne and manicured nails. Constantly being paged by work, never able to stray far from a phone, because the mobile, the piece of technology about to revolutionize Dennis's life, wasn't readily available then.

Compared with Dennis, her student friends in open-necked shirts and leather jackets suddenly seemed shabby and undirected. Dennis was part of the adult, glamorous world to which she was longing to belong. It was the Eighties, for God's sake! Everyone wanted to be mature, wealthy, wearing shoulder pads and gold buttons. Stockbrokers like him were pin-up boys.

He'd just bought three flats in the Docklands and was 'developing' them on the side, whereas she was still living in a tiny little room in her hall of residence.

Eve couldn't remember what she'd talked about, but something must have interested him because he'd asked her out for dinner the next night and she'd shyly accepted, feeling nothing but terror at the prospect.

All three of her best friends had chipped in with things to wear on the date, and in her miniskirt, blazer, fishnets and low-cut bodysuit, she'd looked glamorous and much older than her 19 years.

He had come by taxi to collect her and taken her to a nerve-rackingly expensive restaurant in the West End.

She had only eaten a starter and a salad, because she wanted to offer to pay her half and couldn't afford anything else. But Dennis had settled the bill with a flourish of plastic and then they had gone on, Evelyn still rather hungry, to a cocktail bar where she had become giddy after two pina coladas.

He'd charmingly asked her to come back to his flat, but she had refused with shyness and giggling because he was a thirty-something man who would definitely want sex and she was almost certain that she didn't want to get into all that with him yet. Dennis had made light of the knock-back, paid a taxi to ferry her home and then, for reasons she still couldn't fathom, he had begun a campaign of seduction. Weekly dinners, bi-weekly flowers, phone calls – although these were usually reduced to scrawled messages on the noticeboard: 'your old man Dennis rang'.

After a fortnight, she had heard all about his lonely, unloved childhood and they had shared long, hot kisses in the back of the cab on each journey they had made together. By the time four weeks had gone by, he had told her how much he wanted to settle down and start a family of his own and she had allowed him to feel her breasts. Then after a very swank dinner during which he had persuaded her to share a second bottle of champagne with him, he had produced a jewellery box with a heavy gold choker inside and again asked her to come home with him.

She'd put the choker on, feeling it fasten surprisingly tightly round her neck, and when she looked at him she had felt drunken, turned on and in love.

He hadn't kissed her in the cab. This time he'd sat very close to her and under her coat had moved his hand up her knee, thigh and into the folds of skin at the top of her leg. He'd felt his way into the girlish black cotton pants and watched her mouth as he'd moved gently up and down in the wetness.

He wanted her more than he could remember wanting anyone else. He was 32 years old and had his fingers on a 19-year-old clitoris. He was taking her home and seriously thinking about having her as a proper girlfriend, not just a quick conquer and blow-out. She was sweet.

Long, mousy-blond hair, which he would persuade her to lighten. An attractive, willowy figure: he was sure she could dress up a bit better. He saw firm, smallish breasts moving under the dark clothes she wore and he couldn't wait to see if the nipples were as pink and rosebud perfect as they felt.

As she walked round his flat in amazement, Evelyn was beginning to understand what it meant to be giddy with desire. She had never seen anything like this before. Chrome and black leather furniture, a highly polished wooden floor, a few sleek steel units which served as a kitchen and a spiral staircase right there in the middle of the room which she knew would lead upstairs to his bed.

She sat down on the creaking leather sofa as she waited for him to come out of the bathroom. She suspected he was brushing his teeth, combing through his blond hair, splashing on more cologne and getting ready to seduce her. The thought made her pulse pound with a mixture of fear and excitement.

She thought about what she had let him do in the back of the cab and felt another lurch in her stomach. It was a thrill, this strange new cocktail of terror and desire. Was she really going to do this? Make love to him? Here? Tonight? She put her hand on the choker and felt the warm gold under her fingertips.

When he came out, as she'd guessed, he was fragrant and freshened up. He'd taken off his jacket and tie and approached her now with his shirt open, revealing a creamy neck.

He was carrying two champagne glasses, an ice bucket with a bottle in it and he'd put Sade on the stereo.

If she hadn't liked him so much she would almost have had to laugh at how corny he was being. Dinner, jewellery, champagne and low music . . . was this seduction by numbers? Would he have black satin sheets upstairs on the bed?

They started to kiss and moved together to the sofa, where she tried to ignore the creaky, squeaky leather noises and concentrate on him. This was the best kissing she'd had to date and now he was nudging her dress down over her shoulders as his other hand moved to that warm, tingling, melting place he'd found so quickly in the back of the cab.

Oh yeah.

He smelled of lime soap and her tongue was against his, still fizzing with champagne, she was squeezed tightly against an impeccably pressed City suit and pink shirt. She was about to have yuppie sex and it was knocking the Burlington socks off schoolboy and freshers' week sex – the only other kinds she'd had so far.

'You're so beautiful,' he'd whispered. 'Please come upstairs with me.'

And up the spiral staircase to the mezzanine bedroom they'd gone.

Black satin sheets! She couldn't believe it.

In between kisses, he'd begun to undress her: the cheap dress, horrible tights and when the black bra hit the floor, her breasts, which she was rather proud of because they were small and very white with tiny rosy nipples, seemed to have an overwhelming effect on Dennis.

For a moment she thought he might cry.

'Hey, it's OK . . .' she kissed his cheek. 'They're just breasts.'

'They're perfect,' he told her. 'You are absolutely perfect.'

Hard to resist a grown-up who buys you solid gold and thinks you're perfect. The shiny satin sheets were too cold; lying down on them made her shiver. But Dennis's nice warm body was there to turn to.

He spent the longest time on her breasts. Wetting them, stroking them into points, kissing them and sucking at them. She found it all interesting, but not a huge turn-on. When he came, it was too soon and she was left with her impression intact that sex was a pleasant way to pass half an hour or so but she really couldn't see what the fuss was.

Dennis had dozed in a puddle of gratitude for a few minutes, then roused himself, made coffee and switched on the computer beside the bed. She'd fallen asleep to the sound of him cursing under his breath about stock falls in Tokyo or something.

The sex got better and Dennis spent the next few months styling her into his model girlfriend. She wore lacetop stockings and G-strings, bras that cost more than she would previously have spent on a coat.

Soon, she joined the handful of select students turning up to lectures in cashmere rollnecks, designer jeans and high-heeled boots. Her head was well and truly turned. No-one had ever made such a fuss of her before. Her younger, cleverer and prettier sister, brainy Janie, had always been their father's favourite and there was no mother at home to even things out and make her feel a little bit better about herself. So she had always felt second choice, second best. And when Janie got into Cambridge, no less, to study law, Evelyn had felt even more rubbish about herself than usual.

So the attentions of Dennis were especially welcome. He put her on a pedestal, spoiled her, paid attention to her, treated her if not exactly as an equal, then as someone precious and sweet and special.

And she was so besottedly grateful, eager to please him and turn into the kind of woman he obviously wanted.

Then in that summer term of her first year at

university, several things happened all at once to push Dennis and Evelyn together much more quickly than they might both have wanted.

Dennis's remaining parent, his mother, died. She suffered a few weeks of serious illness, in which she managed to tell him rather dramatically from her bed that it would be her biggest regret not to have seen him marry, settle down and have children. Then she died, leaving him enough money finally to leave his job and set up a 'development' company of his own. In the midst of funeral arrangements, will settlements, Dennis clearing out the family home and putting it up for sale, Evelyn discovered that she was pregnant.

Her first reaction had been terror. What would Dennis think? What would her father and clever sister Janie have to say? It was one thing to become grown-up, sophisticated and sexy. Another to get caught out with an unplanned pregnancy. She didn't tell Dennis for several weeks, and in that time did a little growing up on her own.

She wanted to be Dennis's wife, she wanted to have their children. She would make a good mother, she felt sure of that. He was not going to persuade her to do otherwise. And so, in the aftershock of losing his mother, Dennis learned he was to be a father and Evelyn made it clear she wanted marriage, straight away.

He was too unsettled to make even initial objections, just went along with it and before the year was out Evelyn was installed in her first little Surrey house with baby number one on the way.

Dennis was enjoying success with his small London-based business and although Janie and their father had disapproved enormously, Evelyn's pregnancy and lack of qualifications meant they couldn't see any better solution than her marrying this wealthy boyfriend.

Evelyn herself had seemed so blithely happy about it, waltzing off into wife and motherhood at the age of just 20. Within a year of Denny's birth she was pregnant again and her life took on a shape of its own, with toddler groups and nursery school, lunches, tennis, dinner parties, occasional evenings in town, moving house, redecoration and the little bit of admin work Dennis would give to her when she complained of being bored.

But when she looked back on their seven years of marriage now, she wondered if she hadn't actually been sleepwalking all the way through. Well, she had loved her children fiercely from the start. But between her and Dennis there had been only the haziest of connections. He'd treated her as some sort of cross between a housekeeper and a doll. She had been expected to keep home, cook, look after the children, dress nicely and perform in bed. His end of the deal had been to provide for them, and every year they seemed to get wealthier. New car, more furniture, more expensive clothes. He'd worked longer hours and she'd known less and less about his job. But it had never really bothered her too much. She'd been too submerged in her cosy, pampered, sheltered life.

Chapter Twelve

She could still name the date when it had all started to unravel. April the 3rd had started so absolutely typically with Dennis leaving early for his office in the City while she got the boys ready for the school run. Denny, then six, and Tom only four, in their tiny grey flannel shorts, blazers, caps and brown satchels for the precious private day school they attended.

She remembered being behind the wheel of the sleek black Range Rover spinning along the green and lovely country lanes with her two sons chattering in the back and she'd felt happy, really happy for the first time in ages.

She'd not long turned 26 and she was 11 weeks pregnant with the baby she'd wanted for two years now. It still seemed such a fresh miracle to be pregnant again. Last year she had forced Dennis to come with her to see a specialist, as she'd become convinced Tom's difficult birth had somehow left her infertile.

In fact it turned out that Dennis's sperm count was faltering. The doctor had told him to cut down the stress, cigarettes and booze. But Dennis had shrugged the advice off, saying business was at a critical stage, he couldn't slow up now, needed a drink to relax. In fact, he had started to work even longer hours in the London office, had taken on yet more new clients and had stressed and worried about them all, although the money seemed to be piling in.

But still somehow, almost three months ago now, the magic had just happened. Dennis was pleased for her of course, but she could hardly contain the happiness she felt about it. She couldn't wait to have a baby in the house again. Please, please, a girl. And this time it was going to be different: no bottle-feeding, no leaving the baby to cry in the night, none of the small miseries Dennis had inflicted on her and her boys 'for their own good'.

A new baby would at last punctuate the busy boredom of her days when the boys were at school. Dennis hadn't wanted her to go out to work, he'd made that clear when they married – her, in a soft lacy dress, vaguely embarrassed that she was already obviously pregnant with Denny.

So, Evelyn had stayed home, looked after the children and cooked and shopped and entertained and decorated their progression of larger and larger Surrey houses with taste. She'd held dinner parties, joined the ladies who lunched and done all the little chores (with the help of a cleaner of course) that made up running the household. Without ever knowing if it was what she wanted, she'd turned herself into a model, polished and perfectly organized, Home Counties wife. But since Tom had started school in September, a deep boredom with it all had crept up on her. She knew exactly what she was going to be doing this week, next week and for ever . . . so she longed and longed for the baby to give her a new sense of purpose. At some point on that drive, bowling along the narrow roads, she must have felt the merest hint of a trickle, down there, between her legs. But she hadn't paid it any attention.

She'd driven into the village to do the morning's shopping at the butcher, delicatessen and greengrocer's. She'd picked up the dry cleaning, popped her head round the door of the hairdresser's to book an appointment. All the usual errands.

Back home, it was almost lunchtime. She'd unloaded everything from the car, put it all in the fridge and cupboards and finally headed upstairs to the bathroom. It was there that she'd seen the sizeable splash of dark red blood.

She'd felt strangely calm about it. No, she wasn't bleeding any more, she'd told the doctor over the phone. Get some rest, he'd advised her, take it easy, lots of women bleed in early pregnancy, it's probably nothing. But he warned her to call back if the bleeding got heavier or if she began to feel pain.

She'd managed to eat lunch almost cheerfully and made the few calls she'd been planning. Then she'd persuaded herself to go and lie down and try to get some sleep before it was time to pick her sons up again at four.

An hour or so later, she'd woken up feeling groggy with dull, cramping pains in her stomach. She had pushed back the duvet and been horrified to find herself lying in a pool of blood. It had soaked through her trousers and onto the sheet and duvet cover. Shocked and panicky, she'd rung the doctor from the bedside phone and he'd ordered her straight to hospital.

But she'd had the necessary calls to make first. Her fingers had shaken as she'd dialled the boys' babysitter, Mrs Wilson, and asked her to collect them from school and look after them until she got home.

'Is everything OK, dear?' Mrs Wilson had asked.

'I don't know yet. I have to go in for a check-up. I'm not sure how long it will take, but I'll make sure Dennis is home early,' she'd said, not knowing how she would persuade Dennis to get out of his office ahead of schedule, even in an emergency. She'd punched in his number and listened to his secretary on the other end.

'Mr Leigh is out of the office meeting clients for a late lunch, Mrs Leigh.'

'Do you know where?' She was anticipating no response to his bleeper, as usual.

'Well . . . according to the schedule, it's with a Mr Maxwell at the Savoy.'

'Thanks.' She'd hung up and dialled his bleeper first, leaving as urgent-sounding a message as possible, then she called the restaurant: it had no booking under Leigh or Maxwell. The waiter, sensing her agitation, had offered to go and ask for Mr Dennis Leigh at each of the tables.

She'd waited out the long minutes this took, watching the folded white towel she was sitting on turn red as she'd wondered how she was going to get to the hospital without leaking blood everywhere.

'No madam.' The waiter was back on the line: 'There's no-one here by that name, I'm sorry.'

She'd hung up and immediately forgotten about Dennis, her mind filling up with worry about the bleeding and the hospital trip. She could feel great gouts of blood flowing out of her now. It was ominously dark and she was beginning to feel scared. In the bathroom, she'd stuffed a wedge of toilet paper into her pants, then pulled on dark blue jeans, socks and loafers, before calling a taxi.

Waiting for the car, she'd filled her handbag with things she thought she might need: a magazine to read, more toilet paper, purse, keys. It hadn't occurred to her she might be there overnight.

By the time the taxi was snaking along the busy road to the hospital, blood was seeping out of her jeans and starting to pool in the folds of her raincoat. The driver took her straight to the A&E entrance and wouldn't accept the note she shakily held out for him.

She'd walked across the tarmac, bent double with the pain of the stomach cramps, white-faced and in shock now. When the nurse at the reception saw what a mess Evelyn was in, she ushered her into a side room to sit on a trolley while the forms were filled out.

'A doctor will be here soon,' Evelyn was told, but an age of waiting had followed. Lying on the trolley, she'd watched the blood seep out of her clothes, felt it wet her socks, run between her toes.

Finally, she had been wheeled up to the ward, feet first through the endless, pale green corridors. In the small exam room, a doctor and nurse in those silly paper hats, green pyjamas and plastic aprons had attended to her with a level of quiet hurry which had made her feel even more frightened.

She'd heard herself asking over and over, 'What's happening? Am I going to lose the baby? I need to phone my husband.'

They'd given her only reassuring noises, not answers, as they did the blood pressure, temperature and other checks and helped her out of her sodden, blood-soaked clothes and tied a hospital nightie round her. The hot flow did not stop: she'd felt the sticky puddle growing underneath her, soaking into the back of the nightdress.

At the doctor's request she'd put her blood-stained legs up into the stirrups, but reluctantly; she had not wanted to be examined in these circumstances at all.

Then came the matter-of-fact words she had so hoped not to hear: 'Your cervix is dilated, I'm afraid you're miscarrying. I'll need to get a better look.'

Out came the speculum to crank her open. Lying there on the examination bench, totally exposed to the bright strip lights above, she'd felt the beads of sweat form on her upper lip and armpits.

The doctor began the examination.

'Hmmm . . . the sac is stuck in the cervix,' he said finally. 'You won't stop bleeding until we remove it. I'm going to try and get it out, but we might have to take you down to theatre.'

The sac . . . the sac . . . She barely had time to register that he meant the baby in its little sac of fluid, before the terrible prodding began. It wasn't painful, but it was such a violation of the most tender and secret place. It had felt like sex and like rape, like abortion and like birth all at once.

As he fiddled and prodded, she had not been able to stop herself thinking about the birth she had imagined for this baby, in a warm pool with candles and lavender oil and love. But here she was in a small, hot cubicle having it pulled out of her with tongs, with rivers of blood, with two absolute strangers whose names she hadn't even picked up.

She'd begun to weep then, head flat back against the bed, arms gripping the sides, the tears running straight down into her ears as the nurse stroked her hair with a crackly plastic-gloved hand.

'I'm sorry,' the doctor had said. 'I don't want to hurt you, maybe we should just take you down to theatre and do this under anaesthetic.'

'No, no,' she'd insisted, clinging to some hope that if she just stayed conscious, maybe she could hang onto this baby after all.

He'd probed in with the tongs again.

'Stop, please stop,' she'd asked him as another contraction moved through her, squeezing a fresh stream of blood onto the bed.

He'd told her to try standing up, so some-how, with the nurse helping her, she'd got to her feet and had stood there, loose-kneed, clinging to the bed, feeling the blood run down her legs. Then she'd wished she could faint and be out of this, but her mind was stubbornly conscious.

She was ushered into the adjoining toilet where the doctor put a cardboard dish over the toilet seat and told her passing water might loosen the sac. Racked with sobs she tried to pee, while inwardly clenching every muscle she could to try and hold onto this baby. But the flow had started and she'd felt an involuntary, entirely unwanted contraction inside until – plop – like a smooth and painless birth, she knew her body had pushed the baby out.

She'd stood up and did not need to look to know that her baby was behind her in a cardboard dish, but horrified, she'd turned and looked anyway. All she could see was a surprisingly big bubble floating in a bright red pool of blood and urine. The nurse had caught her glance and had quickly thrown a paper towel over the bowl, then led her to the bed, where a drip was put in her arm and she was helped into the kind of papery pants and sanitary towels she remembered from the maternity ward. So many echoes of giving birth, she'd thought, just no baby waiting for her in a little plastic cot to make the ordeal worth while.

The nurse had sponged the worst of the drying bloodstains from her legs and tried to help her to her feet. But she had buckled on contact with the floor.

'You wait on the bed, I'll get a chair.'

So then Evelyn, in a backless nightie with her pants stuffed full of uncomfortable wadding, had been wheeled along with her drip to a hospital bed, feeling more wounded, hopeless and bereft than she had ever done before.

'I have to make some phone calls,' she'd managed to tell the nurse. 'Arrangements for my boys.'

The payphone had been wheeled to her

bedside and she had rung home first. Denny had picked up.

She'd felt tearful just to hear him say hello, but he was breezy and unconcerned that she would be away for the night.

'Are you and Tom being good boys?' she'd asked.

'Yes. Can we come and visit you?'

'No silly, I'll be back tomorrow. I miss you lots and lots . . . Do you think you could get Mrs Wilson for me?'

After Mrs Wilson had assured her not to worry, she would stay on overnight if necessary – no, there hadn't been any word from Dennis – Evelyn had wanted to speak to Tom.

'Hello, Mummy, where are you?' He'd sounded anxious.

'Hello, muffin.'

He'd giggled a little at that.

'Mummy has to be away tonight, I'm very sorry but I'll be back home tomorrow.'

'Will you take us to school in the morning?' There was a wobble in his voice.

'I might not be back that early, but I will definitely, definitely pick you up from school and we'll drive to the café and have cakes. Would that be a good idea?'

'Yes,' came the whispered reply. 'Is Daddy coming home soon?'

'I'm going to phone him now and he'll be home as soon as he can. And I'll be back tomorrow . . . I promise . . . OK?'

'OK, Mummy. And Mummy, we planted seeds today in pots.'

'Oh, that's great. I love you loads and loads . . .'

'Bye.' He hung up abruptly, the way little kids do, but this evening Evelyn couldn't bear it and hid her face in the sheet to cry.

There was still no word from Dennis. She would have to try him again. So she'd messaged his bleeper: 'Dennis, I'm in the County General, ward 7. Mandy's at home with the children, but when are you coming home? Where the hell are you?' She'd paused, unsure how to end the message, 'I'll be fine,' she'd added. 'But I've lost the baby.'

The receiver back in its cradle, she'd begun to cry again, big heaving sobs which she'd wanted to hide from the other women in the beds beside her, but she couldn't. It was already 6p.m. She couldn't face the food being wheeled round the ward, so she lay in bed, eyes fixed to the wall, too shocked to sleep.

The words 'lost the baby' had played over and over in her mind. 'Lost' hadn't seemed right . . . as if she'd mislaid it, dropped it . . . couldn't find it. In fact, she'd known exactly where it was, in its bubble in the grey cardboard dish, or maybe in a lab dish by now, or incinerated with the rubbish. Dreadful thoughts, but she hadn't been able to turn them off as she lay back against the bank of cushions and watched the ward, watched the clock hands move slowly and felt tears slide down her face, noiselessly now.

It had been almost 9p.m. when Dennis finally appeared.

She remembered how slightly strange he'd looked as he'd sat down on the bed beside her: kind of nervous, agitated and a little dishevelled, although he was still in his pinstripe suit with a vibrant pink shirt and navy polka dot tie.

He'd kissed her on the forehead and asked how she was and as she'd told him what had happened he'd put his arm awkwardly round her, constrained by the seams on his suit.

'I'm so sorry. I'm sorry I wasn't here,' he'd said.

'I couldn't get you. I tried everything,' she'd told him.

'I was at the Savoy, I don't know why the bleeper never goes off in there.'

Evelyn had realized he was lying.

'Were you there all afternoon?' she'd asked, wondering why she wanted to hear him lie some more.

'Yes,' he'd answered, without any further detail.

But she'd pushed him for more, having no idea what to do with her secret information that he was lying. What did it mean?

She'd asked who he'd met, what they'd eaten, where they'd been sitting – as many questions as she could think of.

'Is something wrong?' she'd asked, confused by all this untruth and agitation, as she watched him fiddle with his cufflinks distractedly.

'I can't tell you right now,' he'd said finally, 'It doesn't seem very fair.'

'What can be worse than this?' she'd almost laughed at him.

'Well . . . don't worry about it, right now.'

'What, Dennis?' He was making her frightened.

'Oh Evelyn—' he pressed the heels of hands into his eyes and she realized this was the closest she'd ever come to seeing him cry. 'I'm about to go bust,' he said. 'Well, I have gone bust. And they're going to come after everything – the house, the cars, everything.'

Already in shock from the miscarriage, she could barely register what he was telling her.

'What?' she'd whispered.

He'd nodded at her then begun a halting explanation of how one client was going to bring his whole business crashing down and because he'd always run an unlimited company, everything would go.

He'd known for weeks, of course. He hadn't wanted to worry her, he said. So instead of being allowed to realize bit by bit that something was very wrong, she'd been kept in the dark and now had to endure the car crash shock of this news. When she had finally taken in what Dennis was telling her, her thoughts had wandered to the new leather and beech wood lounger she'd ordered for the sitting room . . . would that go to the receivers too?

'What are we going to do?' she'd asked.

'I've no fucking idea,' he'd answered. 'I won't be able to work here for years . . . not on my own. We'll have to go abroad. The bastards.'

'What about Denny and Tom? What about their school?' Even as she'd said it, she'd realized they would have to leave, because how would the fees be paid?

'I don't know, Evelyn . . . Christ, I haven't worked any of it out yet.'

Chapter Thirteen

The end of her world, or so she'd thought at the time, had come so quickly. She had barely been discharged from hospital when things started unwinding for Dennis in the most spectacular way.

His office was shut, his staff dismissed. He spent several days at home frantically phoning, swearing into the mouthpiece, ringing round for backers, former employers, clients – anyone who could help him out. Then, within several short weeks, it was over. Writs were issued against him, he filed for bankruptcy and the creditors came after him with a vengeance.

Before she had even begun to realize what was happening, valuers had been round the property putting a price on everything: the furniture, the few antiques, the cars and, of course, the house, itself.

The boys had broken up for the Easter holidays and were at home, quietly wondering what was going on as she and Dennis moved in a daze about the house.

She was settling into some sort of numbed shock. First the miscarriage and now this. There had been no time to grieve, to shed tears, to come home, curl up and feel sorry for herself. She came back to find her home muffled, quiet, waiting for the impending catastrophe.

And stupid, stupid girl, it took her days to figure out how bad this was going to be. She'd blithely gone on the weekly supermarket shop, with the boys in tow, and every single one of her cards had been refused at the checkout.

She'd told the assistant not to worry, she would just go and make a quick call to the bank, and she'd loaded the mountain of groceries back onto her trolley and told them to set it aside for her.

In there were all the luxury items she'd grown so fond of: a case of expensive red wine, because she'd felt she and Dennis needed cheering up, fillet steaks for supper, the boys' favourite; finest ground coffees, Belgian chocolates, French cheeses, croissants for breakfast, glossy pots of jam . . . the bulging trolley was stacked full. And what had the bank told her as she called them from the supermarket lobby?

'We're terribly sorry, Mrs Leigh but all those accounts have been frozen . . . the credit cards too seem to be registering suspension . . . yes . . . on the authority of the official receivers.'

She'd fled out of the supermarket in tears, a

159

child in each hand running behind her in confusion.

In the Range Rover, she'd slumped into the driving seat and sobbed as Tom had started to wail because he couldn't understand why they'd left without his juice box. Denny had told him to shut up, and added: 'We haven't got any of the stuff. Mum and Dad haven't got any money.'

The fact that a six-year-old had now worked out what she was only just beginning to understand had made her cry even more.

'What the hell are we going to do? What are we going to eat?' she'd raged at Dennis when they got back from the trip.

He'd taken £20 out of his wallet and handed it to her, ashen faced. 'Just get the basics, to see us through for a few days,' he'd told her. 'I'm hoping to get sorted out with a loan, until I can get to work again.'

So she'd taken the £20 and gone to a different supermarket, on her own this time, and tried, for the first time in her Surrey life, to limit herself to 'the basics' – whatever they were.

She'd put potatoes, bread, milk, Cheddar cheese, mince, onions, carrots and cornflakes into her basket. Wine was out of the question. Never mind, she was sure there was something left in the drinks cabinet. She'd added yoghurt and bananas, then that was it, she couldn't risk buying anything else. If it came to over £20 she'd have nothing left to pay with and she paled at the thought of having to ask the cashier to put something back.

She had no idea how many tiny humiliations, how many small deaths she was going to die inside before this crisis was over.

The very next day, the milkman would be at the door demanding payment and she would be scurrying round the house searching for loose change, spare coins before finally emptying out Tom's piggy bank and handing over the money in two fistfuls of 10p and 5p pieces, close to choking with tears.

'Will you be wanting further deliveries?' he'd asked, making no comment about the handful of change.

She hadn't seen the big For Sale sign yet, which had been hammered in at the bottom of the driveway first thing that morning.

'Emm . . . no, I suppose not . . . well . . . I can let you know if things . . . change. Thanks, thanks for all your . . . help.' Dear God, why was she thanking the milkman for help? 'Deliveries, I mean.'

'No problem. Goodbye then. All the best.'

'Yes . . . thank you.'

And oh so quickly, like pulling at the loose tuft on a piece of knitting, their lives had unwound. The house was sold, the cars were sold, most of the furniture was taken by the bailiffs, along with all her jewellery and even some of her most expensive coats and handbags.

Dennis's computers, the TV and all the related equipment, the expensive stereo, video recorder, their paintings . . . It had been pointless to try and hide anything, it was all comprehensively listed on their insurance schedules, as the bailiffs had helpfully pointed out.

One night, when the children were in bed, Evelyn had looked through her remaining clothes wondering what she could sell herself to raise some survival cash. Nothing would make a fraction of what it had cost to buy. Brown leather Ralph Lauren jeans – original price, six weeks of groceries, or maybe over two months of basics; a four-ply cashmere twinset – the cost of one hundred bottles of cheap wine; her Donna Karan evening dress – Denny's school fees for a term. But now, second hand, it would altogether fetch maybe a few hundred pounds. Still, that was better than nothing, she resolved. So she assembled four of the big cardboard removals wardrobes and began to dismantle six years' worth of assiduously chosen style and taste.

The expensive designer shoes, meticulously kept in their wrapping paper and boxes, went into the bottom of the packing cases. Then she picked through her evening dresses and suits, all shrouded in dry cleaning plastic. The glittering beaded red backless number she had worn to the Christmas ball in London just four months ago, feeling for one night like the most elegant, glamorous creature on the planet.

The chic little French suits, for playing at

162

corporate wife. The suede jeans, jackets and shirts she loved. Might as well ditch them, she wasn't going to be able to afford weekly trips to the dry cleaners any more, was she?

The silk blouses which were perfect, she loaded into the for sale box; those slightly stained, she kept.

She chose the other things she would keep very carefully – jeans, basic jumpers, things that would not be worth anything: T-shirts, casual shirts, all her underwear. She added one perfect black skirt suit, white shirt and black high heels. She felt she needed that in her wardrobe, come what may. A winter coat, warm anoraks, two cashmere rollnecks, the comfortable and well worn shoes. Nightclothes, of course, and her cheap jewellery, the stuff the bailiffs had left after asking her to take the Cartier watch off her wrist, so they could drop it into their box.

The next morning, Dennis had helped her load the cardboard wardrobes into the back of a hired van and she'd driven them herself to the dress agency in town. Suddenly she'd felt she couldn't shy away from this. She had to taste the humiliation, other people's pity, and take it, face up to it. Not let it destroy her.

The woman in the shop had been pleasant and friendly. If she'd known who Evelyn was or why she should be selling almost the entire contents of her wardrobe, she had not let the slightest hint fall.

It was hard, much harder than Evelyn had

expected, to watch each item of clothing be unwrapped and appraised and given a price.

When the red dress spilled out from its plastic wrapper, the woman's eyes had widened. She had known immediately that this dress cost £3,000 plus, just a few months ago, but she offered £400.

Evelyn had nodded, unable to say anything, because the memory of Tom standing in front of her before she left for that magical evening and telling her she looked like a fairy 'all covered in glittery crumbs' seemed too tragic to bear.

The total the woman was offering her sounded like a fortune to Evelyn, well over £2,000. But she could only have half of the money now and the rest would come when at least 50 per cent of the items had been sold.

Evelyn had agreed the deal, but explained she would have to have cash.

'Oh . . . you'll have to come back tomorrow, then,' the woman told her. 'Do you want to bring the clothes back then? Or shall I give you a receipt?'

Hiring the van again was an unnecessary expense and Evelyn needed money now. Supplies were running low, their moving date was just days away and they still had nowhere else to go.

'Don't you have any cash at all?' she'd asked, trying not to think about how desperate this sounded.

'Well, just £50 or so . . . in my purse,' the woman had answered.

Evelyn had decided to ignore the concern in the woman's eyes, take the money and the receipt and leave the clothes there. She would come back for the rest of the cash. As she'd stepped out of the shop, she'd been unable to avoid her friend Delia who was almost level with her on the pavement.

'Evelyn! How are you, darling?' she'd asked as they'd kissed on the cheek. 'What's all this I hear about—' she'd broken off, no doubt wondering if 'your husband going bankrupt' might be a little bald.

'Well, things aren't too good. We're selling up. Have you heard that?' Evelyn had answered, wondering where her slightly trilling lady-about-town voice was coming from.

'No!' Delia had gasped, eyes wide enough for Evelyn to focus on the slightly clumped mascara on the lashes. 'Your beautiful house! What's happened?'

'Dennis is being sued. I don't really know the ins and outs of it.'

'Oh my God, no!' After a little pause, Delia had added, 'Where are you moving to?'

'I'm not sure yet. Depends where Dennis can find work, I suppose.'

'This is *terrible*. Look, I was just going for a coffee, why don't you come and join me?'

They were four doors along from the chichi

little café where Evelyn knew she would be mercilessly pumped for every last detail by Delia, feigning exquisite sympathy, who would then relate all this in thrilled tones to a hushed gathering of the other tennis club ladies.

Evelyn knew this because she was one of them. She'd done the big sympathy routine with some other woman – just getting divorced, just found out about the mistress, the IVF didn't work out, whatever the particular circumstance of the misery – to have a feast to lay before the intimate circle of 'friends' at the next gathering. She knew the next stage in the ritual too: the object of their sympathy would no longer be quite such a bosom member of the group the next time.

'Well, darling, you know I've invited her to dinner several times since then, but she's always alone . . . no-one to make up numbers. And she burst into tears over some joke Dan made . . . so embarrassing.'

She knew what excuses would be made up for her.

'Well, she'll have nothing to wear. Had to give it all to Carole's dress shop in the high street. How awful. And not much to chat about . . . work isn't going well for him, no money coming in and the kids aren't in the school any more.'

She was just weeks away from no longer being one of them, one of the group she'd belonged to ever since she moved here.

She saw now that they would have to move

out of this town. She couldn't face meeting the old crowd and their excuses for why they hadn't rung, hadn't been in touch or visited. Why should Denny and Tom have to start at the primary school and not see all their old friends whose parents would be too snobbish to invite them round?

As she stood on the pavement, declining the invitation to the café, then kissing Delia's smooth crystal-blasted, custom-blended, fragrant cheek goodbye, casually . . . but probably for the last time, Evelyn felt a tight and gripping panic come over her. What a shallow, pointless life she'd been living. Now it was all going to come crashing down around her ears and she had *nothing* more worthwhile to put in its place.

Chapter Fourteen

In the days before the moving-out date, Evelyn had spent most of her time on the phone making unpleasant calls: telling the bursar the boys would not be coming back to school, cancelling lists and lists of monthly direct debits, gym membership, tennis club fees, music lessons, insurances – even their life insurance.

The boys had played football in the garden almost all day long, running the ball from one end of the lawn to the other, making up little rules and games as they watched removals men arrive, fill up a lorry full and drive it away.

'Are they taking everything to our new house?' Denny had asked and it had broken her heart.

'Well . . . I don't know if we're going to need all that old stuff. I mean, we'll definitely have all your toys . . . but . . . you know . . . time for a change,' was the stumbling reply she'd given him.

'So where are we going?' he'd asked and now Tom came to stand beside him so that the two rosy, rapt faces were looking up at her and she had no idea what to tell them, hadn't even broken the news that school would not be starting next week as they expected. She didn't want them to feel as lost as she did.

'Do you think we could move to your father's for a bit?' Dennis had asked over yet another meal of baked beans on toast and too many glasses of wine from a box, taken with the radio on to drown out the anxious, horrible silence between them.

'My father's!' She'd expected Dennis to have a solution for them by now. A new job, a new home, even if it was only rented, some money coming in. She felt she could only begin to start coping if these things were in place. But moving to her father's? All four of them? Was there no other possible solution? It was a fresh reminder of how grim things were.

Her father lived in Gloucestershire, miles away from Surrey.

'For how long?' she'd asked.

'I don't bloody know,' he'd answered.

'I can't ask him if he'll have us and not tell him how long for. And what about the boys? They'll have to go to school.' She resisted the urge to throw down her fork and storm out. It was becoming impossible for the two of them to have conversations of longer than four sentences before one of them became too angry to stay.

They were going to have to try. They were out of this house in three days' time with no money and nowhere else to go. Something had to be arranged.

So it was decided, and in a van filled with the things the bailiffs hadn't wanted – clothes, toys, kitchen stuff, unexceptional furniture from the spare rooms – they had all moved to her father's house.

Evelyn had never had a close relationship with her father. It was generally quite a civilized friendship, although she felt the weight of his disapproval. He disapproved and she 'disappointed' him. That was how it had been since she was small. And boy, had she given him reason to disapprove and be disappointed now.

He sighed and tutted round the house at them, but managed to hold in the lecture he was obviously bursting to give. Her dad. The formal, English solicitor, who still lived in the big family home he'd moved into on his wedding day. Her mother Elsie, only occasionally spoken about now, had died suddenly when Evelyn and her sister, Janie, were children. Over the years, her mother's presence in the house had shrunk down to a few framed and strangely oranged photos out on display and a chest of drawers full of belongings no-one had had the heart to sort through or part with.

After the move, Evelyn was surprised at how quickly they'd adjusted to this odd new temporary life.

Her father had grumpily assured them that they could stay for as long as they needed, so their cases were unpacked, the garage was piled up with their belongings, she and Dennis moved into her childhood bedroom while her sons were installed in her sister's. When the Easter holidays ended, the boys began to go to the primary school she'd gone to as a girl.

'It's just for a little while,' she'd told them soothingly as she walked them all nervous and twitchy down the street for their first day. 'But I bet there are some really nice boys and girls at this school too.'

Dennis, smartly dressed in a suit and ironed shirt every day, either stayed in the dining room, which served as his makeshift office, or took day trips to London to try and find a new job, and occasionally to appear in court.

He'd waved away her offers to accompany him: 'Just means two train fares, doesn't it?'

Her father was away at work all day too. He never gave them money, thought that would be intruding on the situation, but she noticed that he would keep the fridge topped full, would return from work with 'These fish for us all' or 'Lovely lamb chops in the butcher's window today, couldn't resist.'

She spent the hours between dropping the children off at nine and picking them up again at three in a determined housekeeper role, washing, ironing, cleaning obsessively, baking cakes for tea, making supper and trying not to give too much thought to how everything had changed.

At night, she and Dennis would lie side by side in bed, under the ceiling and the walls she'd known so intimately as a child, and say hardly anything to each other. Until one night, after they had been there for five weeks or so, he told her he was going to have to go abroad to work.

'I can't get anything here,' he explained. 'There's been far too much fuss. No-one wants to get involved.'

He'd outlined his plan to take up an offer of work from a former colleague who was now out in Singapore. She didn't remember feeling any particular emotion in response to this news. It was delivered so unenthusiastically. Dennis wasn't presenting it like some fantastic new challenge or fresh start for them all. He simply explained that this is what had to be done.

'I'm not going to be able to have my own company in Britain for years,' he told her with a face crumpled with regret and disappointment. He'd grown so puffy and red-faced in the crisis, she knew he must be drinking far more than he was admitting to. His blond hair was also thinning out rapidly.

When she looked at him she could see no trace of the charming, persuasive, dashing man with a touch of the bounder she'd once found so overwhelming. She saw only a paunchy, stressed-out, City financier. And although she didn't ask exactly what he had done to be in this

172

amount of crap, she suspected he'd not played by the rules and had been severely burned.

So, a fortnight later, he had gone to Singapore. Yes, *he* had gone. There wasn't enough money for them all to go, the job he was taking came with no perks, he'd explained, he could only afford one flight and to rent a small studio apartment. But he'd assured her the situation would change within months; weeks even, once they realized what a good operator he was.

He'd been strangely secretive about it all, left her with only the vaguest contact details, promising that he would phone with all the information once he'd found a hotel, then a flat.

She remembered him packing three enormous suitcases with most of his remaining belongings – even his heavy winter overcoats, she'd noticed – his favourite books, CDs and all his shoes, along with some silver trinkets which had belonged to his own father – a clock, an ornate hairbrush, and a photo frame with a picture of Denny and Tom when they were tiny.

'I don't want to clutter up your dad's place,' he said by way of explanation for the big, heavy bags.

Then he'd left, and she'd not had the slightest idea, as she'd tearfully waved him off in his taxi – he'd refused to let her come to the airport – that he was leaving them for good and she and their two sons would not see him again for years.

Chapter Fifteen

Evelyn had pursued him with a flurry of anxious telephone calls: to the airline, to the parent company of the one he'd mentioned, eventually to the police. All she had been able to establish in those frantic days was that yes, Dennis was alive and well and living over there, but he made absolutely no attempt to contact them.

She had floundered in the knowledge of this. All day trying to carry on a normal existence for the sake of Denny and Tom, in the evening trying to explain what had happened to her incredulous father and at night tossing and turning, restlessly trying to make sense of it.

The novelty of living at Grandpa's house was wearing off for the boys. They were irritable, whingey and naughty. There wasn't anywhere to set up their train track, they weren't allowed to play football in the garden and the more Grandpa disapproved of their behaviour, the more they played up.

Evelyn tried so hard to channel their energy into afternoon swims, trips to the park, even mowing and raking the lawn every second day. But she was exhausted and filled with a barely suppressible rage at what had happened to her. Weeks passed without a word from Dennis. She wrote to him care of the company to ask for some clarification at least, but the letter was returned unopened, marked 'address not known'. She didn't know if this referred to her husband or to the company. She hadn't the heart to find out.

He didn't want to know them. He had abandoned them to their fate. Without the slightest fucking explanation.

One morning Tom had been prancing about the bedroom making an irritatingly slow game of getting dressed as usual and finally Evelyn had been unable to handle it. She'd reached out and slapped him on the face so hard that four accusingly red finger-marks were left glowing on his cheek.

Her son had burst into shocked tears and as she'd hugged him up in her arms, she'd cried too.

'I'm so sorry, Tom. I'm so sorry,' she'd repeated over and over. He was four, none of this was his fault. She couldn't take it out on him.

'I'll be very good. I don't want you to go away like Daddy,' he'd sobbed into her chest.

'I'm never going away. I promise, promise. I'm never going to leave you.' She told both of the boys this every time they even hinted at the fear.

But there was a clinginess to them, a shadow over their lives which had not been there before.

And here she was, back in the town she had grown up in. Back in her family home. Fuck. She was getting a phobia about trips to the baker's shop, the fishmonger and the chemist and hearing the same questions: 'Hello Evelyn, how is your husband doing? When are you and the boys going over to join him then?'

Her father had looked into the legal possibilities of suing Dennis for maintenance and even divorce, but he was in international waters now and out of jurisdiction.

In the long nights she spent alone, awake in her childhood bedroom, Evelyn had time to reflect at length on her marriage. Had she been a bad wife? She had no idea. She had nothing to compare herself with, Dennis had been her one and only serious relationship and now he wasn't even going to give her any explanation as to what had gone wrong.

At first, she just waited, sure that something would happen, some word would come from him, some solution . . . resolution. But weeks and then months and finally the whole summer had slid by until she'd finally realized that she would have to do something. Take charge somehow, not just of herself, but of her two hurt and very needy boys.

Picking up the pieces had felt absolutely impossible. The problems overwhelmed her, seemed to grow bigger and bigger until she couldn't see past them. How would she get a job? How would she pay for childcare and a home? How would she ever get herself and her children out of her father's house? *Why* had Dennis done this to them?

Despairing, Evelyn had spent the hours her sons were at school in her father's sitting room alone at the window: watching the occasional car go past, a mother and buggy, delivery man, whatever. For hours on end, she sat in the room not moving, not crying, not thinking, just stuck.

Dennis had left her here, stuck with the boys, stuck with their care, stuck with no money, stuck in this house which she thought she had escaped for ever when she married him.

It became harder and harder to get out of bed in the morning. And finally, when she had prised herself from the covers, she had gone into auto-mum. Making the children's breakfast, dressing them in their uniforms, walking them to school. The small reasons to be cheerful had eluded her. The boys gave her reason to live, but this was not really living, this was just existing.

One morning, as Evelyn sat on the sofa staring out of the window as usual, she saw a sleek red car pull up. The door opened and out stepped the tall, elegantly dressed figure it took her a few moments to register was her younger sister, Janie.

Strange: Janie arriving unannounced. This

was so unlike her. She'd been down to see them for the odd weekend since they'd arrived at her father's house – but unannounced? On a weekday morning?

'Hello big sis!' In she breezed, kissing Evelyn on the cheek. 'Dad says you're a mess, he has no idea what to do with you and I'm to sort you out. So here I am.'

Evelyn didn't know what to say to this. 'D'you want some tea?' came out instead.

'No, no, bugger tea and sympathy and all that, get your stuff, we're going out.'

'Where? I have to be back for the boys . . .'

'No you don't, Dad's going to pick them up, it's all arranged. And they know, so don't worry about them, OK?'

'OK.'

'I'm not here to tell you what to do,' Janie insisted as they zipped along in the car, 'but you'll have to do something, because you can't go on like this, can you?'

'I suppose not.'

'Have you got any ideas?'

She felt so awkward trying to tell her sussed and sorted younger sister, already a lawyer training for the bar, that she wanted to do something proper and important and a bit worthy . . . oh, and she wanted it to be kind of court-based as well.

But Janie listened, never once snorted or laughed and after several long moments of

178

thought said: 'The probation service, Lynnie. What about the probation service? You won't make much money, of course, but it's everything else you want. And you're great with kids, so why not get into the young offenders side of it?'

It was an unarguably good idea. And like all good ideas, it took on a life of its own. Before Evelyn could raise any objections, Janie had taken her to the social security office to sort out child benefit, study funding, grants. Then she whizzed Evelyn to the library to look up courses, bought her a sharp little suit in the town's one decent dress shop, then took her out for dinner with lashings of red wine.

'How long have you and Dad known I've been married to a shit?' Evelyn wanted to know, once the first course was over.

'Oh God.' Janie looked down at her plate, shamefacedly. 'Don't ask me that.'

'Why not?'

'Because I never wanted you to marry him, but I didn't want to say anything either. You were up the duff, you were so mad about him and would you honestly have listened if I'd said a word? I was 17 at the time, Lynnie.'

'No, I suppose not.' Evelyn wound a corner of napkin round her fingers. 'But is this what you thought would happen?'

'No, of course not!' Janie told her. 'I just thought you were going to be a Surrey housewife for the rest of your life, bored to tears . . . never having found what you wanted out of life for yourself.'

Evelyn let this sink in.

'I'm a single mother,' she told her sister, saying the words out loud for the very first time. 'A single mother who has never had a job and I'm not qualified to do one either. It's very scary, Janie and, as usual, I wish I'd done what you have. I should have re-sat my exams and gone to law school. If I was a lawyer, I'd have enough money and I could buy a house for me and my children and it would all be OK.'

'If you'd re-sat your exams and gone to law school, you wouldn't have had the boys,' Janie reminded her.

'Well, there's one thing at least that I'll never regret.' Evelyn swirled her glass around and drained it.

'You're going to be fine,' her younger sister assured her. 'You've got me and Dad to help you. I promise it's all going to be OK.' Janie so hoped that this was true.

'You're feeling better now, aren't you?' Janie asked her as they finally pulled up outside their father's home.

'I'm feeling a lot better . . . There is hope! Thank you,' Evelyn told her and took a long look at the young woman sitting in the driver's seat beside her. She'd seen Janie as her infuriatingly perfect younger sister for so long now, it was quite hard to take a real look at the woman she'd grown into: smart, driven, really clever.

'I'm proud of you,' Evelyn said.

'I'm proud of you too,' Janie answered. 'You've been through hell. But now it's time to come out the other side ... with a little help.'

'I think I'm going to move back to London,' Evelyn said, the idea just forming in her mind.

'What! With the boys? What about schools? And extortionate rents?'

'I know, I know ... but I liked it there. When I first went – before I met Dennis and all that.' It was hard to explain. She wanted out of her home town, that was for sure, out of the claustrophobia of being recognized at every turn and into the anonymity of the city.

The other thing nagging at her to go back was the belief that in London, before Dennis, she had felt just briefly a very little bit like herself, her real, adult self. She was convinced that she could only find this person again, this who-she-really-was, if she went back to London and started looking.

'There must be plenty of work in London for a newly qualified probation officer,' she told Janie.

'Well, that's true. Come on, hop out. Dad's waiting for us. Let's see what he has to say about all this.'

'Yeah, and then ignore it!'

They both laughed.

The next day, an omen of good arrived for Mrs Evelyn Leigh in the shape of a letter from the secondhand dress shop. Most of Mrs Leigh's wonderful wardrobe had sold and Carole wanted to know if she should forward the £1,570 balance to the same address.

One and a half thousand pounds! The sort of sum Evelyn might once have spent casually on a dress, a chair . . . a new set of curtains, now seemed like the miraculous gift which would allow her to put her newly formed plans into action. Within weeks, she was registered for a probation course in London and she and her sons were moving into a rented one-bedroom flat in a terraced house in Hackney. It was a shabby little upstairs flat in a shabby little street, facing onto a low-rise council estate, but there was a bus stop right outside the door and a church school two streets down which was OK, the letting agent had promised.

The first night there was difficult. Surrounded by boxes, cases and a sprawl of furniture, she had tried to keep her boys cheerful as they all wondered what on earth she had done.

Now that they were in, she saw how tiny the bare white-painted rooms were and felt the damp and dankness of the kitchen and the bathroom. Both had grey spirals of mould on the walls and ceiling.

But she heard herself telling her sons as they ate a fish supper on the sitting room floor, 'I know it looks a bit ropy now, but we're going to decorate it really nicely. You can help me choose the colours of all the rooms, we'll get posters and once we've unpacked our things, you'll see how different it looks.'

And she meant it. This was her life now, she was in charge and it was damn well going to work. She would not let herself be ground down by Dennis, who had chosen to walk out on them and disappear right off the face of the planet.

The three of them slept together that night, crammed onto the fold-down futon, listening to the strange new noises of the neighbourhood. Cars revving up, the noisy chat as drinkers walked home after closing time, the scuffle of cats, she hoped, in the downstairs garden bins. She had a son on each side and she cuddled their sleeping bodies against her long into the night until she finally fell asleep just before dawn.

Over the next few weeks the flat took shape around them – a crazy and unexpected shape. Maybe it was the bottle of Baileys she was taking some comfort in at night, or maybe it was the need to stick two fingers up to the precious Surrey lifestyle she'd spent six years adhering to, but Eve's decorating went wild. With the boys' full approval, the sitting room was painted a rich, claret red with turquoise paintwork to match the lurid turquoise carpet already in place. The boys' bedroom was transformed into a red fire engine, the kitchen had a crude sunset with black palm trees painted onto one wall and the bathroom was, what else – sky blue with white clouds.

It was perfect, like living in a Wendy house, and she was in charge. She didn't have to care for one moment what Dennis, their friends, her dad, or anyone else would think. She no longer had to housekeep to impossibly immaculate standards and neither did she have to fiddle about in the kitchen at the weekends making fussy soups, toasting pine nuts, dissecting star and kiwi fruits, fraying her nerves with *boeuf en croûte* and truffle layers.

Evelyn Leigh was trying to let go, become the kind of person who left things undone, who washed whites and coloureds together until everything was bluish, who watched TV at breakfast (sometimes), who made vegetable stew and lentil casseroles, who had time to spend the whole day in the park with the children. And she was determined to make some new friends and maybe even *have a laugh*.

After only a fortnight in the flat, she felt she was at home. Her shoulders moved away from the position they had taken up right next to her ears and she started to relax. She was finally in control of her own little domain. It felt liberating. She was going to bring the boys up exactly the way she wanted to, let herself become the mum she'd always wanted to be.

One afternoon when they were picnicking in Hyde Park in the drizzly rain under an enormous umbrella, the two boys were laughing hard over a silly school joke and she felt a lightness which at first she couldn't define. Then it occurred to her that maybe it was happiness. It was so long since she had felt anything like it, she hadn't recognized it.

Before she knew it, it was October and she was faced with going back to college for the first time in seven years. That very first morning, when she registered for her classes, she heard herself telling the clerk that there had been a mistake, she was no longer going by the name of Evelyn Leigh, she was *Eve Gardiner*.

That she wanted to revert to her maiden name was not so hard to understand – but *Eve*? She had always secretly called herself Eve, but only now at the age of 26 was she allowing herself to grow into it, let her public self become a bit more like her inner, real self.

Walking into the big refectory with her new classmates and their friends for lunch, she realized how much had changed for her in six short months. Here she was, eating a plate of subsidized macaroni cheese with a group of other women – some her age, but most younger, all in the kind of hippie chic groove-nick clothes, which made her polo neck, jeans and anorak seem so incredibly square. They were talking films and rooms and rents and boyfriends and her past life as Evelyn Leigh – tennis and boutique shopping, private schools and dinner parties – seemed so far away, it was almost as if it had never happened. This was her first day of training to be a probation officer. What would

Delia and company ever, ever make of this? If they ever took the trouble to find out what had happened to her.

'I'm going to have to miss the last class every afternoon to go and get my kids,' one woman was telling a friend. 'I'll have to borrow someone's notes to keep up.'

'Me too,' Eve told her.

Very quickly, she and this woman, who was studying midwifery and introduced herself as Jenna, 'but everyone calls me "Jen"', were doing the bonding mummy chat.

'How old are yours?' Eve asked her.

'Terry is five and John is nine months. I am dragging myself out of the house to do this course.'

'I've got two boys as well, Denny's six and Tom's nearly five. I love boys,' Eve confided with a smile. 'All that footballing and cars and trains and rushing around.'

'Yeah! But they're bloody exhausting,' Jen laughed. 'So where are you from, then?' She had a slight London accent and a tired face set off by unruly dark hair bundled into a ponytail. She looked about Eve's age, maybe a little older, maybe a little more careworn.

Eve told her, skating over all but the merest of details, how she'd been living in Surrey but had moved back to London 'when my marriage ended'.

'So you're a single girl again?' Jen asked.

'Oh, I don't think of it like that, because of the boys.'

'You will,' Jen smiled. 'And you've come to the right place. I've never been anywhere more obsessed with sex. Look around you – couples coupling, flirts flirting, lecturers leching . . . You're going to have a great time. Too bad I've got the old man at home, that's what I say.'

Eve just laughed at this.

'Where are you all living then?' Jen asked and as Eve told her, Jen nodded and asked her the street name, then smiled, telling her. 'That's round the corner from my place! I'll have to take you out and show you the sights.'

And because they left college at the same time and took the bus back to Hackney to collect their kids from the same school, and because they lived just round the corner from each other and had two sons each, it felt inevitable and right that they became firm friends.

Over mugs of undrinkably strong tea in Jen's flat or the college canteen, they talked and gradually learned a lot more about each other.

Jen hadn't always lived in London; at 17 she'd followed a boyfriend down from a small town in the north-west. She'd worked long hours in a clothes shop while he played drums all day, gigged, got drunk at night and never paid his share of the rent. 'I just drifted through my twenties,' she'd confessed.

She'd moved from shop to shop, from flat to flat after a string of hapless boyfriends called Dane, Shane, Wayne and so on until she'd met Stavo, a Slav who at least seemed to have some

187

goals, ambitions, some reason to get up in the morning. But his reaction to her pregnancy announcement had been to head-butt her in the face. She'd knocked him out cold with the first heavy object to hand, the bathroom scales, then packed her bags and left.

She'd had baby Terry, all alone, apart from a midwife holding her hand and buying her flowers in the hospital shop.

'He's named after my dad and John is named after his grandfather,' Jen had explained.

Baby John's father was Ryan, the lovely Irishman who looked after Jen and toddler Terry, who got her out of the house and smiling again.

'You can't imagine how bad it was, Eve, stuck on the 18th floor of a dreadful block with a baby, all on my own. Living off benefits for the first time in my life,' Jen told her: but only the once, because she was a woman who had moved on, pulled herself through and didn't like to dwell on how bleak it had once been. 'Ryan was my reward for all the crap stuff. I've no idea how he finally persuaded me to have another baby, but he promised he would stick with us no matter what.'

In a delighted whisper, so her sons couldn't hear, Jen had confided: 'We're saving up to get married . . . maybe when I finish my course and land my first job. When we'll have enough for a proper party.'

Jen had never forgotten the midwife who helped her through Terry's birth. She told Eve:

'She bought me flowers although she didn't know me from Adam. And I decided I wanted to do that job, give other women help through that terrible time, when you're straddling life and death and wondering which side you and your baby are going to end up on.'

As they got comfortable with one another, Eve had allowed little bits of her own life story to unfold. And eventually, the gilded life and times of Evelyn Leigh became a big joke between them.

'Oh darling, Ralph Lauren does one just like this,' Eve would swoon over Jen's latest market stall purchase.

'I don't know . . . Does it come in suede?' was a catchphrase they used for all sorts of nonsense – dusters, children's underpants, baby's bibs, bin bags.

The Donna Karan evening dress, the silk curtains, the Range Rover with the leather seats – it was a fantasy world Jen loved to hear about. It wasn't painful for Eve to reminisce. It was like the memory of a dream. How she could now joke at the pettiness of it all. She and her new friend would shriek with laughter, as if this was the most ludicrous world anyone could ever imagine.

Eve Gardiner had such a new life now, to go with her new name, a life which revolved around the children, of course, but also college and hip student friends, flat parties, Sunday markets, charity shops and junk stalls, the library, museums, DIY, vegetarian cooking . . .

Every single aspect of her life changed and by the end of her first term she didn't think Evelyn Leigh would even recognize the person she'd become. A better person, she was sure. She spent long hours with the children and rediscovered all sorts of things she'd liked doing as a child, but hadn't done since. She taught them how to knit and they sometimes spent whole afternoons painting: handprints, potato prints, glitter and sparkle paintings and home-made Christmas cards for all her new friends. She made a quick decision not to bother sending anything to the Surrey brigade. She couldn't see the point. Despite the fact that she'd paid to have mail forwarded from her old house to her father's, not a single one of her old friends had tried to get in touch.

About Dennis, Eve felt only a dull anger, but for the boys' sake, not really for herself any more. She put it to the back of her mind. In fact she was surprised at how little she thought about him now. Disappearing Dennis had become something that only troubled her at night as she was falling asleep – and not every night.

Chapter Sixteen

'God, you look so well, I can't believe it!' Janie
was being ushered up the cramped staircase to
Eve's one-bedroomed home for her first visit.
Although she'd been dismayed by the dinginess
of the street her sister was now living in, she was
relieved to see that Eve did genuinely look better
than she had done for ages, as if a weight had
been lifted from her shoulders.

'Prepare yourself for the décor,' her older
sister warned her with a laugh as she showed her
in. 'I got a bit carried away.'

'Oh my God! But maybe you all needed
cheering up.' Janie took in the lurid sitting room
and kitchen, then poked her head into the
bedroom and even the bathroom. 'It's good . . .
cosy,' was her verdict. 'Where are the boys?'

'A friend's looking after them for a couple of
hours. I wanted you all to myself just for a bit,'
Eve told her, noting her sister's heavy, silk-lined
coat and leather overnight bag and registering

how out of place they were in this cheap and cheerful flat.

'Where do you sleep?' Janie asked.

'The sofa folds down. Tonight you get the lower bunk in the boys' room and I cuddle up with Tom, in case you're wondering!'

'It's fine, honestly.'

'So . . . what's the big news?' Eve asked, taking a good look at Janie now. 'Why the rush to come up here and visit us this weekend?'

'Well, I wanted to see you, of course and make sure that everything was OK. I've been so worried about you, but . . .'

It really wasn't hard to guess what else was going on in Janie's life. Her cheeks were flushed, her eyes were shining and she was finding it hard to stop smiling. 'David has asked me to marry him!' She gave a little scream and had to hug Eve all over again.

'Congratulations!' Eve told her. 'Really! I'm so happy for you! He's a very nice man. I don't think there's any danger of him turning out like Dennis,' she couldn't help adding.

'Well . . . I realize this must be hard. Me getting engaged, you . . .' Janie hesitated, wanting the right word . . . 'abandoned' was definitely not right . . . 'Separated'.

'No, you're wrong, Janie,' Eve replied, going into the kitchen for glasses so they could start on the bottle of champagne her sister had brought: 'I'll be the happiest guest at your wedding, honestly, we're doing really well.'

And Janie could see that it was true. Her sister looked scruffier, but more relaxed and happier than she had done for years. She looked *younger*, that was the strange thing. She'd been through all this terrible stuff, but she'd come out the other side looking a lot better. As Dennis's wife, all dressed up and blow-dried, she'd always looked well into her thirties.

'I think student life suits you,' Janie told her as they sat on the sofa together and toasted each other.

'Mmmm . . . beautiful,' Eve said after a long sip and swallow. 'It's been a long time since I've had a glass of champagne.'

'Well, drink up,' Janie told her. 'There's plenty more here.'

'OK and now I want to hear all about the proposal. Blow by blow. Don't leave anything out.'

Janie snorted with laughter here: 'Oh big romantic moment. David rolls over in bed and tells me "I was just thinking I'd like to marry someone like you." I say "*Someone like me?* What about *me*? Don't you want to marry me?" And he says "Well . . . yeah."'

' "*Well, yeah,*" ' Janie repeated. 'Isn't that the most underwhelming proposal you've heard in your whole life? I burst into tears.'

'Oh no.'

'Don't feel too sorry for me though,' Janie added, sloshing some more champagne into their glasses. 'He now feels so guilty, he's buying

me a ruby the size of a golf ball and taking me to
Venice for Christmas. Well, I mean . . . I wanted
to check with you first,' she added guiltily. 'You
know, if you're planning to be at Dad's and
you want me there . . .'

'Don't be silly, go to Venice,' Eve told her, from
the dizzy haze of a champagne high. 'Make lurve
on Christmas morning.' They both giggled.

'We're going to stay here, I've decided. In our
cosy little home,' Eve said. 'Dad might come up
and visit on Boxing Day.'

Once most of the bottle was gone, Janie
quizzed her hard. Was she really OK? Were the
boys coping? Did they need anything? Did she
want to borrow some money?

'We're really fine. I promise,' Eve assured her.
'I know, it's hard to believe, but we're very
happy. I like it, Janie,' she confided. 'It's
very zen! No, honestly. Everything has changed
and I needed that. A shake-up, a paring down . . .
I've been thinking about it a lot.' Eve put her
glass down, crossed her legs and faced her sister,
fixing her cool grey eyes on her. 'I've lost so
much: the baby, our home, our whole way of life,
all the things I loved that I'd surrounded myself
with, Dennis . . .'

Dennis was last on the list, Janie noted with
some relief.

'All I want now is peace, calm and the basics
. . . it's hard to explain. I don't want anything
right now that we don't need and I don't want
anything that can be taken away. I suppose it's a

security thing. I don't want any of us to be hurt any more.'

Janie thought she understood, but she still asked: 'But don't you miss so many things? It's worse than being a student because you don't even get to go home and stock up on all the nice stuff in the holidays.'

'Like what?!' Eve wanted to know.

'Marzipan, chocolates, expensive wine, gin and tonics . . . fillet steaks . . .'

Eve laughed: 'No, none of that, just perfume and my old face creams. The ones that cost £50 a jar. I mean it just seems crazy now!'

'I'll get you one for Christmas,' Janie chipped in.

'No, no . . . It would feel all wrong. But it's funny, there are some things I still have to buy the expensive version of, like chocolate bars and washing powder. And I hate cheap shoes, so I have to wear these—' she pointed to her trainers. 'But I feel like I was the most spoiled little brat ever and now I'm coming back to reality. The boys, too. We'll all be the better for it.'

Janie thought of the price tag on the engagement ring she and David had already chosen and felt hideously guilty.

'What do you want for Christmas?' she asked Eve.

'New hair!' Eve joked, flicking at her overgrown, under-highlighted locks.

'OK. Well there's something I can sort out,' Janie insisted, 'Seriously.'

*　　*　　*

And that was how Eve had met Harry the hair.

Studying on her miniature budget, only too aware that Christmas was just around the corner, she had no idea how she was going to ensure that it wasn't one more big disappointment for her children.

The year before, Christmas Day had been the most incredible, over the top extravaganza. Dennis had gone overboard, buying the boys electric cars they could ride in, remote control trucks, a city of Lego, football strips, boots, signed footballs. Even at the time, in the depths of her affluent Surrey lifestyle, Eve had thought they were being spoiled. She had opened a small gold foil wrapped parcel to find her diamond-studded Cartier watch inside. Ha, things change. She couldn't help glancing at the black plastic £5.99 job on her wrist now. She'd even considered that an extravagance.

Anyway, she had no idea what to do this year. Especially as Tom at least still believed in Santa Claus and how would he cope with the fact that Santa's budget had dramatically shrunk?

She was saving very hard to get them some nice little things. That meant endless variations on beans and lentils for supper and lunch, home-made porridge for breakfast. Absolutely no money spent on anything unnecessary. But she was going to use just a little of Janie's generous 'hair' money to treat herself to a simple Christmas haircut. Her locks had been untouched since the Dennis bankruptcy crisis hit the fan and they looked awful. Her dark mousy-brown roots had now grown down past her ears and the remaining eight inches of expensive Surrey highlights were overgrown, split-ended and out of shape.

The plan was to have it cut into an above the shoulder bob and much as she detested the idea, she was going to have to dye it to natural. There was no way she could afford highlights now.

She'd made an appointment at the salon a few streets away because it was cheapish, but for Hackney, the interior looked surprisingly stylish.

Once she was inside, she'd been gowned up and led to a chair where she'd made the acquaintance of Harry, a solid, black-haired, East-End-Italian performer.

He'd flourished his comb, moved through her locks and given her his deadpan Michael Caine line: 'It's big hair but it's out of condition.' Followed by, 'Now darling, what are we going to do with it, because it's Christmas, every women needs to dazzle.'

So she'd explained the low-maintenance brown bob she'd decided on and he'd shaken his head sadly and said, 'Oh no, mamma mia, I think we need to bring back the blonde in you, dying to get out.'

In the course of explaining why she couldn't afford highlights because she was saving for Christmas presents for the boys and she didn't know how to stop Christmas being a disappointment for them this year . . . because their father had vanished and she couldn't afford anything like the nice things he'd given them . . . oh boy, out it all tumbled and here she was sitting in a hairdresser's chair blubbing, but Harry, a lifelong comforter of sad women, handed her tissues and a cup of tea and told her, 'Now, now, my darling. It's Christmas time and you have to allow Harry to sort out your hair. And once we've done that, you'll feel much better and nothing will look so bad, I promise.'

So he'd cut her a snappy little shoulder-length bob and told her to come back on Thursday evening, training night, when he would do her highlights gratis while his two trainees watched.

'But I can't come in the evening, I haven't got anyone to look after the boys,' she'd protested, finding it hard to accept this kindness from a stranger.

'Bring the boys,' he'd said, waving his arms expansively round the salon. 'We have videos, we have swivelling chairs, bowls of sweets. They'll be fine.'

That was how she stayed blond while she studied. Harry, then the trainees, coloured her hair once every three or four months on training night. And when she got her job, she of course carried on at Harry's paying him as much as he would accept – always well below the list price.

But that wasn't the reason Harry had become

a close friend. Harry was part of her closest circle because of what he had done for her and the boys that first Christmas. While he dabbed bleach carefully onto strands of her hair and watched her two sons climb over the salon chairs and munch all the sweets in his customer dish, he had told Eve that maybe what they needed at Christmas was not big toys but a little bit of magic.

'My mother was half Italian,' he told her, crossing himself, 'and we all used to go out to midnight mass on Christmas Eve and when we came back the house would be transformed. The tree would be up, the presents would be out – fresh tangerines, panettone, tiny chocolates, little wooden toys, balloons – the candles and little lights would be lit. It was magical. This was what our Santa Claus did, not this sinister coming down the chimney, leaving things from the Argos catalogue that goes on now. I still don't know how my mother did this, but my guess is she had everything wrapped and ready in a cupboard and while we were out, a good friend came in and laid it out.

'Now for the two fine boys you have, I would be prepared to be that good friend, Eve. It would make me very happy.'

It was a wonderful idea. And she couldn't think of a reason not to accept it. Harry was in his fifties, not married but with family, great-nieces and nephews he didn't see nearly as often as he would have liked to. Why shouldn't she let him be kind? Accept the hand of friendship being held out to her now.

'Well, I'm not sleeping with you and there's nothing in my flat worth stealing . . . Does the offer still stand?'

So on Christmas Eve Harry was entrusted with a key and after the tiny tree, lights, carefully chosen presents and treats had all been laid out under the bed and in the kitchen cupboards as arranged, Eve took her sons to the 11p.m. service which the school's church was holding.

Eve, not a churchgoer by inclination, was nevertheless quite taken with this church. It was run by a youngish trendy vicar type who was doing the best he could to maintain some interest in religion in the primary school pupils. The Christmas Eve service promised 'carols, old and new' plus mince pies and cocoa or mulled wine afterwards. The church was romantically dimmed and candlelit for the evening.

The boys, wound up way beyond tiredness with excitement, sang everything loudly, even the carols they didn't really know, and listened to the manger story and the short sermon without too much fidgeting.

Still, a quick glance round the congregation and Eve saw they were the scruffiest there. The pews were packed with respectable black families whose scrubbed and polished children sat in absolute stillness.

200

After the service, the boys had three mince pies each. They were amazed to find it was already after midnight and people were hugging them and kissing them and wishing them Happy Christmas.

'It's Christmas already, Mummy!' Tom had said with glee as they walked out of the church, his hand in hers.

'I know,' she'd smiled back.

'Does that mean Santa Claus will have come?' he asked.

'Santa Claus doesn't exist,' Denny had told him in a voice laden with gloom. 'It's just your mum and dad putting stuff there and there isn't going to be much this year, is there?'

Tom had looked up at Eve for reassurance.

'I don't know about Santa Claus,' Eve had said then, knowing she could hardly go back on the explanation she'd given Denny last year that it was a lovely story, based on a kind man who lived a long time ago, that you told little children. 'But sometimes, really magical things happen at Christmas,' Eve had said to them both. 'And I can't think of three people needing a bit more magic right now than us.'

'Shall I wish on a star, Mummy?' Tom had asked. But when they looked up it was a grey, overcast night and the sky mainly looked orange as it reflected back the streetlamps. No star could be seen.

'There's one,' Tom had said, pointing.

'No. It's just an aeroplane, you div.'

Eve let it pass. Denny was upset and preparing himself for a big let-down. He was already expecting a poor show of presents and no word from his dad. He was so down and so gloomy, she began to worry during the walk back to the house that he was going to see her stunt for what it was – a way of dressing up the little money she'd been able to spend on them – and sink into deeper gloom.

She'd unlocked the front door and they had climbed the stairs to their flat's door on the first floor. On it there was a big green wreath tied with a red bow, which hadn't been there when they left.

'What's that?' she'd said, surprised herself. This was one of Harry's personal touches. The keys turned in the three locks and she pushed the door open.

The sitting room was lit with the tiny white fairy lights on the knee-high tree and by rows of flickering tea lights and candles on the window shelves.

'What's happened?' Denny had walked into the room and she felt happy relief to see the amazement on his face. Seven was obviously still too young for real cynicism to set in.

'Santa's been!' Tom rushed in now from behind her legs where he had been nervously watching.

'Oh my goodness,' Eve said, feeling almost as overwhelmed as the boys, because the room looked so beautiful, much more magical than she had expected. The little flames on the windowsills were reflected in the glass and it looked as if hundreds of lights and candles were burning in the room.

'There's a tree as well,' Denny said. 'I didn't know he brought trees!'

'Maybe just for us,' Eve answered. 'Maybe he heard how I didn't want one and he thought, "That's just ridiculous!" ' The boys laughed.

'But how did he? We don't even have a chimney . . .' Denny's musings were interrupted by Tom's more pragmatic question.

'Are these our presents?' he wondered, peering down at the gold and silver wrapped packages. 'And look – sweeties,' he added, seeing the dishes of Maltesers, Quality Street and Smarties which had been set out beside the parcels.

Eve knelt down now and looked at the gift tags she had carefully printed out so that her handwriting would be disguised.

'This is for Denny, this is Denny's, this is for Tom . . .' She divided the spoils until both boys had a little mound of parcels, small and medium-sized, nothing big.

'These three are for me!' She was really surprised now, because she had wrapped up some cheap pants and hair slides for herself, so the boys wouldn't be suspicious, but the other two parcels in shiny red paper were new.

She put them down so she could watch the

203

boys' faces as they unwrapped their goodies.

A wooden box filled with 400 small, intricate building blocks for Denny. He seemed genuinely pleased. Then there were playing cards, yoyos, bangers, indoor sparklers, water balloons, a torch. He seemed to like everything.

For Tom, there were little fire trucks, trains, Jeeps, a wind-up crocodile, toy ducks, a fireman's hat and a spider which jumped when you squeezed its pump. He was just bubbling over with delight, his fingers probing into the crevices and feeling all the surfaces as he made the new things his own.

'Can we eat the sweets as well?' he asked, little face turned up to her with his best pleading, melt-in-the-mouth expression.

'Of course . . . well, a few. We want to save some for Christmas Day!'

They both scooped up as many as they could manage before she put the bowls out of reach on the bookcase.

'What about yours, Mummy?' Denny asked.

'Oh yes, I almost forgot.'

She opened the heavier parcel and out slid two fat bottles, very expensive shampoo and conditioner and, she guiltily thought now, she hadn't even given Harry so much as a bottle of wine to thank him.

The next parcel opened to reveal a sticky block of Christmas cake decorated with a layer of walnut halves and cherries.

'Wow,' Denny said. 'Can we have a piece?'

'Yeah, let's cut a slab and make cocoa and have a midnight feast.' For a moment, Eve was about to suggest opening the parcels hidden under her bed, which she was planning to claim were from 'her' in the morning. But no, she wanted them to have something else to open when they woke up when the little presents, which seemed so glamorous and magical tonight, might have lost their shine.

She got them into their pyjamas while the milk heated, then all three of them tucked up into her bed.

When the cocoa and cake were finished and Tom was already glazed-eyed and almost asleep, Denny cuddled in beside her and said in a teary whisper, 'I wanted to send Daddy a Christmas card, because I want him to know I still love him.'

'Oh, Denny.' She'd hugged him in hard beside her. 'I'm sure Daddy knows that.' How could he not know he'd broken their hearts? she thought with a surge of fury.

'But we don't know his address, do we? So I couldn't send him a card. But he might think it's because I don't love him.'

Just because her children had stopped asking about things or speaking about them, did not by a million miles mean that they had stopped thinking about them.

'Denny, Daddy knows where Grandpa lives,' she told him. 'He could write to us any time or phone Grandpa any time to get our address or give us his. For some reason that I don't understand, he has gone off on his own to another country. Maybe he'll write or come back one day soon, or maybe he won't. I just don't know. All the three of us can do is love each other and get on with our new life now and try and be happy. I'm never going to leave you and Tom, never, ever, ever in a million years.' She squeezed him in her arms and kissed the top of his head, which smelled of his own peculiar sweet sweat and self.

'But what if you die, Mummy? Who will look after us then?'

'Oh Denny.' She smiled at him and tried to make light of this gloom and doom. Although, it was a terrifying thought which occasionally woke her in the middle of the night.

'I'm not going to die for a very, very long time, I hope. But if I got sick and couldn't look after you for a while there would be Grandpa and Aunty Janie and JenJen, lots of people who could help out. Please, sweetheart,' she brushed the hair back from his pale forehead – 'it's Christmas, it's a happy time. Try not to worry about it too much. I'm right here beside you.'

She rested his head back against the pillow and stroked his soft cheek and then his back until his eyelids drooped and he fell asleep.

Then she sat up and moved gently out of the bed. There just wasn't room for all three of them on the sofa bed now, she would have to sleep in their room. She watched the boys for a while after she'd arranged them more comfortably close together, away from the edges.

God damn Dennis for making them so unhappy, her precious children. She would never, ever forgive him for that, for as long as she lived.

Another thought occurred to her as she found the sweet bowl and took a big scoop of chocolates for comfort. She never wanted to be rich again. She thought of Scarlett O'Hara in the potato field, vowing never to be poor, and felt the opposite. She never wanted to be rich ever again.

She and Dennis and their shallow friends really had known 'the price of everything and the value of nothing'. She and her children had once had more than they could ever appreciate and now they had little and appreciated everything, including each other and the kindness of their new friends.

What was the point of putting any store in things which could disappear overnight if the money ran out? She only wanted reality, the important stuff, the things she could truly own and afford now. And not to care too much about them either.

So when, three whole years later, word finally arrived from Dennis – via his lawyers, requesting a divorce because he planned to remarry – Eve had already decided she wanted no maintenance, just a one-off, clean break settlement. She bought herself a small, secondhand car, put the rest of the money in the bank for the boys and tried to erase for ever the memory of the reunion at the lawyer's offices.

Scraping chairs, untouched cups of tea, the joy, hurt and confusion of the boys, and Dennis – browner, balder, fatter – and his lamentably pathetic: 'I know this has been hard . . . I don't know where the time has gone . . . I've been meaning to get in touch.' She had barely been able to speak because of the rage she'd felt on seeing him again and had agreed to everything and his offer to come and visit the boys when he was 'next in the country' with curt nods and the bare minimum of words. When he'd held out his hand to bid her goodbye, she'd kept hers jammed to her side.

Tom had cried all the way home and Denny had stared out of the bus window as furious and as silent as her.

208

Chapter Seventeen

'They're back early.' Deepa looked up from her position, prone on the somewhat decrepit brown sofa, when she heard keys rattling in the door of the flat.

'No.' Tom raised his head from the corduroy beanbag he was sprawled across. 'It's pretty late, almost midnight.'

They had spent the whole evening in front of the TV eating a not entirely bad chicken, noodle and broccoli concoction he'd cobbled together, discussing the pros and cons of three-wheeler buggies, endowment mortgages, crèches and bridesmaids, before moving on to mugs of hot chocolate in front of *Pop Idols* and whatever else was on. Tom had found it all a bit heavy, but at least it was calm. Deepa was five months pregnant now and it felt as if she had been crying or shouting at some point on almost every single day of the pregnancy.

'Hello!' Denny opened the door and came into the room, Patricia following close behind. They'd wangled tickets to a film première and party, so they were looking gorgeous, Denny in black tie and Patricia in long, figure-hugging, backless glittery-black.

'Hello little Ma and Pa,' Denny was teasing them. 'Had a nice evening by the fire?'

'Ha, ha.' Deepa was hoisting herself up onto her feet. Then, hands on bump, she slid her feet into her slippers and headed for the door.

'I'm off to bed,' she told them, 'Good night everyone.'

'Night.' 'Good night.'

'So. Was it fun? Was it showbiztastic?' Tom asked the pair, who were wound round each other, snogging and rumpling hair, as if he wasn't there.

'You bet.' Denny broke off to answer him. 'It's the most bizarre thing though, how tiny celebrities are when you see them in real life. They're like little bonsai versions of themselves, with perfect plastic hair and teensy muscles.'

Patricia started to giggle helplessly at this, then whispered something into Denny's ear, giggled some more and went out of the room.

'Too much champagne,' his elder brother said and that was when Tom saw how lashed Denny was too.

'And the rest?' Tom asked.

Denny tapped the side of his nose: 'Little bit of hokey cokey on the go as well.'

'Oh God, I hate that stuff. Bad taste at the back of your throat for a week.'

Denny just laughed. 'You should have come,' he said, and sat down on the sofa opposite his brother. 'The party was fantastic, never seen anything like it, man. We only left early because Pat's got to work tomorrow. It was going to go on all night.'

'I'm not really in a very partying place right now.' Tom stretched his arms up above his head and gave a huge yawn.

'No. I can see that.' Denny made a gesture at the cocoa mugs, bank and pram brochures strewn all over the floor. 'You're a bit young to be giving up though, aren't you?' he asked. It was meant to come out a bit more teasingly than it did.

'And what's that supposed to mean?' Tom asked.

'Well, slippers and cocoas and prams . . . getting married . . . mortgage. All that stuff. It doesn't have to be like this. I've no idea why you're going along with it all.' Denny pulled his bowtie undone, opened his shirt and leaned back into the sofa. Tom felt like he was being offered advice by some low-budget James Bond.

'I already have a mortgage – with you, in case you've forgotten,' he replied. 'And I'm not "going along" with anything, thank you very much. Deepa's pregnant, which wasn't planned, but we both want to have the baby and we both want to get married.'

'All right.' Even in his pissed state, Denny could see he had really annoyed his brother. 'I'm just telling you that you don't have to give up and become a boring old fart, before the baby even gets here. I mean look at Rich and Jade. Are they boring? Do they drink cocoa in front of the telly every night? Is she mentally moving into a three-bed semi in Surbiton?'

'*All right*, you've made your point,' Tom told him. 'Can you just shut up now?' But now he was thinking of Rich and Jade, unmarried friends who'd had a little girl last year. They ran an ultra-groovy interior design business and the baby seemed to have changed nothing. The couple still partied hard, worked all hours, lived in a fantastic loft, dressed in matching bespoke pinstriped suits – Jade's always worn with a nipple-revealing white vest. Baby Bethany seemed to accompany them everywhere in a sheepskin papoose, dressed in mini Paul Smith and cool shoes, causing no disruption what-soever. It was all rather sickening, really.

And maybe he'd imagined that's what he and Deepa would be like as parents, but he hadn't banked on Deepa being this ill and exhausted, moody and *needy*. She changed her mind about what she wanted from one day to the next. At the moment she was going through a scarily coping, trying to be efficient, organized sort of thing, but any day now and they would be back to tearful, distraught . . . confused.

She'd really needed him to offer marriage. She'd felt better and seemed less anxious as soon as they'd made the decision. But the wedding was taking on a hideous shape of its own. It seemed to have become about what Deepa's parents wanted, what the owner of the hotel wanted . . . what the vicar wanted . . . the photographer . . . Whatever he and Deepa had planned seemed to have been forgotten long ago. But he was frightened to broach the subject with Deepa; she was in quite enough of a state as it was.

And bloody Denny-James-Bond here, what did he know?

'Denny boy, you have to come to bed now.' Patricia was at the door. Only her head, a long swish of hair and shoulder was visible, but both brothers could see the delicate pink strap against her white skin and guessed she was in some delicious silky concoction.

'Lucky me,' Denny said getting up from his seat.

'Yeah,' Tom agreed. 'Lucky you.' Lucky bloody Denny – aged 22, unmarried, childless, a fashion photographer dating a model. He didn't really have too much to worry about, did he?

Left along in the sitting room, Tom put on a CD and went into the kitchen in search of a bottle of wine.

An hour later, he had poured the last of the Australian red into his glass and knocked it back. He still didn't feel anywhere near drunk enough. He wanted to be out of it, he didn't want to think about all this any more. He turned the volume up on the stereo, although he was aware it was after one in the morning.

What about the crusty old bottle of tequila on the bookcase? Maybe that would hit the spot. He held it up to the light. At least two stiff shots' worth were swilling about the bottom. He poured the drink out into his wine glass and took a gulp.

Urgh, disgusting, but satisfyingly strong. Another big glass full and he could be in the state of happy oblivion he was hoping for.

Why was none of this proving to be as easy as he'd hoped? He and Deepa had spent the days straight after the pregnancy test cocooned in some sort of mad romantic dream about how amazing this was and how they were going to be married and looking after this wonderful baby together, la di la. Then the outside world had got in and trampled all over the daydream, and fuck, what a mess it was turning into. Worst of all, Deepa's parents had offered to lend her money towards buying a flat round the corner from her family home in leafy, bloody boring Chingford. And Deepa was trying to persuade him to accept.

He rinsed the last of the revolting fermented cactus liquid around his mouth and swallowed. Then he stood up and realized how quickly, horribly drunk he'd got. This was awful, not the happy numbness he was hoping for at all.

He decided to head for the bathroom and a glass of water.

Once he was in the cramped room, his fuddled brain began to register the inevitable consequences of his uncustomary binge. He knelt down at the toilet, lifted up the seat and began to vomit. Why was he such a crap drinker? He looked at the revolting blood-coloured spew, which the red wine had formed.

He heaved and heaved, feeling vomit chunks move through his nostrils. God, how long was this going to go on for?

'Just what is this supposed to solve, exactly?' he heard Deepa's angry voice demand from the bathroom door.

He turned and saw her framed in the doorway in the baggy knee-length nightshirt she'd bought about a hundred sizes too big because she was expecting to grow into it.

'I don't know,' he answered, trying to muster as much anger as he could from the depths of the toilet bowl. 'I just wanted to relax for a couple of hours. Not think about it. OK?'

'Oh well then, that's all right. Just leave it all to me to think about, why don't you? Have a few hours of fun while I'm stuck without being able to have a sodding drink.'

'Oh Jesus, don't start crying again. I can't stand it!' he shouted back. 'Just stop bloody crying. What do you think crying solves? It just makes me feel like the biggest shit in the world. This is not all my fault!'

'No, it's all mine. I wish I'd never had sex with you, I wish I'd never gone out with you. I wish I'd never met you. And I'm not bloody well going to marry you!!' She stormed off to the bedroom, sobbing.

Tom stood up and washed his face with cold water, then buried it in a towel. He wanted to cry too. This was so hard. He was 20 and not ashamed to admit to himself that right now he needed his mum.

He heard Denny's bedroom door creak open and then close again. All these evenings in and late night rows were not fair on his brother. He and Deepa would have to get it together somehow or find somewhere else to do their falling apart.

He went back into the sitting room and looked through his CD rack. Ha, there was the one Bob Dylan album in his possession, a Christmas present from Joseph. Poor old Joseph, he'd figured in Tom's romantic wedding plans too.

In those three blissful days when Deepa was first pregnant, Tom had imagined a family wedding so happy that all the divisions would be healed. He'd seen himself with an arm round his long-lost dad, smiled on by Deepa's father . . . his mother dancing cheek to cheek with Joseph while Anna and Robbie whirled round them. What a complete pillock he'd been. Instead, he'd stirred his oar into three different seething family cauldrons. And his own relationship was looking far from ideal. Love's young dream was turning into love's young complete fucking nightmare. He went back into the sitting room and slumped onto the sofa.

He knew it was far too late, but he picked up the phone anyway and dialled . . .

'Hello, yes?'

'Mum? Don't worry, it's just me, Tom.' He heard the panic in her voice and felt immediately guilty.

'Is everything OK?' Eve, woken by the phone, was still lying in bed, in the pitch dark, heart hammering in a state of parent terror.

'Yes, everyone's fine. I'm just feeling awful,' he told her and she realized that he was crying. The first time she'd heard him cry for years.

'Is it your head? Have you got a temperature? Rash?' Even only 15 per cent awake, she automatically did the meningitis drill.

'No, Mum! I'm not ill. I'm . . . I just don't want to go through with this. I don't want to be a dad and a husband and have a bloody baby to look after. And Deepa—' big sob – 'she's a mess. She can't handle it.'

'It's OK,' Eve soothed and let him stumble on, spilling out his thoughts, while she switched on the light, shook herself out of sleep and listened.

When he was finished, she tried to calm him in a voice that sounded all thick and furry to her.

'Tom, it's a big thing. A really big thing that you're doing. It's going to take a long time to come to terms with it. But you're all going to be fine.'

217

'Yeah,' he said with a sniff and a teenagey lack of conviction.

'I'm not going to let it not turn out OK,' she promised him.

'It's just not fair,' he added. Ah, the not fair thing. How did any parent reply to that? 'Tom, some people get to be teenagers well into their thirties, some of us have to grow up a lot faster. But it doesn't have to be awful. You've got to think about how to make it work for you both. You don't have to get married,' she told him. 'You don't even have to be with Deepa if it's not what you want. But you have to promise me that you won't walk out on the baby.'

He sort of sniff mumbled a reply to this.

'All my children are going to be really good parents,' she said and it sounded like a warning.

'It's 1.48a.m.,' she told him. 'Not exactly a great time to talk. Will you call me in the morning?'

'OK,' he said.

'And Tom, go to bed. Don't drink any more, you're a really rubbish drinker.'

'Ummm . . .' Had it been that obvious? 'OK. Good night, Mum. Thanks.' He hung up abruptly and within moments, was fast asleep on the sofa.

Unfortunately, Eve was now wide awake. For half an hour, she tried to fall back to sleep again, then decided it was hopeless. She got up, made camomile tea and began to mix up fertilizer for the houseplants; she'd been meaning to do it for weeks.

Children! *Grandchildren*!

There was a sleep god up there somewhere who demanded a trade-off. If you stayed awake and worried about your children's problems for them, they could fall into deep, untroubled slumber. That was the deal.

Chapter Eighteen

'Henry is not stinky. I want to wear Henry . . . waaaaaaaaaaaaaaaaaah!'

'But you wore Henry yesterday and now he has to go in the wash, Robbie,' Eve said. Good grief. Here they were battling it out in front of the washing machine again, Robbie trying to tug the minuscule red pants out of her hands.

'He's not stinky!' Hysterical tears of rage now.

She waited for a few moments, then put her nose to the pants and gave a theatrical sniff: 'Poo-ey!! Henry you need a wash!'

Oh, was that almost a smile from Robbie now? 'Poo!' She did it again. 'Henry, you are whiffing. You try, Robbie?'

He put his nose onto the pants. 'Poo,' he agreed, giggly now.

'OK, why don't you see if you can fit them into the machine?'

He took the pants and paused for just a nano-second, as if he was weighing up the pros and cons of running down the corridor back to his room with the beloved Henry pants or giving in to this scheme of hers to distract him by getting him to put them into the machine.

He put the pants into the machine.

'OK, shall we finish getting dressed now?' He nodded. She followed him into the room, where Anna was at her desk putting some last-minute touches to her homework.

Soon all three of them were at the door, dressed, buttoned up and ready to go. Eve swooped down on her children to cuddle and kiss them. 'I love you to bits,' she told them. Robbie squirmed with delight and even Anna conceded, 'I love you too, Mummy.'

'It's Friday!' she reminded them. 'Tomorrow we can do whatever you want, oh and Tom and Deepa are taking you out in the afternoon, on a surprise!'

Tom had insisted: 'We're looking after them, we need the practice. You have the afternoon off. Go out, have some fun. Don't just hang around the garden all day.'

It was no use telling him that was what she really wanted to do. Get the gloves on, tackle the ivy, which was trailing down off the walls and growing rampantly beyond all control. And the weeds! Nothing else would come through at all this year if she didn't get some serious weeding done and it was high time to set up the tomato plants against the sunny wall and she wanted to plant more herbs . . .

When Tom and Deepa arrived on Saturday, they looked a little more relaxed and happy than Eve had expected.

'Sit down, have tea and chat to me first, or else you're not allowed the kids,' Eve told them.

'Now,' she said as she plonked mugs, teapot, milk and annoyingly over-sticky home-made flapjacks down on the table, 'what's happened? You both look so well!'

'We've chilled out about it all,' Tom said, stuffing a whole flapjack into his mouth. 'Que sera, sera . . . Zen, good karma, all that,' he said, trying not to spray oaty crumbs across the table.

Deepa, swathed in a black stretchy top and trousers, giggled at him and patted his arm. She said the feeling sick and exhausted had finally worn off and she was beginning to enjoy the process.

'And then we had a visit from my Uncle Rani,' she added. 'He's quite a cool guy. He came to see us and then he went and sorted my family out.'

'You'll absolutely love him, Mum,' Tom said. 'Oooops . . . totally not supposed to say that.'

More giggles on both their parts.

'Well, whatever he's done for you, it seems to have worked,' Eve concluded.

'Oh, he was great, Mum, "All parents are students of the profound nature of humanity", I remember him saying. He was great, I was blown away.' Tom reached over for another flapjack.

'So, what's happening with your family?' Eve asked.

'They've chilled out a bit, but boy are they fussing about the wedding,' Deepa said. Tom rolled his eyes and tried to make a joke about it: 'I can see why people only want to do this once in a lifetime.'

'Is it going OK?' she asked, but when they both gave slightly short and huffy answers to this, she thought maybe best leave it alone.

'I think it's going to be a bit too traditional,' Tom threw in. Deepa didn't say anything to this but Eve watched her cross her arms and press her lips together.

'So who is Uncle Rani?' she asked, wanting to change the subject.

'The family black sheep,' was Deepa's reply. 'My dad and all his brothers did medicine and became doctors, but Rani, who's the youngest, is a psychologist. He's pretty good, though. He lectures . . . does family therapy.'

'Ah ha,' Eve said. Then in a stage whisper added: 'Don't tell Anna!'

'Don't tell me what?' Anna had arrived in the kitchen bang on cue.

'You don't approve of psychologists, do you?'

'Well, not if they haven't had any *medical* training,' she replied. 'Psychiatrists do full medical training, then study the mind.'

'Well, I suppose Rani would argue that he

223

spent seven years studying the mind and not a whole lot of organs he didn't need to know about,' Deepa told her.

Eve gritted her teeth, expecting a flurry of disagreement from Anna, but unusually her daughter just said: 'Hmmm.' And helped herself to a flapjack.

'Robbie!' she bawled. 'Mummy's got biscuits in the kitchen.'

And Robbie made them all laugh because he came in running with his mouth open, bouncing the sound out of it: 'Ah ah ah ah ah ah ah ah ah ah.'

'Do they have raisins?' he asked, coming to a stop right beside Eve's chair.

'These ones don't, but I could put some raisins on your plate to eat with it.'

'OK.'

'Ah now . . .' Eve remembered. 'There is something else I want to talk to you about.' She looked up at Deepa and Tom: 'Your wedding present. Hard cash – and as soon as possible, so you can use it for the wedding, towards a flat, towards an all-singing, all-dancing electric buggy . . . whatever you like. No pressure what to spend it on. Please yourselves.'

The two of them looked at her, a touch embarrassed. Eve's super-generous cash gifts always took everybody by surprise. She had come up with lump sums for Denny and Tom when they left school, sorted out their flat deposit, and, Tom remembered now, bought Joseph a stunningly expensive coat and briefcase for his first proper job. Still, this was a woman who had never once been on holiday, considered home-made soup and bread a dinner and had driven the same Peugeot 205 for about ten years now.

'Can I send you a cheque?' she asked, considering this would be the easiest as she didn't want to hear their protests.

Eve was always saving for something, including her fantasy future when she thought she might spend her retirement in the country in a perfectly Zen retreat, the kind of place where everything would be white and calm and there would be a labelled shelf for every single pair of shoes and socks. She would snip at teeny bonsai trees, live on green tea and ornamental rice rolls and spend most of her time tending her water feature, raking gravel and trying to perfect her unsupported headstand.

By the time Robbie left home, she'd have been a mother with children in the house for over thirty years; she thought she could maybe do with some peace, quiet and order by then. But she wanted the children to live nearby, didn't think she could manage too long without them.

But should she be alone? she wondered. Could the fantasy not include a kimono-clad love god waiting for her in the wooden bathtub?

'The aquarium, Mum? Hello?' Tom was telling her. 'We're going to go off to the aquarium. And maybe the cinema afterwards if there's anything good on. Then we'll give them supper and have them back at bedtime.'

'Are you sure?' She was looking at Anna and Robbie, who were grinning at her. Well, obviously that was what they wanted. Robbie was sitting on Deepa's knee now.

'We need the practice,' Tom reminded her and smiled at Deepa. Oh it was cute, they were in love, despite all the anxieties.

'And what are you going to do with yourself?' Tom asked.

'Well I was going to garden for a bit . . .' Everyone groaned at her. 'I like it! Really! Then I might go out for a drive . . . I don't know . . . or just curl up and read something. Honestly, don't worry about me. I'll have a lovely time.'

She kissed them all at the door, then closed it, turned and had the flat all to herself. Delicious.

Now, she wasn't going to waste all this precious alone time cleaning up . . . but there were just a few chores to get out of the way first. And then on to planting. It was already May! And she still had the odd bag of bulbs she hadn't found homes for. Denny had given her a whole sack of mixed gladioli bulbs for Christmas, Gladioli!!! But he'd promised he'd seen them on some cutting-edge garden makeover programme. 'Gladioli are the new hollyhocks – or something,' he'd told her. She was going to bung them in and see what happened; the packaging promised beautiful

226

shades of pink and the soft red she liked so much. Then she wanted to put pink cyclamen and blue violets into the windowboxes at the front because she'd decided that would look much more special than geraniums. She'd had a long, satisfying love affair with geraniums, from palest pink to deep red, with their clean-earth smelling leaves. But it was over. They looked prissy, fussy and old-fashioned to her now. Whereas cyclamen . . . she was in the first flush of passion with pinky-purple cyclamen, the upright, translucent petals looking like brand new butterfly wings.

'I'm completely insane,' she told herself as she took a shiny fork and trowel out from the cupboard under the stairs. 'I've got a crush on a plant variety . . . Gardening has become my sex substitute.'

Was there a glimmer of truth in that? Gardening had become Eve's thing not in Surrey – where every house they'd lived in had come with lawns, borders, even greenhouses, all tended to by part-time gardeners – but in the first flat in Hackney where she'd started with houseplants and windowboxes, then found herself begging the people downstairs to let her mow the lawn and put in a few patio pots. Because suddenly her longing to grow things, to be surrounded by green and flowers and beauty – wasn't it about making their dingy and unpromising surroundings more beautiful and natural? – anyway, the longing could no longer be confined to houseplants and two windowboxes.

At last she flopped down on the sofa with her book after a rare pampering bath. Her hair was wet and lavishly conditioned, up in a turban, her face under a mask. She was physically shattered from the afternoon's work in the house and the garden, but just as she was flat out on the sofa and halfway through the first paragraph, the phone rang.

For a moment, she considered leaving it. Then just the slightest flash of worry that it could be Tom and some sort of child disaster gave her the strength to heave herself up and answer.

'Hello, Evelyn.' It was her father.

'Oh hello, Dad.' They phoned each other once in a while; she went down with an assortment of children to visit once in a while. It was a friendly relationship, not too close, not too personal – just the way he wanted it.

The phone was on a shelf in the sitting room close to one of those fold-down canvas chairs, so she sat down, happy to chat, in her bathrobe and turban and mask. They skimmed through the 'how are yous? on to the children and then their gardens, which was a nice little interest they had in common. Very important to have some sort of neutral topic to chat about with fathers like Eve's. They just weren't comfortable with opinions, emotions . . . they wanted conversation about something concrete. And finally, sandwiched between long, awkward pauses, out it came.

'I've had some rather bad news this week, Evelyn, which you should know about . . .'

'Oh no,' she said automatically, wondering what was to come.

'I've got a tumour in my bowel and it's not looking too good—' this delivered in what she referred to as his army officer mode.

'Oh my God, Dad.'

'Yes. It's a bit of a shock.' He sounded so calm, he could have been talking about someone else.

'Oh my God,' she said again. It still didn't feel as if it had registered. 'How did you find out?' she asked, appalled that she hadn't suspected anything was wrong.

'I've been a bit under the weather for a couple of weeks or so. I thought it was old age or maybe a flu bug I hadn't shaken off . . . finally went to the doctor's, he sent me for tests and here we are.'

Here we are. Jesus Christ.

Her father was 72 and only in semi-retirement. He was still reluctant to give up work completely. He enjoyed having his office and his colleagues to visit several times a week because he was not a man of many friends, or many hobbies. She had often worried about how he would fill his days when he finally decided to leave his partnership. And now she was hit by the awful possibility that maybe he would die.

'I'm going to have an exploratory op in a month or so, they can't do it till my other medication has worn off or something. But they'll know more after that. Bloody doctors,' he added.

'How are you feeling?' she asked.

'Not the best. I'm off my food and pretty uncomfortable.'

This sounded so strange. She couldn't think of a time when her father had been ill. He rarely even caught a cold.

'Oh, Dad,' she managed, 'I'm so sorry. We'll come down and see you as soon as we can.'

'Yes.' Still so calm. 'Janie's coming tomorrow for a few days,' he told her. 'Come when she's here, if you like, or whatever suits you.' He didn't want to impose. Even as a seriously ill man, he would never want to impose.

'I'll get some time off work. We'll drive down tomorrow,' she said. 'And don't go to any trouble. We'll sort ourselves out with food and beds and stuff. Is Janie bringing the children?'

'No,' he said.

They made the arrangements, talking about travel and arrival times, maybe trying to talk around his news as much as possible.

'All right, OK . . . well, so long then,' he said finally. Ending calls was difficult for him. He would never have said the sort of things she did to her kids: 'I love you . . . missing you already . . . take care, darling . . . lovely to speak'. But he felt their absence. 'All the best then,' he managed, stiffly. Stiffly – the word that summed him up.

'Take care of yourself, Dad.' See, she couldn't manage all the love stuff either with him, he

230

made it too hard. He saw an emotion coming at ten paces, ran away and hid. 'See you tomorrow,' she added.

'Bye.'

'Bye.'

Slowly she put the receiver down and stared at it until it became a blur of tears.

Tom knew as soon as he saw his mother that evening that something was wrong. Her eyes were pink and she was smiling too hard at them.

'Hi,' he said. 'Are you OK, Mum?'

She waved the question away. 'Have you had a lovely time? Deepa! Don't carry him!' She saw Deepa lumbering in behind Tom with a whacked-out Robbie over her shoulder. 'Your poor back.'

Robbie was transferred to Eve and he managed a squeezy hug before conking out again. Anna looked sparkly and bright with the excitement of the day.

'Will you stay for a bit?' She tried not to plead but she really, really wanted the comfort of Tom this evening.

'Of course.'

So Deepa, Tom and Anna went to the sitting room for drinks and crisps and chat while Robbie was eased into his pyjamas and tucked into bed.

Only when Anna had been listened to, washed, teeth brushed, tucked in and left reading in her room, did Eve go back into the sitting room and collapse. 'It's Dad,' she told them, Tom really, not able to stem the tears now. 'He's got a tumour in his bowel. They have to open him up and take a look.'

She saw the surprise of this register on Tom's face.

'God,' was all he felt able to say.

'Janie's going down and I'll take Anna and Robbie for a few days as well,' she explained.

She suspected that Janie, much closer to their father, was going to find this very hard to cope with. Janie would manage little chunks of visit, but she wouldn't be able to stay long enough for her or her father to get really upset. Her sister and her father were much more alike, tried to keep most of their emotions locked up safely out of harm's reach.

'This is going to be really hard,' she said. 'We'll have to go down a lot. He'll really need us.' She felt Tom's arm slip round her shoulder.

'Mum, I'm so sorry,' he said, not sure of anything else that would help.

Chapter Nineteen

When Eve arrived at her father's house, in time for lunch as arranged, her younger sister was already there. Had been there for a couple of hours already, judging by the scrubbed-clean look of things.

Janie had greeted her and the children at the front door wearing yellow Marigolds. 'Hello, Lynnie.' She'd hugged her as Eve had wondered, yet again, how she'd managed to acquire three first names in the course of one lifetime. 'Children!' she'd added because Janie, despite being a mother of two, was still one of those people who addressed children collectively rather than by their names.

Anna kissed her politely but Robbie hid behind Eve's legs and felt shy.

'Dad's in the sitting room,' she'd told Eve, but didn't come in herself. 'I'm going to finish the scrub-down I'm giving the kitchen.'

Eve tried not to sigh at her. A decade and a half

of marriage had turned Janie into a fussy, over-anxious mother and a boring cleanaholic. After half a day together, Eve usually wanted to shout at her that not everything in the world could be put right with a jolly good clean.

God! Did Janie come into court in the morning and announce: 'Right, Your Honour, if we just dust down the panelling and hoover the jury box, I think you'll find this trial will run much more smoothly'?

It bothered Eve a lot that she and her sister had lost track of each other and were no longer as close as they had once been. Janie looked exhausted, as always, in a slightly sad, shapeless, greying kind of way.

She always gave Eve – dressed today in a sober (she thought) purple velvet skirt and pink flowered top, with her hair in a plait – a kind of mildly amused, mildly tut-tutting once over.

Eve dumped the bags she was carrying in the hall and went into the sitting room with Anna and Robbie following her. Her father was in his armchair with the *Sunday Telegraph* folded up beside him. Everything looked so normal. The room, his papers, him.

He stood up at once and held out his arms just a little bit apart. She kissed him on the cheek as he squeezed her shoulders.

'Hello, Evelyn, good to see you,' he said. 'And Anna, you've got so tall – and little Robbie, you're growing too.'

Anna proffered a smile and polite kiss; Robbie

was still peeping out from behind Eve's legs, threatening to topple her if she did anything sudden.

She took a seat in the middle of the sofa with a child at each side and felt herself scrutinizing her father as they went through the polite small talk.

She thought he looked tired and maybe a little thinner under the shirt, tie and navy V-neck jumper. His generation's idea of casual Sunday afternoon dressing. To her 'How are you, Dad?' asked with throat-aching feeling, he'd merely answered, 'Not too bad. Not too bad . . . anyway. Anna, I want to hear all about school. What are you reading these days?'

'Where is the poo dog?' Robbie asked, all of a sudden not shy any more.

'Robbie!' Anna ticked him off. 'It's Hardy.'

'But he stinks! Where is he *Drandpa*?'

'Oh God. Outside I hope,' her father answered.

Hardy, who truly did stink – he farted uncontrollably, belched, rolled around in gunge and had some sort of waxy ear problem which further added to the aroma – had come to live with her father several years ago when a friend had died and left him the dog in his will.

'The nerve,' had been her Dad's response. 'He knew how much I hated that bloody dog.'

But there was obviously some sort of grudging companionship going on because although their father complained about Hardy constantly, he walked him twice a day, fed him all sorts of luxurious doggy treats and obviously had no

235

intention of carrying out his regular threats to 'have him bloody well put down'.

And, Eve thought, Hardy added a welcome touch of chaos to her father's prim and orderly household. The dog was one of those shambling furry blond spaniel things. He left pale hairs over everything, would appear, fart, shuffle off, and he often howled for no reason in the middle of the night.

'So what have the doctors said?' Janie asked, pouring coffee as Eve returned from tucking her children up in bed.

'They have to go in and take a look. But they weren't too cheery about it. Let's put it that way,' their father answered with a small smile and a long sip of his drink.

'So they think it might be cancerous?' Janie asked and there it was: the C word, out there in the open for them all to think about.

Long silence, everyone focusing on it. Cancerous . . . Cancer. All the horrible implications.

'We'll have to wait and see. No point worrying about it till it's there,' he said, but they were, of course, all worrying about it.

'At least I've got plenty of time to put things in order' – solicitor speak taking over now. 'I'm going to sell the firm to Jack, put the money in the bank, update the will. Be ready if it's bad news. We've all got to go some time.' He brushed the crumbs on the tablecloth in front of him into a neat line. 'I should be grateful for the notice, really . . . not like your poor mother. So . . . There we are.'

Eve and Janie were too choked to say anything.

'How are you both?' he asked after a pause. 'That's the thing I worry about really, how you're getting on.'

Eve knew this worry was focused on her, mainly. Janie's career was going well, she was married to David, had been for years and years and would be for years and years, unless Eve was incredibly mistaken.

Eve listened to her sister talk about David's promotion and her teenagers, Rick and Christine and how well they were doing at school. Then it was her turn.

'Things are fine, Dad,' she said. 'Work is good and the kids are all great. Have I told you that Tom is getting married in July? That's something to look forward to.' She didn't think the pregnancy detail was needed at this stage.

'Really?!' was her father and Janie's joint response to this news.

'Isn't he rather young?' Janie asked.

'Nowadays, yes . . . But it's what he wants to do, so he has my blessing. I'll be giving them both all the support they need.'

'I hope you don't mean financially,' her father said. Oh no, she'd hoped to cheer them up with good news. Instead here was her dad giving himself some new reason to worry.

'Look, honestly, we're fine,' she said.

'What are your Denny and Tom doing now?' her father asked.

She told him, dreading the inevitable 'Shouldn't they both have done law?' conversation.

'Photography and computers? Well,' he said, lips drawn into what she couldn't help thinking of as his 'cat's bottom' expression. 'Do you think either of those careers will last?'

'What do you mean?'

'Will the world still need photographers and computer software designers in ten years' time?'

Oh . . . she understood now: as opposed to lawyers: 'Well who knows what's around the corner,' she said, hoping to end this line of questioning. 'Careers aren't the lifelong things they once were and I think that's a good thing. I'm really proud of them both.'

Loud silence.

'Look,' she willed herself to be calm – 'we're here to look after you. Let's not go on about all this other stuff.'

'Why don't you go up and have your bath, Dad?' Janie intervened. 'Lynnie and I will tidy away.'

So then she and her sister were alone in the kitchen. Janie *bustling*, the way she did: scraping pots, putting the radio on, keeping up a cheeriness that felt like the last straw to Eve, who now saw her parents' framed and faded wedding photo on the wall, took it down and sat at the kitchen table to look at it properly. Then wished she hadn't, because it made her weep.

'Oh Lynnie . . .' Her sister put a hand on her shoulder. 'You mustn't be like this. We've got to put on a brave face for Dad.'

'Why?' she asked.

'We don't want him getting really down about all this. We're here to buoy him up.'

'Are we? How do you expect him not to get down about the fact that he's going to die, Janie?'

'We don't know what he's got yet,' Janie said.

'Janie . . . he's in his seventies. He's not going to be here for ever.' Eve pressed at her eyes to try and stop the tears. 'Pretty soon he's going to be saying goodbye to us, his home, his friends and everything he loves.'

'Well who knows? Maybe he'll see Mum.' Even as she said this, they both wished and wished they could believe it, but they didn't. There wouldn't be any comfort in that thought.

'Maybe Mum's met someone else.' Eve wrung a little relief from the joke. 'I mean she's been on her own for a long time. And there are all those great people up there . . . Bing Crosby, Spencer Tracy . . . Elvis.'

'Oh for God's sake. What are you like? One minute blubbing your eyes out, the next taking the complete mickey.' Janie was loading the dishwasher and running hot water into the sink for the oven pans.

'You're right. I'm sorry,' Eve said and then quite randomly added: 'You'd have been really good during the war, Janie.'

239

'Oh now what?' Janie snapped, not looking round from the washing up.

'No, I mean that in a nice way. You're very good at battening down the hatches and coping. Anna really wouldn't approve but I suppose that's what the war spirit was all about. I'd have been flailing around in a great big panic, especially if my sons had to go off to fight. How awful! No, I'd have put my heart into being a conscientious objector and begged them to stay at home with me and spread the word.'

'Oh for God's sake,' Janie said again, angrier now, and she was right. This was ridiculous. Just one of those family debates you blunder into and in a minute it would move on to 'Nazis: why Eve thought it was better to be one than get her sons killed' and Janie would hold a grudge against her for years and mention it every Christmas and really, it was ridiculous, it had to be stopped.

'Sorry. Sorry. I'm losing the plot,' Eve said quickly. 'How are you doing?'

'I'm still in shock probably,' Janie said, scrubbing hard at the pan in the sink. 'Dad seems so well. I can't really believe it's going to be cancer and we're going to have to go through this. He's not even properly retired. He's 72! That doesn't seem so old.'

'I know, I know.' Eve stood up to hug her sister.

'If it's cancer . . . Christ. I don't know if I'm brave enough for this,' Janie said over Eve's shoulder.

'Neither do I. But we have to be. We've got each other, OK? We've got each other,' was Eve's choked answer. She gave her sister another squeeze then told her with a sniff: 'I think we should see what's lurking in Dad's drinks cabinet.'

'Good idea,' Janie replied.

First of all they had port, then Baileys, followed with a Martini and lukewarm tinned lemonade, for old times' sake, then it got more adventurous.

'Advocaat?' Eve had offered, opening the bottle and sniffing it.

'Oh God, don't touch that. It goes off, it's got egg in it.'

Eve had crouched down to get to the bottles at the very back of the cabinet: 'Blue Bols?! That's probably been here since the Seventies. Oh, here's the stuff the monks make,' she pulled out a crusted, gunged-up bottle with an ornate label, 'when they want to hallucinate!'

'And crème de menthe,' she added, 'Didn't Mum like that?'

'That's probably her bottle,' Janie said.

And for some reason, they both found this hilarious and began to shake with laughter, until Hardy shuffled in to see what the fuss was, farted and went out again.

Eve was waving a hand in front of her face, tears of laughter streaming from her eyes. 'Oh no . . .' she managed when she'd finally calmed down enough to talk. 'Dad can't die yet because

241

you'd make me take the dog, wouldn't you?'

Janie threw a sofa cushion at her and Eve realized that she hadn't seen her sister drunk or even vaguely tipsy for years, which was a shame, because she liked her quite a lot better like this.

They settled down on the sofa together with more Baileys and Janie asked all about Tom's wedding.

'Oh, I'm just the mother of the groom,' Eve told her. 'I gave them a cheque and told them to get on with it. I'm not expecting to know much about it all until the invitation comes in the post. I think that's perfect, though, I mean I'll help out with stuff if I'm asked but I don't want to get embroiled in the sort of wedding shenanigans people seem to have. Deepa and her family are Indian – have I told you that? I don't know if that means a wedding is an even bigger fuss or not. I'm sure I'll find out when I meet them.'

'Are they Hindu?' Janie wanted to know.

'No . . . lapsed C of Es apparently. Not that it makes any difference to us raving agnostics. Deepa's really nice,' she added, 'I like her a lot.'

'How is her family taking the pregnancy and everything?'

'According to Tom and Deepa, they're getting used to the idea. It's a bit of a bloody shock when your 20-year-old son pitches up at the door and announces he's going to be a dad, I can tell you that for free. So, I can only imagine it's even worse if it's your daughter because of all those extra worries . . . Labour . . . will she and the baby be OK? Will the father stick around, or leave her to get on with it? Very scary. I think her family went nuts for a bit. She's studying medicine and she hasn't decided whether she'll be able to carry on after a break, or what she's going to do.'

'Oh boy.'

'But, you know, they're really sweet together. I think they'll work things out. I hope they will.' Eve took a deep sip from her glass. It was a very big leap for Tom, she really hoped he wasn't going to flake out on them all.

'Oh . . . put this in your scandal pipe and smoke it,' Eve added. 'Dennis Leigh, the man formerly known as my husband, is planning to come to the wedding with his wife and daughters.'

'No. *No!* . . . *Dennis?*' For a moment, Janie wasn't sure if she had understood this correctly.

'Oh, I am enjoying the look on your face,' Eve smiled.

'You can't . . . he can't really be coming? How dare he? It will ruin everything . . .'

'Oh don't be so melodramatic, Janie. I'm sure it will be interesting. It's not like he's turning up just for the ceremony. He's coming over from America with his wife and daughters a few days before, apparently, so we'll all have a chance to get . . . acclimatized.'

'Oh my God. You've never even met his wife and children before, have you?'

'No. I've only seen him a few times since . . . you know.'

'*Oh my God,*' Janie couldn't help repeating, 'I can't believe we'll see him again. The rat.'

'I know,' Eve could laugh at the idea now. 'It's quite brave of him to face us all with his wife and teenage daughters.'

'*Teenage?*' Janie pounced on the detail, 'Has it been that long since he left you?'

'Sixteen years. Intriguing, isn't it? He certainly didn't mention any children when he re-appeared three years later to ask for a divorce. But they must have been around . . . otherwise they wouldn't be teenage, would they?'

'Why on earth does Tom want him at the wedding?'

'He's Tom's dad. Tom's about to have a baby, he's going through a lot of heavy stuff and has decided he wants to get to know his dad. It doesn't seem so surprising. Bit annoying, though. I can't say I'm looking forward to it.'

'D'you think he feels guilty?'

'Dennis?! Er . . . no. I don't think the word is in his dictionary. Well . . . occasionally, he must get some kind of pang, then he writes them a cheque, sends it and feels better again.' She swirled her drink around then swallowed it down. 'What worries me,' Eve confided now, 'is that the boys have always idealized their dad a bit. They couldn't really help it. And now that they are grown-ups – well, sort of,' she couldn't stop the little snort at the idea of Denny and

Tom being grown-ups. When did your children ever seem grown up to you? 'Anyway . . . I think they'll see him for what he is this time,' she continued. 'And it might be very disappointing.'

'Yeah, I'm sure. But never mind,' Janie said. 'They'll realize what a lovely mummy they have instead. You're doing so well with them all, Eve, you should be proud.'

'Oh! Thank you. Now that really is enough about us. How are you and David and your lovely, brainy children?' Eve asked.

'We're fine. All absolutely fine,' Janie answered with a smile and a little tappity tap on the side of the glass which made Eve wonder.

'Can I ask you one thing about Dennis?' Jane surprised her.

'Of course. Nothing to hide.'

'Are you still at all upset about what happened?'

'Oh God no,' was Eve's immediate answer. 'Everything turned out for the best. For us anyway.'

'So not the slightest trace of heartbreak left at all?'

'Heartbreak!! No, definitely not. Dennis has been out of my life for about three times as long as he was ever in it. No,' and then in a burst of candour, Eve added, 'The only person at this wedding who is going to remind me of heartbreak is Joseph.'

'Joseph is coming as well!' Janie just about tipped her drink down the front of her sweater.

'Of course he's coming. He's family. He's Anna's dad . . . and Robbie's.'

'Sorry, Eve. I always liked Joseph.'

'Yeah, me too,' she smiled at her sister, trying to shrug off the sad feeling this was provoking.

'Is it well and truly over with him then?'

'Looks like it. He's just got engaged.'

'Oh . . . So, pregnant Indian bride, the long-lost husband, the ex-lover and his fiancée – this is going to be the best wedding ever!' Janie said, trying to lighten the mood.

'Janie! Just because I don't live in a Victorian villa in Winchester with my lawyer husband and 2.2 children!' Eve retorted. 'I'm the norm these days, you know. You're the strangely unusual, monogamous, married person!'

They both laughed at that.

'What about a boyfriend?' Janie asked.

'What!'

'Shouldn't you be bringing a boyfriend? Otherwise, Dennis will be there with his wife. Joseph's got someone new . . .'

Eve nodded.

'So you really should take a boyfriend along. Isn't there someone . . . ?' Janie was leaning forward curiously.

'Well . . . there's the potential of someone.' Eve shot her a little grin, 'but no-one serious enough for Tom's wedding. No, I'll have to go alone . . . Alone? Ha,' she laughed at this idea. 'I have four children, I am *never* alone! Anyway – what are we going to do tomorrow?'

'Drive out somewhere for a picnic if the weather is nice? If Dad is up for it,' Janie suggested.

'OK, good idea.'

Chapter Twenty

On the top deck of the bus winding its way through Friday afternoon traffic, there was plenty of time for Eve to think as she made her journey from work to collect her youngest children.

She'd come out of a conversation with her boss, Lester, who had appeared in her office just as she was getting ready to go, to warn her that his deputy, Rob Greene, had decided to apply for the top job and so would be standing against her.

'Lester, have I even officially applied for this job?' she'd asked him. 'I mean . . . I'm still not sure.'

'I wouldn't ask you to do this if I didn't think it was a good idea,' he'd said.

But up on the top of the bus, Eve worried. It wasn't really the work side that bothered her, it was essentially the hours and the added stress. She still couldn't decide if it was what she wanted. And now Rob was standing too. Nice man, but he would be an infuriating boss. He was jumpy, moody, found it hard to make decisions, procrastinated . . . Now everyone in the department would want her to have the job, just so he didn't get it. And then if she did, he would have to go elsewhere. Oh bloody hell.

She had enough to think about. Her dad's surgery was only weeks away and Tom and Deepa had decided to postpone their wedding till August to await the outcome and hope he would be well enough to be there.

She willed the bus to move faster through the snarled up roads. She just wanted her little kids round her and to be back at home.

Finally, they were there, back at the flat, deep in their Friday evening routine: Robbie watching Thomas the Tank, Anna finishing off her homework, Eve, casually dressed in a summer skirt and vest, barefoot, trying not to care too much about the fact that Joseph would soon be at the door.

Then the telephone rang.

'I'm really sorry, the traffic's at a standstill,' Joseph was saying, 'I'm still on the M6, I'll be at least another two hours. Is that going to be OK?'

He asked to speak to Anna so he could explain. What a nice dad he was, she couldn't help thinking as she listened to Anna's side of the conversation.

'Yup . . . OK . . . Yeah, I'll snooze in the car . . . That's fine, Daddy . . . Be careful. See you later.'

And it was much later, almost 9.30 when Joseph finally rang at the door. Eve was dozing flat out on the sofa, Robbie was long asleep and Anna had gone to read in her bunk.

'That's your dad,' Eve called to her now from the sitting room, but there was no reply.

'Anna?' She went to the children's room first, on her way to the front door, and peeked in. It looked as if Anna had fallen fast asleep with a book open on her chest. The doorbell buzzed again and she went to let Joseph in.

Anna only opened her eyes when she heard her parents saying their hellos at the door. Her mother and her father had to spend some time together, *alone*, Anna had decided, and she was guessing – quite correctly – that Joseph would need a break from driving and neither of them would want to wake her up until it was time for her dad to go. So this would leave them with half an hour, maybe even longer, alone together. OK, she had to face the fact that it could be too late to save her dad from marriage to Michelle, but until the deed was done, every little effort to get her parents back together again had to be made.

She heard them walking towards her bedroom door and quickly closed her eyes again. 'Oh!' she could hear her dad say and she hadn't seen him for a fortnight, so she really, really wanted to turn and smile at him. 'Aren't they both sweet!'

But then the door was closed and he was obviously taking up the offer of a drink she'd heard her mother make.

Anna picked up her book again and carried on reading with her fingers crossed.

Eve went to make tea and left Joseph taking a seat on the sofa in the cosy jumble of a sitting room he still knew so well.

He sank down into the flowered cushions that were still warm from where Eve had been lying, and saw the dish on the floor filled with apple cores, tangerine peel and a KitKat wrapper alongside an empty wine glass.

When she came in, balancing a tray with the tea things, he pulled the side table in front of the sofa, so she put the tray down and quite naturally, busy with mug arranging and tea pouring, sat down beside him.

They started to talk: how was work? . . . how were the children? . . . Michelle . . . Manchester . . . London bla di bla. They were both tired and a little preoccupied with the worries of the week, so they forgot that they were supposed to be sarcastic to each other and instead found themselves unwinding on the saggy old sofa, chatting, laughing . . . both remembering how good it was to talk together, before the era of sniping and snide comments and the slightly bitter and twisted stuff they seemed to indulge in most of the time.

'What's all this about going to Germany then?' she asked him. 'And environmentally friendly business ideas?'

'Oh yeah . . .' He looked embarrassed. 'There's

interesting stuff happening over there that I'm sure will catch on here eventually.'

'So it's a moneymaking thing?'

'Eve, I'm not all bad, you know. I have some ideals too,' and he fixed the dark eyes on her and smiled.

See? What was going on? Was he changing? Had she totally misunderstood what was happening in his head when she threw him out of her home? She was losing her bearings. But there was one feeling that was clear and undeniable, as they sat together on the sofa, her looking round at him every now and again to catch his nod and reassuring smile: she knew without a doubt that she was still magnetically attracted to him.

'How's your dad doing?' Joseph was asking now and then Eve was telling him about that and about Tom and Deepa and how anxious she was for them . . . and work. He'd obviously not come straight from the office that night, she couldn't help noticing, he'd had time to change into casual clothes: a chunky rollneck, a pair of loose white trousers and trainers. His arms were folded behind his head and he looked really not a bit older than the day she'd met him. He'd muscled up just a little over the years, but he was still the same lean, lithe person she used to practise yoga with on the bedroom floor.

Yoga on the bedroom floor . . . well that had nearly always ended in positions a little more kama sutra than iyengar.

'That's all really hard,' he was sympathizing. 'Poor Eve, you've got a lot on. If there's anything I can do to help . . . Maybe I could take the children for a weekend. *Both of them*,' he smiled at her. 'Because I think you have to let me take Robbie now, he's old enough.'

'Yeah,' she agreed and glanced down to her lap, only to see that her left leg was just a centimetre or so away from his. She could feel the warmth of him through the thin skirt she was wearing.

'Are you going to be OK?' he was asking, so kindly, she looked straight up into his face.

Oh Joseph, how am I ever going to be OK again, now that you're marrying someone else?

'Hey, don't cry,' she heard him say. 'It's all right.'

No, it's not all right. It is not at all all right.

One of the arms behind his head unfolded now and moved around her. He leaned forward and hugged her in against him. For a moment or two she stayed there, very still, head against his shoulder, feeling the tight warmth of his arm around her. Then she looked up and that was when his fingers brushed over her eyelashes, their lips touched together and they began to kiss. And, oh God, it was perfect. All she could think of as she moved her tongue into his mouth and tasted him, as her hands felt across his beautiful face, as she slid a leg over his lap to get closer to him . . . all she could think of was that this was unlocking a physical memory. Details

253

kept in the body long after they'd slipped from the mind. She felt like a pianist oblivious to the music stored in her fingertips until she'd touched the keyboard again. They were moving, quite involuntarily, following the steps in a dance they had perfected in their seven years as lovers.

She didn't dare to open her eyes, terrified that if she looked, she would break this spell. She was kissing Joseph's tea-flavoured mouth as he slipped down the straps of her vest to touch her bare breasts. Down there in his lap, underneath her, she could feel an unmistakable throb.

With a gentle roll, he laid her down on the sofa and wordless . . . wordlessly . . . as if a single sound would ruin everything . . . his hand was feeling for her, his mouth still over hers.

Eyes tightly shut, she let him. She had no idea what it meant but she let him pull her skirt and underwear aside and move his fingers in.

She felt dizzy, oxygen deprived . . . high. She was desperate to groan, to whisper to him, but she bit her lip, terrified that the slightest noise would wake them from this.

Another hand squeezed her breast up into a little mound and he put his mouth, hot and wet over it and bit gently.

Ah, aaaahhh . . . she so wanted to sigh, shout, tell him. But she kept her eyelids scrunched up and the sound bottled inside her. She couldn't bear for this to end. She groped in the tight sofa tangle they'd become for his cock and heard the sharp intake of breath when she reached it and ran her fingers over the velvet skin. Everything was so familiar and yet this was too strange.

His lips were moving over the bare skin of her collarbone, she felt him hot and nudging against her, and that was when she had to open her eyes.

'Joe?' she asked, barely above a whisper, and she saw his eyes open too. 'This can't be a good idea.'

'No.' He sank his head down against her shoulder.

For a moment, she wondered if he was going to say anything, but he just lay there crushed down on top of her, waiting for the blood to stop pounding in his ears and other places, then he gave her neck a small, sweet kiss and sat up.

She pulled herself up too, hooked her vest straps back over her shoulders, smoothed her skirt and stood up. They looked at each other and the smiles were apologetic. What was there to say? This was moment of madness territory . . . wasn't it?

When he stood up, she saw one of her blond hairs on the shoulder of his blue jumper and she reached out to pull it off.

Did she know she was making his hair stand on end with desire when she did that? He had no idea. Not for the first time in his life was he wondering what on earth she wanted from him and what he wanted from her. Jesus.

'I better go,' he said. 'Scoop Anna up and head off.'

'Yes.'

They were looking each other in the eye but there really was nothing obvious to say. Eve broke his gaze and turned towards the door, he followed her out of the room and together they lifted Anna from the bed and into his arms.

'Hello.' Anna said in a drowsy mumble.

'Hello honeybun,' Joseph kissed her cheek. 'I'll carry you to the car.'

'OK.'

Eve kissed Anna at the door but only smiled at Joseph.

'Good night,' she told him. 'Drive carefully.'

When she went back into the sitting room she saw the indents on the sofa cushions, the two empty tea mugs on the side table and she couldn't deny what had happened. She had touched him, kissed him, felt him, let him almost . . . almost make love to her again.

She was still too stirred up about it to even want to cry. She needed more wine, she decided – anything to drive this gale of loneliness from the room.

Chapter Twenty-One

Denny arrived just a shade before 6.30p.m.
because Eve and Jen were meeting in town
tonight and he was babysitting.

'Hello darling,' Eve kissed his cheek,
breathing in a hint of aftershave, French
cigarettes and the general expensive, high maintenance lifestyle he seemed to so go in for.

Robbie, who would dance with ecstasy when
even the meter reader rang the doorbell, was
wrapped around Denny's knees singing his
hellos.

Denny looked at his watch. 'I'm not late, am I?'
Eve looked at it too: clunky chrome with lots of
diving buttons and dials. Oooh, it was new,
something special and very expensive he was
maybe hoping she'd recognize.

'Nice watch,' she said.

'Thanks.' He put his arm down slightly self-
consciously.

'Present from Patricia?'

'I wish.'

'Oh? Are things OK?'

'Yeah.'

She waited a moment, wondering if he would say anything more about his girlfriend, but he didn't. Subject closed, obviously.

'Anna's in the sitting room, finishing off her homework,' Eve told him.

'Hi, Den,' came the shout.

'Robbie, as you can see, doesn't have any homework and is desperate to take you off to the train set. So, all the usual, they've had supper, but they need baths and bed no later than eight.'

'And where are the two of you wild girls off to tonight?' In her outfit of big, fringed gypsy skirt and cowboy boots, it was hard to guess.

'Aha!' she grinned. 'Two classes tonight, regular yoga with Pete the Geek and afterwards –' dramatic flourish with both arms – 'we learn to tango.'

Denny laughed. His mother and her best friend had tried out every adult education class, dance wave and fitness craze going. Just for fun. Just to have 'something to get us out of the house' at least one evening a week.

Some of the fads stayed. Pottery had been big – most of the kitchen mugs were still the ones she had made years ago – and yoga. Eve had been a yoga buff for as long as Denny could remember. It was no longer remotely unusual to come across her lying in the plough in the bedroom or doing one of those strange pelvic bridge things on the sitting room floor as she watched TV.

She hated to sit in chairs for any length of time and always ended up lying across sofas or cross-legged on the floor sitting quite easily and comfortably with perfect posture. He had taken so many photos of her like that, straight-backed, rising effortlessy out of her folded up legs, head balancing lightly on her neck, shoulders loose.

Eve ran up most of the long escalator at Holborn tube station and was scrabbling in her bag for her ticket when the couple snogging on the other side of the turnstiles caught her eye. Well, it was the ponytail. The two and a half feet or so of smooth chestnut silk flicking as the kiss went on.

Eve fed her ticket into the machine and walked through, hardly taking her eyes off the ponytail. This was some snog. Surely Patricia was going to come up for air in a moment though, wasn't she?

Finally, as Eve walked right up to them, the couple stopped kissing and were laughing into each other's eyes. She tapped Patricia on the shoulder and the porcelain perfect face, with lips still wet from this other man's kiss, turned to her.

Eve watched her eyes widen and her colour flush up to pink, then blotchy red. At last, there was a thing she didn't do prettily. Blush.

'Er . . . hello,' Patricia said.

'Are you going to tell him, or am I?' Eve asked now, feeling her stomach lurch and her own face tingle with heat.

'What's this?' the man asked. Eve's eyes

259

swooped up and down him for a moment, just long enough to register that he was older, very smartly dressed and definitely not Denny.

'Nothing, Peter.' Patricia pulled the lapels of her jacket protectively up around her neck. If Eve hadn't been so furious, she might almost have felt sorry for this girl. So pretty, so thin, she was like an impulse summer buy. A gorgeous skirt you had to have even though you knew it wouldn't stand up to a single trip round the washing machine.

'Nothing?' Eve heard herself demand.

'Eve . . . I'm sorry. I didn't want this . . .' Patricia tailed off.

'Patricia? D'you want to tell me . . .' the man began.

But Eve broke in: 'OK. Well, tell Denny as soon as you can, please, it's only fair.' Then, holding her bag tightly under her arm, she turned on her heel and almost ran out of the station.

She pounded along the pavement, thoughts whirling, all the way to the dance school. What a horrible thing to happen. She still couldn't decide if she should have approached Patricia or not. But then if she hadn't, wouldn't that have been like cheating on Denny herself?

'Goodness me, you don't look happy,' was Jen's greeting when they met outside the yoga class.

'No? Well I've just bumped into Denny's girl-friend with her tongue down another man's throat.'

Jen took a little moment to register this.

'No!! Did she see you?'

'Of course she bloody well saw me,' Eve stormed. 'I marched up to her and told her she'd better tell Denny about this, or I would.'

'Oh my God,' was Jen's reply. 'Never, ever meddle with your children's love affairs. That is the rule.'

They sat down, side by side on the bench, pulling off their outdoor shoes.

'I wasn't meddling. I just wanted her to know I knew. What do you expect me to do, Jen?' Eve was yanking at a shoe. 'Sneak around for weeks with the information that my son is being cheated on when I could just clear the air and put a stop to it all? I mean, I don't mind if he still wants to go out with her, just so long as he *knows*. I hate secrets. They make me nervous.' She stood up now, faced her friend and wondered if she was going to confess to the steamy sofa clinch with Joseph.

'Come on, you silly moo. Time to "stretch . . . stretch out and reeeeelax".' Jen did her best imitation of their teacher, Pete the Geek, then stood up and smiled at her.

After yoga, they went to tango class where they partnered each other, as usual, and gossiped in whispers in between the tiny dance teacher's instructions to: 'Squeeze . . . squeeeeeeze your pardnah . . . like you are making lufff', which made them both quake with suppressed laughter.

'The solution to your troubles lies in the sock drawer,' Jen told her.

'What?!'

'There is dating truth in every sock drawer. All the single socks,' Jen explained. 'You've just got to keep putting them back in and, almost always, they do eventually find their partners. Have faith! It is very, very rare to have a truly single sock . . . over the long term.'

'No. It's going to happen to me,' Eve said gloomily, 'I just know it. I'm the turquoise and purple stripy handknit which can't just be lumped alongside the other blue knee-lengths.'

'Who are you calling a blue knee-length?'

'Oh you know what I mean!'

'Why don't you go out with Pete the Geek?' Jen asked her as they sashayed from one end of the room to the other, cheek to cheek, like the twenty-five or so other couples around them.

'No way!' was Eve's horrified reply.

'Why not? You're both yoga buffs, he's thirty-something, single, clearly interested . . .'

'Oh my God, Jen! This is a man who "douches" his nose with salt water.'

'No!' Jen's turn to be horrified.

'*And*, he only drinks Echinacea tea kept overnight in a copper bowl and always "eliminates" before breakfast. And you think I'm a freaky health nut.'

'OK, OK, he's not quite right then. But I do see you turning into the kind of woman who tours Nepalese craft fairs to seduce the ponytailed talent behind the counters.' They both started giggling at this.

'Two . . . three . . . four . . . bend, bend those backs and squeeeeeeeze.' The dancing teacher gave Eve a stern prod.

'Nils is not a hippie,' Eve whispered when they were out of range again. 'He's completely scientific and square. Well, no, he sometimes uses homoeopathy on cats.'

'But he's not quite Mr Right, is he?' Jen was asking from the depths of a backward bend with Eve leaning right over her.

'No.' Eve hoicked her up out of it. 'But he's Mr OK . . . I think.'

'Been for any more appointments?' Jen asked.

'I'm not telling,' Eve answered.

'Ooooh . . . what's eating you then?'

'I snogged Joseph,' Eve said, before she could really weigh up the pros and cons of coughing to this.

Jen braked so hard midway through her twirl, she almost snapped the heel off her shoe.

'NO!'

'Ah ha . . . I have no idea what that was about,' Eve told her. 'I don't think it's a sign. Because we pretended that nothing happened.'

'It's a sign that you both need your heads examined,' was Jen's verdict. 'And at your age,' she added. 'God, you really need to get a grip. He's practically married, Eve. I have got to find you someone else. Quickly.'

'And how's your dad?' she asked in a

deliberate attempt to not dwell on this Joseph muddle that Eve seemed so desperate to get into again.

'We're waiting,' was Eve's answer. 'His op is in two weeks' time.'

'Oh, I'm so sorry.'

'Yeah . . . I know.' She caught the teacher's eye. 'Let's dance for a bit,' she said, and with that she gave Jen – who was always the girl – a hard spin and for the next half an hour they tried to concentrate on the lesson.

When Eve got back home that evening, she found Denny drinking tea and smoking a cigarette in the kitchen, which was totally against house rules even though the windows were wide open.

She hated the fact that her son smoked and considered it a personal failing on her part, but she didn't nag him this evening, just poured herself a cup and made him come out to the garden with her because she had pots to water in the warm dark.

'Janie phoned,' he told her. 'Grandpa isn't well . . . she got a call from the GP. They're trying to move his surgery forward.'

'Oh my God.' Eve gripped the sides of her mug, feeling panicked.

'She says she'll be there at the weekend, and she's hoping you'll go down too.'

'Did she say what was wrong?'

'He's a bit breathless and confused. A neighbour phoned for the doctor or something. She's pretty upset,' Denny told her.

'Does she want me to phone?'

'No, she said she'd call in the morning, she was off to bed.'

Eve bent down to the coils of the hose and started unwinding it slowly.

'Are you going to be OK?' he asked.

'I think so. Hope so . . .'

He let her water in silence, then when she had finished they went to the bench at the end of the garden and sat together in the dark.

'How are you anyway?' she asked him, with a little pat on his arm. 'You look tired.'

'I'm so-so.' He shuffled a hand through his dark hair and took another drag on his cigarette. 'Lots of work on,' he added, 'but hardly any of it has been used yet, so no big pay cheques.'

'Oh Denny.' She tried to rally him: 'You're a photographer, an artist. You can't expect to make the same money as a finance director, or . . . a company law expert. But maybe you get to keep a bit of your soul.'

'Ah well,' he let out a sigh of smoke. 'Maybe I'd rather trade my soul for a bit of filthy lucre.'

'Not if you're my son, you wouldn't,' she smiled at him. 'It's about *being* not *having*, remember.'

'Wise words, but they aren't going to pay for the surfing holiday.'

'Oh – are you going away?'

'Well, I suggested surfing and I was thinking

Cornwall, whereas Patricia was thinking California. Bit of a difference.'

'Hmmm.' With a lurch of nerves, Eve wondered if she should say something about Patricia.

'So . . .' he added and she couldn't read his expression in the dark, 'maybe that's why I got dumped.'

'Oh no.' Boy, Patricia hadn't wasted any time. 'Tonight?' Eve asked.

'No! I've been here all night. Last week. She's finally succumbed to the charms of her agency boss.'

'Oh.' Eve suddenly had to take an intense interest in deadheading the flowers in the pot beside her. *What a total tit I am!*

'Are you OK about it?' she managed.

'Yeah. Bit sad, but it's not the end of the world or anything.' He stubbed his cigarette out on the paving then flicked it over into next door's garden.

'Denny!'

'Oooops, sorry.'

'Are you really OK?'

'I'll be fine, honest.' He turned and smiled at her. 'It wasn't love or anything . . . I was basically sleeping with a very attractive friend. I think you know about that kind of thing, don't you?'

'Who? You mean . . . ?'

'The vet. You're doing the vet, aren't you?'

'Denny! *Doing* him?! I'm your mother.'

'Well, you know.'

'I've had a few dates with Nils. It's not a big thing.'

She got up now and went in search of her snail bucket to avoid further questioning. He watched from the bench, taking yet another cigarette out of his packet and lighting up with difficulty against the breeze. 'What are you doing now?' he asked as she foraged into her shrubbery with a torch.

'Drowning snails. It's best to hunt them at night.'

'And I thought gardening was such a gentle hobby!'

'It's nature – dog eat dog out here . . . or more like snail eat shoot.'

'Anyway . . . Mum?' he asked, but she interrupted him.

'You're smoking too much,' she scolded as she plopped another snail into the bucket.

'I know, I'm going to give up really soon.'

'Anyway, what?'

'Are you OK about our dad coming to the wedding?'

'Are you?' was her reply.

'I asked first!'

'Well . . . I think so.' She didn't turn from her snail search. 'I'm quite interested in meeting his family and seeing him again, I suppose. I'm not wild about it, though.' That was something of an understatement. 'He's not my favourite person

267

on the planet, but if you and Tom want to be in touch with him, I don't want to get in the way of it.'

Denny blew out a mouthful of smoke: 'I feel the same,' he said. 'If this guy wants to get to know us a bit better, fine. If not, fine.'

'I'm sorry about your dad,' he added.

'Yeah.' Plop, another snail hit the bucket. 'You and Tom should come down and see him once the op is over.' She felt the little sob at the back of her throat as she said this.

'I know,' Den replied.

Chapter Twenty-Two

Eve and Janie spent the day before their father's surgery at home with him, trying not to panic at how unwell he looked – thin, tired, a yellow tinge to his face which had never been there before.

The sun broke through after lunch, so they moved deckchairs and a lounger out to the lawn and sat there with him, drinking tea. Eve was taking in the garden: one of those formal, suburban affairs with a bright green lawn, trimmed to a clean-edged square and rose bushes, shrubs and bedding plants spaced neatly round the borders. 'My children,' she heard Janie complaining. 'They're probably going to spend the whole weekend in the sitting room with the curtains pulled shut, watching TV and eating their body weight in cheesy tortillas.'

'It's a phase,' Eve soothed. 'Only a few more months, then they'll be doing the organic vegan thing, promising to "never eat another victim of torture" or tune into "this hypocritical exploitation of the masses pumped into our homes by the government." '

Janie snorted at this and added: 'And I can never get them to go to bed or get up in the morning.'

'Well, that's normal,' Eve smiled at her. 'All teenagers have the right to a lie-in enshrined by the Geneva Convention or something. Tom's going to get a horrible shock when the baby—' She bit the rest of the sentence down. Her father still didn't know about Tom's impending arrival and she had no intention of announcing it to him just yet. He was quite unwell enough.

She gave Janie a brief finger on lips signal, but their father didn't seem to have heard.

'Anna reminds me so much of your mother,' he said all of a sudden, glancing up from his newspaper. 'The same fair-haired seriousness. A bit bossy and strict.' He smiled at Eve. 'Elsie would have loved Anna.'

Her father might not be here either to see Anna grow up or even grow much older. Now, the thought was out there in the open, all raw and awful, and all three of them felt choked up with it.

By 4p.m. it was time for the sisters to drive him to hospital and help him to settle in for his pre-op night. They sat for a while in the rhubarb pink ward, ignoring the brown tea in plastic cups and struggling to keep up a cheery chat.

Back at his house, Eve and Janie did what

they could to keep themselves occupied: cleaned out the kitchen cupboards, ironed. They had filled the fridge with food, but decided to go out for supper, because at least it was a change of scene.

In bed that night, Eve could only think about all the people she loved and the unchangeable fact that one day she would have to say a final goodbye to every single one of them.

It felt unbearable. Lying there in the dark, she couldn't push away her worst fear: that one of her children would die before her. She had four. She had quadrupled the odds! Usually she managed to keep this thought reined in, under control, but tonight it was rearing up to scare the wits out of her. But, she suspected, on some level, life has to be lived like this, in the knowledge that death is around. Can't be staved off with a nice house, or smart car or sense of style . . .

'Oh my God, I'm in the middle of a conversion to Buddhism.' She was staring up at the ceiling half expecting to see some sort of apparition in the lotus position. Maybe she'd read one too many yoga manuals, but she really did want to be at one with the universe, in good karma, looking forward to reincarnation and all that stuff.

Maybe there was a class she could do? Maybe Jen would come? Her next thought was, which night would be suitable? And who would babysit?

271

'This is why I will never be able to meditate, let alone sleep,' she told herself off. Time to get up and boil the kettle for camomile tea. Oh . . . But she was at her father's house . . . nothing but full strength English Breakfast. That wasn't going to help.

In the morning, it was obvious that Janie had also spent most of the night awake. She was pale with tired circles under her eyes.

'Are you OK?' Eve asked her as they made toast and scrambled eggs in the kitchen together.

'Ah . . .' slight trace of tears brimming, 'I'm all right. I think . . .' but then she added in a whisper, 'I'm so frightened for him.'

'I know . . .' Eve wrapped an arm round her, 'I know.'

The day wore on until finally it was time to go and visit him after the operation. He was worse than they had expected – barely conscious, propped up in a starkly white bed in a small side room, both arms hooked up to drips and a pain relief pump, another tube snaking out from under the covers which it took Eve a moment to realize was a catheter.

To her, he looked for the first time like a man who could die. She felt tears spring to her eyes at the sight of him and had to feel her way to one of the chairs beside the bed. Janie put a hand on her shoulder and managed some soothing, bed-side small talk, while Eve took in the backdrop: the click-clunk, click-clunk of the morphine pump and rattle, pause, rattle, pause of her father's breathing. She moved her chair closer to the bed and took her father's hand in her own. It felt lukewarm and papery dry. As she stroked it, she thought about how she'd not done this for decades. Hadn't held his hand since she was a small girl.

'How are you doing?' she heard herself ask and her throat squeezed up with the effort of it.

All the stuff she would have liked to say about how they had loved each other in their own way and how she was sorry it hadn't been more straightforward between them . . . none of it would come out.

'You're all right, Dad,' was all she managed.

There was no news about the operation, the relevant doctor was off duty, so they were told by the busy night staff to ask again in the morning.

After they had eaten quietly together at the kitchen table, Janie went up to her bath then bed early. Eve thought she could hear her crying in her bedroom and wondered if maybe she should go in and comfort her, but the echoes of their childhood were too powerful.

They had lost a parent before and they knew what was to come. The bereftness, the clothes and possessions packed away in boxes, the suddenly precious photographs which no longer seemed to capture any sort of reality, the vague unease and embarrassment of friends and relatives at the funeral and afterwards . . . Surely it couldn't be so raw this time round? Their mother had died one January morning at the age of 40 in a mundane and ordinary car crash. Black ice on an ungritted B road, no other car involved. A district nurse making the mile-long drive between one patient and another, she'd left her seat belt undone and been killed instantly when her car veered off the road and hit a tree.

Nothing so bewildering would or could ever happen to Eve and Janie or their father, ever again.

It had taken weeks – months – for the new reality to sink in. On the first day, they had played house and dolls and giggled and felt strangely excited by it all. No school! People kept turning up at the house with sweets and presents. It was like Christmas. Only much later did they start to ache for Mummy and begin to understand that she wasn't coming back. They would hide in her side of the cupboard and bury their faces into her fur coat and soft jumpers, breathing in the faint snatches of her perfume that were still there and cry for her to come home.

Eve tried to settle now into the kind of evening routine she would have had at home. She finished the house chores, spoke to all four of her children on the phone, which took almost an hour, took Hardy for a walk, then went out into the garden where she deadheaded roses in the last light of the day, then clipped the edge of the lawn, although it was only a few millimetres overgrown.

Back in the house, still feeling restless and untired, she sat cross-legged in the middle of the uninspired beige sitting room carpet and quite automatically began to work through a short routine of poses until she felt calmer.

She moved through the energetic salutation to the sun, *up, down*, grazing her chin on the carpet and *centre* with her hands pushed palms together in front of her. She did the whole sequence several times until she felt warm and limber.

Then the cat: she stretched through her spine pushing her breath out. 'All we have is the present,' she could hear Pete the Geek's intonation in her head. Now she was in the downward facing dog and felt the weight of her body pushed up by her arms. She widened her pelvis, back, ribcage, shoulder blades and breathed, new breath in, old breath out.

'Let go . . . lose the tension, lose the anger, lose the worry. Let go of it. There is nothing in life we can hold onto, it's moving and changing all the time—' Pete's karmic world view again.

But she felt the truth of it tonight. Nothing was for ever . . . her mother, Dennis, Joseph . . . gone. Her father going . . . the children, growing away from her every day. Oh God, she curled up into child pose and cradled her head between her knees. This was very bleak.

But now, she wondered, what would she miss about her father? Unsatisfactory conversations, with neither of them expressing themselves very well? Weekend trips to this stultifying house where everything was so neat and precious that her children could never relax for fear of breaking or spoiling something?

She felt sorry for him. He'd never seemed very happy, he'd never found a new love, or any real closeness with his children and his grandchildren. She felt full of regret for him that he had lived such a careful, controlled life. Kept it all at arm's length. But what would she miss? She didn't know yet. Her past? Her childhood?

She unwound and lay on her back for a few moments before standing up and moving into the stiff, steady warrior pose. She was strong. She was together. Arms wide and straight, one knee bent, ready for action, the other leg rooted to the spot, she was disconcerted to see Janie's face appear round the door.

'What *are* you doing?' Janie asked.

'My poses . . . I can't sleep. It helps a bit.'

'Do you meditate as well?' Janie came into the room now and sat down on the sofa.

'Sometimes. But I'm not very good at it . . . always find myself wondering if I've put the washing on . . . or what to have for supper . . . you know . . . mental whirr.'

'Yeah,' Janie agreed, 'mental whirr. I know all about that.'

There was a pause between them before Janie added with a half-sob: 'I'm scared that Dad is going to die.'

'I know . . . me too.' Eve sat down beside her on the sofa.

Chapter Twenty-Three

Eve walked into her father's kitchen as Janie was taking the call.

'What? . . . What!' Janie repeated.

'Are you sure?' she asked now with a smile breaking out and spreading across her face.

'Are they *sure*? Well . . . That's amazing! That's just fantastic! I don't know what else to say. Yes . . . Yes . . . By Friday . . . OK.'

Eve went to stand right beside her, craning to hear the voice on the other end of the phone, trying to work out what this was, certain it had to be good news. Finally, Janie put the phone down and turned to face her.

'That was Dad.'

'Yes?'

'They've removed a tumour the size of a grapefruit from his bowel – and it was benign. He's going to be OK,' Janie was retelling the words, still obviously not quite believing them.

'The size of a *grapefruit*?' Eve repeated. No wonder he hadn't been feeling too perky.

'And do you know what he said?' Janie looked slightly dazed. She was leaning on the counter-top for support. 'He told me: "*I'm 72 my number's going to come up any day now . . . but not today, Janie, not today.*" And then he laughed – he really laughed. It was a bit strange . . . not like him at all.'

'Good grief,' Eve said. 'How amazing . . . a benign grapefruit.' It was difficult to take in after the frenzy of worrying the two of them had done.

'So he's already feeling better?' Eve asked.

'Yeah . . . Phoning, chatty. Not out of bed yet, but yesterday I thought I'd never speak to him again.'

For a moment they were both silent. The day would come. But as he'd reminded them . . . *not today*.

'Shall we go and celebrate?' Eve asked.

'I don't know . . . don't know if I could. I feel really strange.' Janie was wiping her eyes.

'Come on, let's go buy him a present,' Eve rallied her. 'Then when visiting time is over, we'll have a late lunch with far too much wine and probably feel a lot better.'

Their father was delighted with the gift: a CD Discman with headphones and a selection of jazz and big band CDs to listen to in bed.

He was still in his pyjamas looking white and

drained but, even so, there was a sparkiness, a twinkle to him neither of them recognized.

'What has happened to him?' Janie asked Eve when they were installed in a cosy pub for their lunch.

'I have no idea what the medical term is, but a lot more than a grapefruit got removed from his arse, I can tell you that much.'

Janie gave an outraged 'Lynnie!' but laughed anyway.

'But you saw him!' Eve said, attacking her food with an enthusiasm she hadn't been able to summon for days. 'This could be a whole new lease of life for him. He might get ten more years and do something interesting with them. This could be the best reminder he'll ever get to seize the day.'

'Maybe.'

Was it Eve's imagination or was Janie looking wistful at that? She'd thought all Janie's upset and anxiety had been provoked by their father, but now she wondered if other things weren't amiss in her sister's life. But she knew better than to ask directly; with Janie it was always better to wait, let the story unfold.

'Why don't you stay at home next weekend? I'll come up with the kids and look after Dad,' Eve offered.

'No, no. Don't be silly. He'll need lots of help.'

But in fact he was surprisingly well by the time he was allowed out of hospital. He needed help to move around the house, but he could sit up, talk, eat fairly normally. And Eve was right, something had changed for their father. He was more positive, more alert . . . more interested than she ever remembered him being before.

Nothing demonstrated this better than the crime Robbie committed which, pre-op, her father would never, ever have forgiven.

After breakfast on Sunday, Eve and Janie were summoned to the spare bedroom in their father's house by the sound of Anna wailing.

'Robbie! Robbie! No!' she was screaming.

Eve rushed up, taking the stairs two, three at a time.

'Mum! I thought he was with you!' Anna shouted accusingly as soon as Eve reached the door.

Then Janie was there, just a moment behind her: 'Oh dear God – don't let Dad see this. Oh God.'

Eve wasn't sure which looked worse, the shocked white face of her sister or the disaster her little boy had created along with the dog.

Robbie had found the chest of drawers stuffed full of their mother's belongings. He and Hardy must have been up here, quietly occupied for some time, because Robbie had emptied the two bottom drawers of all their contents and with Hardy's help, had utterly devastated them. Diaries and photos had been torn into little shredded heaps. A gooey old bottle of ink had been trailed all over the carpet, messy piles of papers, a silk scarf. Something quite unrecognizable now must have been thoroughly chewed over, because Robbie's cheeks were smeared in gluey grey and Hardy's drool looked greyish too. There were bits of all sorts of things scattered in a circle right around the pair.

Both Robbie and the dog were looking up at them very guiltily, fully aware that this amount of forbidden fun could only come at a price.

'Jesus, Eve,' Janie was panicky and angry. 'We've got to clean up straight away, see what can be salvaged.'

'What on earth is all the fuss about?' It was their father. He had managed to hobble out of his room to see what was going on.

Everyone was lost for words and Eve instinctively moved to pick up her son. He was only three, he had no idea what a treasure chest he'd been playing with.

'This is all my fault, Dad,' she said quickly, 'I'm so sorry. I'm sure some things can be rescued.'

Her father was heading for the pile on the floor. Janie moved to take his arm and help him as he walked.

He leaned over to look carefully through everything.

'Anna, why don't you fetch the brush and dustpan?' he said finally. 'This is just a lot of old rubbish. Probably your mother's shopping lists and bus timetables and a few bad photos she didn't even like.'

Janie was standing open-mouthed at this.

'I have absolutely no idea why I've kept it all so long.'

He opened the top drawer of the chest now and they saw yellowed hairbrushes, a stack of embroidered hankies and facecloths, and a toiletries bag.

'Oh, I really need to clear this out,' he said as he made a cursory rummage into the things. 'Elsie would laugh at me, she'd kill herself. She really would. The more I think about it, the more I realize I've done all the things she would never have wanted me to do. I mean, look at this place—' He sat down on the horrible pink stool beside the drawers and glanced about the room. 'The house hasn't been redecorated for years and years, I'm still at work – with my pension fund! – I've never remarried. It was terrible when she died. Terrible. But if I'd been the one to go first—' he shook his head a little – 'Eventually . . . she'd have lived it up, girls, holidayed in the Caribbean, put in a new bathroom with a whirlpool, had a boyfriend, maybe several! I've really let her down.'

Eve caught Janie's eye and they exchanged expressions of disbelief. Was this really their father talking? He'd just called them *girls*, he'd just mentioned their mother and the word 'boyfriend' in the same sentence . . . and he was about to brush up her old junk and put it in the bin.

This was all good, Eve told Janie as they said

283

their goodbyes later the same day . . . but that didn't make it any less shocking.

'I'm so proud of you both,' her father told them as she kissed him at the door, ready to make the drive home to London: 'Your mother would have been too.'

So proud of you both????! What had happened to 'of course if you'd got into law school, Eve' and all the other million little digs and disapprovals he usually made?

More than a grapefruit had been removed, that *was* for sure.

'And when is the wedding?' he wanted to know, hoping it hadn't all been put back just because of him.

'August the 17th, Dad,' Eve told him. 'They've postponed it a month, but it's no big problem.'

'August . . . Great . . . I'll be fit as a fiddle by then . . . dancing on the tables.'

Dancing on the tables??? Her father? She was glad Janie was staying on with him for a few days. Maybe this was some side effect of the painkillers . . . a temporary delirium.

But she felt she should take advantage of it.

'Tom and his fiancée are expecting a baby. Have I told you that?' she said with a big smile.

'No! How marvellous. I'm going to be a great-grandfather.'

Now she was sure it was delirium.

Chapter Twenty-Four

Big beams of July sunlight were splashing in the window as Eve sipped tea at the kitchen table. Every season was good, but for Eve, summer was the best. In the garden, where Anna and Robbie had already taken their toys out for the day, pink and orange flowers were bursting out of pots, corners and borders. The vibrant gladioli buds were emerging square-tipped from their sheaths like brand new lipsticks.

'Shall we invite the vet for supper?' Eve asked when Anna appeared at the door. 'Today, if he's free . . . or maybe tomorrow?'

Anna considered this request carefully: she was suspicious of her mother and the vet. But maybe she should watch them at close quarters, try and work out what was going on.

'OK,' she said, not adding anything else to it.

Eve took the lack of comment as a sign that Anna suspected nothing. Oh, why should she? She was only nine.

'What are you and Robbie up to?' she asked with a smile.

'Oh the sandpit . . .' Anna gave a big sigh. 'I'm trying to build a water feature, but Robbie keeps knocking it down.'

'Ah.' A water feature?! In the sandpit? Eve was trying hard not to laugh.

Nils, sounding more than a little surprised to get her call, agreed to come round that evening. 'Are you trying me out one last time?' he'd asked.

'Something like that,' she'd told him. And this wasn't so far from the truth. She'd heard her father regret all the years he'd spent alone and taken a message from it about her own life.

Dinner out in the garden was lovely. Candles flickered, fairy lights twinkled, the children flitted up and down from the chairs, in and out of the house, providing a constant babble and distraction. Eve, dressed in a 'I'm really not *trying* to be this pretty' outfit of vest, flirty, flowery skirt, glitter pink toenails and sequined flip-flops, made a noodly vegetable approximation of chow mein, which everyone seemed to like. Then there were bowls of whipped cream studded with the warm raspberries the children had picked from the two canes she kept in the garden.

She laughed a lot with Nils and together they drank enough ice-cold white wine for her to feel relaxed and happy.

'So, that's the little people tucked up in bed,' she said, as she came back from the twenty-minute tussle of washing, teeth, stories, good-night kisses and last minute pleading requests to stay up 'just a bit later'.

She had a cardigan wrapped round her now because it was growing cool with a slight breeze.

'Shall we go to bed too?' she asked with a smile and sat herself down in his lap for the kind of kissing she'd been looking forward to all night.

'Well that was easy,' he said, putting his arms round her. 'I thought I was going to have to do a whole seduction routine ... woo you ... impress you.'

'No,' was her reply, 'I'm willing.'

She put a raspberry into her mouth then bent down to kiss him, bursting it against his tongue.

Tasting wine, berries and his warm mouth, she felt his fingers move under her skirt. She slipped arms round his neck and let him move into her pants and tease her there. Then she felt for his zip and wanted him, right here on his lap, to the sound of radio, chat and clanking dishes drifting over the garden from the neighbouring houses.

She held his earlobe between her lips, kept her eyes closed and her nose against his hair as he moved quickly inside her.

Later, she sneaked him into her bedroom where they peeled off each other's clothes intending to make love again, this time properly, slowly, soaking up every moment they had together.

But just as Nils was telling her to: 'Please say you're going to come soon . . .' the phone rang. Loud, insistent, threatening to wake up the children, so Eve leapt out naked into the sitting room to answer it.

Bloody hell. Why hadn't she remembered to turn down the volume and switch on the answering machine? She was so out of practice with the whole sex thing.

'Hello?'

'Hello, Eve, it's Joseph. How are you?'

Joseph? Joseph! Another timing masterstroke. Definitely regretting not having the answering machine on now. This was too weird.

'Hello,' she said as perfectly normally . . . chirpily as she could manage. 'I'm fine. We're fine. We're all OK.'

'And how's your dad?'

'He's really good. He's going to be fine.'

'That's great. So . . .' He was getting to the point now. For a moment it flashed across her mind that maybe he would want to talk about *that* night. She felt her stomach lurch. 'Eve . . . you know we talked about me looking after Anna and Robbie for a few days?'

'Oh yes.'

'Would you still like to do that? Maybe you'd like to take a weekend off, go to your dad's or your sister's . . . I thought I'd look after them at your place, because Robbie would probably prefer that.'

A weekend off?!! For a moment, she imagined driving fast down an empty road without *Sesame Street*'s Silly Songs blasting from the tape player.

'It's a great idea,' she told him, 'I'd really like that. But can I call you back tomorrow? I've got someone round at the moment.'

'Yeah, of course. Who is it?'

'Oh . . . no-one you know. Erm, from work. Someone from work.'

'Yeah, of course.' *Someone from work . . . at 11p.m.?* 'Speak to you soon.'

'Yeah . . . thanks for phoning.'

They said their goodbyes and she put the phone down, feeling odd . . . Why had they never talked about that night? Why didn't they want to figure out what was going on there? Or not going on . . . or *what*???

She didn't get the chance to think about it any more because then Anna walked in.

'Mum, why are you naked?'

'Ummm. Why are you up?'

'I've had a bad dream.'

'Well, have a glass of water and go back to bed.'

'Why are you naked?' Anna asked again.

'I thought my pyjamas were in here . . . but they're not.' Pathetic, but the best she could come up with in the circumstances.

'Shall I look in your room?' Anna offered.

'*No!*' Major panic, young, impressionable daughter walking in on naked vet. 'Water and back to bed.'

'All right, there's no need to be so huffy.' Anna was feeling hurt now; usually her mum dropped everything for a nightmare, tucked her in, cuddled up next to her for a bit, told her not to worry. But she went back to her room and Eve slunk into hers.

She'd always thought it was a serious design flaw that children didn't come with a pause button, so that when totally harassed and annoyed and driven wild by yet another toddler tantrum, demand, whatever, parents should be allowed to press pause. Even just for two minutes – any longer and it would be open to abuse. You'd have three-year-olds coming round ten years later to find they'd got all tall and hairy or children would figure out how to pause each other for a laugh. Well, OK, maybe it wasn't such a good idea.

Finger on her lips, she tiptoed across her room. The vet smiled, pulled the sheet over his head and waved at her to come and join him.

She got into bed.

'You're freezing,' he said and cuddled her up against him.

'You have to go,' she whispered.

'What, now, when you're so cold?' He brushed a hand down her back, pulled her in close against him. She could feel all sorts of interested perkings and stirrings starting up between them.

But still she said: 'No . . . I'm sorry. My daughter's having nightmares and wandering about the house. It's definitely time to send you home.'

He gave her one long, long final kiss and got out of bed.

She watched as he dressed himself.

This was the strangest affair she'd ever had. It was about friendship, laughter, sex, and not phoning very often. There was no longing, no passion, no chance of getting hurt. And, it occurred to her, the sex was of the athletic, we're all-grown-ups kind, not the let-me-look-into-your-soul lovemaking that, quite frankly, would scare her to death right now.

She really liked Nils, but if he disappeared tomorrow, it wouldn't matter to her. She wasn't going to let it matter.

'D'you want to come to the wedding with me?' she heard herself ask. *WHAT? Was she insane? Why was she doing this? Please say no, please say no.*

'Your son's wedding?' Nils was asking back.

'Yes, on 17 August.' Maybe he would have something else planned for that day.

'Your son's wedding which is going to be attended by Dennis, the father of your older boys and Joseph, the father of your little ones, oh and Joseph's fiancée, not to mention all your friends, family and the new-in-laws?'

'Yeeeeeees.' *The vet must not come.*

'I'd really like to be there, Eve.' *Oh my God.* 'But I don't think I should. It's too important.' He sat down on the edge of the bed beside her. 'You don't want to distract people with your casual boyfriend.' His eyes were fixed on hers and he was smiling. 'You can come and see me any time, before or afterwards, if you need someone. But it's too important . . . Be strong,' he told her and touched her forehead with his finger. 'Go alone. Be proud to be alone.'

She suddenly felt a surge of teariness. Was she proud to be alone? Or was she too proud to be alone? *Or so proud she was alone?*

'You're a good person,' she told him. 'I'm sorry I don't like you a bit more . . . I mean, I'm sorry I don't *really* like you.'

'You don't really like me?' He was still smiling at her. He'd missed the nuance.

'No . . . no, I mean . . . I'm not in love with you. Well, you know that. But I feel sorry about it.'

'I'm not in love with you,' he said. 'Shall we not be in love together?'

She managed a laugh at this.

'No,' she said, serious now. 'We deserve better. We'll just have to keep looking.'

He nodded his head at her and as he began to do up the buttons on his shirt, she felt a pang of something. Regret? Loneliness? It still felt the more natural state to share your bed, to have someone live, human and warm, dressing, undressing, talking at your bedside. She could get used to this in an instant. It was being alone, making it up as you went along that was hard.

Chapter Twenty-Five

Joseph lay in Eve's little bed and found he couldn't get to sleep although he'd been up since six o'clock that morning when Robbie had burst in, but on seeing him, had screamed and run straight back out again.

It was only 11p.m., but he was worn out by his first full day with the children. His *children*! He had *two* children and this was the first time he'd been alone with them both. Up until now, Eve had never left him in charge of both Anna and Robbie before and it was *exhausting*.

He had found his first day terrifying. Breakfast had started at seven and they had wanted complicated stuff like porridge, boiled eggs, apple-and-carrot juice made in the juicer. He was partly impressed that Eve was bringing them up so perfectly healthily, but partly infuriated by her as well. How did she manage all this stuff and get to work on time as well? Bloody perfect parent. He had stumbled round the kitchen, searching for coffee, but the strongest thing he could come up with was a decaffeinated Earl Grey teabag.

He'd forgotten about all the weird stuff she kept in her cupboards: black unsulphured apricots, packets of pumpkin seeds, organic popping corn, bags and bags of oats . . . did she have a horse somewhere he didn't know about? When he unthinkingly put his teabag into the rubbish, Anna had scolded him and he'd had to fish it out and put it in the composting bin. All the bottles and tins had to be washed out and piled into the relevant – admittedly overflowing – cupboards for recycling. How had he forgotten all this?

He thought about his life of dinners out, throwaway cups of coffee, plastic sushi lunchboxes, wine bottles guiltily slung into the rubbish . . . gas-guzzler of a car . . . Oh, she was infuriating him just with the contents of her kitchen. But here was the thing he couldn't let go of: she was quirky. She was an original. He'd never met anyone like Eve. She was still well and truly under his skin. And these lovely little people chomping their way through their wholesome, wholefoody breakfasts, they were his. They were well and truly under his skin too. Where he wanted them to be. He had taken them out for most of the day on a park crawl, with a visit to a café for lunch, and by the time they were back home at 5p.m. he had been desperate to lie on the sofa with them watching cartoons but instead, he'd had to cobble together some sort of supper. Even though it was his first night on duty and he had meant to cook himself, he was far too tired, he'd bought no groceries and he knew the freezer was bound to be stuffed with the neat little boxes, tubs and jars full of Eve's soups, stews and even puddings, so he'd guiltily pulled out a selection, emptied them into pots and heated them up.

Then at bath time there had been that conversation with Robbie who had suddenly piped up: 'What is a daddy?'

'Ermm,' had been Joseph's first attempt at an answer, as he wondered how much of a 'separated parent' explanation you could give three-year-olds.

'What does a daddy do?' Robbie had asked, looking up as Joseph tried to shampoo him without getting the stuff into his eyes.

'Ermm.'

'Do they play football?'

'Yes!' Maybe this wasn't going to be so hard. 'Daddies play football and read you stories and ... tickle you—' this got a giggle. 'And they give you piggy-backs.' Another giggle.

'OK,' Robbie said finally, with a theatrically deep sigh, as Joseph rinsed the shampoo off. 'You can be my daddy.'

Joseph helped him out of the bath and cuddled the little boy up in a towel.

Then Robbie added: 'Do daddies sleep in mummies' beds?'

'No. Not all the time.'

'But you're sleeping in Mummy's bed.'

'Well, she's not here . . . When she comes back, I'll go to my house.'

'Why?'

'Robbie, what about a game of hide-and-seek?'

Now finally, Joseph was in bed, noticing all the ways the room had changed since he'd lived here with Eve. She'd repainted it a deep, rosy pink and the gilt-framed mirror above the chest of drawers, all hung with beads and chains, was new. There was more space now that their large double bed had been changed for a smaller one and Eve had made it unashamedly girlie with fuchsia sheets and a bedspread and curtains of pink and gold saris.

He had not been able to resist opening her cupboard to look at the clothes: some he remembered but most were new. Apart from her black work suits, all lined up neatly on the left, she liked to buy cheap and update regularly. Tie-dyed pink, fake fur lined denim jacket, shaggy waistcoats, surfer girl tops – she was still totally hip. A forty-something market stall and Top Shop fanatic.

He'd looked through the bookcase and the pile on the bedside table to see what she was reading – a book by the Dalai Lama caught his eye – but he hadn't opened any drawers, knowing that was where she kept papers and diaries and all sorts of private things he had no right to poke into.

She still had the inch-high photo of him with

baby Anna in his arms in an enamelled frame on her bedside table, he'd noted, alongside a bigger snap of Anna and Robbie and a faded primary school portrait of Denny and Tom smiling missing-toothed grins. The sheets and pillowcases were new on, but still when he lay back on the pillow he could smell lavender, sandalwood and rose, the droplets she sprinkled to help her sleep. And something else too, the musky vanilla which was her own particular smell. He buried his nose in the pillow and tried to breathe in a big lungful of it, but the harder he tried to smell it, the more elusive it became.

Best to lie back, breathe gently and catch it in little wafts.

He couldn't help but be impressed with her. She worked, she cooked, she decorated, she gardened, she looked good, she was bringing up the children so well and she did it all alone. He thought guiltily that she must be busy every moment of the day. His own weekday evenings were spent socializing, going to the cinema, going out for dinner with Michelle. In this household, he knew, evenings were a rota of baths, bedtime stories, loading the washing machine, folding socks and collapsing onto the sofa at the end of the day. He'd often wondered why she hadn't found someone else to take his place, and now he suspected that she didn't ever have the time. Why was thinking about sock-folding making him feel sad? And what the hell was that bleeping?

He had been lying there for about twenty minutes now and had thought the low bleep sounding every minute or so was coming from the street, but now he was sure it was in the room.

Bleep . . . bleep . . . he tried to follow the sound. He flicked on the sidelight, got up and walked slowly round the room.

Bleep . . . under the bed? Lifting up the sari, he saw a small black pager with a flickering red light.

Hmmm . . . He flicked the back case off and removed the offending low battery. He didn't think she had one of these. Even the probation service had stretched to a mobile phone for Eve. He put the pager on top of the chest of drawers and went back to bed, not giving it another thought until the phone rang late the next evening and a heavily accented male voice, slightly disconcerted by Joseph, explained that he was a friend of Eve's and was she there?

'No, she's gone away for a few days.'

'I see . . .'

'Can I pass on a message at all?'

'Yes . . . are you a friend of the family?'

'I'm Joe – Anna and Robbie's dad.'

'Oh, I see . . . ummm.' Pause. 'Please tell Eve Nils rang and . . . she won't be able to help right now . . . but I might have dropped my pager when I was round . . . when I came to visit . . . a few days ago.' Awkward clearing of throat.

Joseph felt a surprising lurch of his stomach as

298

he realized he was talking to Eve's lover. He had begun to suspect that there was a man floating around in the background. It wasn't something he'd had to confront until now. A dropped pager under her bed had given her away.

'Actually, there is a pager lying on the bookcase in the hall. A small black one. Maybe Eve found it and forgot to mention it to you before she went away.'

'Ah.'

'Do you want to come by and you can check if it's yours?' Joseph found his curiosity was hard to resist.

Nils sounded relieved and they agreed a time the following evening.

'The Dutch vet who looks after the cats. I think he wants to be Mum's boyfriend' – this was all the information Joseph could glean from Anna. Nils was not very different from how Joseph had pictured him. A chunky, blond guy with a big physical presence.

He took up the whole doorway and made the solid front door seem lightweight. The pager disappeared into his large hands and, after a quick check, into the pocket of his overcoat.

'Hello. How are your cats?' he'd asked Anna and Robbie who had come to the door to see him.

'Well, thanks then.' This to Joseph. 'Sorry to trouble you. How is Eve doing? Is she going to be back soon?'

'I'm not sure,' Joseph had told him, realizing

he was taking some comfort from the fact that Eve hadn't told Nils where she was. They obviously weren't that much of an item . . . Oh for goodness sake. What did he know? What should he care? But he realized he did care and he wasn't sure what to make of the feeling.

When Eve phoned later that evening to speak to the children, after the long menu of the day's events she made him go through, he told her: 'A friend of yours came round to pick up something he'd left here . . .'

'Oh?'

'Nils.'

'Oh . . . What did he leave?'

'His pager. Anna found it in the sitting room,' he heard himself adding because he suddenly didn't want to hear anything from her about who this man was and what he meant to her.

'Oh,' Eve answered and, knowing perfectly well that Nils was never in the sitting room, wondered why Joseph wasn't telling her he'd found it in her bedroom. She couldn't help giving a little giggle.

'He isn't really a friend, you know,' she said.

'Oh,' from Joseph.

'Casual sex . . .' she whispered.

'Oh!'

'I don't really want a relationship now . . . But a bit of adventure, just once in a while . . .' Her voice had dropped to a whisper. Why was this giving him goosepimples?

'It's high time I got over you.' She made this

sound jokey. But there it was, all naked and out in the open: she still had to get over him.

She took a steadying breath and added: 'How is Michelle?'

'Oh, fine,' was all he said.

'Good,' Eve replied and then asked to speak to the children.

As he lay in her bed now, Joseph found it hard to get the giggled, whispered line out of his head 'A bit of adventure . . . just once in a while.' He didn't want to think of her having adventures with anyone else.

He didn't want her to share this room with someone else. He didn't want Anna and Robbie to grow up loving the man who would be sharing this room with her. So what the hell did he want exactly? He lived in another city. He was with someone else . . . he was getting married, for God's sake. What the hell had he expected Eve to do? Not get over him? Ever?

Chapter Twenty-Six

Michelle had come long minutes ago, when she was straddled over him and he was really hard and grasping inside her, when she'd felt him push up and up. She'd run her tensed hands over his lovely stomach, then down to his protruding hip bones and thrown her head back, feeling his fingers squeeze hard over her breasts. 'Yes, yes, yes . . . oh yes, yeeeeees, oh Joe, yes.'

And still he'd ground away under her, up, down, up, down, trying to get some traction in the relaxing, softening wetness.

She'd bent down over him, so she could lick his ear, nipples brushing over his chest, and urge: 'Come baby, come baby,' reaching under his buttocks to knead them and thrust him in. But she could already feel him start to deflate and grow softer until he slid out altogether.

'Oh, Christ,' he groaned and opened his eyes to see her hurt, angry face over his. 'What is the matter with you?' she demanded.

What indeed? She was lovely. Honey hair framing her face, lean honey-blond arms and legs parted over him. He could feel her wet pubic hair resting heavily on his. He looked at the breasts balanced just in front of him and struggled to sit up and suck at a nipple.

'Oh, don't bother,' she said, pushing his face away.

'I love you,' he said. 'I'm sorry, I don't know what this is about.'

There was a long silence, just the two of them breathing, eyes averted from each other, thinking through a cluster of confused thoughts, before she blurted out: 'You don't want this, do you? You can't want it.'

He didn't know what to say in reply, he honestly didn't know any more.

'Every time we've made love since you said we could start trying for a baby, you haven't been able to come. I don't need to be Brain of Britain to work out what's going on,' she said. It was true. It *was* obvious. And he just didn't know where to go from here. Or, more like, where to *come* from here.

She swung one long leg over, so she could move off him, and faced him now with her arms crossed over her breasts.

'You don't want me enough, Joseph,' she told him angrily. 'You don't want us to start a family and you can't get that bloody woman out of your head.'

He didn't know what to say. It was complicated

... It was Eve, it was Anna and Robbie, it was Michelle ... it was him. He had *two* children. It was as if this had only just become a reality for him. He had just come back from London, to Michelle who had told him within about half an hour – the very expensive diamond flashing on her hand as she waved it about in excitement – that the Italian hotel she'd wanted for the wedding was available, that she just needed a deposit cheque to secure it ... oh and thank goodness he was back in time because tonight was a very good night for ... *trying*.

He'd acted the happy guy. He'd looked through the hotel brochure – although they still hadn't had another conversation about whether or not his children would be allowed to come to this wedding – he'd let himself be led to the bedroom, although he was really tired, and somewhere in the back of his mind were all the doubts, worries and troubles which were now spilling out to the fore.

He wasn't ready for another baby. Things were quite complicated enough with Robbie.

And then Eve ... what the hell was that stuff going on there that night when ... ? Should he really be marrying Michelle just yet? Maybe this was all way too fast.

'Haven't you got anything to say?' she was asking him furiously now.

'Of course I do, Michelle,' he told her. 'But it's difficult to explain without hurting you. I don't want to hurt you . . .' He stroked just once, gently down her face.

'Are you still in love with her?' Michelle's hands were gripped tightly to her upper arms.

'I don't think so. But I miss my children. I really miss them.' He detected just the slightest of cracks in his voice and tried to clear his throat.

'Poor Joe,' she said and put an arm round his shoulder. 'That's why we need a baby of our own. A new family for you and me to belong to.'

'Michelle. I can't just drop the other two and start from scratch. They need a dad too. Are you really going to be able to share me with them?' His voice was low, barely above a whisper, but she caught every single word.

'You should never have gone down to babysit,' she said, snatching her arm back from him, 'I knew this was going to be a mistake. She's trying to get you back, trying to get you to feel sorry for her.'

He wanted to laugh at this: 'Eve?' he heard himself ask. 'Sorry for her? She's the most together person I know and anyway, she's got everyone.' He felt the choke at the edge of his voice again.

Something in Michelle's face changed with this and he knew he'd said far too much.

'Me? Or her? Joseph. It's your choice.'

'Oh don't be so melodramatic. There is nothing going on between me and Eve, hasn't been for years,' and he felt his face flush because this was now a lie.

'I'm going to be her friend,' he told Michelle. 'I'm going to be really involved with the children. Maybe it's you who needs to make the choice, Michelle? Me with my kids or not at all.'

'And what about our kids, Joe? Where do they fit in?' she shouted back at him.

'I don't know,' he said, 'I don't know the answer to any of this.' He was now feeling as deflated as the damp and shrivelled-up penis between his legs.

'Well fuck you.' She got off the bed and his heart sank with the ugly, ugly words he hated to hear her say. 'Fuck you, Joseph—' she wrenched open the drawer and began to tug on underwear and a T-shirt, 'I'm 27, I want to get married, I want to start a family. If you're not up for it, I'll have to find someone else who is.'

'Look, it's late,' he said as soothingly as he could, 'Maybe we should sleep on this and talk about it again in the morning.'

'No!' She was brushing away furious tears as she yanked on jeans and boots, then snatched up her phone, her keys and her handbag: 'I've got to get out of here,' she shouted, 'What is the point?'

She slammed the wardrobe door as hard as she could, tears streaming down her face now. 'I'm going to move out, Joe . . . I'm serious. I just don't see any point. What is the fucking point?'

'Michelle!' He got out of bed now and fumbled to tie on his dressing gown.

'Just *fuck off.*' She waved a hand in the air and there was a faint tinkling, rolling noise, then the bedroom door slammed shut behind her.

He sat down on the bed. He couldn't think of anything he wanted to say to her to bring her back. Maybe he should just let her go. The only thing he was sure of at this moment was the huge doubt in his mind . . . he didn't know if he would ever be as happy with Michelle as he had once been with Eve.

But where the hell did that leave him? Stuck in a place from which there didn't seem to be any going back or any going forward.

He ran a hand over the baseboard of the cherrywood sleigh bed . . . with the newly laundered Irish linen sheets. He took in the architect-designed wardrobes, the polished oak floorboards, the outrageously expensive Danish-design lamp on the bedside table. It was all crap. He was still just himself, not any better, not any more important, not any more powerful or intelligent, or knowledgeable for all this stuff.

And, even worse, this flat didn't feel like home. Had never felt like home. This place was just temporary . . . a beautifully designed pose . . . something he'd thought he could do for a while before he finally went back home. And home was still the chaotic little place where tea bags were composted, walls were covered in Blu-Tack and there was always a slightly strange mix of smells like onion soup and lavender.

Oh God. It was far too late . . . she would never

forgive him. And there was someone else for her too . . . And poor Michelle.

'I've completely fucked up,' he said out loud. 'How is any of this going to work out?' It was also just occurring to him what that strange tinkling, rolling sound was: the noise a heavy three diamond and platinum ring might make as it hits a wooden floor and rolls away.

It served him right. It really did. He was never going to fall asleep now. He went into his sleek, black and marble kitchen, clicked on the Starck kettle and wondered exactly when he had turned into such a selfish prat.

Chapter Twenty-Seven

'OK Robbie, that's enough.' Eve took the little index finger off the bell and they listened to the clump, clump, clump of footsteps coming down the hall to meet them. The door swung open and there was Tom grinning, saying hello, squatting down to hug Robbie, and they were all ushered into the flat.

Eve, carrying a parcel of home-made treats, could tell she had walked straight into a big scene. Deepa was huddled into a corner of the sofa looking stormy and Tom was being all awkward and twitchy.

'Just sit yourselves down, wherever you like. I'm going to put the kettle on – and hide!' This was meant as a little jolly-along for Deepa, but she just stared at him and didn't make any reply.

'Come and chat.' Tom directed this at Anna and she got up with Robbie in tow and followed him out of the room.

'Sorry about this,' Deepa said when she was

left alone with Eve. 'We're in the middle of a big fight.'

'D'you want us to come back another time?' Eve asked her.

'No, no, don't be silly,' Deepa said and then she was in tears.

'Oh . . . silly me . . .' she was sort of gulping and sniffing. 'Hormones, isn't it? You're supposed to go completely bonkers by the end and I'm not even there yet.'

'Hey, it's OK,' Eve soothed. 'You're allowed to shout, scream, cry, change your mind, eat bananas dipped in Marmite . . . whatever helps to get you through.'

Deepa managed a little smile at this and was maybe about to say something else when the doorbell rang again.

'That's my mum,' Deepa explained. 'We invited her for tea as well.' Deep sigh, lip wobble.

'Is there anything we can help with? Mums are good . . . try us.'

'I don't know . . .'

Tom was opening the front door now with his cheeriest sounding hello.

'Kalna, come in – lovely to see you. You remember Anna and Robbie, don't you?'

Eve went out into the hall to say hello and then engineered mothers and little children to the kitchen and Tom back into the sitting room to Deepa.

In the tiny kitchen she and Kalna chatted and

fussed over teapots, mugs, the splash of milk left in the fridge.

'Deepa is going to have to get more organized when the baby is here,' Kalna scolded, shaking the almost empty carton. *And other things not to say to your daughter right now.*

'She's got a lot on her plate. It's probably Tom who needs the boot in the bum,' Eve was quick to point out.

'Well, she'll soon give him that,' Kalna laughed. 'Once they know each other a bit better.'

Eve liked Deepa's mother and the feeling was mutual, which pleased them both. When the two families had met for the first time, in the slightly fraught circumstances which came in the wake of the unexpected pregnancy and marriage announcements, the mothers had hit it off straight away, because they both recognized immediately that they were the same kind of devoted mummies, secretly gleeful at the prospect of a grandchild.

Especially Kalna who had two much older, unmarried daughters all caught up with their medical careers who, in her words 'looked very unlikely to produce'. So, Deepa had found her parents' reaction to her baby and wedding news unexpectedly cheerful after the brief period of shock and disapproval had worn off.

'I think they are having a bit of a row,' Eve confided to Kalna.

'What about?' Anna piped up. Oooops.

'Oh I don't think it's anything serious, honey.'

'Pre-wedding nerves,' was Anna's verdict.

'Come on, Anna, you take the mugs and let's go find out.' Kalna picked up the teapot and tray of cakes and gave Eve an infectiously wicked smile.

It turned out to be the wedding, which was just five weeks away now. They'd both gone off the idea – not of getting married, but of the traditional white wedding they had arranged. Tom had never been too hot on it all. But now Deepa had changed her mind.

'I'm going to look ridiculous . . . look at me,' she sobbed over her tea to the two mothers. 'And the hotel is so boring . . . And I don't like the church either . . . or the vicar. It's all just really stupid and it's just totally not what Rich and Jade would do, is it?' Big sob here.

'Forget about them,' Tom told her, beside her on the sofa now, stroking her hand.

'But it's supposed to be about us . . . And none of this is us.'

Tom looked up at Eve and raised his eyebrows in a slightly helpless kind of way.

'What would you like, Deeps?' This from Anna who was sitting on the carpet at Deepa's feet.

'Oh it just sounds silly. I'm a big fat, stupid, pregnant girl who needs to get married in a rush . . . None of the things I want can get sorted out in time.'

312

'Just tell us anyway,' Tom soothed, not at all angry about this any more.

And so Deepa told them, stopping once in a while to dab at her eyes and blow her nose with the big damp balls of hankie she was holding in both hands. 'I want to get married in a field, in the afternoon with home-made vows as well as the real ones . . . and have a pink tent with lots of pink flowers and a pink cake . . .' She broke into tears here, but after a little patting from Tom, she managed: 'And lots of dancing in the open air while the sun comes down . . . and home-made food and everyone just really relaxed and . . . happy for us. And Tom,' she looked up at him, her face all puffed up and tear-stained: 'You won't have to wear a suit if you don't want to.'

He kissed her on the nose: 'It sounds lovely, but we're not going to be able to rearrange everything now.'

Kalna and Eve looked at each other a little bit misty-eyed. A little bit fierce and determined.

This is obviously how the fairy godmother felt when she pitched up in Cinderella's kitchen, Eve thought. *Deepa, you shall go to the ball!*

'How long have we got?' Eve asked.

'Five weeks,' Kalna answered her.

'Field, tent, obliging vicar, lots of food, servers, DJ, flowers . . .' Eve was ticking things off on her fingers. 'Can the other wedding be cancelled?'

'We'd only lose the deposit . . . no big deal,' Kalna told her.

'Are you serious?' Deepa was asking them. 'What about Dad?'

'Oh, leave him to me,' her mother said, as if she cancelled weddings every day. 'Now, if we divide things up between the four of us . . .'

'Denny will help,' Tom added, suddenly all bouncy with enthusiasm. 'He's always location scouting for photos, he'll help us find something.'

'OK, so between the five of us . . .' Kalna looked absolutely calm, just as she had when they'd been organizing things for the first time.

Pens and papers were coming out of drawers now, the Yellow Pages came down off the shelf, Denny was phoned. A rush of excitement was on the loose.

'I wonder what Dennis will make of all this?' Tom said to Eve at some point.

'Dennis?' She was startled by this because she usually managed to keep thoughts of the impending Dennis reunion at the very back of her mind.

'He's going to be here in three weeks' time. Have I told you that yet?' Tom gave a distracted shrug, shuffle of hair.

'*No!* You bloody have not,' she replied.

'Yeah. He's here first on business. Then his family are joining him the week before the wedding.'

'Right . . . three weeks' time?'

'Yeah. August the 7th.'

Why did she feel so panicky? Why did she

314

want to shout: *'NO, NO . . . I'm not ready . . . I need to get myself together . . . be much stronger . . . be able to cope with this . . . be able to face him down'*?

Stupid woman. She told herself off. Get a grip. She put a hand on Anna's ponytail and felt reassured.

Maybe Anna would know how to handle this. Maybe she had a book about it.

Chapter Twenty-Eight

'You know if I'm totally, totally honest with you, I just don't enjoy anything any more.'

Eve watched her sister's plain brown bob, silvered with strands of grey, dip down as Janie bent her head over her teacup.

She stirred at the tea over and over again, although the milk was long mixed in, then *ting ting-ed* on the rim of the cup several times and finally laid the spoon down. Eve had been surprised to get the call from her sister earlier in the week. It had been ages since Janie had come to visit her in London, but here she was, drinking tea in the kitchen, looking so sad and serious.

Watching her, Eve couldn't help thinking that there had been a time when Janie, although never beautiful, would always have been described as striking . . . elegant. But now she looked drab. And even worse, her once uncorkable energy seemed to have run dry.

The bob, no doubt expensively cut, was un-dyed and didn't really suit her long, angular face. Her charcoal grey, unlined linen trouser suit didn't help either. Janie looked dull, Eve saw as she studied her now – saggy, sad and shape-less. Middle-aged was the word that came to Eve's mind.

The lines from her nose to the corners of her mouth were deepening and her face was about to set into a downturned, downcast expression of vague disappointment. She probably had those half-moon reading specs with a long chain somewhere in her briefcase-cum-handbag. And no doubt, if someone was introduced to the two of them now, they would assume that Janie was older than Eve, not the other way around.

Eve didn't think this with any sort of smug-ness. It pained her to see her sister like this. 'You know . . .' Janie looked up from her tea again with tear-filled eyes, 'Cooking, for example. There was a time when I loved to cook, I'd buy the latest books, spend the whole of Saturday hunting down the best ingredients and it was a pleasure. Now I just feel like all these meals are coming at me, relentlessly, day in day out . . . breakfast, packed lunches, snacks, supper, four meals a day at the weekend. It's a nightmare. It's a full-time job just making sure that the fridge is full – and then there's all the bloody housework and washing and homework and listening to all this teenage *moaning*, and I have a full-time job on top of that which is *damn* stressful. And hardly surprising . . . my husband finds me boring. I am boring! And I'm bored . . . bored beyond belief!' Eve saw the little spurt of tears start down her sister's cheeks.

'Oh, Janie,' she said and stroked her sister's hand.

'I don't want to live like this any more,' Janie sobbed. 'Waking up every morning going through a mental checklist of everything I've got to do . . . existing in a house with such a miserable atmosphere . . . someone about to explode with anger or burst into tears at any time. I don't want it. I can't stand it.'

Eve carried on with the hand-stroking.

'What is it all for?' Janie demanded. 'What am I working myself this hard for? Why am I struggling to push my ungrateful children into the best universities? I suddenly haven't a clue what this is all about any more.'

Eve let her cry for as long as she needed to without saying anything.

'And I'm here, Eve,' Janie said finally, smudging at the tears on her face, 'because I always feel there's fun and . . . I don't know . . . a lightness to your life and to your family and I want to know how you do that.'

Janie looked properly round the kitchen now: at the mismatched pottery on the table, the crusted plates stacked on top of the dishwasher, the treasured baby paintings unpeeling from the fridge, plants in luscious health on every windowsill and the remains of cat food clinging to the sides of the bowl by the back door. The place was a mess, the floor was sticky and Janie had found herself scraping crumbs off the waxed tablecloth as she waited for her tea. But . . . but . . . but . . . it smelled delicious. Soup or something was cooking on the hob, the bread-maker was clanking its way through a program . . . and it felt so relaxed. She sat at this table and knew Eve had time. Time for tea, time for talking. Later on, there would be a bottle of wine opened and they would sit out in the garden drinking just a little bit too much. They would eat something cobbled together from the kitchen and Anna and Robbie, currently playing a noisy game of hide-and-seek outside the opened back door would scutter in and out, before finally disappearing off to bed. It was relaxed . . . happy.

Could it have been a bigger contrast to her home??? Where no-one came by unannounced, they came for dinner – proper with three courses and gourmet cheese and vintage liqueurs to follow.

Her house was sleek, white, beige, greige . . . maple floors, banisters which were regularly polished, sofa covers which had to be dry-cleaned three times a year . . . a stainless steel kitchen which showed up four fingerprints every time you opened a drawer.

And in a funny way, Janie thought now, her house was quiet. Apart from door slamming.

David hiding in his office behind a slammed door, Christine in her room on the phone behind a slammed door, Rick going out of the front door in a huff . . . SLAM.

She sometimes had the radio on, quiet Radio Four, but Eve's house was a racket. Robbie and Anna laughing and shrieking, the telly, videos, the phone ringing a lot, Eve's own taste in music which veered from classical to the kind of get down with the kids anthems on in the background now.

'Oh boy . . .' Eve was telling her, with a big sigh. 'We've had our really tough times in this house too, you know. Don't go thinking everything's perfect, because it's not. There's plenty of stuff I fret about in the small hours once in a while. I mean look at me! Why am I still single?!'

'But you enjoy life, don't you?' Janie asked and hoped it didn't sound too accusing.

'Of course I do, hon. Some of it's a drag and some days are a bummer . . . but I'd be lying if I said I wasn't happy to be here.'

Janie looked at her older sister and saw how she oozed – what exactly? A sort of fizz of carefreeness. Yes, maybe that was it. She wasn't burdened with the weight of what other people thought of her all the time, like Janie was. Worried, worried, all the time: did her lawyer colleagues think she was good enough? What would her friends think? Were the other children's parents doing this? What would Dad think? But there was Eve, single, hair far too long and blond for someone in their forties, clothes far too bright and tight, house a state, piss-poor career, accidental *babies*, listening to club music with her tin of marijuana on the top of the kitchen cupboards and she was *happy*. That elusive emotion which seemed to have bypassed Janie completely. And Janie's husband and, even worse, her children.

'I don't have any advice for you,' Eve said, wondering if wine would have been a better bet than tea. 'I don't like giving advice. All I can tell you is that I've tried to work out what really matters to me, what I really want to be doing and . . . well . . . stuff the rest.'

Much later in the evening, when they were two bottles of wine down and Eve had finally persuaded her strait-laced sister to *for God's sake* take a drag, no she wouldn't get arrested and barred from the bench and stripped of her wig and gown for the rest of her life . . . they giggled their way through a very long list of the things that Janie should just stuff.

Doing all the shopping, cooking and cleaning for starters.

'Are you completely mad?' Eve told her. 'Are you not in possession of an able-bodied husband and two able assistants who can do the super-market run while you lounge in the bath under a face pack reading *Hello!* and fantasizing about being married to Antonio Banderas or whoever does it for you?'

Snorts of laughter to this.

'And you know, maybe you should take a holiday, just on your own, Janie, and do relaxing things. Massages, waxing – I don't know . . . What do barristers do to relax? Go and get spanked or something . . . put in handcuffs. Isn't that it?'

More laughter.

'And stuff your perfect house. I mean it's lovely—' Eve wasn't so far out of it that she'd lost all sense of tact completely – 'but it is so high maintenance. I have actually let my children eat off your floors. Well . . .' she ducked down under the kitchen table at this point, 'they eat off mine too. Because there's so much nice stuff down there.' She came back up with a very grubby looking square of jam toast: 'See.'

Janie began to laugh now, so hard that soon her cheeks were hurting and then her stomach muscles.

'God, I'm such a slob,' Eve said. 'You're really regretting this trip now, aren't you?' You're thinking, "If that's on the kitchen floor what the hell am I going to find in the sofa bed?"'

'Stop it.' Janie was crying with laughter now. 'Stop it, I'm going to wee.'

'Oh my God, Janie,' Eve said, deadpan. 'You're scarily high.'

'I'm not am I?' Terrified look on the barrister's face now.

'No. You're fine. This is called enjoying your-self.' Eve said this slowly, as if trying to make herself understood in a foreign country. 'You may have had enough enjoyment for one night now, we will have to bring you down slowly.'

She looked at her sister, flushed with laughter and wine, looking a lot softer round the edges than she had for a long time.

'You need to let go a little, maybe,' Eve added. 'Let go of trying to do everything, trying to control everything. Your kids will appreciate you all the more if you cut them some slack. I promise, they are good kids, they'll be fine . . . in the long run. Who cares if they get into a few scrapes when they're young and silly? That's how they learn. Remember when Tom got hooked into that stupid sales scam? What was it again? Herbal slimming pills or something. God, I can't believe I can't remember it now. It all seemed so big at the time! He was almost £1,000 in debt before he told me what was going on. Silly twink.'

The two sisters looked at each other and burst into fresh giggles.

'And I seriously think you need new hair and new pants,' Eve added.

'What!' Janie shrieked.

'Well, I'd like to drag you out kicking and screaming for a whole new wardrobe. But I think it would be too much hard work, trying to drown out the voice of your inner barrister. But new hair and new pants would be a start, get you out of this sort of boring, middle-aged, frump thing going on here.'

She reached over and twanged at the top of Janie's elasticated trousers revealing, as expected, greying briefs encased in American tan tights.

'Yuck,' Eve said, pulling a face. 'This is all very practical, but . . . yuck. What we want is you sitting in your boring, barrister suits and thinking, "Yes, I know I look dull, but I'm wearing very racy pink pants . . ." '

'And better hair, darlink, better hair.' Eve couldn't help lapsing into Harry speak now. 'Harry must take a look at this bob, darlink, and work his magic.'

And so it was that at about 3p.m. the next day the two sisters pulled up chairs in one of those expensive, marble-topped-table cafés where everything comes with quadruple whipped cream, still in a whirl of breathless *do you like it? Are you sures?* about their new hair. Sneaking peaks in the mirrors, in shop windows, still not quite recognizing their reflections.

Eve's blond tresses had been streaked with bright girlie pink.

'I'm not too old for pink hair, I promise I'm not – and no, I don't want washable, I want permanent pink . . . for the wedding,' she'd assured Harry, who had expressed reservations as he'd gowned her up and listened to her request. But when the striped candyfloss head had emerged, he'd had to agree. No she wasn't too old for pink hair. She looked . . . hmmm . . . a lovely mixture of rosy, flushed and groovy.

Eve's courage had forced Janie to be bold too. She now had sleek, short hair tucked in around her small ears and round the nape of her neck in a dark, conker brown.

'We're looking good, honey, I promise,' Eve told her as they sipped at the ludicrous mountains of cream.

Scrunched up between their feet on the floor were plastic and paper bags full of pants, bras, hipster knickers . . . G-strings! After the initial shock, Janie had decided to go for it – green, pink, orange, turquoise, even glitzy silver smalls were in the bags.

'Promise me you'll wear them in court,' Eve had said loudly in the changing room.

'For goodness sake!' Janie had shooshed her.

But Eve had rather been looking forward to the intrigued look on the face of the saleswoman as they came out.

'I'm sure she thinks we're lesbians,' Janie, flustered, had whispered as they made their way out of the shop.

'I know.' Eve threaded her arm through her sister's. 'Be a shame to disappoint her.' She'd licked Janie on the ear.

'Get off! Are you insane?'

'Just a London girl, you uptight, Home Counties mum.'

'Please can I be just a little bit more like you?'

'Yes. But can I remind you once, way back, when I wanted to be like you too?'

'D'you think you'll actually wear any of them?' Eve was asking her now.

'Of course! You don't think I'd waste money on knickers for the back of my drawer!'

'Will David get to see them?'

'Well . . . ummm . . .' Janie picked up her spoon and began twiddling with it again. 'You know, I think David and I need to be apart for a while.' She looked up at Eve. 'And I've only just decided that today.'

'Hairstyle changes,' Eve couldn't help saying. 'They're scary.'

Janie just smiled at her. Then after a long thoughtful pause, she added: 'I've been married for sixteen years, Eve. That's a very long time. A very long time to be half of a couple, to be a wife, a parent, to be constantly compromising what I want with "What would David want? What would the children want?" I hope I don't sound like the most selfish woman on the planet, but I feel like I've forgotten myself, I've forgotten who I am and what I want or like, God, even what I like to eat or drink. Prawns for example—' she was almost laughing now. 'I don't think I've had prawns, hot, fried with garlic, all juicy in their shells with a little squeeze of lemon . . .' She broke off and tilted her head thoughtfully. 'You know, I've probably eaten them three times since I got married, even though I love them, because David is allergic to them.'

She shook her head.

'We're so up close, together all the time, I can't *see* him. I haven't the slightest idea what it was about him that I fell in love with and if it's still there. And I no longer think there's any hope of finding out until I get away for a while. Have a holiday . . . leave them all to it.'

With another almost laugh, she added: 'God knows how they'll react to that.'

'Try not to care,' Eve said.

'Yes. One long compromise – that's what my home life has become,' Janie said. 'No-one is doing what they want any more. We're all doing what we think we should . . . what someone else wants. I know you can't please all of the people all of the time, but at the moment one of us is always miserable and all four of us have forgotten how to be happy.'

'Well . . . group living is tricky,' Eve said. 'Needs of the individual versus the group . . . I'm sure Anna could direct us to whole bookshelves about that.'

'She is a little bit scary, isn't she?'

'Occasionally, but she's quite a normal nine-year-old most of the time,' Eve said, never wanting Anna to be labelled with any hyper-intelligent tags that she might struggle to live up to later.

Something was occurring to Eve for the very first time.

'Now that I think about it,' she confided to Janie, 'I compromised totally for Dennis. I did everything the way he wanted and tried to be everything he wanted me to be. And with Joseph, it was the opposite. I fought every hint of a compromise all the way. I tried to make him do everything the way I wanted it – even changed his diet, made him give up coffee, cycle to college, recycle everything . . . Oh God! No bloody surprise he turned out the way he is. He rebelled!'

'Scary,' Janie said. 'And you know, I think when people live together for a long time, it's the trickle of water on a stone effect: gradually you change, you get worn down. David's little comments about my clothes: too expensive this, too revealing that, too tight, too bright . . . they've gradually, over the years turned me into a frump. *Me!!* Eve! The girl who used to spend half her wages on the very best Italian clothes Winchester had to offer.'

Eve considered this carefully then said: 'This is obviously why people getting divorced in their mid-forties go on these crazed "I'm an individual" benders. Buy sports cars, groovy gear and pop music.'

'Does it have to be this way? Do I have to get divorced to be me again?' Janie asked her now.

'I don't know.' Eve licked cream from the back of her spoon. 'Only you and David, and maybe the children, can help you with that one.'

Her sister looked down at her cup and began

to stir again, over and over. How hard she was to read, Eve thought, her practised, inscrutable barrister's face.

Finally Janie looked up and said with a little smile: 'I'll have to wear the nice pants for myself for a while . . . Get comfortable in them.'

'That's my girl,' Eve smiled back.

Chapter Twenty-Nine

Eve had allowed the whole work thing to somehow get away from her. Lester had urged her to go ahead and apply for the promotion anyway, because she could always change her mind. And now here she was brushing down her best suit, ironing her shirt and polishing shoes for a day of meetings with the selection panel tomorrow because she was being interviewed for the job along with Lester's deputy and two outside candidates.

All this concentrating on whether or not she wanted it, she'd let slip the fact that maybe she wouldn't get it and suddenly that seemed to be whetting her appetite. Looking down at her note-scribbled diary, she saw the big red ring round 7 August, interview. She had the vaguest feeling that there was another reason she should remember the date, but shrugged it off. Thoughts of the interview were crowding in now . . . maybe she did want to head the department, get things done the way she wanted, take the rap, make the changes . . . Her only reservation was family life and how it would be affected by taking on more work.

But wasn't that the hardest thing to get right? The balance between work and family. It was an art to be in the middle of the push and pull and not be torn apart, to find a way to give more attention to one side when it was needed then move quickly back and redraw the lines. She saw Janie and Jen struggle with it week in, week out and she knew Deepa and Tom would have to play the game too when the baby arrived.

After a long bath, Eve went to check on the children. Like every parent, she loved to watch them sleep – the long lashes, the flushed pink cheeks, the steady rise and fall of the little chests. Asleep, they were always perfect: Anna, an angel, Robbie, a little pyjama-clad Cupid.

Back in her bedroom, she worked through all the most complicated calming poses, then curled herself up small, tiny, tiny into child's pose on the floor and tried to relax.

That night, very soon after she had finally managed to fall asleep, she was woken by the scary sound of stumbling and choking in her room.

When she managed to get the sidelight on, she saw her little son, pale and sweaty, looking up at her with trails of vomit down his chin and pyjama top.

'It's OK, Robbie,' she'd said, going from asleep to fully awake and coping in twenty seconds. She gathered him up into her arms and put him in her bed. 'You get comfy, I'll go and get a cloth.'

She sponged him down, along with the floor, the rug and her work shoes – which had somehow got embroiled in the vomit scenario.

He was hot and listless in the bed. But not too hot, she thought, feeling his forehead, his neck and his tummy, so she gave him a few sips of water, then cuddled up with him and they both fell back to sleep.

In the morning, he woke well before seven and seemed warm but not too bad. He could still go to the childminder's, but for a quiet day in.

Eve had hardly sat down at her desk when the call came from Arlene. Robbie was burning up and wouldn't stop crying for her. Eve didn't need to hear the symptoms to know that he was really unwell, she could hear the horrible high-pitched wailing in the background.

'OK, I'll be right over, as fast as I can. Tell him I'm coming . . . There isn't any rash, is there?' Because it was impossible not to fast-forward to that.

'No, no rash,' Arlene told her. 'But he doesn't look good.'

Eve scrambled her belongings into her bag and went to find Lester.

He couldn't believe what he was hearing.

'I have to go,' she told him.

'For God's sake, Eve, this is really important,' he stormed. 'I don't know if it can be rearranged, and anyway what for? Your son has a temperature! You know what kids are like, he'll probably be much better by the time you get there and you'll wonder what you were so worried about. Isn't there anyone else who can look after him? Just to give you a few hours. We'll try and do your interview first.'

'No,' she'd told him. 'No, Lester. I don't know how unwell he is, I'm not a doctor. All I know is he's hot, miserable and he wants his mummy. I don't have the luxury of being able to send my wife – or Robbie's dad – so I have to go.'

And then for good measure she threw in: 'My family comes first. I want a world where that's not seen as a strike against me . . . that's why I do this job, for God's sake.' Flushed up with anger, she added: 'You bloody know I could head this department really well, because I *am* the kind of person who drops everything for a child who needs mc.'

Lester's gaze fell to his folded hands and he gave a deep sigh. 'OK, OK . . . off you go. Keep in touch and come back as soon as you can.'

'Thanks, I know you'll man the fort for me,' she said, her usual farewell to him when she was leaving early.

'But not for much longer, Eve,' he called after her as she hurried out of the door to the minicab she'd ordered. 'Not for much longer.'

*   *   *

As she ran up the path to Arlene's house, she was shocked to hear her son's piercing cries.

She rapped impatiently on the door and Arlene let her in almost immediately. She rushed to the sitting room, to see her little boy red and sobbing inconsolably on the sofa.

'Oh Robbie, Robbie.' She cuddled him up and he buried his head in her chest. 'I'm really sorry.' This was directed at both her son and the anxious childminder.

'What do you think it is?' Arlene asked.

'I don't know, probably one of those nasty kiddie bugs, you know the ones that go on for 24 hours of hell and then disappear. I'll get him home and see how he goes. We'll phone the doctor for some advice.'

Back at home, Eve washed Robbie down with lukewarm water, changed him into his pyjamas and let him doze on the sofa. He didn't want to let her out of his sight, cried whenever she went out of the room.

He was hot, 39 degrees, when she checked with the thermometer. She stood in front of the bathroom medicine cabinet and swithered – baby paracetamol or homoeopathic belladonna? Reduce the fever or stoke it up? Calpol or belladonna? Calpol or belladonna?

She decided to use belladonna but switch to Calpol if the fever went any higher. So Robbie was dosed, then sponged down with water every half an hour to keep him cool. He was vomiting back even the tiniest sips of water she was spooning into him and didn't perk up at all at the sight of Anna. By the evening, Eve decided it was time to consult the doctor again.

'Sounds like just a virus,' the tired foreign voice at the other end of the line told her. Because this was on-call time and the best you could hope for in this part of London now was a locum who at least knew what he was talking about, even if you couldn't understand him.

'Just a virus? Just a virus??!' she couldn't help snapping back. 'Isn't meningitis just a virus? AIDS . . . Ebola?'

'There's no need to over-react.'

'No,' she agreed, trying to calm herself. 'I'm very tired, my son is ill and I want to know if he's going to be OK.'

'Well, it sounds like gastric flu. You'll have to keep a close eye on him. If his temperature goes up higher, if he gets too dehydrated, or if any sort of rash develops, call us straight back. Give him Calpol and tiny sips of water.'

Here we go with the Calpol thing again. Was this the only medicine available for children under ten?

'Calpol is just paracetamol. It's not a wonder drug,' she heard herself snapping again.

'It will make him feel a bit better, Mzzzz Gardiner. You might both be able to get some sleep.'

*   *   *

335

Mzzz Gardiner put the receiver down when the conversation was over, feeling mightily hacked off. At times like this it was very hard to be on her own. She needed another opinion, she needed somebody calm to look at Robbie, lying in a hot, dry, restless sleep in her bed, to say 'He's going to be fine', to put an arm round her and tell her to get some sleep on the sofa, he would stay with Robbie for a bit.

She thought, with tears welling up behind her eyes, that she needed Joseph. And before she could stop herself, her head was in her hands and she was remembering him covered in projectile vomit from a teething baby Anna, managing to smile and coo at her 'There, there, feeling better now?' while baby sick dripped off his cheeks and pyjamas.

Remembering him nurse her through flus and colds with soup brought to her bedside. He'd once set up the TV and video in her room and forced her to watch Laurel and Hardy films when she was too blue and unwell to make it out of bed.

He was a lovely man.

Was . . . *was* . . . she reminded herself, willing her thoughts to stop. He turned into a jerk, remember, Eve? – that's why he had to go and you packed up his bags and got rid of him.

Robbie woke up hourly throughout the night, to be sick, to cry, to lie listlessly in her arms, willing her to make him feel better because she was his mummy. And that's what mummies were supposed to do.

At one point he woke up and demanded that they go and make a cake.

'What?' she asked him, fumbling for the side-light, hardly able to wake up yet again because she was exhausted.

'I want to make a cake,' he was crying at her now.

'A *cake*??? Oh Robbie, honey, it's the middle of the night.' In fact it was 5a.m. 'Shall we try and get back to sleep and make one in the morning?'

'I want to make a cake, I want to make a cake,' he kept repeating over and over. He was boiling hot and still so dry, not one bead of sweat, there was no sign of this fever breaking.

She needed to sponge him down again and get some water into him.

He was still grizzling on about the cake, so she went into the kitchen and poured flour into a bowl, put a wooden spoon into it and brought it back to the bedroom. I must be insane, she thought, watching her delirious son stir flour until it had settled on his hair, his arms, his pyjamas, her duvet cover, the bed.

He puked up the mouthfuls of water she had made him sip into the bowl and then, moments later, fell asleep in her arms.

Just a few restless hours later, Anna was up offering to make Eve some breakfast while Robbie finally slept deeply.

'So long as you haven't reverted to breast-feeding him,' Anna said, as they sat together at the kitchen table, Eve barely able to hold a spoon, she was so whacked.

'No, I haven't – but you know, if it was what he wanted, I'd have done it, just to comfort him.'

Eve had breastfed Robbie until one month after his second birthday, despite Anna's disapproval.

'He's anxiously attached,' Anna had told her.

'Maybe you're jealous,' she'd countered.

'Yuk, I am not!'

'I'll stop when he's two, I promise.'

So she'd had to explain to Robbie that he was going to get a beaker with milk. They had gone out together to buy a bright red beaker with purple swirls on it. He drank from beakers all day, but this was a special milk beaker.

'I like boobies,' he'd told her, cuddled up in her arms, after just a few sips of beaker.

'So do I,' she'd said. 'But you're a big boy now, boobies are for baby boys.'

'Am I big?' he'd asked with a smile.

'Yes.' And she'd kissed his fat cheek.

That was how the breastfeeding ended. Later that night, she couldn't help crying about it. That was it, the last baby weaned. Her little breasts would shrink up into an even tinier size and never be of any use to her again.

'You look terrible,' Anna told her now.

'Thanks, darling.'

'Is Robbie going to be OK?'

'I'm sure he is. I think he's a bit better already,

338

he's sound asleep and he doesn't feel so hot any more.'

'How come you've got flour in your hair?'

'Oh, long story.'

Yup, she looked undeniably rubbish: sagging, shapeless grey nightshirt, greasy hair with flour, eyes with double bags. She really needed a bath, but then Robbie woke up and had to be attended to and somehow the morning wore on without her having the chance to wash, dress or sort herself out.

Until the phone rang.

'Hello, Evelyn, glad to catch you home.' She registered the American twang before she began to wonder how this voice knew her name – her old name.

'Hello?'

'Hi, yeah. It's Dennis here. I'm meeting the boys at their place at noon, so since I'm early, I thought I'd drop off. Visit you, catch up, see the flat.'

'Dennis?' DENNIS!!!!!! Heart pounding, breath catching shock.

'Yeah, hi. Are you about? Are you up for it? I'm just round the corner, in a cab.'

Round the corner!

'I'll be right there. Thought it would be good to say hello.'

Why was it so hard for her to say no to this man? He was like an unstoppable tide. Still the same bossy voice, just a bit Americanized, coming down the mobile phone at her. She was hardly able to speak, she was so shocked to hear him. Somewhere, there must have been a note of his arrival date, some word from Denny or Tom, but she'd filed it away and forgotten all about it. Avoided thinking about it, more like. Now here he was about to knock on the door, turning up completely unexpected, like a, like a . . . virus.

She said nothing. He wasn't listening anyway. He just carried on, as he always had done, getting everyone else to fit in with his plans.

'OK, does that suit? I'll be there in five. Number 53, right.' Click. Unbelievable. He didn't even wait for her agreement, goodbye . . . anything.

'AAAAAAAAAAARGH!' she shouted out loud with the burring receiver in her hand. 'Get lost! Get stuffed! Leave me alone!' But none of those things would come out when he was actually in earshot, would they? Why not? How did he still manage to make her feel this . . . powerless?

He would be here in five minutes! In the reunion she'd pictured, she'd fussed about what to wear, how to look, what to say. Now she was about to get caught barefoot in her nightshirt, looking like crap. It wasn't fair. It made her want to cry.

She rushed into the bathroom. God, she looked awful. Where to even begin the rescue operation? She brushed through her hair frantically, but that just seemed to spread the flour around. She scraped it back in a ponytail and searched about for some lipstick, couldn't find any . . . raced to the bedroom for clothes. Anything clean would do . . . maybe even ironed, was ironed too much to ask?

The doorbell was ringing as she did up the last buttons on her jeans. There wasn't going to be a moment to straighten up the flat. But still, she picked up armfuls of stuff and threw it into cupboards as she headed for the door. At least Robbie was asleep again, that was one thing less to worry about.

And now here she was, opening the door on the man she had once called husband, the man who had walked out on her and the boys, the man she hadn't set eyes on for almost six years now.

She registered the horrible sick feeling in the pit of her stomach as her hand went up to the Yale.

'Hello, Evelyn.' A pinstripe-suited man with a ruddy face and a blond, balding crop was holding out his hand to her.

'Dennis?' She barely recognized him. He looked so old, well into his fifties of course; even his eyes looked a different colour than she had remembered. But then again, it was probably years since she'd even looked at a photo of him.

'Hello,' she managed at last and held out a hand for him to shake. 'Come in.'

'Had a great flight,' he said, before she'd even thought to ask the question. 'First class – only way to go. Treat you like royalty, in-flight massages . . .' He held forth as she led him down the small corridor into the kitchen.

A mistake, she thought, as she looked round. It was never the tidiest of rooms, but this morning, oh boy. There was even a plastic salad bowl containing a small quantity of sick and a scrunched-up paper towel on the table.

She threw a cat off a chair and gestured to Dennis to sit down. He didn't look too sure.

'My little boy isn't well, we've had a terrible night.' She waved vaguely, wanting to explain away her outfit, the chaotic state of the flat. Wondering why she was caring so much what he thought of it.

'Jeez, this place is tiny. You have just this floor? What . . . two bedrooms?'

She nodded.

'So at some point you, the boys, your boyfriend and your other children were living here? Aren't there laws against that kind of thing?' This was said with a smile as if he meant it to be funny. Some bloody joker he was.

She was about to explain that actually Joseph and the big boys had moved out by the time Robbie arrived. But what was the point? He wasn't listening anyway, too busy critically taking it all in, making his snide little judgements.

'Tea?'

'Ummmm . . . do you have coffee?'

She thought about the tin at the top of the cupboard, about making him a coffee and sitting down to a joint while he drank it.

'Decaf?' she asked instead, deciding she should try and behave herself. Not scandalize him any further.

'Sure.' Not 'thank you' or 'lovely' or anything grateful. Just 'sure'.

She banged the kettle on, thumped and clanged her way through the coffee-making process just to let off some steam.

They tried out some small talk about their children – first the mutual ones and then their second families.

It was awkward and not exactly bonding.

'Well, they've turned out quite well, considering,' Dennis had offered about Denny and Tom. 'A fashion photographer and a software designer – not bad considering they haven't a degree to rub between them.'

'They both went to college,' she snapped.

'I don't think that's quite the same.' His mobile rang, saving him from the eye-scratching he was coming close to.

'Dennis Leigh . . . Ah ha . . . that's great, Guy . . . really great. No, I can reschedule. I'll be there at one for lunch, great . . . yup, fresh off the plane. Ah ha . . . in north London, catching up with some former colleagues.'

Former colleagues. It crossed her mind to have a secret spit in his coffee.

And before he'd paused for breath he was on the phone to Tom cancelling his lunch arrangement and agreeing drinks at 6p.m. instead. No, he wouldn't be able to see their flat today

– he'd do that another day . . . urgent business.

Well, that was Dennis. Didn't see his sons for six years, then would postpone his reunion for a business meeting.

She'd thought he might just have mellowed a tiny little bit . . . but obviously not.

'So,' he sipped at his black coffee, spit-free. 'Still in the same flat, the same job as when we last met?'

She nodded.

'Haven't you managed to step up at all? In *six* years?'

For a moment, she was going to mention the promotion possibility, but then she decided she didn't want him to know even that much about her life at present: 'I've had another baby, been busy,' she said instead.

'Yeah. You well and truly missed that part of the biology lesson, didn't you?' Casual little 'ha ha', and another sip of coffee.

Oh Jesus. Why couldn't she just tell him to go now? She thought of her little boy, lying on the sofa, at last getting a bit better and this creep referring to him as a mistake.

His making might have been *unplanned* but Robbie would never, ever be a mistake to her. She hated anyone even hinting at it.

'This flat is pretty . . . unique . . . isn't it?' he was looking around now. The painted ceramic plates on the table didn't match. The walls were an uneven, yellow-orange. And the place was a mess. Even with a sick child, the woman he'd married would never have let things get out of control like this.

He'd seen Eve occasionally over the years since he'd left her and in his opinion, she seemed to get more and more unravelled. Why hadn't she just made her life simple and married another wealthy City boy, like him? He couldn't believe she hadn't had the opportunity. Instead – look at her! Mad, hippie, vegetarian, *pink haired*, single mother of *four*. Bringing his sons up in some piss-pot little flat in Hackney. But he'd just left them to it, he thought with some annoyance now, he'd been too busy: work, his new wife, his two daughters. He hadn't been able to give Eve and his boys too much thought. Just hoped they'd turn out OK.

He stood up and looked out of the window at the extraordinary garden. It was small, but absolutely brimful, bursting with green and blossom. But he saw only the mess of toys strewn all over it, a little yellow tractor, a sandpit shaped like a turtle, plastic spades and forks and several footballs.

'Keeps me sane,' Eve said, anticipating the usual compliment about her garden.

'I see,' was Dennis's reply and the compliment didn't come.

She looked OK though, he had to admit. He knew she was 42, but she looked much younger. She hadn't sagged or crinkled up much, she was just a little softer round the edges, fuzzier. She still had her girlish, supple figure and he

certainly envied her that. Was she happy? He
had no idea. Was *he* happy? In most ways, yes.
He loved his wife. He knew that, at least, had
been the right decision.

'I'd like to get to know Denny and Tom a bit
better,' he said now. 'I'm going to invite them to
come over and visit, open invitation . . . whenever they'd like.'

'That's nice,' she heard herself answering, but
knew she was just dreading this. With a wealthy,
US-based dad they could both go and work in
the States, and wouldn't they want to do that in
a shot? Especially Denny.

Even now, she could hardly repress the fear,
lurking for all those years, that Dennis would
some day turn up and lure the boys back with the
sheer glamour of having been the missing
parent, the absent one, the fantasy parent, rather
than the one who did the washing, the homework, wiped your nose, took you to the dentist.

'Mummy!' She heard the cry from the sitting
room.

'You should probably go,' she told Dennis,
who immediately flicked a glance at his watch. 'I
don't think Robbie's really up for visitors and
I'm waiting for a work call.'

'Of course, have to go anyway. Can you hail a
cab round here or should I call one?' So then
there was all that kerfuffle, finding cab numbers,
phoning, and now he had to wait around for ten
minutes.

'*Mummy!*'

'I'm coming.'

'Look, you go and see to him, I have some calls to make.'

Finally she was saying goodbye, waving him out of the door, forcing herself to keep that smile up for just a little bit longer.

She slammed the door shut behind him, though. No, that wasn't quite enough, she went into the sitting room and pummelled sofa cushions very hard for a few minutes while Robbie giggled at her.

Fuck him, fuck him, fuck. Fuck. Fuck. Fuck.

OK. That was a bit better.

Chapter Thirty

Denny dropped them at the lobby of the swank hotel and drove off to find a parking place.

This was all Dennis's idea, of course. The big family reunion. She and her four children were scrubbed up and polished, ready to meet him, his wife and his daughters.

OK, she knew it was pathetic, but she'd taken ages trying to decide what to wear. The black work suit had been put back in the cupboard because it was too formal, the hipster jeans and a variety of bright tops had been tossed to the floor because they were too informal. Finally, she'd decided on a long, clingy satin skirt, green, and a black blouse with her best turquoise beads and arm cuffs. She had been worrying about whether the turquoise clashed with the green, but then Anna came in to discuss her own choice – an unusually girlie pink party dress someone had given her as a Christmas present, but Eve wasn't going to disagree – and then Robbie demanded juice and a biscuit and a video and when were they going? and was it nearly Christmas? . . . So the skirt and the mildly clashing jewellery stayed and in the back of Denny's car, Eve even did lipstick and sparkly eye shadow because this was a special occasion after all.

Denny made them wait for him in the lobby on pain of death: he didn't want to miss one second of this big get-together. When he finally got back, Eve and the children were directed to the residents' lounge where 'Mr Leigh and family' were waiting.

Deep breath.

'OK, everyone,' she summoned her band. 'Off we go.'

As soon as they walked through the door, Dennis waved with a casual-sounding 'Over here,' and stood up as they got closer.

The three women sitting around him got up too and the two groups faced each other, Eve feeling dangerously unbalanced with a suddenly shy Robbie pressed hard against the back of her knees.

Dennis did the introductions and there was a flurry of handshakes.

'This is my wife, Susan,' Dennis was saying now. 'My daughters, Sarah and Louisa. Anna, hello, I'm Dennis and this must be Robbie . . . hi there.'

Eve was shaking hands with the women now – Susan, a well-padded helmet bob blonde in stiff lilac with pearls constraining her neck. Why did

Eve have the feeling she'd seen her before? She was in her late forties at least. Older – that was a surprise to Eve.

But it was the girls she was shaking hands with now.

They were *so* adult, in lipgloss, low cut tops, tight jeans. Was this how quickly girls grew up in the States?

'Gosh, you're so grown-up!' she couldn't help telling the older one – who was it again? – Sarah.

'Well, I am about to turn 16—' This said with an undoubtedly teenage defiance.

Dennis heard his daughter's words and glanced at Eve, who was flushing up with an emotion he took to be shock, even as she turned to the younger girl to shake hands. *Sixteen!* she was screaming in her head as she managed 'Hello, nice to meet you', to Louisa.

Sixteen. Wasn't Sarah just exactly the age her lost baby would have been?

Sixteen. Didn't that mean this girl was already on the way when Dennis left?

Sixteen. So Susan was pregnant when Dennis left Eve?

Susan? Susan? Her mind was like some demented search engine racing through data all on its own and *ping*! Up came the answer. Susan Mitchell, the financial director of one of Dennis's favourite clients . . . Well, that's what she was back then. Eve looked over at the blond helmet head and couldn't believe she hadn't recognized her straight away. Why was Susan pretending not to know her? This was completely bizarre.

'Hmmm?' Louisa was looking at her as though she expected an answer.

'How old is your little girl?' Louisa repeated.

'Oh . . . Anna, she's nine, going on nineteen. Come and say hello.'

Denny and Tom were chatting to Dennis and Susan. They were laughing, sounding polite, interested. This was not the moment to ask about her ex-husband's infidelity with his current wife.

She put her fingers up to her burning cheeks and felt tears forming at the back of her eyes. Fuck him though. Why hadn't he told her this before? Why had he left her to figure it out and muddle through the shock?

She knelt down to speak to Robbie, who was still clinging like a limpet to her legs. She hoped to stay down there for a few minutes, until she could pull herself together to deal with this.

'Hi, are you OK?' she asked her son.

'I don't like that man,' he said.

'Which man?'

'That old man—' he pointed at Dennis. It was almost impossible to hide any emotion at all from a small child. They had in-built radar for this kind of thing.

She wasn't going to ask why, but Robbie blurted his reasons out anyway: 'He looks like the Fat Controller and he makes me sad.'

'What can I get you to drink?' Dennis tapped her on the shoulder.

'*Go away!* You fat man,' Robbie yelled at him.

351

'Errrrrrr . . . Robbie, stop that.' She wanted to laugh – and cry. This was appalling. Why did she feel as if her life, the one she'd carefully constructed for herself over the past sixteen years, was falling apart? Why the hell did Dennis still have this effect on her? Like he was always able to be the one in control? The one who could wind her, wound her, still pull the rug out from underneath her? Fuck, this still hurt. All those days, long evenings, even longer nights waiting for him to call, come home, get in touch. All the tears she had shed for him, for the baby she should have had fifteen, sixteen years ago now. It felt as if it was all opening up again. FUCK. Like a seam, ping, ping, ping, she could almost hear the stitches.

'I think a drink would help.' Dennis's voice now.

'Maybe several . . . maybe you could line them up along the bar for me.' She tried to sound breezy but he knew she knew, had worked it out.

'We'll have to talk all about this some time. I should have given you a better explanation.'

'Aha,' she agreed.

'*Go away*,' Robbie ordered again. Then to Eve and Dennis's surprise, he sank his teeth into Dennis's thigh.

'Ouch!' Dennis said quite loudly. No wonder. It bloody hurt when Robbie bit you.

'Robbie!' Eve admonished him. She knelt down beside him again, feeling flushed and horribly embarrassed.

'I don't like him!' Robbie yelled, then smacked her quite suddenly in the face.

'Robbie, NO.' Wasn't it fun being part of the transition generation? She thought, not for the first time in her life, we are the people who get hit by our parents *and* our children.

Robbie burst into noisy tears, but fortunately Tom was there and whisked his little brother outside before it all became a hideous scene.

And somehow they stumbled on through it. Eve making small talk with Susan, both of them pretending not to recognize each other. Talking about the States and how much London had changed.

Denny and Dennis talking about the States and how much London had changed, as far as she could gather from the snatches she overheard, and the girls in a little huddle. When Eve passed her daughter, long blond ponytail bobbing animatedly, she thought how sweet Anna looked trying to fit in with the big girls and she couldn't help tuning in.

'You've been in rehab? Cool. I got some therapy when my mum and dad split up, but rehab? You actually got to stay there, full time. *Cool*. I want to be a psychiatrist when I grow up,' Anna was saying.

Oh God, this was terrifying.

Walking back towards this weird family grouping, she saw Dennis put his arm round Susan's waist to give her a reassuring squeeze and Susan turned to smile at him. Just a tiny thing, it surprised her. Up until now, she thought she'd have to feel sorry for anyone with the misfortune to be married to Dennis, but when she caught that little moment, she knew they were actually in love. Well, wasn't that one of life's little ironies? Dennis the deserter was the one who'd ended up in a long and happy marriage. She'd never wanted to be like her dad, a long-term single, settling into her own eccentric little groove. But that was exactly where she was headed. Even Dennis had someone who loved him. Wasn't she worthy of that? Oh hell . . . she swirled the ice round her glass . . . two gin and tonics and I'm a bloody wreck.

When Dennis suggested dinner in the hotel's restaurant, she told him no, it wasn't suitable, she wanted to go somewhere more relaxed, nearby, and she'd already made the reservation.

That surprised him – and her. But she'd made a resolution earlier that day that she was not going to let him push her about. He was only here for a short time, but too bad. She was her own person, nothing to do with him any more.

At the restaurant, she felt like an observer, rather than one of the group taking part in this odd event.

She watched her sons, eagerly polite and curious about Dennis. And saw how even Anna wasn't impressed with how sulky and sullen the teen daughters were being to their parents. Fortunately Robbie was given a balloon. He didn't worry about how anyone was interacting with anyone else, he simply ran about making train noises until he was so exhausted, he fell asleep on Eve's lap.

Eve focused on her little girl, so ladylike, so wishing she was a grown-up and yet so nine-ish at the same time.

She watched her unfold the napkin, put it across her lap and eat her pasta elegantly with a fork and spoon, wiping her lips whenever the pink sauce strayed.

The American girls stuck gum to their side plates before eating and whispered conspiratorially before trotting off to the toilets together. Rehab or not, Anna was less and less impressed with them.

And Dennis was starting to bray now: 'Well, I'm hoping to send the girls to medical school. If they ever open a book and think about passing an exam, that is.' On cue, the girls looked at each other and rolled their eyes. 'Only way to make money in the States, as far as I can tell,' Dennis continued. 'Doctors . . .' Blah, blah, Eve tried not to listen.

'Are you OK?' she asked Anna.

'Yeah, fine,' Anna answered. 'It's all very interesting,' she added in a whisper.

'Aha.'

'It'll never be like this with my dad though, will it?' she asked now.

'You mean, not see him for years and years? No, sweetpea, your dad and I are friends and we both love you very much.'

'I think Daddy's still in love with you,' Anna said matter-of-factly, pushing another forkful into her mouth.

'What makes you think that this time?' Eve asked with a smile.

'Because I could tell he was really sad when you came back from Grandpa's and it was time for him to go home.'

'Ah ha.'

'And I told him you always slept in his old pyjamas and he said that was sweet.'

'I don't sleep in his pyjamas!'

'I know, but I just wondered what his reaction would be.'

'Anna!'

'And Michelle makes him very grumpy. We never have a laugh when she's around.'

'Ah ha.' This she could believe, but she didn't think it had anything to do with him being in love with her.

'And . . .' Anna was getting ready for the big one now: 'There's a picture of you in a little frame hidden under the jumpers in his cupboard.' Never mind that Anna had put it there, her dad had never removed it, she'd checked every time she went up.

'Well . . . that's very nice,' Eve said. 'But you really shouldn't be looking through Daddy's cupboards and as I said, we're good friends,

356

Anna, and we both love you, that's the main thing.'

After that, Eve tried to carry on eating and behaving normally, but it was no use. *I am so pathetic*, she told herself. 'Why is my heart pounding like a teenager's over a photo in his jumper pile? I am a pathetic, sad and lonely old bag, I really need to get a life. I need to go out with the vet immediately. And why do I keep calling him "the vet"? Nils . . . Nils.' Thoughts of Nils . . . Did they help?'

When they got home, there were about eight messages on the answering machine from Jen.

'For God's sake woman . . . I don't care how late it is, get your children into bed, pour yourself another glass of wine and phone me back. I want to know all about it.'

'How are you feeling?' Jen asked her, when she'd heard Eve tell it all right from arriving at the hotel down to the very last detail of the evening.

'I'm still furious with him,' Eve said. 'But I hardly think it's worth telling him now. I don't want to go there, get involved, be fighting with my ex. But I certainly don't want him to come back and play the big glamorous daddy-figure when he's been so absent for all these years. I don't want the boys to like him!' she blurted out. 'I know that's unreasonable and it's only fair for them to want to get to know him . . . blah . . . blah . . . But actually, I just wanted: Dennis comes back, it's obvious to everyone what a big shit he is, Dennis goes away again.

'And how come I was never told about his wife? About the fact that she was pregnant when he left us? That was quite an important thing he left out there.'

'He's a prat,' Jen reminded her. 'He thinks about himself almost all of the time. We know all this, Eve. But I have to say, I'm so looking forward to meeting him.'

'What?'

'At the wedding! There is still going to be a wedding, isn't there?'

'As far as I know – but what do I know? I didn't even know about my ex-husband's other woman. God! I was supposed to be the one who was so together and I feel totally undermined.'

'Because you haven't got a husband?' Jen asked with some indignation.

'Maybe . . . or a glamorous job . . . or any sort of fuck-off lifestyle to show off.'

'EVE!!! I just can't believe I'm hearing this from you! You had nothing. He left you with two little kids and nothing else. You've done it all yourself, so please stop having a wobble.'

There was a small silence before Jen burst out again: 'I can't believe he still has this effect on you. Hello!!! You know, I might have to pretend you didn't say any of these things and you'll wake up again in the morning the woman I know and love. The woman who can grow her own potatoes, find fifty-five different ways to cook them, answer A-level algebra questions, have sex in the lotus position, and still hold down a full-time job.'

Eve had to laugh at this: 'Sex in the lotus position!'

'Try it. It's a challenge,' Jen cackled back at her, then added: 'You're going to be fine, you silly moo. Call the vet.'

'No, no. I couldn't.'

'Call the vet,' Jen said again.

'It's Nils. Why do we keep calling him the vet?'

'I don't know, it sounds much dirtier. What's Dennis's wife like anyway?'

'She's OK . . . she's the kind of wife Dennis should have: businesslike, groomed, confident, runs her own company . . . has driven her daughters to drugs,' she couldn't help adding, a tiny bit gleefully.

'Really?'

'Well, I don't know. Anna said they've been in rehab, but for all I know, it could have been chocolate addiction, you know Americans. I'm being a bitch, I've only just met these people.'

'Are you glad it's not you? Married to Dennis, living in the States, running your own company and whatever else?'

'Yes,' Eve said, without having to think about it.

'Well, that's OK then. He hurt you all really badly but it's turned out OK.'

'You're right,' Eve said finally. 'I think we're doing a good job.'

'We're doing the best we can. What more is there?'

There was a pause in which they both smiled and felt the warmth of each other's affection, acknowledged each other's support over the years, through the happy times and through the really tough times.

'What are you wearing to the wedding?' Jen asked then.

'Oh wait till you see it!'

'When?'

So they made their arrangements to meet up and finally said good night.

Eve tiptoed into the children's room and smoothed covers, patted hair and kissed cheeks.

Anna had fallen asleep with her book open in her hand: it was her well-worn copy of *Families and How to Survive Them*. Eve had to smile at that. She gently eased it out and put it down on the bedside table.

She went into the kitchen and did her chores, then made tea. In a life full of little rituals, this was one of Eve's favourites: the gentle *whump* the tea caddy lids made when she pushed up the latches with her thumb, ahhhhhh, the smell of the tea – her own mix, two-thirds Earl Grey, one part Darjeeling – the rustle of the leaves when she dug in, and the clank of the spoon as she stirred the boiling brew round her favourite old teapot.

When the cup was poured – yes a little blue and white porcelain *cup*, with saucer and teaspoon, for private tea drinking – she took it through to her bedroom, turned on the gentle orangey sidelight and got undressed, letting her clothes fall into a heap at her feet until she was naked.

It wasn't a bad body for 42, little breasts with solid nipples, a stomach with soft skin but firm muscles underneath. She ran her hand down from her belly button to the quiff of hair on her pubic bone and twirled it in her fingers for a moment. Mummy muff . . . that still made her smile.

She opened the door of her wardrobe now and took out the dress she had chosen for Tom and Deepa's wedding. She slid it off the hanger and smoothed it over her head down onto her naked body.

It was perfect. A below the knee, cream coloured, crocheted dress. Pure 1970s with sleeves that flared out from the elbow and an on the bias thing going on which made it slither over her hips and thighs. It was secondhand of course, vintage in fact. From the kind of shop she popped into on the odd occasion to buy presents: cutesy little handbags, brooches or scarves.

It was the first time she'd bought a dress there. A whole dress. But this was her son's wedding after all. They'd also kitted her out with a big floppy straw hat and a crocheted bag. She had just the right shoes, which she strapped on before taking a long look at herself in the mirror. It was just what she wanted, Faye Dunaway with pink highlights.

This was how the dress should be worn, with nothing underneath. But when she'd shown it to Anna like this, there had been a horrified reaction: *'Mum!! Nipple alert, nipple alert!'*

So she would wear glossy beige underwear underneath. One didn't want to upstage the bride by causing any sort of nipple sensation.

She couldn't help herself from thinking that she could get married in this dress . . . this was the perfect outfit for foxy forty-somethings to take their vows.

Oh listen to me . . . Did she really think she'd be a bride again, fall for that romantic dream? Only youth and optimism, like Deepa and Tom, could go for that now. Well, well, sip of tea. Stop being so bleak. Who knows what lies around the corner? Didn't life always throw up the biggest surprises just when she thought she knew exactly what was ahead?

Chapter Thirty-One

Eve was finding it hard to resist touching the sculpted buttock moving up and down within arm's reach of her face. The muscle tone was incredible: curved, hollowed, sinewed with steel. That was lap-dancing for you, night after night of doing squats in high heels, you got the bottom of an Olympian Greek.

'Don't let her sit on your skirt,' Tom was shouting in her ear, in an effort to be heard above the belting music: 'You'll never get the fake tan off.'

'You do the money thing . . .' Eve shouted back, 'I'm too nervous.'

'Na-ah. You have to do that. I'm a married man . . . almost.' Tom grinned at her and took a drag on his cigar. *Cigar?* How much had they drunk for Tom to be smoking a cigar?

There was a glass of something pink and pretty in her hand. She took a sip and had

absolutely no idea what it was, but . . . gorgeous.
She took another sip.

The dancer's long fake brown legs were on
either side of her knees now and she was shaking
a minuscule triangle of sparkle bikini in front of
Eve's face. Eyes fixed on this little silver triangle,
Eve wondered if she should really have accepted
an invitation to Tom's stag night.

'It'll be cool, Mum,' he'd assured her. 'Everyone's coming.'

Everyone consisted of about three tables full of
a very eclectic crowd: young Tom-types from
work, medical student friends of Deepa's and
then a lot of 'Tom-friends' – the office sandwich
lady, a variety of neighbours, that kind of thing.
His wedding was going to be very interesting.

She slipped a rolled-up tenner into the
dancer's hand rather than her bra or stocking top
or . . . well . . . anywhere else. And now Denny
was asking her if she was OK and she felt as if
she was answering in slow motion.

'I'll be fine . . . drunk a bit too much.' She tried
to smile but her face didn't seem to want to obey
instructions.

'Dennis. Now he's a bit of a wanker,' Denny
said and took a big swig from his glass.

She put hers down on the table and told herself
once more not to pick it up again. 'So you spotted
that then,' she said.

Denny sent a wobbling smoke ring up into the
air above them.

'Well. I don't know . . . I hardly know the

guy. He's very into his work, isn't he?'

'Who is?' Tom leaned into the conversation now, breathing cigar smoke all over them.

'Dennis,' Eve explained, trying not to cough.

Tom launched straight into the booming Dennis voice he'd been rehearsing: 'Boys, things are so hot for me right now – look out. Don't touch . . . smokin'. I'm moving into so many new markets, I can't keep track of them all.' Tom waggled his cigar and winked.

'And Mum,' he added, 'will you please just tell him where to get off when he starts annoying you? You don't have to sit there and take it for us, OK?'

'Right.' She was glad of the blessing.

'What *exactly* does he do?' she asked then, shouting it into both of their ears in turn.

'No idea,' said Denny as Tom shrugged his shoulders. 'Financial services . . . consulting . . . Tom and I talked to him all evening about his work and we're still none the wiser.'

'Do you think you'll go and visit him some time? In the States?' Eve wanted to know.

'Yes,' Denny replied.

'Definitely,' from Tom.

'But please don't move there.' She grabbed for both their arms and bit her lip so that she didn't burst into drunken babbling tears.

'Shall I get you some water or Coke or something?' Denny asked her. 'You're looking a bit funny.'

'Water's a good idea,' she said.

So Denny got up, leaving her snuggled against Tom. She waved his cigar smoke away and asked: 'Still happy about marriage?'

'Yeah . . . I think so,' he grinned at her. 'The wedding's going to be great. Deepa has everything planned down to the most annoyingly tiny detail. I would quite like to turn up on an elephant or something mad just to surprise her.'

'Please, not an elephant!' Eve said. 'I won't be able to get Robbie away from it. But, Tom . . . marriage?' she had to ask. 'You're definitely ready for the big M?' It was only four days away now. She had to be sure he was sure.

'I think so,' Tom replied, smiling at her seriousness. 'Hey – if we don't like it we can always get divorced.' Waggle of cigar.

'You're just saying that.' She felt a bit shocked . . . but in a way, why shouldn't he see it like that?

'Well, yes and no . . . nothing ventured, nothing gained, Mum.' And then he surprised her with: 'So, why didn't you and Joseph get married?'

She tried to shrug the question off: 'Oh . . . I don't know. Just as well. I'd be a double divorcee now, wouldn't I?' *Would I? Should we have? Nothing ventured, nothing gained . . .*

Denny came back with a tray of bottled water and glasses just in time to hear Tom say: 'I always imagined myself happily partnered up with children, at some point, so maybe that's why I don't feel too freaked out about it.'

How had she imagined the future? she

wondered. She'd always said she didn't like what Joseph was growing into, but what had she expected? Him not to grow up at all, not to make the slightest change from his 22-year-old self?

'Have I told you about my promotion?' Tom had their full attention now. 'Yeah – it's great. I'm going to take charge of a new system we're developing *and* I'm getting a profit share if it takes off.' Big, excited grin.

'Oh my God,' Denny was groaning. 'You're not only going to be married before me, you're now going to be a multimillionaire as well. I can't cope with this.'

He laid his head on the table and pretended to cry.

'Den! It's just another little step up the ladder, really.'

Denny lifted his head and held out a hand for his brother to shake: 'Mate, I'm really pleased for you, honestly. Now can you and your ever expanding wife please think about getting a new home, so I can buy you out of your old one?'

'Yeah, that's the next plan . . . And not in Chingford either. I think we're sticking with Hackney. We both like it there, so why change? We're a bit young to go out to the burbs.'

'He's so grown-up, Mum.' Denny lit a cigarette as consolation. 'At this rate, Anna will be married before me.'

'Anna!!! Married!' Eve laughed, and took a deep sip of water. She was feeling a bit better already.

'The poor man,' she added. 'You realize he'll have to undergo three years of analysis with the shrink of her choice before she'll be able to agree.'

'Has Patricia ever been in touch?' she asked then, hoping her little adventure with Denny's girlfriend had never come to light.

'Pretty Patsy and the head of her modelling agency are currently holidaying in his yacht off the coast of Sardinia.'

'Do you miss her?'

'Not really, it's just that I always imagined myself with my own modelling agency and yacht.'

'Poor Denny.' Eve laughed and reached over to stroke his head, which was back down on the table again. 'It's OK. The girl in the silver bikini is heading this way again.'

Chapter Thirty-Two

They bumped along in the Peugeot through the open gate and into the bright green field. Anna and Robbie were giggling with excitement on the back seat, but Eve was worrying about her boxfuls of food in the boot and willing them to have survived the journey.

She'd expected a field, but this was just perfect. The perfect field! Close cropped emerald grass, eye-wincing sunlight . . . She followed the rope fence into the parking area, trying to tear her gaze from the adorable pink and blue marquee, the wooden open air dance floor decorated with bunting, plastic palm trees and big bunches of flowers.

Up on the brow of the hill, 300 or so yards away, seats were set out in a big semicircle, ready for the service.

The sky was blue, there wasn't a breath of wind, it was only 12 noon but it was obvious the weather was going to be superb.

Once she was parked, Denny bounded out of the tent to meet her.

'Mum! Hello! The fridge is misbehaving, Deepa's having "practice contractions" or something, no-one has any idea where Tom is . . . Otherwise it's all perfect!' He gave her a little kiss on the forehead as Anna and Robbie tore past them to go and check out the venue.

'What?!! What do you mean no-one knows where Tom is?' was her reaction to this spate of news.

'Well, we don't. He wasn't in the flat when I got up this morning. His mobile is off. I can't get hold of him and neither can Deepa.'

Denny gave a little shrug: 'We're not worrying about it just yet, OK. We've still got—' he glanced at his watch, 'hours.'

'I've got all the stuff in the boot. And what else does Deepa want us to do?' Eve asked.

'I have my instruction book.' Denny took a thick roll of typed pages out of his back pocket and smoothed it open. 'See!'

She saw pages and pages of information along with sketches of where to put flowers, how to arrange chairs, where to tie ribbons . . .

'She was here earlier doing the cake and folding millions of napkins, but now she's gone home for a rest,' he explained.

'Was she worried about Tom?'

'Not really, but it's hard to tell with her. She's like a mad thing about the wedding anyway. Are you worried?' he asked.

'*Very* . . . Can I borrow your phone?'

'Yup, but let me take these.' He started to unload all the boxes and Tupperware dishes from the boot of the car.

'Is the fridge going to be OK? Otherwise, I should take them back – or we should think of something else.'

'I think it'll be OK.'

She felt nervous, fussy, slightly crazed . . . realized this was mother of the groom nerves with bells on because the groom was AWOL.

She punched in Tom's number and clicked through to his voicemail. For a moment, she hesitated about what to say: 'Tom, this is your mother. Will you please phone us? Or at least phone Deepa . . . just let us know that everything is OK.'

Then she hung up, wondering if she should have been a bit sterner. What was he doing? Trying to give everybody a heart attack?

She made her way to the beautiful tent, all Barbie-pink, draped and dreamy inside with fairytale spindly gilt tables and chairs.

'Oh, it's wonderful,' she told Denny, still fluttering with nerves that Tom was going to blow this whole thing apart.

Rows and rows of champagne glasses were lined up beside cutlery and vivid pink napkins. All the tables were decked with little gold stars, trails of glitter and big, messy flower arrangements – bright pink roses scrambled in with sunflowers and a tangle of ivy.

371

Deepa's touches were everywhere: in the kitschy paper windmills dotted about, the sari-clad Asian Barbie kissing a T-shirted Ken on the enormous white and pink cake. It was fabulous and, more importantly, it was so *them*. They were going to get the wedding they had wanted . . . so long as Tom turned up.

Anna and Robbie were already racing up and down the wooden floor holding hands, pretending to dance.

'What else can I do?' Eve asked Denny.

'Not a lot. We've been here since 8a.m. We just need Tom.' He gave what he hoped was a re-assuring smile. 'Come and see the view from the hilltop.'

He took his mother and the two children up the path to the semicircle of chairs set out for the ceremony. It was a small hill on their side, but from the top the land fell away steeply on the other side and a great carpet of landscape opened out in front of them with dark green woods, small villages, church spires, red roofs. In the strong sunshine, they could have been in Italy; this was how beautiful Kent could be, occasionally.

'Oh wow,' she said. 'I'm going to cry already and it's still four hours to go.'

'I know, me too,' Denny smiled.

'Is Tom OK?' she asked him. 'Did you see him last night?'

'Yeah, he went out with some friends and

came in just after eleven. He seemed fine . . . normal. Well, nervous, but OK.'

Denny put an arm round her and she forced a smile.

'Maybe we should just go home, get dressed up and be back here nice and early. I'm sure he'll turn up – in his wedding jeans.'

'*No!*'

'I've no idea. He's kept his wedding outfit very quiet.'

'Not much else we can do,' she agreed, and taking in the dark circles under her son's eyes, she added: 'You really need some sleep, Denny.'

'I know . . . but not today.'

'Do you really think he'll turn up?'

'Yeah. Why not? They're a good couple. I hope it works out for them.' So casual. Kind and genuine, but casual. What more could you say at weddings these days? You hoped it worked out, at least for a while, and that they made each other happy, at least for a while, and that if they divorced – which was at best 60/40 at any wedding, now – you hoped they would be amicable and have some really good times to remember.

'Mum, why isn't the vet invited?' Denny asked as they headed down the hill.

'Ah . . . It's too big a day really . . . And we're . . . I think we're on a go-slow,' was the best explanation she could come up with. 'I've had too much other stuff going on, really.'

373

'I see,' Denny said, but he felt a bit sad for his mother.

'So, who am I sitting beside?' Eve asked. 'Joseph, by any chance? Has Anna nobbled the seating arrangements yet?'

'No, no. You're beside Deepa's very attractive, mature, *single* uncle. I have no idea what that's about,' Denny smiled.

'Neither do I, I'm sure.'

Back at home, in between washing down children, ironing outfits, polishing shoes and fiddling with her hair, she kept trying Tom's mobile. No reply. Just voicemail. It was hard to know what to leave: stern messages? Sympathetic messages? She left both, then decided to speak to Deepa.

But her mother answered the phone and told Eve that Deepa was asleep.

'Is she OK? Not worried at all?' Eve clucked.

'Worried? No? She's very happy, very relaxed. What's to worry about?'

Hmmm. That either meant all was well on the Tom front, or that Deepa hadn't shared the information that her fiancé was nowhere to be found.

'I hate my hair!' Anna returned from the bathroom where she'd gone to inspect her bridesmaid's ribbon-trimmed bun looking dangerously tearful.

'Well what do you want? I'll try and do it whichever way you like.'

'Just a ponytail. Nothing fancy.'

374

'Are you sure Deepa won't mind? She asked me to do it the other way.'

'I don't care.' Big sulky huffy face. 'It's bad enough having to wear this stupid sari.'

'You look adorable in the sari,' Eve fibbed. Fuchsia pink and gold had turned out to be a very bad choice for Anna. She looked like a vampire victim.

It was one o'clock, time to cram into the car, crank the fan on full blast against the heat and head back to the wedding venue again, praying that Tom would show up.

When they arrived, there was only one other car already in the parking area – Denny's. But as they climbed out, she could see Denny, all handsome and suited, coming down the field towards them, waving.

'He's here!' she made out. 'Wait till you see him!'

They hurried along to the other side of the marquee, directed by Denny.

'Oh Tom!' was her first reaction.

'Aaaaaargh!' Anna gave a half-scream.

Her son was standing in front of them in a white, high-collared Teddy boy suit with a blue frothy shirt and the first short back and sides haircut he'd had since he was 13. He looked amazing. Transformed. And he knew it. He was grinning at them.

'Sorry, Mum,' he said, giving her a big smile and then a hug. 'I didn't mean to freak everybody out. I just looked at myself in the mirror this

375

morning in the outfit I was going to wear and thought "nah". This is major. I'm going to get married. I'm going to be a dad. I need change.'

'All this time I've been panicking about you, you've been shopping and having your hair cut!!'

'Well, I was thinking too. Walking and walking . . . thinking.'

'And what have you thought?' She was trying to be stern but you couldn't with Tom, he was young, a bit daft, but so kind at heart.

'I think it's going to be cool.'

'Cool? Cool?! Well so long as it's going to be cool . . . that's all right then.' Her arms were crossed and she still didn't feel she'd had the satisfaction of being angry with him.

'And I've rewritten all my wedding vows. Everyone's going to blub, guaranteed.'

'No way,' Anna told him. 'It's all sentimental guff.'

'Anna! You believe in all that stuff! Don't even try and pretend that you don't. Anyway, isn't Mum looking fantastic?' Tom said.

'I'm very grumpy with you,' Eve replied. 'Don't try and wriggle out of it.'

'You're gorgeous,' he smiled at her. 'I *luuurve* what you're doing to your hair!'

Anna and Robbie giggled and it was no use, she was going to have to cool down and let Tom off.

This was his wedding day after all.

'Come on . . . time for the first bottle of the day.' Denny went to raid the marquee fridge.

What they managed to chat and joke about as they picnicked in the sunshine on the grass – polishing off the sandwiches, fruit and cake Eve had brought, along with two icy bottles of champagne – she couldn't remember.

Well, apart from Tom's: 'Egg sandwiches! Mum! I can't eat them . . . the groom can't have egg breath.'

'It's OK. I came prepared,' Anna had told him, fishing in her big black rucksack. 'I have Tic-Tacs just for you.'

She watched her four children laughing and teasing each other, her heart feeling like it might actually burst with pride, and tried to push away the thought that this was an ending. The next time they had a family picnic, Deepa and her baby would be there to share it. That was nice, not sad, surely? So why was it making her feel so upset?

The first guest to arrive, shortly after 3p.m. was Joseph. He pulled up in his silly little car, which she didn't think suited him at all. He was too tall for it. He boinged out like a character in a pop-up book, dressed in white linen and alone . . . by the look of things. He was smiling at them, waving and carrying a big, wrapped parcel, which he hugged up against his chest as Anna hurtled into him.

Eve looked at Robbie, who hadn't run down to meet him but was standing up on the rug then jumping up and down with excitement.

'That's my daddy, Jofus, that's my daddy, Jofus,' he was saying over and over again, which was cracking them all up.

Joseph kissed everyone, even Denny and Tom, and Robbie was scooped up for a hug. 'So, how are you Tom?' Joseph asked.

'I'm cool.'

'Of course. Very. Love the shirt . . . And how's the missus?'

'Fine . . . about three and a half weeks to go, we're cutting it a bit fine. But she's great.'

He handed over the parcel and before Tom took it off to the marquee, Joseph added: 'There's another little present I want to talk to you about, when we get a moment . . . before the service, OK?'

'OK, you really shouldn't have, you know.'

'Yes I should!'

Joseph sat down on the rug beside them, Anna tucked under one arm, Robbie coming over to play with his shoelaces.

'So Evie, the first one is flying the nest. How are you coping?' He was smiling at her. And she was trying hard not to notice how well he looked.

'I'm fine, absolutely fine. Just don't make me cry again. I may as well not have bothered with make-up.'

'Where's Michelle?' Denny asked. 'Is she OK?'

378

'Errrm . . . lots of apologies, but she couldn't make it. She's put her back out.'

'Oh, poor thing. What did she do?' Eve hoped this sounded sincere, but really she couldn't have been more relieved that Michelle wasn't coming.

'Oh . . . at the gym or something,' Joseph batted the question away and patted Anna's hair. 'You look lovely,' he told her.

'D'you like it?' she smiled. 'I'm Deepa's mini me.'

They laughed at this.

'So . . . I'm looking forward to meeting Dennis.' Joseph turned to Eve and gave her a smile.

'Ah ha!' she said. 'Well, you'll have to tell me what you think.'

He nodded at her and raised his eyebrows.

A convoy of cars was heading for the field now. It was time to fold up the picnic rug, brush themselves down and start the ceremonies.

Eve wanted to give Tom one last hug and sidled up to him.

'Well, this is it, then . . .' She stroked the newly shorn hair at the back of his neck. He looked into her brimming eyes.

'Are you ready?' she asked.

'Yeah.' He put a hand on her shoulder and drew her in for a hug. 'Are *you* ready?' he asked back.

'I think so,' she managed, her cheek pressed tightly against his jacket. 'I'm so proud of you,' she told him. 'Sorry,' she sniffed, 'I didn't realize how hard this was going to be.'

'You'll be fine,' he told her.

'Yes. We love you,' she said.

'Love you too,' he said and gave her a blokeish pat on the back.

Then it was time to mingle, welcome the guests and show people to their seats. Jen and her husband Ryan were walking up the hill towards them with Terry and John in tow.

'My God, your boys look gorgeous,' Eve said as Jen hugged her. 'And I love your hat.'

'How are you coping, you old bag?' Jen asked. 'You look like you've been blubbing all afternoon.'

'Do I? Oh no.'

'No – no, just joking.' What was she doing inducing further panic in the mother of the groom? 'You look fantastic,' Jen corrected herself, 'and this is just amazing.' Then she caught a glimpse of the groom. 'Look at Tom! My God! I can't believe it!'

'*Eve!!!*' And now, here was Janie. A radiant, tanned, back from her solo holiday to South America Janie. And David beside her looking relaxed and happy . . . and the kids – they looked appalling! But Eve thought that was good to see. Christine was in the all-black Goth uniform with eyeliner 14-year-olds should be entitled to and Rick was entering the phase Tom had just said goodbye to . . . long hair, falling down jeans and 'Hardcore' plastered over his T-shirt.

The important thing was, Janie had let them

come like this. Everyone looked happy. This was so good.

She gave her sister a big hug.

'How are you bearing up?' Janie asked.

'Oh, I'm a mess. You have to sit next to me so you can pinch me when I start snivelling.'

'Dad is on his way up the hill,' Janie added in a funny sort of wait and see voice.

'Oh God, does he need any help?'

'No, no, no . . . Look here is, with his *laydee friend, Martha!*' Janie stage-whispered.

Eve turned to see her father, almost within earshot of them now, looking like some ageing English screen star, all buttonhole, suit and bright white shirt. On his arm was a curvaceous, dazzling blonde who could hardly have been a day over 60.

'Met at the hospital, apparently,' Janie explained.

'No!!' Eve was stunned.

'Evelyn!' Her father had spotted them. 'Got someone here who'd love to meet you. Martha – she wants to do a bit of yoga, you know.'

Eve kissed her dad and wanted to start on a list of questions but . . .

'*Is that Dennis!!!!????*' came Janie's frantic whisper now.

Eve turned to look and nodded.

'Hello, Dennis, Susan . . . come and say hello to Janie and her family.'

It was all perfectly restrained and civilized, lots of polite handshakes and 'Good to see yous' exchanged. Eve and Janie exchanging surreptitious glances and waggling eyebrows at each other. Their father making a reasonable effort to hide his disapproval of this man.

Eve thought it was funny how surprisingly English Dennis and his family looked. Morning suit for him, lime green taffeta and hat for her. She thought almost two decades of living abroad would have de-Anglicized them a bit.

Their teenage daughters had cleavages and legs on display in bright minidresses with matching jackets. They looked ravishing and when she went up to say hello, she could smell clean hair, melon perfume, the juiciness of being 14 and 16.

Finally, everyone was in place and it was time for Deepa to walk slowly, calmly up the path to the top of the hill on her father's arm with Anna following behind.

Eve took long, deep breaths, put a smile on her face and tried not to cry at the first sight of them.

She was in the front row with Denny on one side, Robbie squirming on the other, Janie and her family beside them.

Joseph was in the row behind and Eve imagined that Dennis and his family weren't too far away either.

She tried to keep her eyes on her little son and his stack of wooden trains as Deepa and Tom took their marriage vows and then began their home-made promises to each other. She hoped, with Robbie as a distraction, she would manage to get through it. But every once in a while she looked up and saw Deepa, eyes fixed full beam on Tom, delirious with happiness, and she choked up all over again.

Tom was holding her hand, not letting go of her with his gaze, as he said: 'I'm going to love you, cherish you and honour you, Deepa – as best I can – apparently, it won't always be this easy.'

He got a little audience laugh at this, but continued, so sincerely: 'When things aren't going so well, I promise I'll think of today and remember how we felt.' Down to an almost-whisper, he added: 'Because today is perfect and there is enough love here today to last a lifetime.'

Eve couldn't contain it any more, she began to sob as quietly as she could manage. Robbie and his trains were fading into a tearful blur. *Enough love to last a lifetime . . .* Oh God. She was gasping with the effort of trying to keep her sobs under control. She felt a hand on her shaking shoulder. And she held onto it tightly. Had she once had enough love to last a lifetime? Only to push it away? The thoughts were avalanching in her mind and coming to rest at the realization that maybe this was never going to get any better. She saw now that the hand was Joseph's not Denny's and it made her cry even more. Was she going to regret breaking up with him for the rest of her life?

*   *   *

383

With a lot of pausing and eye wiping, Deepa was trying to get her promises out too and now the pair were kissing over her luminous pink bump to claps and cheers. Eve looked at them, Deepa in sparkly sandals and a mad pink sari – the white satin and froth dress had gone back to the shop – Tom with short hair in a suit. The two of them, barely in their twenties, understood commitment so much better than she ever had. They hadn't *changed* for each other but they had worked out that they had to grow towards each other, be prepared to meet in the middle. Or else there was no choice but to grow apart.

With her handbag full of hankies, she started a tear-stemming operation and managed to stand up, clap and smile.

'They're going to be good, aren't they?' Joseph was saying behind her.

She turned and smiled at him: 'Yeah, they are.'

'Are you OK?' he asked.

'I'm fine. Fine. Honestly,' she smiled, broke the eye contact and looked away.

And then she was caught up in the wedding whirl . . . photos and confetti throwing and the noise of 100-odd guests greeting, talking, congratulating. Amidst all this hubbub, Eve managed to get to Deepa and Tom as well.

'You cried, didn't you?' Tom asked her over the hug. 'You gushed.'

'Yes, I did, darling. It was beautiful.'

'Look at my ring!' Deepa, an arm round her new husband, was telling her. 'Look at it! This is what Tom pulled out of his pocket to marry me with, I nearly had a heart attack! I can't get it on my fat fingers but it's gorgeous!'

Eve looked at the outstretched hand: three substantial diamonds were strung across her pinkie on the daintiest of bands.

'That is lovely,' she agreed . . . and way out of Tom's budget.

'Please tell me you haven't spent the entire flat deposit?' Deepa asked just what Eve was thinking.

'Er . . . no. I've got a little bit of explaining to do on the ring front . . . but you won't be cross. I promise,' he told her as the next wave of relatives came to claim them.

In the marquee, Eve hoisted Robbie up into her arms and looked at the crowd to see who she should talk to next.

'Hey, Robbie, I almost forgot, I've got something for you.' Joseph was coming up to them again. She really didn't want to see him right now, still felt too shaken by the wedding ceremony.

He pulled a little train engine out of his suit pocket and gave it to Robbie.

'Thank you, Daddy Jofus.'

'Oh God,' Joseph groaned. 'That name makes me feel about a hundred and I can't get him to stop using it.'

'Poor Daddy Jofus,' Eve managed to smile.

'Oh, what a lovely couple.' One of Deepa's old

aunties sailed up to them now. 'Look, your outfits even match, and is this your little boy?' Oh God, she meant *them*.

'Yes,' they answered together. Their outfits matched? She looked at his cream suit and supposed they did. He had admired her dress already, but now he took another long look at it.

'Oh, he must bring you so much happiness. How old is he?'

'Three,' Eve replied.

'Is he your first?'

'Ah!' Eve smiled, unsure what to say. The whole saga of how she was the groom's mother, but she and the groom's dad had long parted, and she had two children with Joseph but they'd split up before Robbie was born . . . it all seemed too long and too complicated.

'No, we've a daughter as well,' Joseph said.

'Oh that's lovely. One of each. How lucky. Are you going to have more?' This asked with the cheekiness only ageing aunties can get away with.

'Oh well . . . we'll see.' Joseph again, sparing everyone's blushes.

'I think Deepa wants a boy,' Eve said, hoping to steer the auntie off their case.

'Oh yes. And look at the shape of her. It's a boy all right,' the auntie smiled at them both and then sailed off to accost more innocent victims.

'Is Nils here today?' Joseph asked.

'No . . . he couldn't come, unfortunately,' Eve lied. But this was easier to tell him than the truth and anyway, she wasn't sure she wanted Joseph to know that her most significant relationship since him had broken up so quickly.

'We need to have a chat . . . probably not today,' he added, taking in the sea of guests she had to go and mingle with. 'But I'm moving back to London.'

'Really?'

'Yes . . . the environmentally friendly business projects,' he smiled. 'I'll tell you all about that . . . but what I want you to think about is letting me have the kids two or three nights a week. Shared care.'

'Right.' Oh God, massive step. Two or three nights a week! She wondered if she could do it – and at the same time felt so happy that he wanted to.

'Eve, there you are!' An arm went round her waist and she turned to see Janie. 'Oh Joseph, hello . . . it's been ages.' Janie looked very pleased to see him. 'How are you?'

And was it Eve's imagination or did he squirm slightly at her: 'So you're getting married?'

When Joseph took Robbie off in search of juice, Janie couldn't stop herself from telling her sister: 'He's absolutely lovely. Far better looking than I remember.'

'I know,' Eve said. 'He gets better with age. It's not fair.'

'And he's so good with the kids.'

'Janie!' Eve warned. If Janie was warming up for a 'why did you let that man get away?'

lecture, she'd picked the wrong day. 'Tell me all about your amazing holiday.'

The meal whizzed past, the speeches . . . she had a million people to speak to. Deepa's entire family, not to mention charming Uncle Rani, carefully name-placed beside her for the meal because the bridal couple hadn't been able to help themselves from a bit of optimistic match-making. A psychologist by profession, Rani had wheedled her whole life story out of her – well, that was how it felt – between Robbie distractions.

Now it was time for dancing and Jen was by her side, with a glass of fizz – no non-alcoholic-it's-my-turn-to-drive fruit punch nonsense for her – still wearing her hat, boobs spilling out of something black, silver and tight.

'Your children all look beautiful,' Jen told her. 'And so do you, you skinny cow.'

'Look at you! You're gorgeous, I love you,' Eve smiled, full-on emotional mess now.

The music had begun at sunset and Jen's youngest boy, John, was jiggling alongside Anna on the dance floor. Robbie was copying them from a safe distance.

'Are you all tearful and mother of the groom-y?' Jen put an arm round her.

'Of course. Don't get me started.'

'They're a lovely, lovely couple. I'm sure they're going to be fine.'

'I hope so.'

'That's all we can do, darling, keep hoping.' Jen took a slug from her glass. 'Terry's going to be OK now, I think.'

Terry, 21 now, had been a terrifying teenager, but did seem to finally be calming down.

Jen gave a subtle point in the direction of her smartly turned out older son. 'He's decided to become a plumber,' Jen told her.

'A plumber! Fantastic . . . He'll make more money than a rock star,' Eve laughed.

Lizzie from work came up to them now: 'Your ex-husband, by the way,' she told Eve. 'Total tosser. Your ex-boyfriend – bit of a different story.'

'Yup,' Jen agreed.

Eve was only half listening, she thought she'd heard something about a bamboo roof and a bamboo floor float over from the sound system. She tuned in to it now . . . yup, a song she hadn't heard for years was being played. A silly, silly song Joseph had been obsessed with one summer. She'd never even heard it anywhere else, 'The House of Bamboo': she'd assumed he had some obscure, one-off recording. And now, here he was, smiling at her, taking the glass out of her hand and pulling her onto the dance floor: 'For old times' sake.' *For old times' sake?* What was that supposed to mean? 'Did you bring this record?' she asked him.

'No. Nothing to do with me.' This was true. He'd been just as surprised to hear the song as she had.

It was the verse which rhymed 'magazine, oh' with 'cappuccino'. She'd forgotten how silly it was, hadn't thought about it for years but now found she knew all the words, including all the 'dum dum di dum' bits.

Anna and Robbie were already dancing, and Deepa and Tom. Even Denny and a girl she didn't know were headed for the floor.

She, Joseph and her children couldn't help singing along and doing all the stupid moves they'd made up that summer. Other dancers held back for a moment, aware this was a family thing, but they were waved to join in.

In the end, the DJ played the song three times in a row. Later, he would give the record back to Anna, who would pack it away in her rucksack without mentioning anything to anyone.

During the song, Eve kept her eyes on Anna and Robbie and laughed with them – anything not to think about the hand on hers, on her shoulder, round her waist. Joseph pulled her in, pushed her away again in a sort of jivey thing . . . *do do dee do*. Whenever she dared to meet his eyes, they were fixed on hers.

She couldn't know that at some point during the dinner Joseph had looked for her and seen her talking and laughing with Deepa's uncle, as she spooned food into Robbie's mouth. Joseph had watched her hands, small but strong, short gardener's nails, one gripped round the thigh of their son as she held him on her lap, the other balancing the spoon expertly. He'd looked long and hard at those hands and had a feeling of calm, of coming to his senses as he'd realized with total clarity that Eve, Anna and Robbie were the loves of his life. Everything else was just bollocks. Now all he had to do was make her see it that way.

'All warmed up?' the DJ's voice boomed from the speakers. 'Then it's time to salsa.'

Eve and Joseph had slowed to a stop. She thought she should probably stop dancing with him now because she was feeling so ridiculously flustered.

'Shall we?' he asked. He hadn't let go of her yet.

'I only salsa with Jen.' This sounded so breathless, she was starting to blush.

'Why?'

'I always lead.'

The music was pumping up, warm and irresistible. Only a strip of gold and pink sunlight remained on the edge of the velvet blue sky so the dance floor was growing darker, more secretive, lit only by a row of flaming torches.

He pulled her closer and together they stepped back down into the throng. 'So, lead me,' was all he said, but the words so close to her ear, his body so close to hers, his neck almost touching her face . . . What was he trying to do to her?

'I'm sorry, Joe.' She broke out of his hold. 'I really need a drink . . . to cool down.' She turned and walked away as quickly as she could, hoped he wasn't following.

From the safety of the bar, she watched the dancers. Deepa was really going for it, positively bouncing. Eve wondered for a moment if she should go and tell her to calm down. But then thought she was being too much of a clucky mother hen. Deepa was a medical student who knew her own body. It was her wedding, let her dance if she was up for it. Tom was laughing with her, twirling her round.

And then Eve's father was by her side, insisting she sit down and have another drink with him. 'Something a little stronger this time, surely?' He eyed her orange juice suspiciously.

'So . . . Martha seems very nice,' she challenged him.

He spoke about his new *friend* and the wedding . . . Tom . . . her other children, but the only words she really heard, really registered, were said in the serious, hand on arm moment when he told her: 'It's never too late, Eve. When you get to my age, you don't regret the things you've done, just the things you haven't done.'

'What are you talking about, Dad!?' She shied away with a smile.

'Your dancing partner.'

'Ha . . . right.' Deep swallow of the champagne he'd pressed into her hand.

'Robbie needs a poo.' Her two youngest children were in front of her now. Robbie white with exhaustion because it was hours past his bedtime, both of them damp-haired with sweat from the evening of dancing.

392

'Duty calls,' she told her father and carried the toddler off to the Portakabins at the back of the marquee.

'Eve,' Jen crossed her path: 'There's something I've got to tell you . . .'

'Can it wait a moment? We're on our way to the loos.'

'Joseph's socks . . . It's a sign,' Jen said and just walked off. *What?* Eve put it down to too many glasses of champagne.

Squeezed into the tiny cubicle, with Robbie asleep, head in her lap, she listened with horror to the goings-on in the cubicle beside hers.

Dennis's daughters, Sarah and Louisa, were in there sniffing coke, making hyper-giggle jokes about getting the drugs free from the DJ, 'but you know that means he'll want something later' – more hilarious, drugged-up laughter.

Eve couldn't bear it. These two beautiful girls – one of them could have been hers, she couldn't shake this illogical thought – with everything ahead of them.

But she couldn't face them herself, didn't feel it was her place.

So when they'd finally left, she bundled Robbie up in her arms and marched out to find Dennis. He was on his own at one of the smaller tables, looking round the room with a big tumbler of gin and tonic in front of him.

'Hello, Dennis.' She managed a smile and pulled up a chair so she could sit beside him, Robbie asleep in her lap, dead weight on one arm.

After their polite chitchat about the wedding, she worked up the courage to tell him about his daughters.

'I see,' was his reply. He picked up his drink, drained the glass dry and then pulled at his cufflinks. Weirdly, she remembered this habit of his and it seemed so odd not to know someone at all any more and yet remember their nervous tics.

'They're "in the loos",' he said finally. 'That's very Evelyn of you, isn't it? Shouldn't hip and groovy Eve say "crapper" or "shithouse" or something a bit more with-it?'

'That's hardly a very grown-up response, is it?'

'Well, what the hell do you expect me to do, *Eve*?' He said her name with a sneer.

'Can't you stop them? Can't you at least talk to them?' she asked. 'They're your children.'

'If £15,000 worth of rehab can't help them, what the hell am I supposed to do?' He waved the barman over and gestured to his glass. 'I'm just their father. The guy with the deep pockets who goes on paying – for clothes, for schools, for horses, for holidays. And I'm so looking forward to paying for cars, abortions and nose jobs. That's all they want, my money, and then they throw this crap back in my face.' He was speaking too loudly now.

'Oh for God's sake,' she hissed at him hoping to quieten him down.

'Well, what do you expect me to do?'

'Jesus, Dennis.' She felt furious with him, out of all proportion to the situation. A floodgate was loosening and any moment now . . .

'Maybe they want you to love them, to pay attention . . . to be a *parent*, for God's sake,' she heard herself spitting out. 'To parent, Dennis, it's a verb. It's about putting in the hours: wiping bottoms and noses, helping with homework, teaching your children to walk, to talk, to read, to swim. You watch wet and cold football matches every week, you patch grazed knees, read long and repetitive bedtime stories, listen to long, complicated girlfriend woes. You make breakfast, lunch and supper, day after day, week in, week out and persuade them to eat it . . . And your reward for this, d'you know what it is?' Her voice was starting to crack with effort. 'Your reward is happy, well-adjusted children who love you to bits, but grow up, move out, move away and start lives and families of their own.'

He took a mouthful from his glass, swallowed, then told her: 'Well you always were the perfect parent. No-one can fault you there. But a lousy wife,' he added. 'The kids always came first. And you know what? It doesn't surprise me that you're on your own with even more children. There was never going to be room in your life for anyone else. How could there be, when you're so busy being the perfect mother?' She felt as if he'd slapped her in the face. Tears were springing up in her eyes. How dare he?

'Just shut up, Dennis,' she said furiously. 'You

have no idea. You have no bloody idea. I've had to do it all on my own. Don't you think I wanted to get close to someone else? But what you did made it too hard.'

She was aware that someone had stepped up behind her chair, but she was too upset to stop.

'The boys don't need you now, Dennis, they don't need your money, or to be impressed by you, or to admire your job . . . They needed you when they were small. And you let them down.'

Dennis's wife Susan had come up to the table and both Tom and Denny had materialized. There were hands on her shoulders, rubbing her neck.

'It's OK, Mum,' Tom was saying, crouching down at the table, trying to be the peacemaker.

'If you and the boys want to get to know each other now, fine,' she said, much more calmly. 'But I'll never understand what you did and I'll never forgive you for it.'

Dennis picked up his glass and drained it down, then set it carefully back on the table. When he looked up at her, it caused her a stab of pain to see tears in his eyes. 'I'm sorry, Eve. I'm sorry to you all,' he said. 'There doesn't seem to be much else I can do.'

'Well . . . sorry is a start.' This was Joseph's voice. It took her a moment to register that it was Joseph standing right behind her, that his hands were on her shoulders once again.

'I think we should go now,' Susan told Dennis.

'Do you know where the girls are?' He gave a bitter laugh in response to this and stood up.

'Good night, everyone. Enjoy the rest of the evening,' was all he said. Then he took Susan's arm in his and together they walked out of the tent.

Denny let out a gasp of air and a: 'So that's that then.'

Eve was wiping tears away with Joseph kneeling down at her side: 'It's fine. You're going to be fine,' he said. 'He deserved everything you said, OK? Every word.' They looked at each other and Eve was aware that something important had happened, some final hold Dennis had still had over her was falling away.

Tom felt he was interrupting but there was something he had to ask his mother: 'This isn't exactly the perfect moment,' he said, 'But do you know where Jen is?' Eve saw the anxiety on his face. 'Deepa wants to speak to her because she's feeling really odd and she's starting to worry.'

'Oh my God!' Eve passed her sleeping toddler to Joseph, jumped up and sped round the tent.

When Jen and Deepa came back from the toilets, where they had adjourned for a cramped examination, Tom and Eve could tell by the excited, if somewhat surprised, expressions on both faces that something was definitely happening.

'Yes, it's labour,' Jen told Tom nice and quietly, so the assembled crowds wouldn't all be in on the act. 'Three centimetres. Time to get back to London.'

'But we're only half an hour away from the big send-off,' Deepa protested. 'Can't we just wait for that and then we'll zoom off in our wedding car as planned? We'll just take it straight to the hospital.'

Jen wasn't so sure. 'Twenty minutes, max,' she compromised. 'And I'll go in the car with you, in case you need a midwife sooner than you think.'

The couple smiled at this, because it just seemed too ridiculous.

'Look at me, I'm fine now,' Deepa told her. 'It's not anything more than a stitch every once in a while.'

'Yeah well . . . things will probably be really slow and steady and nothing will happen for hours, but you never know, your waters might break and it'll be a great big rush.'

The suggestion of her waters breaking at her wedding seemed to galvanize Deepa. 'OK, everyone into a circle for the send-off.'

It was the perfect ending. All the guests encircling the couple, clapping and singing to the music as Deepa and Tom went round kissing and hugging everyone in turn and trying not to get too overcome with emotion. It was hopeless by then, Eve just gave in and sobbed horribly loudly, one arm round Janie, one round Denny.

Deepa had told her mother and sisters what

was happening and gradually word was getting round. The send-off was reaching a hysteria level of excitement and concern.

'Oh Deepa, take care', 'We love you', 'God bless', was being shouted to them as they climbed into their wedding car – a shiny white chauffeur-driven VW Beetle – and told the alarmed driver of the change of plans.

'Are you staying on a bit?' Joseph asked Eve as the car moved out of sight, relatives being almost mown down in their final attempts to kiss the bride and wish them the best.

'No!' Eve told him. 'She's in labour, they're headed for the hospital. They're waiting at the first parking place on the road for me to bring Jen. You know, in case—'

'Oh my God! Come on, then. Why don't you and Jen get going? I'll follow on with Robbie and Anna. You might need another car . . . or another person.'

'Well . . .' She saw how fired up he was . . . hard to refuse. 'Well, I need Robbie, I've got the car seat, but why don't you take Anna home and wait for news, OK?' She handed him her house keys.

The little Peugeot engine hummed and rattled all the way up the M23 to London. She'd lost the Beetle miles back, but she was determined to get to the hospital vigil in time. In fact, she kept checking the hard shoulder, scared that the Beetle would be pulled up there with her first grandchild too well on its way to be stopped. They were with Jen, she reminded herself, they would be fine.

She looked at her little boy, zonked out in his car seat in the back, and remembered Jen bringing him loud and kicking into the world. She hadn't let Joseph come to the delivery. She'd thought it was too weird, considering they were apart and he was seeing someone else by then. But he had rushed down anyway, to the same hospital Deepa was heading for now. And she had let him see his son when they were both bathed, dressed and ready for visitors.

He'd held the baby on his lap and stroked the damp silken hair, too moved to say anything.

The perfect parent? A lousy wife? Dennis's words were still ringing in her ears. They had hurt so much because weren't they, in some ways, true? There was no room in her life for a partner, because she didn't want there to be. She had told herself that she wouldn't have to face the pain of losing another love, if she didn't have one.

She pushed her foot down harder, hummmmmm, the roads were empty but the car was straining to get past 90. If the police caught her now, they were going to enjoy her explanation.

By the time she made it to the labour ward waiting room, running down long lino-ed corridors with a still sleeping toddler in her arms,

Deepa and Tom were in a delivery room with Jen alongside them.

'It's going well,' the nurse at reception told her. 'She's having a slow first stage but she's coping very well. There's nothing to do but wait, I'm afraid.'

Eve was only halfway down her first cup of vile hospital tea when she was astonished to see Joseph approach the reception – Joseph and a very pale Anna, still in pink sari, holding his hand.

He was trying to explain to the nurse why he was there when Eve went up to greet them.

'Oh hello.' He was relieved to see her. 'Anna insisted. She just absolutely would not go home when the rest of you were here. And, I . . . well, I could see her point.'

'Is the baby here yet?' Anna's obvious excitement was going to keep her awake all night if necessary. It was already 1.30a.m.

'No. But Deepa's doing fine. You'll just have to come and drink tea with me. If it's OK with Sister Leanne.'

Sister Leanne said she would prefer it if they all went to the hospital canteen and she would send someone with news straight away.

A little group of Styrofoam cups had gathered between the four of them . . . because Robbie was now awake, bright-eyed, wanting to play, before the news finally came just before 4a.m.

Jen appeared in the canteen, flushed, hair all over the place, red marks on the back of her neck where the plastic apron had been tied over her party clothes.

'Congratulations,' she'd hugged Eve, in a voice edged with tears because she had just delivered her best friend's grandson and it still felt like a present: 'You're a grandma. You're a grandma now. They've had a beautiful boy, 8 pounds 10 ounces and Eve, he's perfect. He's absolutely perfect.'

Everyone was on their feet.

'How is she doing?' Eve managed to ask. 'Can we go and visit?'

'Of course! She's fine . . . tired. But wait till you see them, they're just thrilled!'

Chapter Thirty-Three

They were all allowed in, even Joseph who was initially stopped at the door by Sister Leanne, who told him 'family only', to which Tom said, 'It's OK, that's my dad.'

Eve wondered fleetingly what Sister Leanne made of that, but then there they were in front of her, the brand new family of three – Tom, Deepa and their tiny curled up, folded in caramel kiss of a baby.

'Oh . . . oh . . . congratulations.' Eve hugged and kissed her son, who looked exhausted, but dazed with happiness in his sweat-soaked wedding T-shirt, 'Well groom-ed' spelled out in silver across the front.

Then she moved on to her daughter-in-law, all cleaned up and starchy white in her hospital bed with the baby asleep in the crook of her arm.

'He's just beautiful,' Eve whispered and let Anna and Robbie get right up to the bedside for a look. 'Are you OK?' she asked Deepa.

'Yeah . . . that was a bit sore, though. To put it mildly.' Deepa managed to take her eyes from her son to look up at Eve now. 'But he's wonderful,' she whispered and for a moment they almost all cried all over again.

'Well done, darling,' Eve said, kissing the top of Deepa's head. 'Do your family know yet?'

'Yeah, Tom's made a few calls.'

'There'll be no problems remembering our wedding anniversary now,' Tom added, not able to tear his gaze from his wife and their baby.

'What are you going to call him?' Joseph asked.

'I think we're going to name him after Mum,' Tom replied.

'Eve?' Anna asked, a little taken aback.

'No . . . Adam,' Tom said, smiling. 'If you see what we mean.'

'Oh! Sweet!' was the general consensus.

'Thank you,' Eve said, too overcome to add anything else.

'Deepa? Will the baby drink milk from your boobies?' Robbie wanted to know.

Finally, it was time to go home. Eve carried Robbie and Joseph carried Anna back to their cars.

'You'll need some sleep before you drive back to Manchester, won't you? Or a cup of tea or something?' Eve asked when they were back at the flat, desperate for him not to go. This had been too much of a day. She needed him to stay just a bit longer.

'Maybe I could kip on your couch for a bit. If that's OK?'

'Of course. I don't think I'm going to be able to sleep at all. Ever again!'

They bundled Anna and Robbie into bed, party clothes and all, each of them noticing the other kiss the children and stroke them tenderly.

In the kitchen, he sat down at the table and watched her make tea, in her faded rose-patterned dressing gown with her pink and blond hair clipped up all wonkily on top of her head and her face scrubbed clean, because she'd taken off her tired and smudged party make-up as well as her party dress.

She went to the two tea caddies and spooned out tea leaves from each just the way he expected her to, poured in the boiling water, stirred it meditatively. He felt a pain, which he knew was heartache and homesickness. This was his home. This was the place he should be and this was the person he should be with. The feeling was so strong that he was going to have to do something about it. Say something. At least try. Was there ever going to be a better moment?

She brought the pot over with two mugs.

'Why did Tom thank you for the ring?' she asked before he could say anything. 'Did you lend him the money?'

'No . . . I gave him the ring. I thought Deepa might like it.'

Eve was frowning at him, awaiting further explanation.

'It was Michelle's,' he said.

'Oh.' She was frozen, teapot in mid-air.

'We've called it off. Split up ... You don't need to say anything sympathetic,' he added: 'It was entirely my fault.'

There was a big, expectant pause hanging between them. Eve hardly dared to breathe. She set the teapot down again.

'I think you only know how much you've loved someone when it's over,' he said, suddenly developing an intense interest in a stain on the tablecloth, which he started to scrape at: 'I didn't love Michelle nearly enough to marry her ... But what happened between you and me still seems really important and I sometimes wonder if I'm ever going to get over it ... If I even want to get over it.'

Her gaze dropped to the floor and rested on the caramel suede boots he was wearing underneath his suit. He was jiggling his foot a little and with every jiggle she could see a flash of his socks. That was when Eve saw what Jen had meant. They were probably very expensive socks – Paul Smith or something groovy – but nevertheless, they were stripy socks ... and quite incredibly, they were purple and turquoise stripy socks.

She looked back up at him and tried to read his expression. She didn't know that he was rolling all his courage up into a ball to ask her:

'Eve?' he said, clearing his throat slightly, 'has it ever occurred to you? I mean, have you ever thought that maybe? For the children . . . we should, perhaps . . .'

Her eyes were fastened on his and for a moment he wavered. What was she thinking? Was he about to make a terrible mistake? He glanced round the room for any sort of sign. And as he paused, her hand moved against her mug with the slightest of clinks and he looked down to see that she still, after all this time, wore the ring he'd given her. The slip of platinum and emerald which hadn't been thrown back at him. It must count for something. Surely? OK, deep breath.

'Eve, I'm so in love with you still,' he said, voice barely above a whisper.

Long silence.

'Do you realize that I'm a grandmother?' she said finally.

'That doesn't matter.' He almost laughed.

She looked at him for a long, long time. He felt in fear of what she might say next. 'Do you really think we can do this?' she asked him, head tilted to one side. 'Go back?' *Could he really know how much she would like to go back?*

'No. We can't go back.' He put his hand over hers. 'But maybe we can go forward.'

'I don't know if I can believe in it all again.'

'Then believe in it a little. Take a chance.'

Nothing ventured, nothing gained, Mum. Tom's words in her mind.

She looked at the warm hand held over hers.

'What about the children?' she thought out loud. 'I couldn't bear to see them hurt all over again.'

'I love the children, Eve,' was his answer to this. 'Don't use them as an excuse when they're another reason to try again.'

She looked at his face – so serious, so sincere, so downright, perfectly lovely. Who wouldn't want to wake up next to this face every day of their life?

'This is all wrong,' she told him.

'Is it?' He sounded very worried.

'Yeah, you should definitely have started with kissing. Loosened me up with a bit of kissing and then moved on to the big speech.'

'Should I?' A wash of relief over his face. 'OK . . . Keep me right. Kiss now? Would that be any good?'

'Ah ha, kissing now . . . very good.'

He leaned towards her and kissed the tip of her nose, very lightly. 'I've missed you so much,' he said. 'Every single day.'

'And night,' she added, leaning in to kiss him on the mouth, wrap her arms round him and let herself fall . . . fall into him, fall back in love with him, fall forward into love with him.

He tasted, just as she remembered, he smelled, just as she remembered, he felt, just as she remembered, from the very best of her dreams.

The kiss finally melted apart and they were

looking at each other, very close up, nose to nose. Big wide pupils fixed on her.

'Come outside with me,' she said and led him by the hand out of the kitchen door into the garden.

And there, underneath the tallest palm plants, pressed up against a trellis of sweet pea flowers, they began to kiss again. Again . . . again. He was perfect. She ran fingers through his hair, pulled him in against her, impatient to feel again every single thing that had once been so amazing between them. How had she lived without this? Lived without him?

Her dressing gown fell to her feet and she fumbled over his shirt buttons, in too much of a hurry, licking and kissing at his soft, salty neck, tugging at his zip and feeling him wrap his arms and his jacket tightly around her.

And only when he was inside, their bodies pressed right up against and into each other, moving with intent, did she dare to open her eyes.

'It's OK,' she whispered against his ear. 'It's OK.'

She meant the practicalities – no further surprises on the baby front – but 'it's OK' covered everything else right now. The strangeness and the familiarity, the newness and the known of making love to him again. Her man. His face pressed hard against her neck. Her one and only. She knew the little breathe and catch sound, breathe and catch, he was making. The love of her life. His hands on her hips, moving her with him until she was breaking apart, breaking into pieces underneath him, mouth and nose buried into his shoulder skin. This was how it was meant to be. She was *so* coming, unwinding, unravelling all the way through him.

Joseph could hear only the blood pounding in his ears as he reached the very edge of letting go. He was being rushed to the top of a mountain and aaaaaaaaaaah, pushed down over the other side into freefall.

'I'm coming . . . I'm *coming* . . . Eve,' he was sighing against her ear.

'Yeeeeeah,' was her reply.

'Oh . . . you've no idea.' He wanted to let her know how good it was to come again. It had been so long. To feel the rushing and *the relief*!

'Oh . . . wow,' he managed. He didn't want to open his eyes yet. The earth was actually spinning and he would have to come back down slowly.

He leaned back into the crushed sweet peas, realizing he'd probably stained the back of his new suit irredeemably but, fuck it, who cared?

'Hey, lovely person,' she said and he prised his eyes apart to look at the smiley, fuzzy face pressed up against his.

'You did, didn't you?' he asked.

'Oh yeah,' she nodded. 'But sex isn't everything, you know.' Little laugh caught in the back of her throat.

'No. But it's a very good start.'

'How is this going to work, then? Have you thought about it much?' she asked.

'I call it a day in Manchester and move back in with you,' he answered.

But she shook her head.

'No?'

'We're going forward aren't we, not back?' she reminded him.

'It's OK. I'm a changed man. I'm going to bike to work, recycle everything, save money . . .' he told her.

'Shhhh,' she grinned at him. 'Silly boy. Of course you are. But we can't live here. It's too small.'

And all of sudden it seemed easy. She would stop struggling against all this stuff and just let go, let it happen. Make the changes. She would take the promotion at work, offered to her two days ago, she would sell the flat and the garden and maybe the four of them would move into the big house on the corner. The one she walked past almost every day and dreamed about. The solid but shabby square house with broken windows and the huge, wild, unloved garden. They would fix it all up and make it home.

'Shall we buy a house together?' she asked him.

'A house?'

'Yeah. There is this house on the corner, three streets down. It's a mess, huge garden, totally wild . . .'

411

He saw the light in her eyes.

'An expensive house? Big loan? Having to earn lots of money situation?'

She was nodding at him.

'And this isn't worrying you?'

She shook her head, but said, 'Well a bit . . . But I've got you. You'll help me out of my little rut, won't you? Because we both have to change . . . just a little.'

'Put your dressing gown on before you freeze,' he said and kissed her on the lips.

She tied the gown on, then turned to him, cupping his face in her hands, smoothing down his dark brows.

'Is this really going to work? Can it be as good as it was?'

'I love you,' he said. 'It'll be better. I promise. This is what I really, really want. And I'm not the only person.'

He was right, Anna would love it and probably Robbie would too.

'Don't answer this question now, Joe, don't say a word.' She put a finger over his lips, took a deep breath and asked the question that until tonight would have terrified her: 'Will you think about marrying me?'

He pushed her finger away, face breaking into an irrepressible grin: 'Yes, yes, yes.'

'Don't answer now!'

'Why? Are you scared?'

'Yes!'

'Too bad. The answer's yes.'

'You've only just got unengaged.'

'I know, I'm like a toilet cubicle . . . Engage me, please.'

She laughed at him, feeling even more of a fizz of happiness inside, and told him: 'It's just I really like the dress I wore today and I've got nowhere else to wear it.'

'That would be a shame. So marry me.'

'We'll see.' She knew she meant yes, just couldn't quite bring herself to say it . . . yet.

'That's a very mumsy answer.'

'Mumsy? I'm a granny now – which is quite scary and you should be warned.'

'Not scary to me . . .' He clasped both hands round her back and leaned in to whisper in her ear, 'Less youth . . . more experience.' It sounded filthy.

They kissed again mouth to mouth, eye to eye, holding hands, breaking off to laugh at each other. This was the way it was meant to end for them, or rather, begin again for them. They saw that now.

'Are we really back together. Really, really?' he asked.

'Honey, I don't just sleep with anyone,' was her reply.

'Honey, that's not what I heard.'

'How jealous were you of the vet, then?'

'He took one look at me and threw in the towel,' he joked.

She laughed at this and he held her in to kiss again.

'Promise me all this isn't just about you feeling jealous?' she asked.

'I promise. This is all about me doing what my daughter wants me to do,' he joked.

'I know,' she smiled. 'We are but pawns in her paws.' Then she pulled him away from the wall and surveyed the damage. 'Oh the poor sweet peas . . . completely mashed.'

'Eve, this is all very picturesque but it's very cold and we have to go inside now,' he told her. 'And I'm still going to sleep on the sofa.'

'Why!?'

'Because you gave away our bed and the one you've got now is far too small for two.'

'Too small to sleep in, maybe. But we're not going to sleep just yet, are we?'

'Oh really! But we all have to fall asleep eventually, though. Even you.'

'When I finally fall asleep today, I'm going to sleep so well, you'll have to make the kids breakfast.'

'Deal – but first I'm calling in a few favours.'

'If you make breakfast, you can have as many favours as you want, honey.'

Their arms wrapped around each other, they hugged their way indoors, too caught up in the moment to notice the small face at the window watching them.

Anna, woken up by low voices and laughter, had lifted the curtain to peek out and see what was happening. She had been amazed to see her parents together, kissing in the garden.

Her first thought was that this was some sort of regression, relapse . . . nostalgia night on both of their parts. Then she saw them walk towards the door and she broke into a broad smile too.

That look on both of their faces, she recognized it immediately, even though she'd only seen it in one place before: on the video clip, when her father had given her mother the little ring.

'You see!' Anna was whispering to herself, there could be happy endings, or happy new beginnings if you had a little faith and maybe also a copy of 'The House of Bamboo'. *Do, do, di do.*

THE END

THE PERSONAL SHOPPER
Carmen Reid

Meet Annie Valentine: stylish, savvy, multi-tasker extraordinaire.

As a personal shopper in a swanky London fashion emporium, Annie can re-style and re-invent her clients from head to toe. In fact, this super-skilled dresser can be relied on to solve everyone's problems ... except her own.

Although she's busy being a single mum to stroppy teen Lana and painfully shy Owen, there's a gap in Annie's wardrobe, sorry, life, for a new man. But finding the perfect partner is turning out to be so much trickier than finding the perfect pair of shoes.

Can she source a genuine classic? A lifelong investment? Will she end up with someone from the sale rail, who'll have to be returned? Or maybe, just maybe, there'll be someone new in this season who could be the one ...

A fabulous read. A sexy read. A Carmen Reid.

'If you love shopping as much as you love a great read, try this. Wonderful!'
Katie Fforde

9780552154819

CORGI BOOKS